Lark

BEWARE OF THE WIDOWS

USA TODAY BESTSELLING AUTHOR

LEXI C. FOSS

Lark

Editing by: Outthink Editing, LLC

Proofreading by: Katie Schmahl & Jean Bachen

Cover Design: Jodielocks Design

Cover Photograph: Christopher John (CJC Photography)

Cover Model: Skyler Simpson

Interior Images: Stock from DepositPhotos

Published by: Ninja Newt Publishing, LLC

Digital Edition

ISBN: 978-1-68530-405-8

Print Edition

ISBN: 978-1-68530-406-5

AI Disclaimer: This book does not contain any elements of AI content. All art was designed by real artists, and all of the words were written by the author.

To those who love a badass STEM heroine. I see you. <3

noun: something done for fun, especially something mischievous or daring; an amusing adventure or escapade.

Lark

When they catch their little hacker, they'll make all her dreams come true.
And maybe some nightmares, too…

Lark. A mischievous and appropriate name that I picked for the Dark Net.
I thought I was clever. Daring, even.
But somehow *they* found me.
And now they've kidnapped me.

I thought they wanted their money back.
But no.
It turns out they simply want *me*.

Johan is the cunning one. The fellow hacker who uncovered my real identity and the location of my nest.
Noah is the psychotic one. Yet he's nurturing and caring when it comes to me.
And Lazarus is the one in charge of the pack. As a mafia don, his word is law, and his claim is just as impactful.

The problem is, I don't want to be a mafia queen.
But these men are determined to make me reconsider that stance.

You're ours now, little hacker.
Let us show you what that means.
We promise you won't regret it…

A NOTE FROM LEXI

Lark is a fast-burn standalone "why choose" romance in the Beware of the Widows shared world. While there is character overlap throughout the series, the books can be read in any order. And all of the stories feature contemporary omegaverse as a central theme/genre.

While the shared history between Lark and the other Widows is rather dark, this book is more medium gray to light gray in terms of darkness levels. Please be sure to check other books in the world for their darkness ratings.

SOME NOTES THAT MAY INTEREST YOU REGARDING CONTENT:

✓ Consent (between Lark and her men)
✓ No Other Woman or Other Man Drama (No Cheating)
✓ Pregnancy (Not a Central Theme)
✓ MM (Alpha-on-Alpha) Content
✓ Group Play Scenes
✓ Alpha (m), Alpha (m), Alpha (m), Omega (f) Dynamic
✓ Kidnapping
✓ Forced Proximity
✓ Mentions of Trafficking (History of the Widows)
✓ Psychotic/Assassin MMC (Noah)
✓ Mafia Don MMC (Laz)
✓ Kinky Genius MMC (Johan)
✓ STEM Heroine (Lark)
✓ Possessive Over The Top Alpha Males
✓ Touch Her and Die Vibes
✓ Knotting, Nesting, Purring, Growling, and Scent Matches
Enjoy! <3

```
" + x + " y: " + y);
" + x + " y: " + y);
void go()
t y)
println("in method go: x: " + x + " y: " + y);
x, y)
x + " y: " + y);
println("in method go: x: " + x + " y: " + y);
println("in method go
a, int b)
arameters: a: " + a
void falseSwap(int x, int y)
println("in method falseSwap
arameters: a: " + a + "
a: " + a +
arameters: a: " + a + " b: " + b);
println("in method falseSwap: x:
public class PrimitiveParameters
void moreParameters(int a, int b)
a: " + a +
println("in method moreParameters
public static
int x =
a: " + a + " b:
println("in method moreParameters
```

WELCOME TO WIDOWS PEAK

Once upon a time, six omegas came together in a dark and twisted fate.

They were taken by a cruel alpha.

Taught how to be the perfect Doll for a future pack.

Put on display and offered up for auction.

Then escaped and ran into the mountains where they found an abandoned town—*Widows Peak.*

There, the six females manifested a new beginning. Widows Peak became a place where all omegas were safe. And a decade later, it's thriving.

Only there are secrets that threaten the foundation of what they've created.

Secrets that only one omega knows.

Lark.

She found the abandoned town, led the six omegas there to rebuild, and never told them *how* Widows Peak came to be their new home.

But if there's anything Lark understands, it's that everything comes at a price.

Now it's time for her to pay back what she's stolen.

Or everything she's fought for may be lost in the process…

There you are, sweetheart.
Our beautiful little hacker.
Our intended omega.

You thought you could hide in the Rocky Mountains.
But we know where you are now.
And we're coming for you, sweet Lark…

PROLOGUE

LARK

Ten Years Ago, Henderson Estate

I HATE CLOCKS.

All they do is tick, tick, tick. And I need more time.

This is a complicated hack, one that's about to be thwarted by one of Gideon Henderson's goons. *Come on, come on*, I think, sweat dotting my brow.

The internet connection is spotty, mostly because I'm running my process through seven different servers. Not to mention the rotating satellite.

Biting my lip, I narrow my gaze and move the device on the windowsill again.

Just a little closer to the edge. Enough to try to—

There!

The bar inches along, making my foot tap. *So close, so close…*

A door slams, the echo of it causing me to freeze.

I'm wrapped up in Viv's clothes—a sweater and a pair of jeans that I stole, both of which are too long for my shorter frame. But I needed to mask my scent. And who better to borrow from than the Beta in charge of my torture?

Of course, she doesn't call it that. She says she's our "trainer."

God, this place is a nightmare.

I could have escaped it three years ago by simply giving Gideon my real name. If he had any idea which omega his guys had picked up off the streets, he would have put me on the first plane back to New York City.

But I didn't want to leave Luna behind. It was her they came for that night. I was just a "bonus omega," as one of the goons said.

"What's your name, blondie?" one of them asked as he combed his fingers through my hair, stroking me like I was his personal pet.

I almost told him.

However, I knew he would either knock me out—causing me to lose Luna—or kill me out of fear of me giving his description to my father.

So I simply said, "Lark White."

A play on my hacker name.

"No family," I lied. "I'm an orphan."

They were giddy as hell, thinking they would score big points with the boss.

And they did.

Points I fully intended for them to lose once I broke Luna and myself out of purgatory, but then I met the others.

Lexi, Silva, Aries, and Briar.

And escaping became a lot more complicated.

We're almost ready, I think, listening as footsteps sound down the marbled floors of the corridor. I'm not supposed to be in this part of the estate. Hopefully, Viv's clothes do their job and keep me hidden.

Because she's allowed to go wherever the fuck she wants here.

Her job is to turn the six of us into the perfect little "Dolls" for a future pack of Gideon's choosing.

"Now, you must understand that these packs pay handsomely for Gideon's products," Viv told Luna and me after introducing herself to us at the beginning of our captivity. "It's my job to make sure you meet certain… criteria."

Cooking.

Cleaning.

Entertaining.

Sex.

More sex.

Ugh.

I'm just glad the sex part didn't require hands-on experience. Gideon likes his Dolls to be "mostly untouched." I'm firmly in the "never been touched" category, so I'm a little concerned about what that means for some of the other girls.

However, I haven't asked.

And I never will.

There are just some horrors of this place that deserve to die here.

I wish I could do more than save only us, I think, my heart skipping a beat as I think about all the other omegas being housed in the Henderson mansion. It's impossible to help everyone. I know that. But maybe we'll find a way to come back and take Gideon down in the future.

Alas, I can only focus on the present for now.

Which means I need this damn thing to move faster.

I push up the window just a little bit more so I can slide my whole hand and arm outside. It's not ideal. In fact, it increases the chances that someone will see me.

But it's nighttime.

And the guards are more focused on the omega wings than on this area of the estate.

Except the one patrolling the hallway, I think, still listening to his heavy footsteps. *An alpha, definitely.*

Which means he might be able to smell my natural perfume under all these clothes.

My brow pinches, and I push the window open even more, just in case I need to jump out of it. Maybe the fresh air will help conceal my scent, too.

Regardless, it feels nice. I inhale deeply and attempt to control my racing pulse.

It doesn't work.

The repetitive thrum echoes in my ears, all while I strain to hear those footsteps outside the door. *Did he pause?* I wonder, suddenly holding my breath.

However, I hear him pass in the next moment, the goon—Viv calls them *guards*—leaving.

Thank. God.

I'm in a sitting room of sorts, one I found over a year ago after noting the strategic location in the mansion. The windows are exposed to the elements, making it easier to connect to the satellite network overhead, as there's no roof or overhang to block my connection.

That it happens to also rarely be used is simply a bonus point. I've hidden several "borrowed" devices in here, including the tablet I'm staring at now. It's one of the many items I've taken from the security room stash. No one seems to be missing it. But if it's found, I've already programmed a fail-safe to wipe all evidence of my use if the wrong code is entered three times.

Fortunately, that fail-safe hasn't been needed since my items have remained untouched.

Which means I've been able to accomplish almost everything we needed to prepare for our escape.

This is the final step.

The completion of the transfer.

Final payment for all the property deeds…

I just need this bar to inch over one more digit, and it'll be done. Everything will be settled. The town will officially be *ours*.

But the others can never know.

Only me and Luna.

And even then, I've kept her in the dark on certain aspects. Like *whom* I've taken all this money from. She just helped me with the legal side.

If Luna doesn't become a lawyer after all this, I'll be shocked. The omega has a knack for legalese and research.

"What's that?" a deep voice says outside, causing my eyes to widen.

Shit.

I pull my hand back in and watch the connectivity bars disappear. I was so close. *So. Fucking. Close.*

I flip the screen off to kill the glow, but it's too late.

"Did you see that?" the same voice asks.

"See what?" another mutters.

"I dunno. It… it looked like something was in the window up ahead."

Wincing, I duck down and try to make myself as small as possible beneath the ledge on this side. Being on the ground floor means they'll be able to look in the room.

And if they peer over to glance downward, they'll see me and my toys…

Closing my eyes, I count to five, then start to think through my options.

Maybe if I ball myself just right, I can look like a pile of clothes. I'm small. Only five foot two. Viv has several inches on me, as evidenced by her oversized clothing. So it might work if I—

"You probably just saw the curtain blowing out the open window," the other says, sounding bored.

"Why's it open?" the first one, whom I've nicknamed Deep Voice, presses.

"I don't know, genius. Ask the housekeepers," his buddy

grinds out, his tone full of irritation. "I'm hungry and not interested in investigating a damn window."

There's a pause before Deep Voice mutters, "All you ever think about is food."

"That's not all I think about," the other drawls, the insinuation in his voice making my skin crawl.

Fucking alphas.

I know they're not all bad. But the ones here certainly give their designation a bad name.

Although, the same could be said about the betas here, too.

Everyone in this organization is evil. Which is saying a lot, given my background and familial history.

Their footsteps eventually echo off into the distance, just like the ones from the hallway, leaving me very much alone in here again.

Thank God.

I fire my tablet back up, along with the cellular device that I repurposed for satellite connectivity. Moving the latter item out the window, I again search for a solid link. Once the bars pop up, I click on the tablet's internet icon and then watch as that remaining bar slowly loads.

This had better work, I think, nervous that it's going to make me start all over again since the connection was interrupted.

But after two nerve-racking minutes, I receive the sweetest of messages. *100% Complete.*

"Holy shit," I breathe. "It's done."

I check several screens, needing to be absolutely certain.

However, every record shows the right set of names.

We own the town.

Widows Peak is ours.

It's all legal on paper. All the deeds are evenly dispersed between the six of us. Bought and paid for through means I'll never tell them about.

Hell, I might not even share the deeds part.

All they need to know is that we'll be safe there, nestled in the mountains of Colorado.

Gideon and his goons will never be able to touch us again.

Not that I'm concerned about him and his criminal underworld. The one I just stole all this money from is much, much worse.

But they'll never find out that it was me.

I'm good at what I do.

And it's not like they'll miss the funds.

Lazarus Ferraro is rich beyond sin. His organization is constantly moving money around, both legally and illegally. I just skimmed a little… off the top.

It was for a good cause, I think. *Plus, it gave me an opportunity to provide some sweet revenge.*

The Ferraros have history with my family.

History that I just honored in the best way possible.

Smiling, I shut everything down for the last time. This project is finally done. And next week, we'll escape.

Widows Peak… here we come…

CHAPTER ONE
LARK

Current Day, Widows Peak

It's time to come home, Aurora.

I bite my lip as I read the message for the fiftieth time. It hasn't changed. Not that I expected it to. But part of me keeps hoping it'll disappear. Not exist. *Go. Away*.

"Ugh." I pick up my coffee and take a sip, wishing the caffeine would ease the ache growing inside.

"*Ugh* is right," Luna says as she plops down across from me at the bakery cafe. "I don't know how you drink it like that."

I glance at my cup of heavenly liquid and look back up at her. "You mean… you don't know how I drink coffee the way it's intended to be enjoyed?"

She rolls her russet-brown eyes. "Says the woman who refuses to try a cappuccino."

"Why would I want to spoil a perfectly good cup of coffee with *milk*?"

"It's so much more than that, my dear Lark," she replies, her slender fingers clasping together on the small table as she leans toward me. "Now tell me why I'm risking my 'one baked good a week' rule by hanging out with you here."

I twist my lips to the side. I called her because she's the only one I can talk to about this. She knows enough of my history to understand my predicament.

"We really should get a donut," I admit, glancing at where Emma is standing behind the counter. She's currently helping a beta pick out a sweet treat. "Or maybe a dozen donuts."

One of Luna's dark mahogany eyebrows wings upward to her matching hairline. "That sounds ominous."

"Because it is," I mutter, then show her my phone.

The use of my legal name—*Aurora*—is a dead giveaway. She's the only one in Widows Peak who knows my true identity. And very few people outside of this place refer to me by my given name.

"Fuck."

"Yeahhh," I drawl, then take another sip of my coffee.

"You're going to need something stronger than a donut," she says, leaving me to go stand in line.

When she returns with a pair of warm cinnamon rolls, I almost smile. *Almost.* But the message on my phone is still there. Still reads the same way. Still gives me the same instructions.

Come home.

My stomach twists. "My father must be in bad shape for Gio to send me that message," I say softly.

Luna's brow furrows, probably because talking about my father makes her think of her own.

Our fathers were colleagues of a sort. If criminal syndicate members can even be called that.

Her father is also dead. While mine… mine was very much alive the last time I checked. But Gio's text this morning suggests that status is about to change.

I should care.

I should want to go home and say goodbye to the man who helped create me.

But we were never that close. I was a pawn. A bargaining chip he couldn't wait to play.

That's why I've stayed here—in Widows Peak—to hide.

The only member of my family who knows where I am is Gio. Everyone else probably thinks I'm dead. Not sure. I've let Gio handle all that.

However, his assistance has always been associated with a certain price. *You will come home when I tell you to,* he said years ago.

I agreed.

And it seems he's decided it's time for me to earn my keep.

I pick up the cinnamon roll, not caring at all that it's messy and sticky, and shove part of it into my mouth.

Luna watches with a wary expression. She knows this life better than anyone else in Widows Peak. Although, her background is cartel related, while mine is the mafia.

My father is a don. One of three in New York City, part of a trio of old families that once split up the land into three even pieces.

Bianchi.

Ricci.

Ferraro.

I shiver just thinking about the history between those names. I'm a Bianchi. A coveted omega daughter. The ultimate prize in my father's world.

Yet I disappeared.

Not on purpose at first. But I just never went home.

I'm not naïve, though. I know why Gio made me promise to return when he requested it. He might be a good older brother, but he knows I'm valuable.

"Gio won't auction me off, though. Not like my father probably would have, anyway." The words are for me, not Luna. "Which means he has something else in mind."

"Maybe a leadership role?" Luna suggests, not at all bothered by my wayward commentary. She's used to my chaotic conversation style. I often change topic or discussion direction mid-sentence.

I snort. "That doesn't happen in the infamous mafia trio. Omegas are kept and bred. That's it." I saw what my father and his two enforcers did to my mother. They treated her like a toy.

A very expensive, well-dressed, pampered toy. But a toy nonetheless.

"I mean, you could just… not go?" She utters the words slowly, phrasing them like a question. "What's the worst that could happen?"

"Oh, I don't know," I drawl. "Best case? Gio sends some enforcers to retrieve me. Worst case? He comes himself. Either way, my secret is revealed, and I'll probably be kicked out of Widows Peak for causing trouble."

Luna gives me a stern look. "That would never happen and you know it."

"Which part?" I ask, feigning innocence. "Gio coming to get me or my identity becoming town knowledge?"

"The Widows would never kick you out," she tells me, referring to the six of us who founded Widows Peak. "We're bonded in a way that's impenetrable. And if you think you're the only one here with secrets, think again."

I study her, wondering if she's referring to herself. Or maybe someone else has shared something in confidence.

Regardless of what it is, I don't pry. If anyone can respect the right to privacy, it's me.

I pick up my cinnamon roll again to take another bite, then use a napkin to wipe the icing off my hand.

Meanwhile, Luna uses a fork to eat hers.

I normally would, too. But today is not the day to care about manners.

We eat in silence for a few moments.

Then Luna gets up without a word to go grab some bottles of water from Emma. "On the house," Luna tells me as she sets them down. "I guess Emma can tell it's not a great day."

I glance at the petite omega and force myself to give her a thankful smile.

Then I look back at Luna and say, "You know I have to go back."

"Yeah," she replies. "Yeah, you have to go back."

I growl and pick up my coffee to finish it. "I was hoping you would be the voice of reason."

"I tried that by suggesting you just stay here, and you turned me down."

"Because Gio would just come get me."

"Because Gio would just come get you," she echoes. "Maybe he simply wants you to visit?" Her uncertain tone tells me she knows how ridiculous that sounds.

However, I huff a laugh at it anyway and mutter, "Anything's possible, I guess."

"Pigs could fly tomorrow," she agrees.

"They could."

"And alphas could stop obsessing over their knots," she adds, making me snort.

"Now, we both know *that* is never going to happen." I take the final bite of my cinnamon roll, the flavor doing little to calm my nerves. "I guess I'm…" I trail off as my phone lights up with a new message. My brother's name scrolls across the screen, causing my stomach to dip. "*Fuck.*"

I pick up the device to read what he's written and feel my heart stop in my chest.

"Are you fucking kidding me?" I breathe, reading and rereading his words. "You didn't even give me twelve hours!"

"Lark?" Lexi's familiar voice drifts through the bakery, making my shoulders stiffen.

I love all my omega sisters here—the Widows I escaped

Henderson estate with—but I'm not sure I can mask my mounting fury.

And fury leads to questions.

Which leads to me having to reveal secrets or lie. And I *really* don't want to lie.

Not sharing the full truth of why Widows Peak was a safe location for us all to run to… was a choice I made to protect my friends. However, not sharing my past—my *real* name—was a choice I made to protect myself.

"Everything okay here?" Lexi asks as she walks toward us. She must have heard my tone when she opened the door.

Shit.

"Oh, yeah," Luna replies, waving a dismissive hand. "Lark's just annoyed about a message someone sent her. Probably work related or something."

She shrugs and pushes her plate to the side.

"I need a cappuccino," Luna adds, intercepting Lexi. "I assume you're here for a box of maple donuts?" Her dark eyes lower to Lexi's belly, where a baby bump has started to show. "Pregnancy cravings?"

"*Ughhh,*" Lexi groans. "Yes. All I want to do is *eat.*"

Luna's lips twitch. "Good thing you came to the bakery, then." She loops her arm around Lexi's neck and guides her away from the table. Then she glances back at me to ask, "Want another coffee?" Her voice and tone are even, but her eyes show a hint of concern.

She didn't get a chance to read my brother's message, but she clearly knows it wasn't good.

"No. I… I need to pack." Because I have thirty minutes before a driver named *Noah* is coming to get me.

"Pack?" Lexi echoes, looking at me again. "Where are you going?"

"New York City," I mutter, standing. "I… I need to deal with some family stuff." I wince at how lame that sounds. Then cringe when I see her blue eyes light up with interest.

"Family stuff?" She frowns then. "I... I don't think I know anything about your family." She looks at Luna. "That's weird, right?" Her eyes widen now. "Oh my God, I'm a bad friend. A *really* bad friend."

"No, you're not," Luna inserts before I have a chance. "You're an amazing friend. The best. And you need to eat, remember? Maple donuts?"

Lexi glances between us, her eyes welling with tears. "These pregnancy hormones are *killing* me." She swipes furiously at one of the drops that falls down her cheeks. "All I do is eat, cry, and..." Her cheeks pinken. "Well, that part I don't mind."

By the way her peaches-and-cream scent heightens, I assume she's now thinking about sex with her new pack.

Two sexy alphas and a sinfully handsome omega.

Yeah, Lexi hit the jackpot with her men. As did her twin, Silva. Both omegas only recently found their packs, making it all pretty fresh and new.

The law enforcement links with both their pack mates made me a little nervous at first, but their presence here only bolsters the security of the town. And it's not like any of them specialize in wire fraud or property deeds.

Not that I left any evidence behind of my tampering, I think. It was all legal... on paper.

Clearing my throat, I stand and walk over to give Lexi a hug—because she looks like she needs one—and meet Luna's gaze. I don't say anything out loud but promise her with a look that I'll be in touch when I can.

Then I pull back to meet Lexi's gaze. We're roughly the same height, making it easy to do. "You're going to be an amazing mom, Lexi." I feel the need to say those words in case I never see her again.

Unfortunately, they're the wrong ones to voice because she starts to cry again.

Luna's eyes widen, and she takes over hugging our friend. "Emmett?" Luna mouths, referring to Lexi's omega lover.

I nod and go grab my phone. It feels good to swipe my brother's text off my screen, almost like I'm ignoring him.

I can't, though.

Not for long, anyway.

Dismissing the nerves twisting my insides, I pull up Emmett's name and type out a quick message. *Lexi is having big emotions in the bakery. You or one of those alphas of yours should probably get over here. Stat.*

Emmett's reply is immediate. *OMW.*

Slipping the phone into my pocket, I take in Luna and Lexi's embrace and feel my stomach twist again.

Widows Peak is safe.

It's home.

It's ours.

Leaving feels unnatural and wrong. But that note from Gio was pretty fucking clear. *Noah will be there in thirty minutes to retrieve you. The jet is waiting.*

Luna's comment about me being *annoyed* is an understatement. I'm annoyed *and* pissed. Because how fucking dare he not give me time to accept his summons.

I could have booked my own flight, I start typing, letting my fury guide my fingers. *I don't need to fly home on the family jet, Gio.*

Actually, maybe I should refuse.

Tell him I already booked something for tomorrow.

Or later this week.

Give me a few days to *process* his demand.

And I don't know anyone named Noah, I add. *Why would you send a stranger to pick me up?*

Which has me wondering if this is even legitimate at all.

What if someone else has Gio's phone?

What if something's happened to my brother?

Eyes narrowed, I delete everything I've typed so far and respond with one word. *Tuna.*

If he doesn't respond with the appropriate reply by the time I get home, then I'll know something isn't right.

But if it's the response I expect… I'll let Noah take me to the jet. And face my fate.

CHAPTER TWO
JOHAN

"Tuna?" Noah demands. "What the fuck sort of reply is *Tuna*?"

"It's her safe word," I reply, already aware of the phrase Aurora Bianchi uses with her darling brother.

Just as I'm aware of his usual reply.

But I don't send it right away. Giovanni Bianchi is a busy man. He loves his sister, but he wouldn't be able to immediately reply. However, he wouldn't let her message go unanswered for long, either.

I glance at the clock, giving it two minutes.

"So she knows something's up?" Noah demands. "I thought you said this plan was flawless."

"It *is* flawless," I promise him. "I've thought through every potential play, including this one. We're fine. Just calm your dragon fire and let me work."

Noah mutters something about stabbing me with a spoon and stalks over to the bar.

I ignore him. He knows better than to fix a drink right now. Our prey's life will be in his hands when he goes to pick her up.

Something that's exquisitely dangerous, given his profession of choice.

But I know he won't hurt our little hacker. Not… permanently, anyway.

Noah's proclivities are darker than mine, his penchant for pain something I've enjoyed watching more than experiencing.

Of course, Laz takes it all to a whole new level.

I've played separately with both of them. Normally, we all prefer to put a woman between us. Or we used to, anyway. Before finding Lark.

However, even then, Laz and Noah have never shared anyone before. I don't think there's a soul in this world who could handle group play with the pair of them.

Though, I'm hopeful that the one I'm currently messaging might be up for the task.

My sweet little black hat.

Lark.

That's not her real name, but I rather like it. So I've taken to referring to her as such.

Except, I use a completely different nickname now as I type, *Chill, honey pot, or the wasps will come out to sting.*

I give it another thirty seconds before I hit Send.

Which is just enough time for Noah to come up behind me and read it over my shoulder. "Honey pot?"

"It's what Giovanni calls her. I assume it has something to do with her scent." A thought that nearly has my knot throbbing to life.

I've fantasized about her scent since the moment I discovered her existence on the dark web. That she ended up being the daughter of a business rival was just the icing on the cake.

"Honey-flavored pussy," Noah says slowly. "*Fuck. Yes.*" He plops into the executive chair beside me. "God, I'm hard, and I haven't even gone to pick her up yet."

I snort. "Pretty sure you're always hard."

He lifts a shoulder. "I'm an alpha in my prime. Comes with the territory."

It's on the tip of my tongue to argue that point, but I'm distracted by the ping of an incoming message. *I can't believe you didn't even give me twelve hours to book my own flight, Gio. I don't need the family jet. I'll fly commercial.*

My eyebrow wings upward. I've studied Giovanni's communication style for years, not just because of his ties to our little hacker, but because of his business dealings.

Bianchis do not fly commercial, Aura, I type, doing my best to assert dominance while also being somewhat soft by using his other nickname for her—which is basically a misspelling of Aurora. *And the matter is urgent,* I add. *You know I wouldn't be asking this of you if I didn't have to.*

Little dots appear as she begins to respond. Then they vanish. This happens three more times before the screen goes dark.

So I tap out another message. *Noah will be there in fifteen minutes. I suggest you be ready.*

Those dots begin once more, only to die again in a flash.

Nothing.

Hmm.

"Did she buy it?" Noah asks slowly.

"Only one way to find out," I reply, leaning down to grab a wallet from my bag. "Time to go play chauffeur, Mr. Dragon." I hand him the wallet with the fake ID facing upward.

He glances at it and grunts. "Original."

I smile. "I wanted to make sure you remembered it."

His hazel eyes roll, and he tosses the wallet into the cupholder of his chair. Then he pulls his long, fiery hair back into a bun at his nape. That hair is what earned him the dragon nickname.

Well, that and his penchant for using fire to creatively take out his marks.

And the tattoo on his cock.

Although, the latter was a result of the nickname growing on him, so he decided to memorialize it in the way only Noah ever could.

"No weapons," I remind him as he stands. "Sheriff Syrus is likely going to frisk you."

"Sounds kinky."

"Pretty sure he's taken by one of the other *Widows* in town." I've picked up on that use of a nickname through the chatter between the six females who own the town.

A town they bought with *our* money.

It took me seven very long years to track it all down, and imagine my surprise when I found a pretty little blonde omega as the culprit behind the hack.

That surprise only grew when I discovered her true identity.

And then the obsession began.

For the better part of the last few years, we've been developing a plan on how to exact our revenge.

Not on the Widows, as they like to be called, but on *her.* Our Lark.

For a while, we waited to see if she would return to the city to visit her brother. That would have been the easiest course of action for us. But as I continued digging through her history, it became apparent that she didn't want to come home.

I thought she might return for her father's funeral six months ago, and we prepared to grab her then. However, Giovanni never reached out.

Which was what birthed my idea to pretend to be him.

To lure her out on our own.

Take her home on *our* family jet.

And have a long-overdue conversation about the money she stole from us.

"Why are you still here?" Laz asks as he exits the jet's bedroom in a freshly pressed dress shirt. He finishes rolling up the sleeves to the elbows, then goes straight over to the bar area to fix himself a scotch.

"Because I haven't left yet, obviously." Noah pops up out of his chair like a lethal cat, all athletic agility encased in a six-foot-three frame. "But you should be sure to save some of that tender energy for our new pet, boss."

"Call me that in front of her and I'll make you choke on my knot," Laz returns without missing a beat.

I arch a brow. "You basically just guaranteed that Noah's going to do exactly that." The psychotic enforcer has been wanting an opportunity to suck Laz off for years. But Laz won't let Noah anywhere near his dick.

Instead, I'm the one he turns to when he needs to get off.

An understanding that seems to glint in his gaze as he stares me down now while taking a sip from his glass.

Shit. I know that look. I also know why he disappeared into the back cabin to shower and change.

He's pent up with need, waiting for our omega to finally arrive.

She might not be our scent match. But we don't fucking care. We fully intend to keep her.

Assuming she'll have us, anyway.

However, that's what courting is for. And this is our first move—taking her for a ride on the jet back to New York City.

Might not be the most traditional way to woo an omega. Though, nothing about our arrangement here is normal.

She stole from us.

Now she'll pay us back by giving us her time.

Or that's the plan, anyway.

Noah saunters toward Laz, all arrogance and grace, and pauses right in front of the slightly taller man.

Dark chocolate and cinnamon notes swirl in the air as their scents combine in a tangible sparring match.

These two have danced around each other since the day they met, both fighting for dominance.

I learned long ago not to even try. Maybe that makes me the weakest alpha of our pack, but I've always identified more with beta energy. I just happened to present at eighteen with a knot, an experience that shocked the shit out of me about nineteen years ago.

"Not going to warn me not to touch her first?" Noah asks, a thread of a taunt underlining his words. "Johan says her pussy is like honey. I may not be able to resist."

"I speculated that her scent is honey-like," I clarify when Laz looks sharply my way. "I haven't smelled her yet."

His jaw visibly ticks. "I get first lick."

"Pretty sure that's our pet's decision, not yours," Noah drawls. "And guess who you're sending to meet her first?" He bats his long red lashes at Laz, then turns to leave.

I stiffen. "No—"

"Weapons, yes, I heard you, tech boy genius," Noah interjects, flashing me a dazzling smile. "I don't need weapons to kill a sheriff, Johan. You know that better than anyone."

He leaps out of the jet before I can amend the rules to strictly say *no killing*.

Not that he'll listen to me, though.

"If he kills Syrus, or anyone else for that matter, Lark will never accept us," I mutter, running my fingers through my hair.

"A fact he's well aware of," Laz replies, his voice deep and filled with a familiar rumble. He pushes away from the bar to walk over to where I'm sitting. With the way he's looking at me, I half expect him to yank me out of my chair and force me to my knees.

"I have to monitor the phones and track Noah," I remind

Laz. "While I'm amazing at multitasking, I refuse to let anything—even you—jeopardize this mission."

His lips curl up on one side as he takes over Noah's vacated seat. "I like watching you work, Johan. That'll content me for now." His words are underlined with a knowing lethality, one that has me a bit concerned for Lark.

If he's in this mood when she meets him, he might forget the meaning of consent. Laz already sees Lark as his, which is a sentiment I share. But I want Lark to desire to be ours rather than force her.

Which means I'll probably need to be the buffer between them.

Fortunately, it's a role I know how to play well.

However, it means I'll be taking the brunt of all that alpha need later. And Laz has stamina that can go on for days.

Ignoring my thoughts of what's to come, I focus on the present and pull up Noah's tracker. Lark still hasn't responded to her brother. So either I said something wrong—which I don't believe I did—or she's preparing to submit.

Or, I think, considering a third alternative. *Or she's planning for a fight.*

Wanting to test that theory, I send a final text. *Be sure to warn Sheriff Syrus that you have a driver coming in to get you. His name is Noah Dragon. He's a newer enforcer with the family. Don't test him, honey pot. He's a wasp you don't want to piss off.*

Dots appear, and I wait with bated breath.

Only, she stops again a second later.

"This is going to be interesting," I murmur to Laz. "Think she'll go easily or give Noah hell?"

"If she's the omega I think she is, it'll be the latter." He lifts his ankle to settle across his opposite knee. "But it won't be inside her precious town. She cares about it too much to cause a scene. The fight will happen here." He looks at me. "And I can't fucking wait."

CHAPTER THREE
LARK

He's a wasp you don't want to piss off.

My brother's words have my stomach twisting with dread as I zip up my suitcase. I've only packed five days' worth of clothes. Everything else, I'm leaving here. Including most of my gadgets and technical toys.

Because I'm coming back.

I… I *have to* come back.

I'm going to *demand* that he allow me to come back.

That's the plan, anyway. A plan I will carry out the moment I set foot on the jet. I'll tell this wasplike enforcer to put my brother on the phone. Then I'll draw the gun I've tucked into my boot and threaten to shoot Noah if my brother doesn't promise to let me go home in a few days.

It's a weak plan.

Okay, it's a terrible plan.

I don't even know if this Noah Dragon means anything to Gio. Though, I imagine he does if he's trusting the *wasp* with my kidnapping.

Maybe that's a strong word. But it's an accurate one. I didn't consent to this.

Actually, no, that's not true. I agreed to do this long ago, when my brother helped me out with the whole Gideon Henderson mess.

He was my man on the outside. The one with all the files that could destroy Gideon and his omega trafficking ring.

Of course, my brother would never have sent everything over to the authorities. He would have handled it himself, something he offered to do a decade ago after I escaped. But I told him we needed our own form of closure. I didn't expect it to take as long as it did. However, it's done, thanks to Silva and her pack.

Gideon's dead.

His organization—*Gideon's Dolls*—no longer exists.

And Gio has asked me to come home.

The timing feels a little too coincidental. *Does Gio know we killed Gideon?* I wonder. I didn't tell him. But maybe he has eyes on me?

God, it would be just like my brother to have a bodyguard watching over me. Like father, like son.

I nearly grab my phone to call him and shout at him. To demand answers. But his goon is almost here.

He gave me a thirty-minute warning and then a fifteen-minute one.

Followed by that command to give Syrus a heads-up.

I obeyed only because I don't want any trouble. The past is best left buried. And I'm going to keep it that way by playing along for now.

Until I board the jet.

Then all bets are off.

I pick up my bag and look out the window as an all-black vehicle approaches. It's sleek and expensive-looking, telling me it's my ride.

But before I can leave to meet the *wasp*, my phone rings and Silva's name pops up on the screen.

I nearly groan.

Because I know why she's calling. *Tattletale,* I think, the word for Syrus.

"Hey, Silva," I say, forcing my most nonchalant tone. "What's up?"

"Where are you going? And why is there an assassin escorting you?" She doesn't waste time beating around the bush. But that's Silva—direct and to the point.

My lips twist. "I don't know if *assassin* is the right description," I say slowly. "More like a bodyguard."

"He's six foot three with crazy eyes and a too-charming smile," she says. "He has 'assassin' written all over him."

"Is that your description or Syrus's?" I wonder aloud. "And I'm guessing Syrus frisked him, right?"

"He didn't bother. He said the guy looked lethal enough to kill with his hands alone."

"Sounds kind of like a compliment," I joke, deflecting. "Maybe they can be friends?"

"Lark." There's a subtle bite to her tone. "Tell me what's going on."

"It's nothing," I promise her, hoping I'm not lying. "My brother just wants me to come home for a bit, and he sent someone to pick me up. That's all."

She's silent for a long moment, and I know she's not buying any of this. "If you need help—"

"I don't," I interject. "But if I did, you would be the first one I'd call." That part isn't a lie. Silva's a badass. And her pack is… intense. She would be the best person to get me out of a bind.

But this isn't her battle to fight; it's mine.

"I'm going to be okay," I tell her. "It's a simple family thing."

"A family you've never mentioned."

"I'm sure there are parts of your past that you haven't mentioned either," I point out.

Silence fills the line, confirming my suspicion.

Still, I want to put her at ease, so I give her just a bit more to pacify her. "Remember my guy on the outside? The one I gave all that information to about Gideon?"

I pause for a breath, not needing her confirmation but wanting to provide her with a chance to process my words.

"Yeah," she confirms, sounding wary.

"My brother was that guy, Silva." I swallow, aware that what I'm telling her is directly linked with why I have to go home now. "So everything's good. I'll be back in a few days."

She's quiet for a long moment. "I don't like this, Lark. Something feels off."

"It's the outsider effect," I reply, infusing a hint of nonchalance into my tone. "Once Noah's gone, it'll feel okay again."

"Doubtful," she mutters. "You'd better text me when you get to… Wait, where are you going?"

"New York City," I admit, wanting to give her the truth. "And I'll message you and the others. Don't worry."

"Famous last words, Lark."

I smile. "I'll be fine." I pick up my bag, as the car has been parked outside for a few minutes now. Fortunately, the "assassin" hasn't stepped out yet. I know because I've been watching for him. "Talk to you soon."

"Okay…" The hesitation is clear in her voice. "Text me about bubbles, and we'll come find you."

"Bubbles?" I repeat with a laugh. "Really?"

"It's the first thing I thought of," she grumbles at me. "You got a better safe word?"

Honey pot, I think. But I don't share that with her. "*Bubbles* is fine. I'll find a clever way to use it. Like in reference to a bubble bath or something."

"Good." I can practically see her clenching her jaw. "Be safe, Lark."

"Always," I reply. "I'll be back before you know it."

I really hope that isn't a lie.

And I'll do everything in my power to ensure it's not.

We say goodbye, and I pocket my phone. It's the only piece of tech I'm bringing with me. It's innocuous enough that no one will be suspicious of it.

Well, my brother will be suspicious. But that's just because he knows me well.

Here goes nothing, I think, locking up my place and heading out to where the vehicle is quietly idling.

When the driver's door opens, I pause and take in the sight of the large, muscular alpha unfolding from his bucket seat. I'm honestly surprised he fit in the sporty sedan. Because he's huge.

And I suddenly understand Syrus's concern.

Yep. Definitely an enforcer.

Or an *assassin*, as Silva called him. In my old world, those two terms were pretty much synonymous.

"Ms. Bia—"

"Lark," I interject, not wanting him to give my identity away. "Just… *Lark*."

One of his eyebrows—a dark red slash—lifts. "All right." He walks around to the back of the car as the trunk opens. But he doesn't pause there to wait. He continues toward me with a predatory grace that makes my heart skip a beat.

Lethal feels like an inadequate adjective for this man. He's outright dangerous.

I take a step back on instinct, his eyes holding a touch of insanity that causes my heart to halt in my chest.

But then his natural cologne hits me.

All cinnamon and spice and *alpha.*

My eyelashes flutter, my pulse kick-starting into overdrive. And I realize with a start that this male—this exquisitely beautiful, homicidal male—is my scent match.

My lips part.

The world stops.

And I find myself gaping up into a pair of multicolored irises.

His hand is somehow on my hip. The opposite on my arm as he stares down at me in concern. "You all right, little bee?"

I sway, dizzy from his nearness. And… and the realization that this male… this male is *my scent match.*

Is that why Gio sent him here? Did he somehow know?

"Aurora?" Noah whispers, his voice low and edged with an emotion that's difficult for me to define. There's no way this deadly male is worried about me. Or even cares about me. That's not how the crime world works.

If he's my brother's enforcer, then our scent match doesn't even matter. He's not high enough in the organization to claim an omega of my standing.

My father would have him executed, actually.

And Gio…

What will Gio do?

He couldn't possibly know. Unless… unless he was trying to send me a gift?

I…

A deep rumble ignites from Noah's chest, causing me to blink. *A purr. He's purring. God, why is he purring? Alphas only do that for… for their chosen mates. Their omegas.*

Me.

I'm his…

Oh, fuck…

I close my eyes and try to find my brain. It's somewhere inside me. Somewhere hidden beneath the toxicity of this instant bond. This need. This… *Ugh!*

Pretty sure I growl out loud.

When the alpha stills in front of me, I'm certain I did.

Yet he continues to purr. Which both infuriates me and delights me at the same time. "Can you… stop?" I ask, hating that it sounds like I'm begging. Because I feel helpless. His cinnamon aroma is overwhelming. And I swear there's a note of hot honey beneath it all.

Which matches my own scent.

Brown sugar and honey. Like a damn bakery, one that has only heightened in power since my eighteenth birthday.

Sometimes being an omega is frustrating.

Scratch that. Being an omega is *always* frustrating.

Especially right now as my body sways toward the dangerous man and not away from him. All because my instincts are telling me to rub up against him like a cat in heat.

That's enough, I tell myself. *This is not happening.*

Noah must agree because his purr ceases. Or maybe that happens because I asked him to stop. Not sure.

"Want me to get your bag?" he asks, his voice deep and slightly accented. Not Italian, though. More… Irish.

Which is strange.

The mob doesn't usually associate with the mafia.

But maybe he's just from Ireland? Or has an Irish parent?

It's not a very thick accent, so I suppose anything is possible.

"Aurora?" he murmurs, his lilt exceedingly evident as he rolls the *r* sounds in my name.

"Lark," I correct him, trying to steady myself. He uttered my legal name in a low enough voice that no one else could have overheard him, but that doesn't mean I want to risk him saying it again, as he's already said it twice. "And no, I'll get my own bag, thank you."

I use those words as a reason to step around him and walk over to the trunk to deposit my suitcase in the back.

When I turn around, I find him right behind me, the lethal predator moving on silent feet. I don't jump. I don't even wince. I just… stare up at him. "How long have you worked for my brother?"

He smiles. "That's the question you want to ask me, little bee?"

"Little bee?" He called me that once before. "Seriously?"

He leans down, crowding into my space as he presses his nose to my neck.

Shivers break out down my spine, followed by a trail of goose bumps as his cologne drowns me in a wave of cinnamon and hot honey.

"Mmm, I can't wait to make you buzz," he whispers against my ear. "My sweet little bee." His lips brush my cheek, then he steps back and gestures toward the car with his chin. "Let's go."

"You realize my brother will kill you if you touch me, right?" I demand, not following him as he goes to the back door and opens it.

The smile Noah flashes me is borderline mercurial. "I'm sure he'll try, yes." He cocks his head. "Now, are you going to enter the car willingly? Or do I need to start shouting your real name?"

My jaw clenches.

"Ms. Bia—"

I step forward. "Stop."

He simply grins again, and I understand why Syrus called Silva.

Because the Widows Peak Sheriff was right.

This man—this *wasp*—is insane. I can see it in the way he looks at me. He's probably a psychopath, actually. No emotions. No remorse. Just a calculated killer.

And he's my scent match.

Fucking fate.

I skirt around his muscular form to slide into the car. His natural heat practically bathes me in a warm wave of alpha energy, ensuring I feel him on every inch of my skin as I settle onto the leather seat.

Then he closes me inside, and I'm suddenly surrounded by his scent.

A scent that deepens when he takes over the driver's side of the sedan.

I'm so screwed, I think, closing my eyes for a second.

But then an idea hits me, and I pull out my phone to type a furious message off to my brother. *I can't believe you sent a scent-matching alpha to escort me home. Dad is going to end up killing this poor man now.*

I almost giggle at that last part because *poor man* is not a good description for Noah Dragon. Something tells me if my father tries to take him out, he'll fight back.

He'll lose, of course. They all do. But he won't go down easily.

My phone buzzes with a reply, almost like my brother was waiting for my reaction.

But his response confuses me. *Noah's your scent match?*

You're really going to play dumb? I fire back.

How could I know he would be your match? he returns. *Don't you dare let him touch you, Aurora.*

I snort at that. *You know what? Just for that, I think I'll let him knot me on the jet. Fill it all up with our pheromones, just for you and dear old Dad.*

Dots appear and disappear.

Then nothing happens.

I would worry about my brother trying to hop on a jet to stop me, but he doesn't currently have access to a jet since he sent it here to get me.

Feeling oddly satisfied by that, I slip my phone back into my pocket and look up just as we pass through the small town center.

Club 21 will be hopping soon, the hangout place one I've been to probably a hundred times now.

The Widows own it. But Silva mostly manages it with a few of the others performing there every now and then. I've never been the performing type. However, I handled the tech and security when we first set it all up.

It's a safe space.

One that used to not allow alphas.

That's changed. As has the town.

But the overall haven-like atmosphere is still very much alive here.

I'm coming back, I promise myself as Club 21's sign grows distant behind us.

This is just a short trip home.

I hope…

CHAPTER FOUR
NOAH

My mouth is watering.

My knot is throbbing.

And my dick is fucking leaking.

Yet I've never been more elated in my entire existence. Because our sweet little pet is my goddamn scent match.

She smells divine. Like brown sugar and sweet honey. It makes me want to kneel for her and beg for a lick between those alluring thighs. Her tight jeans provided me with a pretty good idea of what those legs of hers will look like without clothes.

Though, her baggy sweater hid her tits and waist.

I'm guessing a B cup. Soft tummy—perfect for me to lay my head on. And hips designed for my hands to grab while I fuck her from behind.

Mmm. I don't bother to tamp down my interest. I just let my scent drown her in my desire.

She's mine.

Ours.

To share. To play with. To worship.

God, I can't wait to get her on the jet. Take her home. Create a nest. Show her what it means to be our queen.

I knew there was something special about her the moment Johan showed me her profile.

A hacker. Brilliant. Stole money from us—which made me like her already because that took some major fucking balls.

Though, I paused on the praise when I found out she used all those funds to buy some abandoned town in the middle of the mountains.

Still not quite sure why she did that or how she's related to the other girls who jointly own Widows Peak.

It's on my list of questions.

Ones I'll ask her after we address the more important items. Like how she prefers to have her pussy licked. If she enjoys knots in her ass. Favorite ice cream—for food play. Date of her next heat. Bondage preferences. Cock-warming limits.

The usual.

Then we can get to the semantics about our past.

I glance at her in the mirror, noting the way she's worrying her bottom lip as she stares out the window.

Night is quickly creeping up on us, cascading shadows throughout the car. But her expression is still clear in the low lighting.

She's nervous.

And aroused.

The former is coming off her in waves, and the latter is evidenced by the luscious scent of welcoming slick.

She's wet. But of course she is—we're a match. It's a natural response between our dynamics. That doesn't mean I'll take advantage of it.

I want her to ask for my knot.

Tell me to eat her cunt.

Beg me for a kiss.

Yeah, I have a consent kink. It's at odds with some of the other shit I like to do, but there's just something so fucking hot about a woman—or a man—giving me permission to destroy them in bed.

I also really enjoy making my conquests plead for more, even while crying out for me to stop.

I bet Aurora will cry prettily for me. Those beautiful brown eyes, damp with her pleasure-induced agony. *Mmm. Yes, fucking please.*

It takes considerable effort to return my focus to the road. But I need to deliver our queen safely to her future nest. If she's amenable, we can play on the jet.

Then I can stare at her for however long I want.

For eternity, hopefully.

I swallow, my heart beating harshly in my chest. Her scent is like a drug. I'm addicted already and eager for more.

The urge to growl hits me hard, intrinsic desire running hot through my veins.

My omega is finally here.

That I've spent the better part of the last few years obsessing over her existence doesn't help. I haven't fucked anyone outside of our pack since learning about her.

God, Johan must be tired of sucking my cock.

I've used him as my primary relief, all while thinking about the pretty little bee humming in my back seat.

Well, I thought about him, too. And the things I intend to make him do to her.

Soon, I think. *So. Fucking. Soon.*

The makeshift airfield we used to land on isn't too far from the town. An abandoned farm—one we bought after finally locating our intended pet.

Laz hired some guys to turn one of the fields into a small runway. It's not the smoothest surface, but it works.

And now we're getting to use it for its intended purpose—to bring our omega home.

She's quiet in the back seat, still looking out the window. So I'm surprised when she doesn't say anything as I pull into the old farm's driveway and head toward the run-down house at the end.

When I park, though, she frowns. "This isn't the airport."

"It's our airport," I tell her, exiting the car and moving to the back door to open it before she can try to hit the locks.

She peers up at me. "Did you borrow someone's old farm and land a jet in their backyard?" Surprisingly, she exits while she speaks, making my job rather easy as I close the door behind her and go to the trunk.

"Something like that," I admit. "We didn't want to deal with the local airport and their traffic control."

"Hmm."

That's all she says, and I wonder if she's starting to question who I am. However, she doesn't stop me from grabbing her bag, and she follows me around the house toward the waiting jet in the field.

It's all lit up and pretty, just waiting for us to board and take off.

My lips curl. *The fireworks are about to begin.*

Because the moment our girl sees who's waiting for her on board, she's going to backpedal fast.

Which is why I pause at the bottom of the stairs and wave for her to head up first.

I'm about to be the wall that closes her in.

She gives me a once-over, her perfume sweetening the air. I almost ask her if it's an invitation to taste her, but she starts up the stairs before I get a chance to speak.

That's fine.

Her actions provide me with a delectable view of her hips and her tight ass. *Definitely knotting her there.*

My dick leaks a little more, making me wonder if I'm about to go into a rut.

Every part of me is strung tight, my muscles clenching as I admire my omega's athletic legs. *Mmm, fucking exquis*... My brow furrows as the thought trails off in my head. *Is that...?*

My eyes narrow at her ankle, the hint of a bulge that shouldn't exist causing my breath to halt.

I nearly bark out a laugh, utterly entertained by what I assume is a weapon of some kind.

Dear God, I think I'm in love.

Our omega is packing.

Oh, Laz is going to lose his ever-loving shit when he realizes I didn't frisk her for toys.

My lips curl, eagerness hammering through me as I all but sprint up the stairs after her.

I've got to see what she has planned.

She walks into the jet like she owns it, her blonde hair glowing like a damn halo beneath the lights. Only, she freezes upon seeing Johan seated in an executive chair, his laptop balanced along one leg as his ankle is propped up by his opposite knee.

Laz is nowhere to be found, which suggests he's either stepped into the back for a call, or he's planning some sort of grand entrance.

He's the only one our omega might recognize. And once she does, all bets will be off.

I set her bags in a compartment overhead, wanting my hands free for whatever is about to happen.

"Is my brother here?" the little bee demands.

Johan's lips twitch. "No."

"And who are you?" Her haughty tone is all mafia princess. I love it. I love her. I'm ready to make this happen.

My best friend cants his head, the action sending his thick black hair into his eyes. He adjusts his dark-rimmed glasses on his nose, ignoring the unruly mop on his head. "Johan."

Aurora stares at him like she's waiting for him to elaborate. When he doesn't, she folds her arms and asks, "Are you an assassin as well?"

Johan looks around her at me. "You told her you're an assassin?"

"Nope." I shrug. "She must just assume I'm good with my hands." I step closer to her so I can whisper in her ear as I add, "Which I am, by the way. *Very* good with my hands, I mean."

She shivers and steps away from me. But it's not fast enough to mask the fresh wave of her alluring scent.

My little bee is aroused.

Does that mean Johan is a scent match, too? Is she even close enough to tell?

Granted, the entire jet smells like a bookstore cafe that specializes in mixing expensive chocolate into its coffee drinks. That's a combination of Johan and Laz, something I'm sure our omega has picked up on by now.

That could explain the subtle shivers teasing the hairs along her exposed skin. I admire the reaction, enjoying the way her body is naturally responding to ours. It makes me want to wrap an arm around her waist and bury my face in her nape. Lick that throbbing pulse point on her neck. *Bite.*

A growl threatens to rumble free from my chest. But I swallow it, needing to tamp down my rutting instincts.

She has to consent.

No. More than that. She has to *beg.*

"Who are you?" she whispers, looking back at me and then at Johan again. "Something isn't right here."

"A comment I made roughly ten years ago when reviewing my account finances," Laz says as he steps into the cabin.

Ohhh, the show is about to begin.

I move to block the exit, eager to watch the fireworks. If only I had some popcorn. It would go so nicely with the moment.

Our little bee buzzes to life, stumbling backward as her pretty eyes widen. "Lazarus."

Laz arches a dark brow as he slips his phone into his pocket, his expression taking on what I joyfully call "arrogant don" mode.

Here we go, I purr inside, eager to clap. Because I fully expect our bumblebee to sting in response to whatever Laz is about to say to her.

Hopefully, that sting will present itself as a gun.

Go on, little bee, make my night…

"Most omegas refer to me as *sir* or *Mr. Ferraro*. Omegas that have stolen from me, well, I think the formality should be accompanied by a bow. Perhaps a plea for me to spare one's life. Show mercy. Entice me perhaps… with an offer?"

And there goes the buzzing.

She's practically vibrating.

Ready to pounce.

I'm about to grin, to cheer her on, when I realize that the vibrating isn't driven by anger, but by another emotion entirely. She's *trembling*.

And a sour note tinges the air.

One I… I don't like.

The brown sugar and honey is so beautifully smooth. This… this has a bitterness to it that has my lips curling downward instead of upward.

Our bee is… is she going to cry?

Ah, fuck.

That's not at all what I want to see. I was hoping for yelling. Maybe a good punch to the groin. Some sort of fight.

Not *this*.

"Are you…?" The quiver in her tone has me utterly conflicted between growling and purring.

Growling because I'm disappointed. And also pissed at Laz for upsetting our pet.

And purring because… because I want to comfort her.

Fuck. A. Duck. There goes my erection.

This is *not* what I'm into. Not at all.

"Am I?" Laz asks, his voice silky and layered with undeniable threat.

I glance at Johan, note the way his brow is pinched, and

realize he's fighting an urge similar to mine. He wants to comfort the girl.

Well, there go my plans for the night.

"How did you find me?" our omega asks, her voice so small that it takes effort not to wrap her up in a hug.

Which is asinine.

I make grown alpha males cry on the daily.

Yet the first sign of tears from this female has me wanting to drop to my knees and beg forgiveness. And I didn't even fucking do anything.

Laz did this.

He upset our omega.

Yet he doesn't seem to care at all, both his hands now in his pockets as he saunters toward her like he's the king of the jet.

Which I suppose he is as the don of the Ferraro Mafia.

That won't stop me from introducing my fist to his face when we're alone later. He's ruined our entire fucking night. *Asshole.*

"I didn't. Johan did." Laz glances at tech boy genius, then focuses on our omega as he pauses right in front of her. "You provided quite the challenge, princess. Have anything you'd like to say before I destroy your pretty little world?"

Her shoulders stiffen. "You're going to take the town?"

He considers her for a moment. "It would be an appropriate punishment, wouldn't it? You bought it with *my* money, after all."

Laz doesn't mean it. We've talked about this a thousand times. All he wants is the omega—*Aurora Bianchi.*

Not only did she win all of us over with her antics, but her name and birthright are an appropriate match for our pack.

The fact that she's also our scent match is just... fate being fucking awesome.

Only, Aurora doesn't seem to feel the same way. Her head

falls. Her buzzing has all but stopped. And she's suddenly kneeling on the floor like she's going to weep.

God damn it. I take a step forward, ready to string Laz up by his neck and force him to fix this, when the little bee on the floor whirs to life and the sound of a cocking gun fills the air.

"You will *not* touch Widows Peak," she snarls, pointing the barrel right at Laz's knot. "Or I will fucking end you."

I blink down at the little ball of fiery energy.

She's on her knees, which has her perfectly poised to blow Laz's junk clean off.

A laugh escapes me, and my palm covers my heart. "Ah, fuck yeah. I'm definitely in love." I go to my knees beside her, utterly taken by this beautiful woman. "Marry me, little bee. Please?"

CHAPTER FIVE
LARK

I BLINK, SO UTTERLY STARTLED BY THE INSANE MALE *PROPOSING* to me that I don't realize what's happening until the gun disappears from my hand and ends up in Lazarus Ferraro's palm.

Shit!

I shouldn't have let the redheaded sin-on-a-stick alpha distract me.

A growl leaves me, and I launch myself at him, no longer caring about anything else other than unleashing my fury.

These damn alphas.

Lazarus fucking Ferarro.

Finding me.

Tricking me—still not sure how they did that.

And threatening my town!

Then proposing to me as a distraction while strangling me with his intoxicating scent. *All of their scents*, I think, dizzy from the cafe-like atmosphere and that decadent hint of chocolate. *Focus, Lark.*

I scratch my nails across Noah's face and snarl at him like I'm just as insane as he is. And maybe I am. Maybe I have gone a little crazy.

Because these fuckers are here to take Widows Peak from us.

Never going to happen.

"Whoa!" Noah shouts, grappling for my wrists.

The world spins, and I'm suddenly flat on my back with him on top of me, his hazel eyes burning down at me in an array of beautiful colors. *Blue, green, auburn.* Such a unique combination of pigments, the intensity momentarily stunning me.

Or maybe it's the air leaving my lungs that does that.

Because *ow.*

He has my wrists caught beneath one big hand, his opposite at my throat. But he's not squeezing. Instead, he's… he's *petting* me.

"Calm down, little bee," he murmurs, his chest vibrating against mine as he *purrs.*

What the fuck is happening right now? And why am I going limp in response?

"That's it, sweet girl," he coos, his Irish lilt seeming to soften his tone even more. "God, you're killing me." He drops his head to my neck and inhales, the motion causing my eyes to nearly close.

Until I meet Lazarus Ferraro's obsidian gaze from above. My gun is nowhere to be seen. Not that it'll help me now. He's staring down at me with an indifferent expression, his chiseled features ones I would recognize anywhere.

Because he's a fucking god of an alpha.

Tall. Broad shoulders. Thick black hair that falls past his ears. Tan skin. Intensely dark eyes. Square jaw decorated with an elegantly trimmed beard. Full lips.

It's like the heavens above chose to give him every single beautiful physical trait, just to make him that much more lethal.

Because inside is a heart so black that even the most dangerous crime lords fear him.

I've heard the stories.

I know what he's done. Who he is. *How* he does business.

That's why I chose the Ferraro family to steal from. If anyone could stand to lose a few dollars to a good cause, it's him.

"The next time you pull a gun on me, I suggest you use it," he says, his cultured tone causing my stomach to twist.

Not just because his deep alpha voice is an aphrodisiac to my inner omega, but because his *natural cologne* is swirling all around me.

Dark chocolate with a hint of cherry.

Another damn scent match.

Three, actually.

Because that hot guy with the glasses is *also* mine.

Which means they're a pack.

Of course they're a pack. I knew that the moment I stepped onto the jet and smelled their combined fragrances.

That's why I questioned Johan. Something didn't feel right.

Or rather, it felt *too right.* Because of the instant scent match.

There was no way my brother sent these alphas to get me. I determined that before Lazarus stepped into view.

But seeing him confirmed my suspicions.

And brought all my worst fears to life.

"I'm not a forgiving man, Ms. Bianchi," he goes on, still holding my gaze. "I fully intended to destroy the one who stole all those funds. And I still might. But it won't be in any way that you've imagined."

My stomach twists. He's talking about killing me. "My father will annihilate you," I promise. "I'm an omega and his only daughter. Hurting me is a death sentence for you."

He stares down at me, his indifferent mask seeming to flicker with some sort of emotion. It's not fear, though. Or anger. It… it looks like pity.

Which doesn't make sense.

Why would he pity me?

Or is that regret I'm seeing? That would make more sense.

"Kidnapping me is a mistake," I add, hoping I'm reading that sentiment wrong. "Release me, and I'll just go back to Widows Peak. And we'll… we'll forget this ever happened."

His expression hardens. "That's never going to happen, princess. Now get up. It's time to go."

Noah groans on top of me. "But I'm comfortable."

"Stop fucking around," Lazarus growls at him. "You can play with our omega later."

I bristle at that. "I will not be playing with anyone." My body might be reacting to their scents and my inner thighs might be slick with need, but I have no intention of letting their knots anywhere near me.

Well.

No intention of letting them *closer* to me, as I can feel the one currently throbbing against my overheated center. It's almost like I'm naked. Like Noah's naked, too. Because I swear I can sense his pulse through my clit.

"You wound me, little bee," Noah murmurs against my ear. Then he rolls off of me and moves deftly to his feet, his actions lithe and reminding me of a panther more than a hulking alpha.

When he holds out a hand for me, I glare at it.

"You're the one who came clawing at me," he reminds me softly. "I merely defended myself."

"By pinning me to the ground?" I snap.

"Okay, so I defended myself… and I enjoyed it very much." He drops his hand. "Any time you want to spar, I'm your alpha."

"You're not my anything."

He shrugs and wanders over to the jet's exit—which I realize is still wide open.

Or it *was* wide open.

Until now as he closes it.

I frown. "Kind of hard to leave when the door is closed."

He glances at me, confusion in his expression. "We can't fly with the door open, pet."

"I'm not your pet," I mutter at him. Only, my frown deepens. "Wait, *fly*?"

"That is what the boss man meant when he said it was time to go." He waggles his brows at Lazarus. "Right, *boss*?"

The Ferraro don growls. "You're just begging for a demonstration right now."

"I did say you practically invited him to play," Johan inserts from his seat. He hasn't moved from his executive chair, a laptop still perched on his leg. Yet he's watching me with his beautiful ice-blue eyes.

He seems to be the least lethal of the group. Yet I can tell that doesn't mean he's *soft*. He's just… a different kind of deadly, maybe.

"How did you figure out it was me who stole the funds?" I ask him, my stomach knotting for an entirely different reason.

Because I'm pretty sure I know how.

And it has everything to do with that laptop on his lap.

"If I asked how you hacked into our accounts, would you tell me?" he counters.

"No."

He smiles, and the beautiful man now has dimples, making him even more alluring. "Then you'll understand why I'm not going to answer your question," he replies, confirming that his laptop is indeed his weapon of choice.

A fellow hacker.

Great.

Just fucking great.

I'm not sure who to fear more—the psychotic assassin who just proposed to me, the mafia don, or the lethally handsome hacker.

Probably all of the above.

And they're my scent matches.

Ugh.

I want to roll onto my side, curl into a ball, and just… disappear into the floor.

But the floor is now *moving.*

Or rather, the jet is *moving.*

Because we're about to fly.

I sit up suddenly, my gaze going to Lazarus. "You're going to attack from the air?" I ask, dread filling my veins. "Are you…?" I can't finish the question. I… I can't stomach to even *conceive* what I intended to ask.

He said he was going to *take* the town. Not *destroy* it. But maybe I misunderstood?

All my friends…

"Please," I whisper, staring up at him and not caring at all that he can probably see my heart breaking. "Please don't hurt them."

He gives me an unreadable look. "Your family?"

"They're like my family, yes." I probably shouldn't have admitted that out loud. "We've been through hell, Lazarus. I wouldn't have stolen your money otherwise. But they needed a safe place to be… to be *free.* The omegas have started over there. They've built that town from scratch. *Please* don't destroy it."

A myriad of emotions seem to tumble through his features, the chief among them—*fury.*

He's angry that I have the nerve to ask him for anything. I get that. But I couldn't live with myself if I didn't try to save my friends.

"Please," I add again. "I'll do whatever you want. They don't even know what I did. Please don't punish them for my sins. They've… we've…" I close my eyes. "Please… *sir.*"

I'm aware I look weak. Broken. *Stupidly naïve.* Especially as a tear escapes my eye. But this is my worst nightmare come to life. A trap I idiotically waltzed right into.

I was suspicious. However, then my brother used the *bee* references, and I… I thought it was really him.

Only now I realize it was Johan.

God, he's good.

In another situation, I would be impressed.

Though, right now, I'm anything but.

"What *hell* have you been through?" Lazarus demands.

"Gideon Henderson?" Johan suggests. "It would explain why she went on that mission last month."

My eyes spring open, my focus on him in an instant. *He knows about that?*

God, of course he does.

What don't these men know?

"How long have you been watching me?" I demand, aware that my emotions are having whiplash. But I… I deserve answers.

Or, well, I probably don't.

However, I'm going to push for them anyway.

"Years, little cat," he replies.

Little cat? I nearly echo.

But my chin is suddenly caught in Lazarus's hand, and he's bending so that his chiseled features are the only ones I can see. "*What hell*, Ms. Bianchi?" he repeats.

I swallow. "The Doll program," I whisper, feeling the need to be truthful with him. Maybe if he realizes what happened to us, he'll… he'll be compassionate.

Though, just thinking that nearly has me snorting.

This is Lazarus fucking Ferraro. Compassion *doesn't exist in his world.*

"Elaborate." A single word, uttered with such dominance that I nearly whimper.

This is an alpha in his prime. Maybe thirty-eight or thirty-nine years old. I can't remember his exact birthday. But I know he's deadly. I know he's a don. And I know… I know better than to ignore his command.

"Gideon Henderson trafficked and groomed omegas to be Dolls for alpha packs. He… he kidnapped the six of us—the ones who own Widows Peak—during our eighteenth year, then tried to sell us when we turned twenty-one. But we escaped." I swallow again. "He takes six a year…"

I trail off, aware I spoke that in the present tense when it should have been the past tense.

So I amend by saying, "He used to take six a year. Kept us in the Henderson mansion. Trained us as a group with beta handlers. However, it's done. Gideon's dead. As are the beta handlers."

I don't really know what else to say.

But I try one more time to save my friends. "Please don't hurt them, Mr. Ferraro."

His responding growl echoes through the cabin.

Only to be overshadowed by the roar of the engine as the jet begins to really move. *We're taking off.*

He looks up sharply, then suddenly I'm flying through the air as he lifts me into his arms and takes me to the seat beside Johan. I startle as a belt is buckled around me… *and* Lazarus.

Because he has me in his lap.

Noah takes the chair across from us with a skip, completely unfazed by the ground tilting around us. He casually snaps himself in, then winks at me.

I glare back at him.

Which has him grinning like a damn loon.

Because he's nuts. They probably all are, honestly.

And now I've just been officially kidnapped by them.

This is bad.

Very. Fucking. Bad.

CHAPTER SIX
LAZ

THE URGE TO PURR HITS ME HARD IN THE CHEST. AND IT'S directly at odds with my need to *kill*. To annihilate. To *fucking destroy*.

Yet I have no one to take my fury out on because the object of my ire is already dead.

Gideon. Fucking. Henderson.

I've been aware of his existence for a very long time. The sleazy wannabe who fancied himself a crime boss. He trafficked omegas for a living. There's nothing honorable about that. Nothing even remotely admirable either.

I may do some horrible shit. But I don't involve myself in the trafficking of omegas. I certainly don't touch children, either.

There are lines that should never be crossed. Lines that organizations like mine actually understand and respect.

Gideon Henderson didn't understand any of that.

Yet I'm pissed that he's dead. Because *I* want to kill him.

He tried to traffic my intended, I think, staring at her pretty blonde hair. I want to comb my fingers through it, see if it's as soft as it looks. Purr for her as I hold her. Nuzzle her slender neck.

She's fucking gorgeous. Smells like brown sugar and honeyed chocolate. I think maybe that's me altering her scent a little. I like that. It's as though I've already claimed her as mine.

Mmm, biting her will be fun. I can't wait to mark her.

But first, she needs to understand a few things. Because clearly, we did not get off on the right foot.

"I'm not interested in touching Widows Peak," I say against her ear, aware that she seems to be under that misconception.

She trembles in response but doesn't speak.

"I don't want to hurt your friends," I add, ensuring we are clear on this. "And while your family may piss me off on occasion, I rather like Giovanni and have no desire to harm him either."

I purposely don't mention her father… since he's dead.

Alas, I don't have the heart to share that news with her.

I almost did when she said her father would kill me if I hurt her. It was an intrinsic response, one that very nearly rolled off my tongue.

However, sadness overwhelmed me in the next moment. Sadness for her. Sadness that she doesn't know about her father's death. Sadness that I would be the one to tell her.

I don't want to break her heart.

I want to protect it. Cherish it. *Earn* it.

Not crush it.

Fuck.

I nearly bend my head to take in her sweet aroma, to calm my raging pulse by simply hugging her.

But I don't.

Because she's not truly mine. *Not yet.*

"We are heading home to New York City," I go on, trying to placate her with the facts. "You will be staying with us for the foreseeable future. And Widows Peak will remain untouched."

I don't elaborate on that last part, purposely pairing the sentences together. There's an implied *if you cooperate, I won't bother with Widows Peak* in my statements.

In truth, I have no desire to alter the town she's built. I'm more entertained by her stealing my money than I am angry.

We came here for her. And her alone.

She's ours.

The fact that she's our scent match just makes our intended claim that much more powerful.

Giovanni is already aware of our intentions, too. I sent him a missive an hour ago, informing him that his sister is now mine to care for. It was a necessary action on my part, as he was about to learn the truth anyway from Aurora's bodyguard. He would no doubt see us taking her and report back. I figured it would help to get ahead of the problem.

Of course, that didn't stop Giovanni from calling me right before Noah and Aurora arrived.

"What the fuck are you doing, Ferraro?" he demanded as soon as I picked up the phone. "Don't touch my fucking sister."

I calmly explained that I didn't answer to him and that I would absolutely be touching his sister.

It was the wrong thing to say.

All he did was curse.

So I politely ended the call with a "We'll catch up soon, future brother-in-law."

He's probably going to have an army waiting at the airport when we land.

Which is precisely why we'll be going to a private airfield closer to the Hamptons.

Perhaps we'll even stay there for a bit at our family estate instead.

Realizing that I said *New York City* to Aurora, I decide to amend by saying, "Actually, we'll likely be going to the Ferraro estate, which is in the Hamptons. I think you'll like it there, princess. The weather is cool right now, but the scenery is still beautiful."

Like you, I add in my mind. *So fucking beautiful.*

The jet starts to even out in the air, which means it'll soon be safe to stand again.

I'm not sure I'll let her go to try, though. Because I rather like the feel of her in my lap. Her subtle curves are quite enchanting. It makes me want to press up against her ass, just to relieve some of the pressure building inside my cock.

I've wanted her for years. Thus, I expected this yearning.

But the scent-match aspect has me borderline ready to rut.

God, I meant it when I said I might destroy her. She's going to take my knot in so many ways… drown in my cum… fucking live with me inside her for hours or days.

It's going to be phenomenal.

I wanted to start the moment she boarded the jet.

However, her interpretation of events altered my expectations.

Now I have to be patient.

And of all my virtues, patience isn't one.

But for her, I'll try.

"Seriously?" Noah groans. "I fucking hate it there."

"Then you can go to the city and manage the tower while Johan and I entertain Ms. Bianchi at the estate," I tell him.

His hazel eyes flicker with annoyance. "Fuck. Off."

I arch a brow. "So you don't want to manage the tower? Alone? In New York City?"

He unbuckles himself and stands, then stalks off toward the bar while flipping me off over his shoulder.

"I guess he's coming with us, then," I say conversationally to Johan.

"Looks like it," my second-in-command murmurs.

He's not a typical second. Mostly because he's not blood.

But I'm an only child. I never had a brother to help me run the organization. I've only ever had Johan and Noah.

The latter is too insane to be my second. He's an excellent enforcer, though.

Johan sets his laptop to the side and focuses on the female in my lap. "Would you like anything to drink, Lark?"

Lark, I think with a mental snort. I know that's her chosen hacker name, but I've always thought of her as *Aurora*.

Because that's her name.

Aurora Bianchi.

Mafia princess.

Omega.

Mine.

The beauty of the situation is that she very well could have been mine for years, my lineage and birthright essentially setting me up to request her as a bride.

It's customary in our world for arrangements to be made that solidify business relationships. And our two families have been on the cusp of forming an alliance for decades. A union between us would have been natural.

Except she disappeared.

I've also never fancied the notion of an arranged marriage. It feels antiquated and traditional, two aspects of my role that I've fought since becoming the head of the Ferraro family.

My "advisors"—the old guard who supported my father—will be absolutely thrilled by this union. Their approval is possibly the only negative aspect of this situation.

Given all the other positives, I'm willing to overlook that.

"Lark?" Johan prompts. "Are you all right?"

I frown, realizing that she's stiffened against me. She hasn't spoken a word since telling us about Gideon Henderson.

Is she reliving some sort of trauma? I wonder, my frown deepening. *Have we triggered her in some way?*

I suppose we did just take her against her will.

But I have no desire to turn her into a "doll." I want an equal. An omega who will aim a gun at me and not hesitate to pull the trigger.

Though, my balls are grateful she didn't make it that far.

Still, knowing she was strong enough to try is exactly the kind of spirit I need in my future wife.

"Does my father know about this?" she asks quietly.

"No, but your brother does," I tell her, again not wanting to elaborate on her father's status. But I could seriously kill Giovanni for not informing his sister about their father's death.

I expected him to reach out to her months ago and demand that she return for the funeral. Our plan was to take her afterward.

Except Giovanni never made the fucking call.

Which is how we ended up just outside of Widows Peak, waiting in a jet on old farmland.

"May I speak with them when… when we arrive?" The slight stammer in her voice tugs on my heartstrings and makes me want to comb my fingers through her hair again. But it's nothing compared to the way she broke earlier when she thought I meant to hurt her precious town.

That display nearly brought me to my knees.

I never intended to hurt her. Since the moment I learned of her involvement in stealing my money, all I've ever desired is to make her mine.

She's the ideal female to help me lead.

A strong, intelligent woman with a wicked talent for computers. It makes me wonder what else she can do.

But I need to answer her question first. "You may speak to your brother whenever you want," I tell her honestly. "I'm not going to cut you off from your family or your friends. But I am going to make you stay with us for an undetermined amount of time."

She shifts on my lap, causing the seat belt to pull

uncomfortably. I reach around her to unfasten it, giving her space to move.

At first, she's still, like she expects me to do something.

Then she very slowly slides off my legs.

I don't move, nor do I comment on the feeling of loss I experience as she stands.

After a moment, she walks over and takes the chair across from Johan. The executive lounger looks large around her small frame, something that's highlighted even more as she tucks her legs up to hug her knees.

Noah returns to take over the seat beside her, but not before setting two glasses down. The first is his trademark martini—one he makes on every flight. The other looks like sparkling water, except there's a cherry tint to it.

"I made you a Shirley Temple," he informs Aurora. "Seemed like a sweet drink a pretty bee might like."

The glare she shoots him is adorable. "I prefer black coffee."

He blinks. Frowns. Then stands. "Got it."

"No, I mean—"

"Got it, got it." He waves her off and heads back to the bar, presumably to put on a pot.

"I don't want any right now," she mutters. "I'll be up all night."

"I think you'll be up all night regardless," Johan says, his voice softer than usual. "It's a long flight, and something tells me sleep is your last desire at the moment."

"There's a bed in the back, though, if you do want to rest," I offer awkwardly, wanting to be part of the conversation.

"I thought you were going to destroy my world," she returns, some of the fire seeming to reenter her expression. "A fitting punishment, right?"

"Destroying Widows Peak would be a fitting punishment,"

I reiterate, agreeing. "But you're not an ordinary adversary, Ms. Bianchi."

She straightens a little, her beautiful brown eyes catching and holding mine. "And what does that mean, exactly?"

"It means my punishment for you is going to be… unique to our situation." I thread a hint of sensuality into my voice, my chest nearly igniting into a seductive purr.

Because I very much want to begin. *Right now.*

Except her brow simply furrows, her gaze narrowing. "That doesn't tell me anything."

"He's saying that violence isn't part of the equation," Johan interjects. "When someone steals from the Ferraros, their families are often destroyed, and their deaths are… extended. But Laz has no desire to hurt you in that way, Lark. None of us do."

I glance at him, a little irritated that he spoke on my behalf. But his focus is entirely on our omega.

"Widows Peak is safe," Johan goes on. "We've actually been pushing more money into the town for the last few years, ensuring it remains stable and allowing it to thrive. The Ferraro family has no interest in seeing it destroyed. The inhabitants will remain not only untouched but also protected."

My jaw ticks. He's part of my pack, making this his information to share. However, I'm not pleased that he's the one informing her of our influences.

"Prove it," Aurora dares him, causing my second's brow to arch.

"You just want access to my laptop."

"No, I want proof that you're not going to bankrupt Widows Peak and sell it off to the highest bidder," she counters.

His lips twitch. "I'm not naïve, little hacker."

"Neither am I," she fires back.

He shrugs. "If you want to play, we can play." He grabs

his computer and opens it, then starts typing across the keys. After a moment, a buzzing sounds and he arches a brow. "I believe that's your phone, Ms. Bianchi."

She scowls, then pulls it from her pocket.

"Did you not frisk her at all?" I demand, my attention shifting to the enforcer, who had a very simple job—pick up our omega and deliver her safely.

"Safely" includes *disarming* and *frisking*.

"You seemed averse to me being the first one to touch her, remember?" Noah doesn't face me as he replies, just continues fussing over the coffeepot.

We have a flight attendant who could help, but we told Mari to stay in the cockpit area for now with Leo and Tomás. The trio is our favorite flight crew. However, we don't trust anyone near Aurora.

Rather, *I* won't be trusting anyone near her for a while.

Except for Noah and Johan, of course.

"You were all, *I get first lick*," Noah goes on, doing a poor job of imitating my voice while also making me instantly regret my *trust* in him around our omega. "Ergo, I didn't frisk her."

"Because you intended to check her for weapons with your tongue?" I demand.

He shrugs his big shoulders and finally faces me. "I can think of a lot of creative ways to *frisk* our omega."

"I'm not yours," she inserts, her gaze on her screen. Although, she's clearly listening to everything we're saying. "What the fuck did you do to my phone?"

"Cloned it," Johan says. "Obviously."

"*When*?" she snarls at him.

He merely smiles. "If you figure that out on your own, I'll let you see my laptop."

She glowers at him. "You're a menace."

"That's a bit of the pot calling the kettle black, yeah?"

Her resulting growl makes my dick harden, her ire an

aphrodisiac that has my inner alpha wanting to rumble right back at her.

Except, she appears to be pissed at Johan. Not at me.

Which is a shame.

I think I would enjoy wrestling her for dominance while she fights back.

The way she attacked Noah a bit ago also made me jealous. Why was he the source of her anger and not me?

I wouldn't mind pinning her to the ground.

Then kissing her senseless.

"You had no right to do this to my tech," she snaps at Johan.

"Hmm, shall we have a discussion on the moralities of hacking?" he returns as he sets his laptop off to the side again, his icy gaze seeming to glow through his glasses. "How much money did you steal, again?"

She pushes off her chair. "Not enough." She stomps off toward a door at the front, which has my eyebrow lifting upward.

"Do you intend to meet the pilots?" I call after her. "Because I should warn you, they're armed." Not a lie. But they would be fools to pull a gun on her. They know who she is, that we intend to keep her as ours.

They don't know the details, of course. But they're not paid to understand our choices and decisions. They're paid to carry out orders—effectively and smoothly.

Aurora pauses and turns around, then heads in the opposite direction toward another door. "I'm going to sleep," she informs us. It's a lie, clearly. I suspect she wants to go fuss with her phone. Which is fine. I can respect her need for space.

But that doesn't stop me from standing and moving to intercept her.

When she sees me coming, she freezes, her expression shifting from determination to a hint of fear.

"If you wish to rest, I suggest you use the bedroom, not a closet," I tell her quietly, then turn to lead her to the appropriate door.

She doesn't immediately follow.

However, when I push through the threshold to show her the clean space, she finally starts to move again. Then carefully skirts by me like she's afraid I might grab her.

I don't.

But I do follow her inside the cabin and shut the door behind me.

"There are rules, Ms. Bianchi," I tell her quietly, causing her shoulders to stiffen. "I'm going to start by sharing two of them with you, as they're pertinent to our current situation."

She seems to stop breathing, her back still to me as I approach her from behind.

I lean down so my lips are near her ear, but I'm careful not to touch her. Just keep a few inches of space between us to ensure she feels my presence and hears me clearly.

"The first rule is that you will not share any details about me or my pack with anyone else. That includes our location. Our plans. Our business." I pause, waiting for her to acknowledge my words. "Say 'yes, sir' or nod so I know you understand."

Her throat works, the swallowing action one I hear more than see. And it makes me want to wrap my palm around her delicate neck so I can feel the movements.

But I refrain, my focus on her acceptance of rule number one.

"Yes, sir," she says, a little growl accompanying that final word.

A growl that once again has my cock throbbing with need.

However, I ignore my impulses and instead say, "Good girl." I move around her, wanting to see her brown eyes as I voice the second item. Because it's important.

She stares up at me with a wary expression, one that

doesn't match the honeyed perfume coming from between her thighs.

Aurora may not be pleased by her current circumstances. But she's not disinterested.

It could be our scent match messing with her instincts. Making her crave something she shouldn't.

Though, I suspect this mutual attraction goes so much deeper than that.

Our bloodlines practically made us for each other.

Over time, she'll understand that. Respect it. *Embrace it.*

I can't wait. Yet I *will* wait… for her. For her consent. For her acceptance.

And that's the heart of what I intend to say next.

"The second rule, Aurora, is that none of us will touch you unless you ask us to." I cant my head, realizing I should probably amend that statement a little since I technically pulled her into my lap without permission.

And whatever happened on the ground with Noah also contradicts what I've just said.

So I need to be clearer.

"What I mean is that we'll never force ourselves on you. If you want our knots, you'll have to beg for them. Only then will we touch you, princess." I run my gaze over her beautiful form, then lean in so my lips are near her ear again. "And trust me, darling, you're going to want us to touch you."

Precum saturates my dick, causing my cherry-chocolate cologne to deepen in the air between us.

She shivers, telling me she's noticed.

Her blossoming perfume suggests she likes it, too.

I inhale, ensuring she hears me breathing her in, then I exhale against her ear, wanting her to feel my warmth. "Enjoy your time alone, Aurora. If you need anything, we'll be in the other room."

I start toward the door as she replies, "I'll never beg."

My lips curl as I glance at her back. "We'll see." I grab the knob, only to pause and add, "But feel free to watch, Ms. Bianchi. It'll give you an idea of what's to come."

She spins toward me. "Watch? Watch what?"

I simply wink at her.

Then leave the room—without closing the door—and head straight for Johan.

CHAPTER SEVEN
LARK

MY HEAD IS WHIRRING.

My vision is… is *darkening*.

And my lips are parted.

Because I have no idea what Lazarus Ferraro is talking about.

I understood his "rules." Scoffed at his commentary about *begging*.

But now, I'm… I'm confused by his parting words.

Watch what? The thought echoes in my head, rivaling what I said aloud.

Naturally, he didn't respond. And he didn't close the door either.

I stalk forward, determined to slam it shut, mostly to punctuate the finality of the moment. However, I find myself grasping the wood instead and hanging on as Lazarus yanks Johan out of his chair with his grip around his throat.

What the fuck? Is he punishing him for…? My thought trails off as he pulls Johan into a kiss.

A wild, hungry, *furious* kiss. The kind only two alpha males can enjoy. Because it's virile. Masculine. *Violent.*

Johan tries to shove him back, but Lazarus's grip on his throat is unbreakable.

He's *squeezing.*

Is he going to kill him? I wonder, my heart suddenly in my throat.

Lazarus is a cold-blooded murderer. A calculating mastermind. An intimidating masterpiece of exquisite art.

Okay, that last part is my assessment.

The other two descriptions are tied to his reputation. A reputation I seem to be witnessing in real time as he walks Johan backward into a nearby sofa and pushes him down.

He has my gun, I think. *I… I never saw it again. What if he pulls it out and—*

"Coffee?" Noah asks casually, joining me in the doorway with a cup of… of *coffee.*

I gape at him. "Are you crazy?"

He seems to consider my question for a moment before shrugging. "*Crazy* just feels… inadequate. I prefer *psychotic.*"

A growl rips through the cabin before I reply to that asinine comment, the source of it seeming to be Johan. "*Fucking prick,*" he snarls.

"You like it," Lazarus replies, lying down on top of Johan. "Now shut up and take it."

My eyes widen as Johan flips Lazarus off of him and onto the floor, the move impossibly fast and resulting in a snarl from the mafia don.

I grab the doorframe for support, worried that I may need to shove myself backward and lock myself in the bedroom. But all that happens next is Johan pinning Lazarus and kissing him much like he was kissed seconds ago.

It's feral in nature. Borderline intoxicating.

I… I can't stop watching.

Because they're tearing at each other's clothes now. Buttons fly. Fabric shreds. And groans fill the air. "I've always preferred exhibitionism over voyeurism, but watching your reaction right now is rather satisfying. You're practically buzzing, little bee."

I should reply.

No, I should stop watching.

But I can't.

Muscles. So many muscles.

The alphas are *ripped.* Lazarus is all tan skin and defined lines. And Johan is all lean, athletic man. He's still on top, kneeling now as he stares down at the other man.

They're shirtless but still wearing shoes and pants.

Johan's hand goes to his belt buckle to deftly unfasten it.

Lazarus watches with narrowed eyes. "You're taking my knot first."

"Am I?" Johan practically purrs back at him. "Because I'm the one on top, *boss.*"

Lazarus growls, his hand suddenly around Johan's throat again as the pair of them grapple across the floor.

"He doesn't like that title," Noah whispers loudly. "Threatened to choke me with his knot earlier if I called him *boss* in front of you. Sadly, it was yet another false promise."

He pushes into the bedroom, making me spin a little with him—because he's too big to just slide around me.

Or maybe he wasn't trying to.

He sets the coffee cup down on the nightstand, then plops onto the bed, making me frown. "What are you doing?"

"Having a nap," he says, putting one arm over his eyes. "It's either that or go jack myself off in the shower. Alas, I don't think that's going to help anything." He peeks at me from beneath his elbow. "I would use Johan, but his mouth is about to be otherwise engaged."

He adjusts his arm, bracketing his eyes once more, and sighs.

"I would love to share him," he says, sounding sad. "But I don't think he can handle me and Lazarus double-teaming him."

A groan from the other room has me looking back at the dueling men.

Lazarus is on top again, only he's spun around and he's… he's pulling out Johan's…

Oh. My. God.

Johan's dick is… *massive.*

I mean, most alphas are. Or, well, from what I've *heard*, they are. I've never actually taken a knot before.

But *wow.*

He's long. Pale. And… and *going into Lazarus's mouth.*

"*Fuck,*" Johan growls, grabbing the other man's sides like he's about to shove him away again. Except he clings to him instead. Then runs his palms down to Lazarus's waist and around to the front.

Slick pours from my center as I watch him unfasten the don's pants.

No boxers.

And if I thought Johan was large… I… *That will* never *fit inside me. Or Johan, for that matter. Or* anyone.

Except the alpha proves me wrong by opening his mouth around Lazarus's head and taking him with practiced ease.

At least until the don punches his hips downward.

Johan grabs Lazarus's ass, swatting at him. But that doesn't stop the other man from starting to *thrust.*

God, he's in his throat.

They're both… they're both… I can't even… This is… *madness.*

It's so savage, the way they're forcing each other to take their cocks. Even Johan is pumping upward.

And all I can think is what they must look like inside a woman.

Inside me…

My thighs clench.

This is dangerous.

Their scent is everywhere. Intoxicating me. Drowning me. *Tempting me.*

Dark chocolate and cherries.

Leather, paper, and coffee beans.

Cinnamon and hot honey.

The last one is coming from behind me, but it's mingling with the other two and creating an erotic ambience that has need scorching through me in a molten wave of intensity.

I've never experienced anything like this, not even during my heats.

The scent match.

The captivity.

Their vicious sounds.

The growls are reverberating around the room, overriding the hum of the jet. It's almost as though they've unleashed a mating call.

And yeah, I guess they kind of have. Because they're in the throes of passion, face-fucking each other with an abandon that has me longing to slip between them.

This is insanity. They've kidnapped me. They plan to punish *me.*

Although, Lazarus didn't confirm *how* he intends to do that. Just told me it wouldn't have anything to do with Widows Peak. He also claimed my family and friends would be safe. Except, that latter part seemed to be contingent on me behaving.

But then he said he wouldn't touch me unless I begged.

So he's not going to hurt me. Or force this match.

Just… just show me what I'm missing by fucking Johan's mouth instead.

My nails dig into the doorframe, my legs shaking as I fight the urge not to go to my knees and crawl to them.

I am not this omega, I tell myself. *I am not going to go let them stuff me with their knots just because they smell good.*

Well, they look good, too.

Really fucking good.

They're not even fully naked, their pants still on as they use each other for relief.

"Who do you think is going to come first?" Noah asks, suddenly right behind me, his breath warm against my ear.

I didn't even hear him move.

He's the deadliest of the trio. Yet I let him sneak up on me. And I'm not even afraid to have him near.

In fact, all I want to do is melt back into him and let his masculine strength soothe my raging desires.

Only that would probably stoke my need that much more.

"My money is on Johan," Noah continues, his voice low as his warmth begins to bleed through my clothes and seep into my skin. "All Laz needs to do is use his tongue a little bit on the tip, and it'll set tech boy genius off." He chuckles. "At least, that's all I need to do when I suck his cock."

I swallow, imagining Noah now joining the mess of limbs on the floor.

"I've tried biting, too," Noah murmurs. "He doesn't fancy that as much. Seems pain isn't his thing. Too bad, though. I'm a bit of a sadist at heart."

Shocking, I think. I would utter that word out loud, but I don't quite trust my voice right now.

"What about you, little bee?" His voice feels somehow closer now, his presence that much more imposing at my back. "How do you feel about a little sting with your pleasure? Maybe some teeth in your neck?" His lips ghost over my pulse—which is now thudding—as he speaks.

He hums, the vibration of it making me shiver.

"Mmm, I'll take that blossoming fragrance between your slick thighs as a yes." He exhales the words against my neck, nearly making me whimper. "What about your clit, pet? Can I nibble you there? Maybe your nipples as well?"

Oh God, I feel faint. Dizzy with desire. Warmth blossoms in my lower belly, spreading sensation to my nerve endings. It's like I'm about to explode. Yet I'm not even being touched. I'm just watching and listening. *And imagining…*

His words have me nearly turning into him, to see what it would be like to feel his teeth in my flesh.

No, I tell myself. *No. No. Fuck no. No!*

A muffled snarl halts everything inside me, the bookstore-like fragrance suddenly overpowering everything else in the room as one of the men explodes.

Johan, I realize, his head seeming to thrash beneath Lazarus as the bigger man pins him with his cock down his throat.

He can't breathe, I think, the snarl having been cut off mid-sound.

"Choke on it," Lazarus demands, his hand around Johan's knot as he strokes the other man to completion.

Johan has a lethal grip on Lazarus's hips, his arms bulging with masculine fury as his cock unleashes ropes of cum.

Into a shirt, I suddenly understand. *What…?*

I don't even want to know.

Yet I can't stop watching Lazarus squeeze the other alpha's dick. His movements are rough. Cruel, even. Yanking up and down while twisting Johan's knot.

It looks like it hurts.

Only, Johan is still coming. So it must not be that painful?

Lazarus lifts, and a wheeze comes from Johan, only to be cut off again as the don punches his hips back down. "Don't swallow," he demands, fucking Johan in earnest now. "I want that cum."

Noah huffs a laugh. "Good luck with that. Looks like tech boy genius is going to asphyxiate on Laz's load. Ah, well, worse ways to die."

His heat leaves my back, suggesting he's returned to the bed. But I don't hear him. Nor do I check to see where he is. I'm too busy watching Lazarus unleash his brutality on Johan.

I shouldn't be turned on by this. I should be appalled. And I certainly shouldn't wish I were Johan right now.

Yet I do.

I'm absolutely fantasizing about being beneath Lazarus as he destroys me in every way imaginable.

I'm broken. Messed up. Utterly insane.

This… this is going to feature in my dreams going forward. Every night. And I'll never be able to stop it.

That knowledge is only solidified as Lazarus looks right at me, his dark eyes smoldering with intensity as he growls my name. "*Aurora.*"

And then he stops moving.

For a moment, I hold my breath, wondering if he's about to come get me. But his snarl shatters that expectation as his body begins to convulse.

He's coming.

Johan's hands move, one going to Lazarus's knot, like he's trying to prevent the alpha from lodging it deep in his throat.

Can that even happen? I wonder dizzily. *Wouldn't he die?*

Except now I'm wondering if I could handle something like that during a heat.

Definitely broken, I think, echoing my thought from seconds ago.

Johan slams one palm against Lazarus's back, resulting in a snarl from the man on top, but he rolls off of him in a pant of sound, his hand reaching down to take over the motions against his cock.

I swallow as Lazarus meets my gaze again, his hand moving as strands of ecstasy leave his massive head. I have no idea how Johan took that into his mouth. There is no way I am going to ever be able to do that.

Nor will I ever be able to handle that much cum.

Because he's still going, making a mess of his stomach as he unleashes his pleasure.

All while staring me down.

With a hunger that has my thighs quivering.

Johan grabs the shirt from him and spits into it, the liquid abundant and fragrant. *Alpha seed.*

It's everywhere in the cabin now.

Highlighted by their scents.

Driving my inner omega mad.

I'm mere weeks away from my next heat. But if they continue this, I'm going to end up falling into my estrus faster than expected.

By the time Lazarus is finished coming, I'm no longer caring about the mess between my own thighs.

He knows what he's doing.

Johan, too.

They're torturing me. Overwhelming me with their natural colognes. Seducing me with their growls.

And now looking at me with feral intent in their gazes.

However, only Lazarus is daring enough to move. He tucks his massive dick into his pants, but doesn't bother to zip himself up more than halfway, and stands to walk toward me.

Every part of me screams with a need to retreat, to slam the door and hide.

Yet my legs refuse to move. And my core simply weeps with expectation.

What's he going to do to me? I wonder as he prowls forward.

But he stops a foot away, then uses a shirt—the same one Johan saturated with his orgasm, the same one he also spit into—to wipe up the mess on his abdomen.

My mouth salivates over it, my inner omega longing for a taste.

Only for him to drop the shirt at my feet. "In case you want that for a future nest," he tells me. Then turns and walks away while saying, "Sweet dreams, Aurora."

CHAPTER EIGHT
JOHAN

I'M STILL STRUGGLING TO CATCH MY BREATH, MY BODY TENSE with renewed need.

That orgasm barely took the edge off of what I'm feeling. Probably because Laz was a dick and didn't finish it properly.

Or, more likely, because there's a very aroused omega standing at the back of the plane.

A very aroused and now pissed-off omega standing at the back of the plane, I amend as her pretty eyes narrow at Laz's retreating back.

Poor thing thought he was coming over there to play.

But Laz isn't that kind.

When he told her she would have to beg, he meant it.

Though, Noah might not honor that rule. Pretty sure he'll break his own spine if Lark simply asks him to.

Laz crouches down near where he left me on the floor, blocking my view of our omega. He brushes his knuckles along the fine stubble decorating my jaw, the tender motion at odds with all his hard edges and violent tendencies.

"You good?" It's a soft question, one he always asks me after one of our rougher sessions.

"Yeah," I force out, swallowing. It's all I can manage, given how raw my throat feels.

He knows it, too. Because he frowns and his touch drifts down to stroke my neck.

Then he stands and heads straight to the bar, all while ignoring the simmering omega in the doorway.

Noah has moved to stand behind her, his gaze on me over her head. He's checking in as well, aware that Laz can be a dick when he wants to be.

Of course, Noah can be, too.

They're both harsh lovers. But the sex is always phenomenal between us, so I don't mind their brands of sensual violence.

Lark is in for a treat.

However, I don't think she's ready to indulge in us yet. She's still glowering at Laz. "I don't need or want your cum rag," she snaps at him.

Then turns around and walks right into Noah's chest.

His eyebrows fly upward. "Whoa there, little bee. No need to sting me."

She releases a string of creative curses before demanding, "*Why* are you so creepily silent?!"

I sit up and tuck myself back into my pants as Noah replies, "It's not intentional." His tone and expression remind me of a wounded puppy dog. "I'm sorry."

"*Ugh*," Lark groans. "Just… just go away. Please. I… I want to be alone."

"Okay, little bee," Noah says, sounding crestfallen. "But if you need anything, like more coffee, or food even, let me know. I'll get whatever you want."

He starts to move around her but pauses as she says, "How about my freedom? Can you give me that?"

My eyebrow glides upward as I wait to hear how he'll respond to that.

"In time, I think you'll find that the three of us can

provide you with a freedom you never even knew existed." It's a thoughtful response that's underlined with innuendo, and he utters it with sincerity because he means every word.

That's the thing about Noah—he doesn't lie. He can deflect, and potentially withhold the truth, but anything he does say is spoken with honesty.

An assassin with morals, as he once told a mark.

"That's not what I meant," Lark huffs back at him.

"I know, little bee." He gives her an indulgent smile. "But I think you know exactly what I meant." He grabs her hips and lifts her out of his way so he can vacate the room.

It wasn't necessary. He could have moved around her. However, Noah obviously wanted to touch her. I understand, as I feel the same way.

She releases an adorable little growl and grabs the door.

Noah bends, picks up the shirt, and tosses it onto the floor inside the bedroom just before she slams it shut. His lips turn up, and he waggles his brows our way as the omega inside releases a roar of fury.

Then he casually grabs the knob to hold it shut when she tries to open it.

More growling sounds from behind the wood, making my dick throb against my partially undone zipper. "Can you imagine how that'll feel while throat-fucking her?" I ask, groaning as my tip leaks with cum. "I wonder how loud we can make her scream."

"I'm all for finding out," Noah replies. "But Laz decided to create a rule without discussing it with the pack."

"So, what? You're going to lock me in here now?!" Lark shouts through the door.

"It's for your comfort, little bee." Noah's voice vibrates with his purr. "Just enjoy the scents and have fun. There's a vibrator in the nightstand if you need it. No dildos or knots, though. If you want those, you'll need to ask nicely."

Something shatters against the door.

By the scent, I suspect it's the coffee mug.

Noah looks down, his brow furrowing. "Well, that's just wasteful, Aurora. But I'll brew you another cup for later."

He releases the doorknob and heads to the bar area, where Laz is standing.

The two square off as Laz refuses to move, his hands holding two glasses of water.

"I respect you as our pack leader, *boss*, but no more rules without a group discussion," Noah tells him flatly. "And I'm licking her pussy first."

"I thought we decided that was up to her?" Laz counters.

Noah grins. "Oh, it is. I'm just letting you know that I'm the one she's going to invite into the nest first. So I'll be tasting that sweet, honeyed slick before either of you is even considered."

My lips twitch as the door to the bedroom opens and the shirt is tossed back out into the cabin. "In your dreams, *Noah Dragon*," she snarls, clearly having heard his proclamation. "None of you are having my slick. Or *ever* being invited into my nest."

Her gaze meets mine as her nostrils flare, and a hint of uncertainty flashes in her brown irises.

Then she slams the door shut, and the sound of a lock echoes through the cabin.

"Hmm, seems Ms. Bianchi hasn't chosen any of us yet," Laz muses. He lifts one of his glasses toward Noah and adds, "May the best alpha win." He takes a sip before sauntering toward me and handing me the other glass.

"You can't make a toast with water, boss. That's just bad luck," Noah tells him.

"As your *boss*, I can do whatever the fuck I want," Laz replies as he squats in front of me like before. His knuckles brush my jaw again as I take a sip of cool liquid. "Any better?"

I allow myself a few swallows before I reply, "I'm fine, Laz."

His doubtful expression irritates me.

I grab his wrist and yank his hand away from my face. "I'm fine," I repeat slowly and clearly. "I can fucking take your cock, Laz. I have for years." My voice is hoarse, but the words are clear.

"I know," he says, his gaze running over my torso and down to where my dick is still rock hard. "I just want to make sure you're ready to go again before I knot your ass."

"Why do you get a second round before I even get a first?" Noah demands before I can reply. "It's my turn."

"Here's a thought," I interject. "How about you two fuck it out and give me a damn break."

Laz arches a brow and looks pointedly at my erection. "You just said you're fine, baby. Now you need a break?"

I roll my eyes. "Don't call me *baby*." I hate that nickname and he knows it.

The asshole merely smiles. "Make me."

Fuck. He's baiting me.

And I'm two seconds away from giving in by introducing my fist to his face. Because he always knows how to push my—

A beep sounds from my laptop, instantly snagging my attention.

My gaze narrows.

Setting my glass on the ground, I return to my chair and pull the computer into my lap. My dick practically throbs against the metal, my pants still not fully fastened. But that sound is a warning.

Pulling up my screens, I search for the source and feel a smile crest my lips as I find Lark trying to undo the locks I've placed on her phone.

"You two play," I tell Laz dismissively. "I have a hacker to bait."

Rather than listen to me, Laz slips into the chair beside me and places his ankle on his opposite knee. "I'll wait."

"I'm going to try not to take that personally," Noah mutters, the sound of drinkware clinking by the bar. "Actually, no, I'm going to take that fucking personally. Because it's *always* personal."

Laz sighs. "We'll rip each other apart, Noah."

"Yeah, but it'll be a fun way to die." He joins us and picks up the drink he barely touched earlier. I suspect it's not as fresh now, but Noah doesn't seem to be bothered. "So. What's our bee doing?" He leans forward. "Wait, tell me there's a camera in there."

"No camera," Laz informs him.

"Well, that's a missed opportunity. Kind of like how you haven't let yourself feel the wonders of my mouth yet."

"Can you not proposition me for one second?"

"Sure." A beat passes. "Want me to kneel now, *boss*?"

Laz sighs again.

And I start ignoring them.

Because Lark is quickly breaking through all my layers, trying desperately to find a connection she can use. *Who are you going to call first?* I wonder. *Your brother? Because that line has already been compromised.*

I let her maneuver through my safeguards, impressed by the speed with which she's shattering my programming.

Of course, she hasn't removed the cloning tool—which is what I'm using now to watch her.

If she finds it, I have a backdoor I can access.

But she seems to be more focused on finding a way to make a call.

When she slips past the final layer, my heart gives a pang.

Because her father's name is the one she brings up on her phone first.

I intercept it before she can even hear the first ring and say, "Nice try, little black hat. You'll have to do better than that." I hang up her line and hit a stroke on my keyboard that re-enables every layer on her phone in a matter of seconds.

A shriek sounds from the other room.

Followed by another crash.

"Think she threw her phone this time?" Noah asks conversationally.

I shrug. "We'll find out soon enough."

The door opens to display a pissed-off omega—one who happens to be missing a shoe. *Ah, so it was a boot she threw at the door, then.*

"You said I could talk to my family. Was that a lie?" she demands.

Laz looks at her, his expression a mask of boredom. "You may speak to your brother anytime you would like, but you'll need to use my phone if you wish to call him right now."

Her eyes narrow. "So I am a prisoner."

"A pretty pet," Noah corrects her. "One we're going to cherish and take care of in every way."

That appears to be the wrong thing to say because she scowls. "I do not want to be a *pet*. Nor do I want to be a prisoner. I want to be free."

"Then follow the rules, and you'll earn your freedom," Laz tells her. "Do you remember the ones I've given you thus far?"

She simply glares at him.

Which causes him to smile. "Rule three, then, is I expect you to take care of yourself." He looks down at her bare feet, which are standing in the remains of the coffee cup she shattered. "As of right now, you do not appear to be obeying rule three all that well. I suggest you reconsider."

Her nostrils flare. "Fuck. You."

He arches a brow. "Is that an invitation, darling?"

"It's certainly not me begging," she snaps back at him.

And proceeds to slam the door closed again.

"You have thirty minutes to take a shower," he calls after her. "If you don't, I'll come in there and supervise you while you obey!"

I type all that out in a text message to send to her.

The response I get is instant, and it's a middle-finger emoji.

When I show Laz, he smiles. "Please inform her that I look forward to showering with her in thirty minutes."

"Why do you get to be the one who ensures she follows the rules?" Noah demands. "Maybe I want to bathe our pet."

"Because I came up with the rule."

"One you again didn't run by us," Noah points out while I type Laz's words into my computer and hit Enter. "I'm getting really tired of you making all the decisions, *boss*."

"Says the assassin who usually enjoys my commands," Laz returns. "Are you saying you don't want our omega to take care of herself?"

Noah doesn't answer. Just grunts.

Because of course he wants her to be safe and look after herself. We all do.

But he does have a point about the rules.

However, I'm too entertained to comment on it, as Lark just returned a string of creative emojis.

I tilt the screen so Laz can see the array of weapons coupled with several more middle fingers. Noah gets up so he can view the response, too.

"That reminds me, where'd you put her gun?" he asks Laz.

"Why?" Laz asks.

"Because I want to know."

Laz stares at him for a moment, clearly wary. "I set it in the only working drawer over there for now," he says, gesturing to the armoire that serves as a front for our onboard safe. He was obviously planning to set it inside at some point.

But Noah is already walking over to retrieve it.

"What are you doing?" Laz demands, shifting in his seat but not following.

"Getting our girl a toy so she can feel safe again."

Laz's expression shifts to irritation. "Noah—"

"Nope," he says, cutting off the don. "I know what I'm doing."

Laz moves to try to stop him, but I hold out my arm. "I'm actually with Noah on this one." Giving the gun back to Lark is a risk. But… "She needs to feel like she can protect herself."

"And what about us?" Laz demands. "It's not your knot she threatened with that thing."

I grin. "We both know that made you hard."

"Not the point, Johan."

I shrug. "What's life without a little danger? Isn't that what you always say?"

He simply shakes his head. "Lunatics. Both of you."

"Thank you," Noah murmurs, giving a bow. Then he knocks on the door. "I'm coming in, little bee. Try not to sting me, yeah?"

CHAPTER NINE
LARK

NOAH RETURNED MY GUN.

I thought it was a trick. Because it *had* to be a trick.

Yet I couldn't figure out the catch.

The bullets were still in place. The trigger mechanism appeared to work. Everything was *normal*. Exactly as it had always been.

And all he said when he handed it back to me was "Keep it close, Aurora. If we do something that makes you want to shoot us, then do it. Because if we scare you, we deserve to be shot."

With those words, he left and returned with cleaning supplies to mop up the coffee and sweep up the broken shards from the shattered cup. He also attempted to wipe off my boot, which I threw at the door earlier when I realized Johan was taunting me with his hack on my phone.

After setting the boot aside, Noah finished cleaning up my mess and said, "Rule number four should be us ensuring you can handle rule number three."

Then he winked and disappeared.

And shortly after that, my phone buzzed with a message from an unknown number. *The locks on the doors work. Use them if you need to. We won't disturb you until we land. Sweet dreams, little black hat. xx Johan*

I responded with another middle-finger emoji.

Then the bastard replied with a black heart and a top hat.

I snorted at it. And I definitely didn't smile. Not at all. Not even a twitch of my lips.

Because I hate him. I hate Noah. And I *loathe* Lazarus Ferraro.

They might smell like a sensual bookshop stocked with a myriad of books written to fulfill every one of my fantasies, but that doesn't mean I want them.

No.

Definitely not.

Which is why I took a very cold shower. Somehow there was still steam coming off my skin. Or, well, it seemed that way. Because I was basically simmering by the time I finished.

Then I couldn't fathom putting on my jeans again because everything felt too sensitive to the touch. Unsure of where my bag ended up on the plane, I started opening drawers to search for something else.

And found a collection of women's clothes.

That's when I picked up my phone again and shot off another message to Johan. *Do these outfits belong to one of Lazarus's mistresses? Or is she your whore, too?*

Okay, so that was a bit harsh. I don't typically refer to anyone with language like that. But I was *furious* to find evidence of whoever was on this jet before me.

However, that fury vanished when Johan replied, *Check the sizes, little hacker. And the brands.*

Frowning, I set my phone down and found that everything in the drawer was *my* size. Plus, the brands, as he mentioned, were some of my favorites.

You've been our obsession for years, Lark. There's no one else. Just you.

Those words scrolled across the screen as I put on a pair of black stretchy pants and a tank top.

And they're the last ones I've received from Johan.

True to his word, none of the men "bothered" me for the rest of the flight.

At some point, I clearly fell asleep, but the tilting of the plane stirred me on the bed, the landing gears loud all around me. I woke with a start, only to find myself still blissfully alone. The gun tucked beneath a pillow with my phone—right where I left them. And the door still *locked.*

Now that the wheels are on the ground, I'm waiting for the inevitable.

The jet stopped moving about ten minutes ago. So any second now, there's going to be a knock. Or maybe just the click of a key.

Because I have no doubt those three alphas know how to get in here. That lock is flimsy enough that even I could pick it.

However, nothing happens.

All the windows are closed, so I can't peek outside.

And everything is silent on the other side of the door.

I sit up slowly, swallowing.

What's happening? I don't like the quiet. It's ominous. It reminds me of my childhood. *The calm before the storm.*

The Bianchi estate was *never* silent. Not unless something nefarious was happening outside. An attack of some kind.

Is Dad here? I wonder. *Have his people surrounded the jet?*

That would be just like my father, waiting until we landed to take Lazarus by surprise.

My stomach twists with the notion. Because Dad won't hesitate to give a kill order. Fellow don or not, Lazarus kidnapped a Bianchi. That's punishable by death. I warned Lazarus. I told him what would happen.

So why am I suddenly nervous? I think. *Why do I even care?*

Lazarus might be my scent match. But we are *not* going to be together. Ever.

Only… only, I don't really want him to die. I mean, he's not a good man. He's a notorious killer. Ruthless. *Violent.*

Yet rule number two implies consent. I frown. *And everything he's done thus far is… not at all what I expect from the don of the Ferraro Mafia.*

I stole money from him. *A lot* of money. I know what happens to hackers in my position. However, all he's really done is kidnap me.

And force me to watch an erotic show between him and Johan.

Except, he didn't actually force me to watch anything. I *chose* to stand there while they deep-throated each other.

My thighs clench with the memory, a fresh wave of brown sugar and honey teasing my nose. It mingles with the other scents in the jet, creating a decadent bookstore cafe of aromas that have me falling back onto the bed with a groan.

Something buzzes beneath my head. *My phone.*

My *compromised* phone, thanks to Johan.

His hack is… exquisitely intricate. I hate that his technique intrigued me. He's skilled. As a fellow professional, I can respect that. But it infuriates me to no end, too.

Another vibration has me fishing the compromised tech out from under the pillow. Two messages are waiting for me, both from the unknown number, which apparently has a full name in my phone now. *Johan Greco.*

I arch a brow, wondering if that's his real last name.

Then I read his first text. *Time to go, little hacker. Laz's team just gave us the green light.*

I snort.

And then scroll down to the second message. *There's a car waiting for us outside. Noah and Laz are going to meet us later at the estate.*

I blink at that. *Noah and Laz are no longer here?* I wonder, sitting up again. *Where did they go?* My eyes widen a little. *Are they dealing with my father?*

I didn't hear any gunfire outside.

But maybe the jet's walls are insulated or something, masking sound.

Shit.

I grab my gun and phone, then roll off the bed while ignoring the rush of sensation to my head. I need to make sure my dad is okay. Not that we're close. But I don't really like the idea of anything happening to the members of my family.

Especially Gio.

I march toward the door and shove my bare feet into my boots, slip the gun into one side, and exit.

"Where's Lazarus?" I demand.

Johan stares me down from his position near the executive chair. He's wearing a midnight-blue dress shirt, one that looks freshly pressed. The sleeves are rolled to the elbows, and the top button is unfastened. His legs are casually crossed at the ankles, and his hands are in the pockets of his slacks.

The epitome of indifference. Undisturbed. And annoyingly calm.

"He's with Noah," he tells me cryptically. "Shall we go?"

"I'm not going anywhere with you until you tell me what's going on."

He cants his head, the motion sending his dark hair over the rim of his black glasses to hide one crystal-blue eye. I *hate* how attractive he looks like this. All rumpled and delicious. Intelligent. *Sexy.*

Ugh.

The alpha even has dimples.

Which he displays now as his lips curl up on one side. "We're going to the Ferraro estate in the Hamptons, just like Laz said."

"And they're not with us because…?" I prompt.

"Because Laz and Noah have business to attend to."

"What kind of business?"

"The kind we're not going to discuss," he replies, pushing off the chair. "Let's go."

This time, it's not worded as a question but as a statement. A *command.*

However, I have no interest in *behaving* when my family is likely being threatened or hunted or worse. "No."

Johan's eyebrow lifts. "No?"

"No," I repeat. "I've already said I'm not going anywhere until you tell me what's going on."

His gaze narrows. "You might be our scent match, sweetheart, but you're not family yet. Once you claim us, we'll talk."

"I'm not claiming any of you," I bite off through my clenched teeth. "*Where* is my father? Does Lazarus have him? My brother? Are they all fighting outside?"

Johan's brow smooths out, a hint of understanding flashing across his features. "Ah, I see." He turns around to dig in a bag on the chair behind him. "Here." He walks over to me, holding out his hand. "I was going to give it to you in the car, but now seems like a more appropriate time."

I take the phone from his palm and frown at the familiar hardware. "What model is this?" I ask, confused. "This… this can't be what I think it is, right?" I slip my other device into my pocket, then power up the one he just handed me. "Holy shit, it is."

This brand and model isn't available yet.

It's supposed to be released next year.

"How…?" I trail off, deciding it's a moot question.

He's linked to the Ferraros. They own a technology empire as one of their legitimate businesses. Of course he got his hands on a future release.

"It's actually a prototype," he tells me. "Well, *the* prototype. With a few alterations." He shrugs. "I figured I owed you a new phone, so I wiped this one, copied over your contacts and a few other things from the cloud, and put a location blocker in it. Otherwise, it's clean."

I scroll through some of the apps, recognizing everything I use on my compromised device. "You expect me to believe this isn't layered with listening malware and hasn't already been cloned?" I deadpan, trying to pass it back to him. "Yeah, no, thanks."

He ignores the gesture and reaches down to grab his bag, then pulls the strap over one shoulder. "You can check it out in the car. Call your brother. Hell, I won't even stop you from throwing it out the window. Although, I will be a little heartbroken. But it's yours to do with whatever you want."

"I can call Gio?" I ask slowly, surprised by that.

"Of course." He considers me for a moment. "Actually, I kind of insist on it. He needs to know you're safe. And he's about to be really disappointed when he realizes the jet Uriah's tracking isn't ours." His expression turns a bit boyish in nature. "I may have played with the air traffic control logs."

I gape at him. "*What*?"

He shrugs. "Uriah was stalking the inbound flights. I had to give him something to chase to ensure a smooth landing and transport. So I sent them to New Jersey." The boyish glint returns. "They're tracking a jet full of rescue animals. Maybe they'll adopt one?"

My lashes flutter. "You… you tricked Uriah?" That feels unlikely. Uriah is the one who introduced me to my first computer. He's my father's main technology guru. The alpha who taught me how to hack. "That's impossible."

"I assure you that it's *very* possible. If you don't believe me, then call your brother and ask him if he's enjoying that New Jersey air." His crystal eyes glitter with mirth. "You can talk to him while we disembark. Pretty sure Tania is getting impatient outside."

He starts toward the door while I gape at his back.

The phone he handed me is no doubt rigged. But if he's going to let me talk to Gio…

I pull up the contact and select Call while trailing after Johan.

A petite female with spiky black hair waits for us at the bottom of the steps. A petite female who is sizing Johan up like he's a delicious snack she's about to enjoy. A petite female who has me narrowing my gaze and suppressing a growl.

"Hey, Tania," Johan greets her, his sensual baritone grating on my nerves.

"Hey, J," she coos at him, her use of a nickname making my stomach twist. "Nice flight?"

I'm about to cough or snort or *something* when the call connects and starts to ring. The delay is probably related to whatever spyware Johan installed on my phone. Or maybe there's a cell phone jammer on the jet. Who knows? I'm just thankful it works.

"Aurora?" My brother's voice travels down the line, nearly making me stumble on the stairs as relief and a myriad of other emotions echo through me all at once.

"Gio," I breathe. "Are you okay?"

"Am *I* okay?" he asks, sounding incredulous. "Are you fucking kidding me right now? Where are you? Are you okay? Did that asshole touch you?"

"Who? Noah?" I blink.

"No, Lazarus," he growls. "But Noah is there, too? God, I assume that means Johan is with you all."

"Uh, yes and no," I say slowly, then shake my head. "Wait, where are you? Are you really in New Jersey?"

Johan glances back at me with a humored look, ignoring whatever the spiky-haired omega is saying to him. She has her hand on his arm, though. His exposed forearm. And she's… she's dragging her nails along his skin like she has a right to touch him.

Which is really not okay.

"Hold on," I tell Gio, interrupting his reply, which I now realize I wasn't listening to. "Can you stop doing that?" I ask, looking straight at *Tania*.

She frowns back at me. "Doing what, babe?"

"First of all, I'm not your *babe*. And second of all, *that*." I gesture to where she's stroking Johan. "He's not your scent match; he's mine. So fuck off."

Okay. I might be… losing my mind.

That's fine.

Everything's fine.

"*Scent match*?" my brother roars down the line.

Okay. Not fine, I decide, clearing my throat. "Uh, yeah. Unfortunately."

Johan arches a brow. I'm not sure if he's reacting to my comment to my brother… or to Tania.

"You're scent-matched?" Tania asks, yanking her hand away. "*To her*?"

Johan's attention returns to the now-simmering omega. "Yes. I am. Is that a problem?"

Tania looks wounded, like she's about to cry.

And now I feel like an asshole for even commenting.

"*Aurora*," my brother snaps, making me realize that I've missed something else that he's said.

I really need to focus, I think, shaking my head and making my way down the rest of the stairs. "Are you with Dad?" I ask my brother, wanting to assure them both that I'm okay. "And are you really in New Jersey? Sorry if you already answered that, but I missed the response."

Gio is silent for a long moment. "Can you put Lazarus on the phone, please?"

I frown. "No. He's not here."

"What do you mean, he's not there?"

"I mean he's somewhere else," I return, rolling my eyes as I start toward the black car that's waiting for us on the tarmac.

"Why do you need to talk to him? Don't tell me you're friends."

Gio heaves a long sigh. "Aurora… a lot has happened while you've been gone."

"Yes, I can imagine," I deadpan. "Never a dull moment in the Bianchi household, that's for sure."

He's quiet again before saying, "That's not what I mean, honey pot. There's… there's been a lot of changes lately."

My steps slow a mere foot from the door that Johan has just opened for me. "Okay," I reply. "That's cryptic, Gio. Tell me what you mean."

"I'm the don now, Aurora," he tells me softly.

I stop breathing. "The don?" It comes out in a whisper, what's left of my oxygen leaving my chest.

Because that… that can only mean one thing…

"Dad's…?" I don't have enough air to finish the question.

Not that I need to.

Because I already know.

And when I meet Johan's gaze, I realize he knows, too.

Which… which means they all knew…

My father… my father is dead.

CHAPTER TEN
JOHAN

SHIT.

What a fucking brilliant time for Giovanni Bianchi to announce his recent ascension. Everyone knows what that means.

The trio of families that rule New York City only pass the mantle on via one tried-and-true method—*death*.

Laz became the don of the Ferraro Mafia after his father passed away a decade ago.

Just as Giovanni became the don when his father passed, which Lark has clearly ascertained now.

"*When*?" she demands, her eyes filling with tears. But they're not ones born of sadness.

No, my brilliant little hacker is *pissed*.

As she should be.

"Six months?!" She sounds ready to kill her brother. "Why didn't you tell me, Gio?" The first tear falls, and it takes everything within me not to reach out to wipe it from her cheek.

She does it for me, anyway, though. Her hand a furious swipe against her face as she scowls at whatever her brother is saying.

I lean against the car, still keeping the door open, and wait.

Tania makes an impatient sound from inside—she's already in the driver's seat—but I ignore her. She's a good employee, one I've been friendly to because that's my role in the pack. I'm the "nice guy."

She's always mistaken my kindness for flirting, though.

Lark set the record straight almost immediately, a fact that amuses me greatly. Her little possessive intervention made me want to grab her and kiss her.

But then her brother answered the phone.

"You still should have called me. I would have come home," she tells him. Whatever he says back to that has her wincing in response, and a glimmer of doubt creeps into her features. Followed by guilt.

I'm not sure what he's saying to her, but I don't like it.

I'm two seconds away from taking the phone from her when she surprises me by holding it out toward me. "He wants to talk to Lazarus. Since he's not here…" She trails off, her fierce tone from before no longer existent. Instead, she sounds defeated. Which I strongly dislike.

I gladly accept the device and say, "Talk to my omega like that again, Bianchi, and I won't hold back the next time I see you."

"Your omega?" Giovanni returns. "*Your* omega? Fuck, you're just as bad as Ferraro!"

"In regard to my possessive feelings? Probably," I admit. "So, how's New Jersey?"

Silence transcends for a beat, Giovanni no doubt considering his options. I've known the alpha for a long time. As have Noah and Laz. We all went to private school together.

While the families might be competitors, they're also allies in many ways.

That's what keeps New York City from being taken over

by any other syndicate—the Bianchis, Ferraros, and Riccis look out for one another where it counts.

"Where's my sister?" Giovanni asks quietly.

Deciding that we're a safe enough distance away, I decide to answer truthfully by giving him our airport name. "But we're in the process of leaving," I add. "We're planning to have a late dinner at the Ferraro estate."

It's just after two in the morning, the flight from Colorado having taken three and a half hours. With the time change, our schedule is a bit out of sorts.

"Your pack will never get away with this," Giovanni seethes.

"I believe we already have," I tell him, then gesture with my chin for Lark to get in the car. "I'm handing the phone back to your sister now. But before I do, you owe the incoming jet a check."

"A check?"

"Yes. They received word thirty minutes ago of a generous donation being made by the Bianchi Family Foundation."

Giovanni's growl causes my lips to twitch.

But it's Lark's expression that amuses me more. She's staring at me like I've just given her the moon.

"The missive said the CEO was en route to meet them at the airport and to hand over the check personally. Oh, and several news agencies were copied in on the announcement."

The growling turns to cursing.

"Now, I might not be a marketing guru," I go on, "but I think it would look bad not to deliver on such a heartfelt promise, yeah?"

"You fucking—"

"I hope you wore something photo appropriate, Mr. Bianchi," I interject. "I suspect the news vans will be arriving any minute now. Enjoy!"

I hang up before he can say anything else and hand the phone to Lark.

"Do you think your brother will adopt one of the animals?" I ask her conversationally. "Or does he travel too much?"

She simply stares at me.

Then huffs a laugh and shakes her head.

"My brother's going to enjoy killing you," she informs me as she slides into the car.

I follow as I reply, "He's certainly going to enjoy trying to, yes. But I'm not an easy mark, Lark." The car starts to move, prompting me to reach over and buckle my omega into her seat. I follow suit before changing the topic by asking, "Fancy anything specific for dinner tonight?"

The estate chef is waiting for my orders. She's an older beta who *loves* to cook. She didn't exactly enjoy being messaged at midnight with instructions to get the team together, but she's used to our unique hours of operation.

And if she's a little miffed, that sentiment will vanish when she meets Lark.

All Chef Harmony has wanted for years is a Mrs. of the household to dote on. A mafia queen, really.

That's all any of us have desired, actually.

And Lark is the perfect one to fill that position.

If she's willing.

Naturally, that's the unknown of this equation.

"Honestly?" Lark sounds tired, but her eyes are bright as she gazes back at me. "Being in this part of the country just makes me want a proper pizza."

"Want something flown in from the city? Because I can make that happen."

She smiles and shakes her head. "I would be fine with whatever is local." She frowns then. "Except I doubt anything is open."

"Oh, Chef Harmony is a wizard in the kitchen. She can make anything happen." I send a message to the woman in question, then add how I would really like a salad, too. "Want anything, Tania?" I ask, aware she can hear us just fine from the front seat.

Lark scowls beside me. "Oh, I think she made it quite clear what she wants."

My eyebrows lift.

And Tania blows out a sigh. "I'm sorry, Ms. Bianchi. I didn't realize you were his scent match. I promise, it's nothing personal. And thank you, Mr. Greco, but I ate before coming to pick you up."

I nod and inform the chef that pizza and a salad will suffice. Knowing Harmony, she'll still whip something up for Tania. She's her mother, after all.

"Don't apologize," Lark grumbles. "I just… I didn't sleep well on the plane. And everything is… confusing right now." I can't see her cheeks all that well in the dark, but I suspect they've brightened with color.

It's adorable.

She's jealous.

Granted, if an alpha tried to touch her in front of me—one not part of our pack, anyway—I would kill him or her.

"And please call me Lark. Ms. Bianchi is my mother." Lark frowns. "Gio didn't tell me anything about her. Is she okay?" The way she asks it makes me wonder about her relationship with her parents, as she doesn't sound particularly sad, just resigned.

"From what I've heard, your mother has relocated to Italy with your father's former finance advisor," I tell her.

"Bjorn?" Lark's eyes widen. "Really?"

I shrug. "As I said, that's what I've heard. There are ways I can find proof of it, if you'd like," I offer, enjoying the idea of having something I can present to her as a gift.

But she shakes her head. "No. It's fine. I was never very close to my mom. She…" Lark trails off, her lips twisting. "She spent most days in her nest, only leaving when her pack needed her for appearances or, uh, other things."

Hmm. From her tone, I gather what she means by "other things." Which makes me want to ask why those "things" weren't done in her mother's nest.

But I suspect that's not a conversation Lark wants to have about her parents.

I'm also starting to think that however her mother was treated by her pack may have impacted Lark's view on being a mafia queen.

That would explain her mother running off with Bjorn—who wasn't part of her mother's original pack. Her other two alphas have stayed behind to help Giovanni run the empire, similar to how Laz's elders have remained to *advise.*

"I just hope she's finally happy," Lark adds in a quiet voice. "Or happier, anyway."

"The offer stands," I murmur. "If you want to know how she's doing, I'll find out."

She nods. "Maybe I'll call her instead. I don't know. It's been over a decade since we last spoke."

"That's a long time." At least it feels that way to me. But my mom and I talk a few times a week. She's always checking in. My dad, too. "Do you miss her? Or your father?"

Her lips twist. "I don't know. It's hard to miss a parent who was never really there."

She turns her focus to the window, watching as the nightscape passes us by. There isn't much to see since the moon is covered with clouds and the lights out here are minimal.

"Gio basically raised me," she whispers. "But our father wasn't a bad alpha. He was like Lazarus, I guess. A don. Always in charge. Always demanding something from someone." She shrugs. "It's a big job. I respect it. But I left for a reason." Her brow furrows. "Rather, I didn't *return* for a reason."

I wait for her to say more, but she falls silent, her gaze still on the darkness outside.

So I decide to comment on something she said, something I feel needs to be clarified. "Having met your father, Lark, I can promise you—Laz is nothing like him."

She scoffs at that. "You're right. He's worse, isn't he?" She looks at me. "He's pretty well known for his ruthlessness."

"He is," I concede. "He's also passionate, loyal, and exceptionally strategic. Your father was someone who expected everyone to bow to him and work for him. Laz is someone who expects everyone to pull their own weight and work *with* him. He's not an authoritarian. He's a leader. There's a difference."

She stares at me. "And you? What kind of alpha are you?"

I huff a laugh and shake my head. "Truthfully?"

"That would be nice, yes."

I nod, deciding to give her honesty. "I'm not an alpha at heart. Physically, yes. But I always thought I would present as a beta." I lift one shoulder in a partial shrug. "As for who I am, I'm also loyal. However, I'm less strategic than Laz. I love puzzles, though. Especially technical ones."

Lark's expression is masked by the shadows, but I think I see her lips curling a little. "I like puzzles, too."

"That doesn't surprise me at all. You're quite talented with a computer, Ms. Bianchi."

"Likewise, Mr. Greco," she returns. "But I'm going to clean up this phone." She holds up the one I gifted her. "And then I'm keeping it for good."

I smile. "You won't have much to clean up. I already told you—all I did was make it untraceable, primarily so your brother can't find you. Though, your location isn't much of a secret. If he decides to visit, Laz will let him enter."

"He will?" She sounds surprised.

"Of course he will." I frown at her. "Laz isn't the monster you believe him to be." Well, actually, that's not entirely true. So I amend with, "He'll never be that way with you, I mean. For you, maybe. To you, never."

That's a very distinctive difference, one I hope she understands.

"He said he's going to destroy me," she mutters. "That's pretty straightforward."

I lean over to press my lips to her ear. "He meant that sexually, Lark."

She freezes.

"He wants to destroy you in the best way, sweetheart," I add, then brush my lips against her temple. "We all do."

Maybe it was bold of me to say.

But the fresh wave of brown sugar and honey filling the car tells me it was also the right thing to say.

I reach for her hand and give it a little squeeze, wanting to offer her some comfort. Tonight has been… a lot. So the action just feels needed. Though, I fully expect her to pull away.

Except she doesn't.

Instead, she threads her fingers through mine and simply holds my hand.

A purr ignites in my chest, eliciting a sigh from my omega. Pretty sure I hear one from the front seat as well, but I ignore that.

I'm purring for Lark and only Lark.

She leans her head back against the seat, then slowly drifts toward me until she's snuggled into my shoulder. I don't say anything, not wanting to spoil the moment.

Rather, I just exist with her. Purring. Offering support. Soothing her nerves.

It's nice.

It's peaceful.

And it's how we spend the rest of our drive to the estate.

Lark seems to doze off, not reacting at all to the guards greeting us at the gate. Though, she does stir when we pull up in front of the main doors to the mansion.

I help her out of the car, then keep her hand in mine as I

lead her inside. She smiles as I introduce her to staff members along the way but remains mostly quiet as we eat. She doesn't ask where Noah or Laz is, which I'm thankful for, as I don't want to elaborate on what took them away.

Business is business. And while we fully intend to share all aspects of our organization with Lark, she's not on the inside yet.

It's going to take time… for all of us.

"Thank you for the pizza," Lark says to Chef Harmony. "It was lovely."

Harmony beams, then asks Lark about her favorite foods and meals.

I watch their conversation unfold, amused by Lark's minimalistic approach. She clearly doesn't want Harmony to fret over her and is trying to be as easy as possible.

So different from the other mafia princesses I've met over the years. There have been several sent Laz's way, as well as a few daughters from cartel and bratva families.

This whole world is about making business arrangements.

But that's never what Laz wanted for the pack. It's not what Noah and I wanted either.

We've desired a partner, not a trophy.

That's why Lark piqued our interest after we discovered she was the one who stole all that money. And when we realized why she did it, she stole our hearts, too.

The fact that she's our scent match is an exquisite bonus.

After Harmony finishes asking her questions, I politely thank her for the meal and then escort Lark through the mansion to her new accommodations. It's nestled in the middle of the residential wing, with Laz's room across from hers, mine to the left, and Noah's to the right.

I don't tell her that part, but I'm pretty sure she knows from the scents lingering in the air.

Instead, I just show her around her bedroom and en-suite bathroom.

"My bag has already been unpacked," she says, frowning at the dresser's contents.

"Yeah, that would be Noah's doing." I palm the back of my neck and stretch my shoulders a bit, exhausted from traveling all day. "He and Laz stopped by to drop some shit off and change before heading out again. I'm assuming Noah decided to unpack for you first. Probably irritated the crap out of Laz, too."

My lips turn up, amused. I can practically hear Laz growling at Noah in my head.

"Anyway, do you need anything else?" I ask as she sets both of her phones on a nightstand. "Charge cables are in the desk over there, by the way." I gesture with my chin toward the study nook that's attached to her bedroom. "Or you can use the clock charger out in the living area."

She nods, her lip catching between her teeth as she chews nervously. "Thanks." She doesn't look at me when she says it, her shoulders caving a little.

Frowning, I move into Lark's space and use my thumb beneath her chin to tilt her head back. "You good?" I ask her softly, my gaze searching hers.

She swallows. "I…" Her brow furrows. "I want to be alone."

"Oh." I drop my hand. "Right. Of course. I'll check on you in the morning?" It comes out as a question because I'm not sure if she wants me to check in on her at all or just… leave her alone indefinitely.

She doesn't reply, just frowns.

So I turn to leave, not wanting to upset her any more than I already have. "Good night, Lark."

I only make it a step before she grabs my hand.

Electricity shoots up my arm at the contact, my heart skipping a beat in the process.

"No, I mean, I want to be alone. Or I should want that. But I… I don't. I…"

She's frowning when I glance back at her.

"You want me to leave?" I ask, somewhat confused by her grip on my hand.

"Yes," she says. "But no."

One of my eyebrows lifts. "Kind of sending me mixed messages right now, sweetheart."

Her brow pinches even more. "I know. I just..." She releases me and growls at herself. "I'm not scared. I'm... I don't know how to describe what I'm feeling. I'm not weak. I'm not this girl. I'm not... I'm just *not*. Okay?"

None of that makes any sense to me. But I reply, "Okay." I just want her to feel comforted.

Which is when I realize what she may need.

My purr.

It ignites in my chest before I even finish the thought, and her shoulders instantly relax. Her eyes fall closed. And the next thing I know, she has her nose pressed against my pec and her arms are winding around my waist.

I hug her back, my purr deepening, and she sighs.

She's been through some trauma today. Or a lot of trauma, I guess.

Because of us.

And also because of her brother. Her family. Her *birthright.*

But mostly because of us tricking her and more or less kidnapping her.

The least I can do is offer my purr.

So I do.

I pick her up and sit with her on the bed.

She curls into me, her cheek rubbing against me like a cat marking her territory.

I love it. Pretty sure I love her, too.

That thought becomes confirmed when she falls asleep on me, her soft little snores making my purr intensify as I shift her onto the mattress.

Her golden hair splays across the pillows, but her lips pout as she reaches for me in her sleep.

"I'm not going anywhere," I promise her. "Just making us both more comfortable."

I reach down to remove her boots and find her gun tucked inside. I frown, not at the weapon but at the imprint it left against her skin.

Hmm. I make a mental note to suggest that Noah buy her a proper holster for the firearm. Maybe even a better make and model, too. Because this one was clearly purchased from a secondhand shop.

Our girl deserves the best money can buy. And that applies to everything in her life.

I set her toy on the nightstand, then massage her foot a little. I want to make sure she's not too sore tomorrow. Once I finish, I tuck her in beneath the blankets, all while purring.

Yet she still tries to grab me, clearly not wanting to be left alone.

Maybe it's just our scent match messing with her instincts, but I can't deny her. So I slip out of my own shoes and slide into the bed with her.

She instantly rolls into me, burying her face in my chest like she's trying to get as close to my purr as physically possible.

I chuckle, then hold her while she sleeps.

I only realize I've dozed off as well when a vibration on the nightstand stirs me awake. It's her phones—both of them—lighting up with an incoming message.

I glance at it and see it's a text from her friend Luna.

Followed by one from Silva.

And another pops up with Luna's name attached to it.

Not wanting the sound to disturb my resting omega, I turn off the vibration effect on both phones.

Lark can catch up with her fellow "Widows"—a term I

learned while researching her—after she's slept. I'm sure they'll have a lot to discuss.

CHAPTER ELEVEN
LARK

The scent of leather, paper, and coffee surrounds me, causing my nose to twitch. *Did I fall asleep in a bookstore?*

And why am I so warm?

I force one eye open, peering at the masculine wall I'm currently snuggled up against.

A naked chest.

A very toned, very sexy male chest.

And it's purring…

My lashes flutter, the events of last night slamming into me with a start.

Only for my body to relax instinctually as the vibrating sound rolls through me.

Did Johan hold me all night?

And when did he lose his shirt?

Is he wearing pants?

I subtly move my leg, which I now realize is intertwined with his, and freeze at the hardness I feel against my upper thigh.

Because yep.

Yep. I'm not just snuggling his purring chest—I'm touching his *knot.*

Cool. This is fine. Everything's fine.

Actually, everything's hot. Like, *really* hot.

"When did you lose your clothes?" I mumble, certain he's awake. Because there's no way he's sleeping with an erection like *that.*

"Shortly after you started trying to rip them off in your sleep," he murmurs back to me.

I freeze. "What?"

He chuckles. "You're a very active dreamer, Lark."

And now my face is on fire. "It's the scent match," I mutter.

He hums, and I'm not sure if that's a sound of agreement or something else. But suddenly I'm on my back with him hovering over me. Electricity zips through me as his cock settles right against my core, his size and presence overwhelming my every instinct.

"Don't worry, little hacker. I've been a perfect gentleman all night. Even when you tried to grab my knot."

My eyes widen. "You're lying."

"I'd never lie about you trying to touch me. Nor would I lie to you about anything else." He balances on his forearms, effectively caging me beneath him. "Maybe I can make rule number four be about honesty. Think Laz will approve?"

"I thought rule four was about ensuring I can take care of myself… or whatever Noah said."

"Hmm, I suppose you're right. Rule number four can be us ensuring you're safe. Rule number five will be about honesty—no lying between any of us."

"Seems like a rather bold rule to be making without consulting the other members of our pack," a deep voice says from far too close to the bed.

I shiver and look over to find Lazarus standing there in a freshly pressed all-black suit. His eyes are on Johan, though. And they're narrowed into a glare.

"Are you saying you don't value honesty, Laz?" Johan asks

silkily, his body seeming to settle even more intensely on mine. "Because I have some truths I wouldn't mind voicing."

"You know I value honesty," Lazarus returns, finally looking at me. "Would you like that to be rule five, Ms. Bianchi? Honesty between *all* pack members?"

I swallow, unsure how to answer that.

Because I… I don't know if I want to be honest with him. Or any of them, really.

"Honesty can be so refreshing, sweetheart," Johan says, his nose skimming my cheek to go to my ear. "For example, do you have any idea how badly I want to kiss you right now, Lark?"

My breath catches in my throat as he presses himself more firmly into my center.

"It's all I can think about," he goes on, his lips brushing the shell of my ear. "Kissing you. Using my tongue between your pretty thighs. Licking your cunt. Nibbling your clit. *Tasting* your slick."

Oh God… I'm fairly certain there are flames dancing across my skin.

At some point, my eyes closed while he was speaking, so I open them now to check my arms, yet I get caught in Lazarus's stare again. He's watching me intently, his nostrils flaring. "Is Johan breaking rule number two? Did you ask him to touch you?"

The male on top of me stiffens ever so slightly, his purr diminishing.

There's a lethal edge to Lazarus's tone, one that makes me shiver despite the warmth flooding my veins.

"Aurora." Lazarus says my name with authority, causing my stomach to flutter in response. "I need to know if my second has broken rule number two."

Johan slowly pulls back, his expression flashing with something akin to hurt, yet his tone is all quiet fury as he says, "How long have you known me?"

"I'm not speaking to you right now. I'm speaking to our omega." His dark gaze holds mine without flinching. "Answer my question, Aurora."

"With honesty because of rule four or five or whatever we're on?" I ask, arching a brow and feeling a little irritated that he's ruined my moment with Johan. "No, I didn't verbally ask him to touch me. But I touched him first."

Something ticks in Lazarus's jaw.

"No one has broken any rules, *boss,*" I go on, purposely calling him that since Noah mentioned he doesn't like it. "In fact, if Johan wants to kiss me, he absolutely has my permission."

Okay, that might be a bit far.

But I'm annoyed.

And I really didn't like the way he stiffened and stopped purring because of Lazarus's question. While I appreciate him checking in to make sure I'm okay, he should trust his second-in-command.

Yet clearly he doesn't.

I stare Lazarus Ferraro down as I utter the words, "Please kiss me, Johan."

He rumbles on top of me, his purr reigniting. "Was that enough begging for you, Laz?"

"No." Lazarus grabs Johan and yanks him out of the bed so quickly that I yelp. "Sparring room. *Now.*"

Johan glares at him. "You're going to make me deny our omega?"

"Yes, I am. Because she's not asking for the right reasons. She just wants to piss me off. And I won't let her use you to achieve her goal."

My lips part. "Excuse me?"

"You're not excused," Lazarus bites back at me. "But you are." Those three words are directed at his second.

I look at Johan, expecting him to tell Lazarus to go to hell.

But then I catch the hint of sadness in his crystal eyes. It's accompanied by a look of understanding.

Wait, he believes Lazarus? I realize. "Johan—"

"It's okay, little hacker," he says, reaching for something on the nightstand.

His glasses, I think as he slips them onto his face. They don't mask the emotions rolling through his features, though.

Regret.

Disappointment.

Acceptance.

That last one bothers me. Because I… I don't want him to *accept* what Lazarus said. Even if he was partially right. I was trying to piss him off. But I… I do want Johan to kiss me.

I think, anyway.

His purr soothed me all night.

And his scent… it's intoxicating.

I actually think I want Johan to do a lot more than just kiss me. Which is terrifying because I shouldn't want him. Or them. Or any of this.

I should want to go home.

Back to Widows Peak.

Where I'm safe and alone.

"I'll be there in five minutes to spar," Lazarus says, still glaring at me. "Go, Johan."

The other man gives me one last longing look and heads for the door.

Then he disappears, leaving me alone with a furious Lazarus Ferraro.

"Rule number six." He annunciates each syllable a little too clearly. "You will *not* lead my men on. I don't care how pissed off you are with me; you will not use Johan or Noah as a tool for revenge. *Ever.*"

I gape at him. "That's not—"

"Yes, Aurora, it is." He moves forward, his knee hitting the mattress.

I attempt to scoot back, or away, or *something*.

But his murderous gaze holds me captive, forcing me to stare up at him as he continues speaking.

"You wanted to prove a point by kissing Johan, not realizing that my second would shoot himself in the foot if you so much as asked. Fuck, I'm pretty sure Noah would stab himself in the heart if you desired it."

"I would never—"

"Which means," he goes on, cutting me off, "you wield power unlike anyone else in this house. And I will *not* let you use that to hurt them." He grabs my chin and leans down until we're almost nose to nose. "Do you understand me, Ms. Bianchi?"

His fury is so palpable that I'm shaking. "I would never hurt them," I whisper.

"Not purposely, perhaps," he growls back at me. "But you just hurt Johan."

"I didn't mean to."

"And that excuses it?" he demands.

My throat works, my insides suddenly icing over with the realization that, no, it doesn't excuse it at all. But I… I'm pretty sure I *want* to kiss Johan. So it wasn't a lie. However, I… I was annoyed with Lazarus when I voiced the request.

Therefore, he's right.

"I'm sorry," I whisper.

"It's not me you owe an apology to, Ms. Bianchi," he replies just as quietly.

Those words settle between us, his lips scant inches from mine. This close, I can see the brown flakes in his otherwise dark eyes. They're not as black as I thought, just really dark brown. Intense. Beautiful. Decorated with thick, long lashes.

I swallow for a completely different reason now as his scent overwhelms me. *Chocolate and cherries*. My own aroma joins his, and together we smell like dessert.

His gaze goes to my lips, then slowly trails back upward. "I need to go tend to Johan. Feel free to roam today. But don't leave the property. If you try, I'll know. And I won't be pleased." He pushes away from me and leaves the room without another word.

I lie there for a long time, staring at the closed door, struggling to breathe.

So much has happened.

So much has changed.

How was I just in Widows Peak yesterday? I wonder, dizzy from the last twenty hours or so of my life. *And how the hell am I going to survive here with all these intimidatingly gorgeous alphas?*

"Ugh," I groan, rolling over to bury my face in a pillow.

It's the wrong decision.

Because the linen smells like leather and paper. *Books.* Underlined with a sweet scent that's all me.

My combined aroma with Johan.

It's addictive. Perfect. *Ours.*

Which can mean only one thing.

I'm so fucking screwed…

CHAPTER TWELVE

LAZ

Fuck. I run my hand over my face, my heart pounding in my chest. *Fuck. Fuck. Fuck!*

I'm furious.

I'm aroused.

And I'm fucking *devastated.*

Those tears shining in Aurora's eyes threatened to destroy my soul. But I can't let her use my men as a form of revenge. If she wants to hurt me, she needs to do it directly. Not play a dirty game by tempting my second into a kiss under false pretenses.

Someone tsks as I walk down the hallway, and I don't need to turn around to see who is bold enough to be taunting me in my current mood.

"That wasn't very nice," the suicidal maniac sing-songs at me. "Should we make 'no bullying our omega' rule number eight? Or are we on rule number nine? I'm losing count."

I ignore Noah and continue walking.

Knowing him, he'll just follow.

After last night's events, we're both pent up with blood rage. Add in the sweet, honey-scented slick permeating our home, and we're all on the edge of a fucking rut.

I walk swiftly out of our residential wing, Noah hot on my heels, and practically skip steps on my way down the main staircase.

"What about a rule that requires her to walk around naked?" the unhelpful assassin suggests. "Maybe clothes should just be forbidden for all of us."

Of course, his words inspire images.

Images I don't want to think about.

Images of a very naked Aurora. Wet. Panting. *Begging.*

Fuck.

My dress shoes sound loud to my ears, echoing across the marble foyer as I head toward the basement stairs.

We have a full gym underground. Pool. Workout space. Sparring rooms. Even a fucking racquetball court.

I head to one of the fighting areas, aware of which one Johan typically favors. He's a fan of bōjutsu. So I'm not surprised at all to find him waiting for me with a bō in his hand. He's put on a pair of black track pants. Nothing else.

I take off my jacket and hang it up on the wall. A whoosh of sound echoes behind me as Johan begins to warm up. I don't look at him, just continue to undress while a series of subtle whistling noises taunt the air.

"You and your stick," Noah drawls.

"You love my stick," Johan returns.

"I do," Noah admits. "I really fucking do." It comes out as a groan, causing my eyes to roll.

"I want to fight, then fuck," I tell them both, my shirt joining my jacket on the hook. "In that order, preferably."

"And you always get what you want, yeah?" Noah's sarcastic tone has me glancing at him in the doorway. He's leaning against it, still dressed in his outfit from last night's hunt. All black. *To hide the blood.*

I suppose he's not in the mood to work out after all that. He did most of the heavy lifting with our "interrogation." Not that he looks tired, though. If anything, he appears to be energized and ready to play.

Which is dangerous.

Noah's version of *playing* usually involves mutilation.

"What if I want to fuck first?" he asks, his hazel eyes glittering with challenge. "Hell, what if I don't want to follow any of the *rules* you've created and go manifest a few of my own with the little bee upstairs?"

My shoulders stiffen. "We're a pack, Noah."

"Are we?" He pushes off the doorjamb and starts toward me. "Because it seems as though we're all just obeying your orders, *boss*."

"Something you've never had a problem with," I point out. "Until now."

"She changes everything." His words are quiet. No longer playful. *Deadly*. "If I want to touch her, I will."

"With her consent," I press.

"Sure. But I'm not going to force her to beg me. And if she wants to use me to piss you off? I'm okay with that, too."

My jaw ticks. "That rule is meant to protect her, too, Noah." Because something tells me she would regret using them to upset me. Maybe the guilt wouldn't come right away, but it would eventually rear up. And I don't want to risk any potential erosion to our pack dynamic.

"Still, it's my choice to be used," he stresses.

"Even if it'll hurt her in the end?" I counter.

He frowns. "It won't."

"You may not feel guilt, Noah, but I'm certain she does." I slip out of my shoes and socks, leaving me in just my dress slacks. They're not the most comfortable athletic wear, but they'll do. "As I said, it's not a rule to protect just you. It's for her, too."

His jaw clenches, his arms folding across his chest.

But he doesn't say anything else. I assume because he's considering what I've just said.

While he plays the part of psychotic enforcer, deep down, he's more like a golden retriever. At least for those he cares about.

Everyone else… he's just psychotic. Lethal. *Terrifying*.

The two assholes we intercepted in the early hours today only saw that side of Noah. They literally pissed themselves shortly after my enforcer finished introducing himself.

Useful skills for an assassin.

And admirable traits for a pack mate.

Anyone who so much as looks at Aurora the wrong way will meet Noah's wrath before I even have a chance to react.

She'll forever be safe in our care.

Taming his affections for her, though, will likely be a challenge. However, I strongly suspect our feisty omega will be more than able to handle it.

I walk over to retrieve a bō, then meet Johan on the mat. "All right, baby. Let's dance."

CHAPTER THIRTEEN
LARK

I DON'T BOTHER WITH A COLD SHOWER. IT WON'T HELP. SO I make it hot. Too hot. And just stand beneath the spray for… a while.

Every part of me is burning.

I feel ashamed. But also incredibly aroused. Which then fuels the shame even more.

It's horrible.

I… I *hate* this.

I hate Lazarus, too.

Except, I'm not sure if that's true anymore. He's nothing like I would have expected. The ruthless, cunning, intimidating mafia boss known for striking down his enemies and killing without compassion.

Yet he's… he's basically gentle with me. Harsh, too. Yet he hasn't touched me in a way that's made me feel unsafe.

And Johan is everything I find attractive in an alpha. Intelligent. Handsome. *Kind.*

Noah, I don't know well enough yet. But he seems kind of goofy. In an adorable, sweet way. Something that's probably insane to even think, given that he's also clearly an assassin.

I shake my head, sending water all over the place.

This is all really confusing. And the shower isn't helping.

Growling, I turn off the water, step out, and wrap myself up in the softest towel I've ever touched.

Everything about this place is opulent and lush. I know the Ferraro family has money. My own does, too.

But there's something exquisitely decadent about this estate. Something masculine yet beautiful.

I'm not sure if that's from Lazarus and his pack or if it's related to his familial history.

Regardless, I like it. And I kind of hate that I like it. Because I feel like I'm betraying my Bianchi roots.

Sighing, I dry myself off, fix my hair, and then head out to grab some of my clothes from the drawer Noah unpacked for me.

Except… all I brought were lounging clothes, mostly to piss off my father. The Bianchi household has a strict dress-only policy for the women. Which is why I stuffed my bag full of sweats and oversized T-shirts.

Now I don't really want to wear those.

Why I don't want to… is something I don't want to consider at the moment.

So I ignore the impulse to analyze my mind and wander back into the bathroom to the attached closet space, curious as to what I'll find there.

My eyebrow inches upward at the wide array of choices.

Pant suits. Dresses. Sweaters. Jeans. There are even some shorts and tank tops at the back.

I open some of the drawers of the dresser situated in the middle of the space, and my lips part.

Lingerie… and jewelry.

Having come from a life of wealth, I recognize real diamonds when I see them. And wow… "You have got to be shitting me."

I'm about to go text Johan to demand that he tell me what

woman occupied this space before me, but all of the glittering items still have their tags.

Tags that make my eyes bug out of my head. "*Holy crap…*" The collective value in this drawer alone is worth more than the money I stole from them. "This is insane."

I go check all the hanging items, find that they're some of my favorite brands—which are thankfully a lot less expensive than the jewelry brands—and all in my size.

These guys prepared this entire suite for me.

I… I don't know how to feel about that. Spoiled? Lucky? Intimidated?

They tricked me and kidnapped me. I definitely shouldn't feel *flattered*.

And yet…

I close my eyes and shake my head. "Stop thinking, Lark," I mutter to myself and grab a sweater at random. I pair it with jeans, then pause to look at the lingerie again.

My eyebrow inches upward as I take in the various sets. There's a black set that's actually rather pretty. Just a bra and a thong. But a floral pattern is etched into the lacy texture. "Screw it." I grab them and walk over to the changing area to get dressed.

Because of course there's a changing area attached to the closet. One surrounded by mirrors with a round bench at the center. I can only imagine what the guys have in mind with this.

Actually, I *do* imagine.

Because I can totally picture Lazarus sitting right there in the center, arms splayed along the back, watching me with those dark eyes as I try on the lingerie he picked.

This set is totally from him. Simplistic. Black. Sexy as sin.

I swallow when I see my reflection in the mirror. And for a moment, I almost hope there's a camera in here.

Do you like what you see? I wonder, preening in case the men are watching.

Then I realize how stupid I'm acting and quickly throw on the clothes.

It's dangerous to crave their attention. Scent matches or not, it's not healthy to want them. They're rivals of the Bianchi family.

Sort of, anyway.

Not really.

"*Ugh.*" I've clearly not taken my own advice to *stop thinking.*

Shaking my head, I leave the closet, take care of a few items in the bathroom—such as pulling my hair up into a ponytail—and head back into the bedroom.

Lazarus said I could wander. So I think I'll do just that.

I head toward the door, only to realize I should probably take my gun. It's on the nightstand beside both of my phones.

I definitely didn't put those there. Which means Johan did. He obviously took off my boots, too. I spy those near the bed but don't bother putting them on.

Instead, I pick up both phones and examine the screens. The new one has a bunch of missed messages and calls. "Oops."

I'm about to sit down to go through them when I spot the balcony doors off my room and get a better idea. Lazarus said not to leave the estate. He didn't say I couldn't go outside, right?

Wandering over, I twist the ornate handle and find it unlocked. Then I step outside onto a beautiful terrace that appears to wrap around this entire level. Or at least the entire level on this wing, anyway.

"Wow," I whisper, in awe of not just the beautiful balcony but also the view of the beach and the ocean beyond.

I knew we were in the Hamptons.

I wasn't aware we were also on the coast.

Though, it seems obvious now. There's no way a family with as much money as the Ferraros would live out here and not choose a secluded property away from all the others. And they would definitely require a view.

My dad and his pack were the same.

Only, the Bianchi family prefers the city, owning several properties throughout Brooklyn, with one main tower in Midtown Manhattan.

The Ferraros own most of Manhattan. But not that tower. Or the one across from it that's maintained by the Ricci empire.

Regardless of all that, I like it here. With the ocean scents in the air. The soft sound of water rolling against the sand. It's peaceful.

Unfortunately, though, the messages on my phone are quite the opposite. Not because my friends are applying any sort of pressure, but because they're all very clearly worried.

I scroll through Luna's first, wincing when I realize I never texted her when we landed. I was a little… overwhelmed.

Her messages grow increasingly worried, with the last one being time-stamped ten minutes ago saying, *I'm booking a flight.*

I close my eyes and blow out a breath. Then I select her name and call. Because a responding text isn't going to calm her down.

She answers on the second ring. "Are you okay?" she demands.

"Yeah, I'm fine," I tell her. "Things have, um, been a bit hectic." That's an understatement, but I don't really know what I can share with her. Rule number one is practically roaring in my head.

And after witnessing Lazarus's quiet fury before my shower, I'm not sure I'm ready to test the limits of his rules right now.

"I'm sorry I didn't call you when I landed," I go on. "Honestly, I was exhausted and fell asleep on the plane. Then I had a late dinner and fell asleep with my phone on silent."

Luna is quiet for a long moment. "I feel like you're not telling me something, Lark."

Because you know me too well, Luna, I want to reply. Instead, I opt for giving her part of the truth. "There's a lot going on that I can't talk about right now. But I promise you that I'm safe." That word just kind of leaves my mouth, causing me to frown, as it didn't feel like a lie.

Lazarus and his pack have made it pretty clear that they're not going to hurt me. And so far, all their actions have proved that.

Johan's, especially.

He could have easily taken advantage of me last night and didn't. Except, he just purred for me while I slept.

Those aren't the actions of an alpha who means me harm.

Noah also treated me kindly and even offered marriage—albeit as a joke, I think—but doesn't strike me as all that cruel or ill-intentioned.

And Lazarus, well, he's still a threat.

Except he was clearly angry before my shower and didn't assert any power over me. All he did was chastise me for hurting his friend.

Which I probably deserved.

"You know I'll come get you if you need me to, right?" Luna asks quietly, causing me to smile.

"Yeah, I know. But I'm okay. I promise." And I mean it. I really am okay. For the moment, anyway.

"Then when will you be home?"

My lips twist to the side as I consider how to answer that. "I don't know," I say slowly. "I suspect I'm going to be here for a while."

She's quiet for a long moment. "But you're really… okay?"

I laugh a little since I've already told her that. She's just being a good friend, and I appreciate that more than she could ever know. "Yeah, I am. You'll be the first to know if that changes."

More silence. "I don't believe you, Lark." She speaks the words so low that I barely hear them through the phone. "You always try to handle everything on your own. But you don't need to. Not anymore. We'll all help you."

"And I love all of you for that. I do. But I don't need help. Actually, all I want right now is a cup of black coffee. So I'm going to go find one." The phrase is purposeful.

A long time ago, shortly after escaping Gideon, we decided that if anything were to ever happen to one of us, I would tell her I'm enjoying a cup with creamer in it. And if she were in trouble, she would comment on her black coffee.

So saying that I want a normal cup—the way I've always enjoyed it—is my way of trying to subtly convey to her that I really am fine.

"I want a picture of that coffee," she tells me. "In fact, I'd like to see you right now. I'm hanging up and video-chatting you."

"Luna—"

The call ends, making me grumble.

When it starts to ring again, I answer it because I don't really have a choice. I know Luna. If she's threatening to hop on a plane, she means it.

"Happy?" I deadpan, staring at my best friend on the screen.

Her brow furrows, her eyes narrowing. "I don't recall an ocean in New York City, Aurora Bianchi."

"What?" *Oh, fuck.* I quickly spin around so the mansion is behind me, not the beach.

But it's too late.

Far too late.

And Luna just full-named me, too.

Damn it.

"Okay, I'm still on the East Coast," I tell her. "Just… outside of New York City."

The door opens behind me, something I only see because of the tiny screen in the corner displaying what Luna can see on her end.

I wince, aware that I'm probably about to get chewed out by Lazarus.

Only to sigh with relief when it's Noah.

"Who ya talkin' to, little bee?" he asks, peering over my shoulder. "She's pretty."

My brow furrows, and I shift my focus to him. "Excuse me?"

"What?" He blinks his hazel eyes innocently. "It's a compliment. That's a good thing."

"To hit on my friend?" I demand.

"You think I'm…?" His eyes widen a little, and he releases a low chuckle. "Oh, little bee, no. That's not me hitting on someone."

I scowl at him, ready to correct him, but he grabs my hip and pulls me closer, nearly forcing me to lose the phone.

"If I'm going to hit on a woman—which would only be you, by the way—I would say…" He leans in, his lips at my ear. "You're so fucking beautiful that it makes my heart ache, Aurora."

I roll my eyes, not at all impressed.

But he's not done.

"All I want is to strip you naked right here so I can watch the sun paint colors across your flawless skin. See the glow reflect in your golden hair. Watch the colors come alive in your brown irises. And memorize the scene so I can commission artwork later to memorialize the moment."

I swallow. *Okay, that's… that's a little better.*

"God, little bee, all I want is to kiss a path down your exquisite body to that space between your thighs, taste your honeyed slick, and make you scream my name so loud that everyone on this side of the United States hears you claiming me as yours."

My cheeks flame. *Umm, well, this is…*

"I want them to hear you beg for my knot," he continues. "Make it clear that I'm yours in every way. So that no one dares to even look at you. Because I'm a possessive man. And I will kill anyone and everyone for you. Even myself." He presses a kiss to my raging pulse, then takes a step back. "That's how I talk to my omega, pet."

I… I think I forget how to breathe.

"Nice to meet you, friend of Lark's," he adds, winking at something.

I frown.

Then shake my head to clear it. Because I'm still on the phone. Luna… Luna just saw all of that. Or part of it. I… I don't know. I dropped my hand at some point, and the phone was angled…

Oh, it doesn't fucking matter!

I lift it and find Luna gaping at me. "Who is that?" she demands.

"Noah Dragon," he replies, suddenly over my shoulder again. "Lark's future husband."

I close my eyes. I don't even know how to begin responding to that.

"*What?*"

"Well, she hasn't said yes yet," he goes on, apparently talking to my friend now. When my hand begins to shake, he reaches around to help me hold up the phone. "But I think my chances are pretty good that she's going to agree soon."

Luna gapes at him.

Meanwhile, I just twist my lips to the side. Because what the hell am I supposed to say? I can't break rule one. And I… I really don't want to involve Luna in any of this.

"Any suggestions?" he asks, making me blink. "On how to win her over, I mean. Like favorite flowers. Or does she prefer chocolate? Oh! Does she have any enemies I can take out for her? I'm pretty skilled with a kni—"

"I think that's enough," I interject, my voice a little hoarse. "I promise I'm fine. But I… I need to go now."

"You're getting married?" She sounds a bit shrill. Which, yeah, it's… it's a lot.

And also really not true.

Yet Noah says, "Yep."

Which has me quickly clarifying, "*No.*" I finally spin away from him. But of course he follows with a big, goofy grin on his face. "Noah's kidding. He didn't really propose."

"You wound me, pet," he murmurs. "But if you want a proper proposal, I'll handle it." He tries to get in the line of sight of the phone again as he adds, "Any pointers, pretty friend of Lark's?"

I scowl at him. "Stop saying that."

"You want me to clarify how I hit on a woman again, little bee?" he asks, moving into my personal space. "Because I'm happy to do that all day."

I'm suddenly up against the window, his palm resting on the glass beside my head, the opposite on my hip. The intensity in his eyes nearly causes me to drop the phone.

"Luna, I'm going to have to call you back."

"Luna," Noah repeats. "That's a pretty name for a pretty friend."

I glare at him. "Use *pretty* to describe my friend one more time."

He smiles. "I like that it makes you jealous."

"I am *not* jealous," I snap at him. "I'm overwhelmed. And… and… *all I can smell is cinnamon and hot honey*."

"Mmm," he hums. "Well, all I smell is brown sugar and honey, and it's making me wonder if your slick is just as sweet, little bee."

I growl at him.

He rumbles back.

And Luna clears her throat. "I'm still here, Lark."

I close my eyes, then lift the phone to look at her. "Sorry. I'm… I'm in the middle of something."

"Yeah, something hectic," she echoes, using my word from when we first started talking. "Fiancé of my best friend—Mr. Dragon, was it?—tell me where you're keeping my friend, and I'll give you some advice."

Noah steals the phone from my hand before I can comment and skips off onto the balcony. "Ferraro estate, new bestie of mine. The Hamptons." He tilts the phone toward the coastline. "See how pretty it is?"

He starts showing her the balcony, then goes into the bedroom, causing me to chase after him as he begins to show her around my guest quarters.

I scowl at him when he homes in on the gun on the nightstand. "She pulled that on Laz last night. Funniest shit I've seen in a while." Then he skips off to the bathroom and growls in delight. "God, Aurora's aroma is like heaven. We're scent matches, by the way. Not sure if she told you that."

"She didn't," Luna grumbles.

"Probably because of rule number one."

"Rule number one?" she echoes.

Noah grunts. "Yeah, Laz has a thing for rules. Mafia shit and all that." He finally looks at me. "She knows about your past, I assume?"

"Well, if she didn't, she does now," I deadpan.

"You said she's your best friend, little bee. Best friends know everything."

"That they do," Luna interjects. "So tell me what your intentions are with my best friend."

I feel like burying myself beneath a mound of pillows and never resurfacing again.

"You want all the details of how I plan to knot her?" he asks.

"No!" I shout at the same time Luna does. "Oh my God,

give me my phone." I march toward him with my hand held out, but Luna is already talking.

"I want to know if you're going to hurt my friend."

"Only if she asks me to," he replies.

"What does that even mean?" Luna demands.

"Well, we'll discuss limits, like knot warm—"

I yank my phone out of his hand, cutting him off. "*Stop.*"

He frowns at me. "I'm trying to impress your friend."

"You're doing a horrible job of it," I inform him.

"Well, actually, I'm not sure…" Luna says slowly, causing me to gape down at the screen. "He seems… interesting."

Sure. That's one adjective for Noah Dragon.

"I'm protective, possessive, madly in love, and will literally die for Aurora, dear bestie," he sing-songs. "She's safe here. Scout's honor."

"Were you even a Scout?" I ask him.

He snorts. "Fuck no. But I didn't think you would like me saying *assassin's honor*, since, you know…" He shrugs. "A lot of people assume assassins don't have honor at all. However, we do. A lot of it. And I will absolutely honor you." His gaze dances over me. "In *every* way you allow."

My eyes widen, the innuendo not lost on me.

"Yeah, I like him," Luna murmurs, causing Noah to beam and fist-pump in the air.

"His ego didn't need that stroke," I mutter back at her.

"I can tell you what does need to be stroked, though," he says without missing a beat, his auburn-colored eyebrows waggling at me.

"*Ugh.* I really need to get off the phone." The words are for Luna.

Not that Noah seems to care.

"Off the phone or *get off*?" he asks, following me as I spring back out onto the balcony.

"I'll talk to you later, Luna," I tell my best friend. "Please let the others know I'm fine. Silva's worried. Pretty sure Aries might be, too. I saw a bunch of texts from her."

Aries owns a self-defense studio in Widows Peak. I don't know everything about her past, but I know there's a reason for that vocational choice.

And I would bet good money that Silva mentioned my abrupt departure to Aries, which probably inspired her to worry.

"Everyone is worried, Lark," Luna informs me softly. "But wait, did you say *Ferraro* estate?"

"Yeah, Laz and Johan are her scent matches, too," Noah says, popping up behind me *again*. I don't know how he keeps doing that.

"Isn't that like the Bianchi family rival?"

"Ally," he corrects her. "Sort of. But we're all about to be family soon, if you feel me."

I close my eyes for the millionth time and pinch the bridge of my nose. "It's complicated, Luna."

"Complicated chaos, yeah. Yeah, I got that."

I wince. "I really need to go."

"Call me later." It's not a request but a demand.

"I will," I promise her.

Then hit End and turn to glare at Noah. "You're a menace."

He grins. "Why, thank you, beautiful bee."

"That wasn't a compliment."

"I'm going to take it as one anyway." He steps into my space, walking me back into the glass window again. I'm not even sure how he keeps moving this way and that. It's like he's a natural shepherd, corralling me with his body or shifting around me to corner me.

And now I'm staring straight up at him, into those alluring multicolored eyes.

He's no longer smiling.

No hint of teasing.

Not even a glimmer of humor.

"We broke rule number one by telling an outsider where we are, little bee," he murmurs. "Laz isn't going to be happy."

My nostrils flare. "*We* didn't break that rule. *You* did."

He nods solemnly. "True. But I don't like rules, Aurora. Especially ones I didn't agree to."

I swallow, my pulse skipping a beat, as I'm not sure I like where this is heading.

"Rule two is solid. I'll never touch you without permission. But I'll never make you beg, pet. And if you ever want to use me? Even if it's for revenge against Laz for being an ass? I'm game." He pulls back. "I'm yours to command, Aurora Bianchi. Always and forever. That's my wedding vow."

With that insane line of commentary, he turns to leave.

Only then he pauses with a snap of his fingers and looks back at me.

"Right. I was supposed to tell you that we're all going out tonight, so you'll have the house to yourself. We just have some business to deal with. But Harmony says she'll make you whatever you want to eat. Your wish is her literal command."

He winks and disappears, leaving me feeling oddly alone.

What business? I wonder. *And why do I suddenly feel like a damsel-like princess being left behind in a tower?*

CHAPTER FOURTEEN
LARK

Two days.

It's been *two days* since I saw Noah, Lazarus, and Johan.

I have no idea where they are or when they'll be back. The only one I can contact is Johan, yet he hasn't answered a single one of my texts.

And I'm *pissed*.

Noah came by to tell me I would be eating on my own and that they would return after handling their business. I assumed he meant later that night.

Nope.

It's now been two days. More than two days, actually, because this is my third dinner alone.

Harmony made me chicken pot pie from scratch. I should be in heaven. I should be *loving* every bite. But I can barely swallow because I'm too angry to enjoy this delicious meal.

How dare they drag me out here and leave, I seethe, stabbing at my plate. It scrapes loudly across the porcelain, and I don't care. *This is ridiculous.*

I should just call my brother and ask him to pick me up.

But I don't really want to go to New York City. That

feels… too heavy right now. I also haven't spoken to my brother since he told me our father is dead.

Something I still can't believe he kept from me.

My phone vibrates on the table with an incoming message. I grab it, hoping it's from Johan but seeing Aries's name on the screen.

Got a minute? she asks.

I have several, I think, sighing. Then I push away from the table and tell Jimmy—a beta who assists Harmony in the kitchen—that I'm finished.

Once I'm back in my room, I head out to my new favorite chair on the balcony and dial up Aries via video chat.

It's not my preference, but it seems to be the best way to placate my friends lately. They're not used to me being out of Widows Peak. And they all know something is happening, just not *what* is happening.

Well, Luna knows, thanks to Noah. Sort of, anyway. But she's kept my confidence. And she won't tell anyone until I'm ready to share.

Not that I have anything to share since the pack that kidnapped me has disappeared.

"Hey," Aries says, her screen black as she answers. "Hold on a second."

"Are you jogging?" I ask, hearing the subtle sound of quick steps.

"Yeah, just getting out of the gym so I can better hear you and see you." The screen shifts from black to color, allowing me to see Aries's gray-blue eyes. "Hey."

"Hey."

"Sorry, I didn't mean for you to have to call me," she says, reaching up to fix her blonde ponytail. I'm wearing my hair the same way, something we often have in common. "I just had a quick favor to ask."

"I'm all yours," I tell her earnestly. "Please cure my boredom."

She smiles. "I had no idea New York City could be boring."

I snort. "Trust me, it can be." I don't elaborate on the fact that I'm not actually in New York City. Apart from Luna, everyone thinks I'm home with my family. "Now hit me. What do you need?"

"Just some information about a pack that wants to come in to use the gym while visiting for work. Two alphas, specifically. I want to make sure they're solid before I grant them access."

I nod. "Understood." I've done this for her before. Hell, I've done this for all the Widows in some capacity. We're constantly running background checks on strangers, making sure they'll fit in with the Widows Peak demographics. "Just shoot me their names, and I'll do my thing."

"Awesome, thank you." She studies me through the screen, her shrewd gaze instantly putting me on edge.

Aries specializes in self-defense for a reason.

She knows when someone is in trouble.

And while I'm currently safe, she can probably see the stress in my features. But it's not for any of the reasons she could imagine.

"You okay, Lark?" she asks, the question one I've heard too many times in the last few days.

"Yeah." I smile. "Just bored, like I said."

Bored. Worried. Pissed off. Lonely. Confused.

Yep. A whole smorgasbord of emotions.

Aries studies me for another beat. "You're always helping us, Lark. Just know that we're here to help you, too."

I force myself to smile even though it feels weighted somehow. Sad. Because I know she's right. I know my fellow Widows would do whatever it took to save me, if I needed it.

But I don't.

I just want my scent matches to come back. *So I can kill them,* I think.

"I love you all," I say to Aries. "And if I were in trouble, I would tell you. But everything is good here. Just… heavy. I'll explain whenever I come back home."

Or at least give them enough details to placate their interest.

They don't need to know about the sins of my past or how Widows Peak became such a safe place for us all.

That's my burden to bear. Not theirs.

"All right." Aries doesn't look like she believes me. But she doesn't press me for details. None of the Widows do. We all have our dark pasts, some worse than others. However, trauma bonded us. And we'll forever respect each other's wishes as a result.

"Shoot me the names, and I'll send over full profiles in a few hours," I promise her.

"Thanks, Lark."

"Anytime, Aries."

She waves at the camera, and I wave back. Then I hang up and glance up at the moon.

"I don't have a computer," I realize out loud, my brow furrowing. "But I bet Johan has one I can borrow…"

I've refrained from going through their rooms even though I've figured out by scent who lives where.

But given that they've basically abandoned me, maybe snooping is allowed.

If I get caught, I'll at least have a good excuse for poking around Johan's room.

Smiling, I shoot Johan a text. *I need to borrow a computer. Consider this me asking for permission to enter your room.*

I don't bother waiting for a reply. If he decides to finally reach out, then he can see what it's like to go unanswered for a while.

I walk back inside, set the phone on the nightstand, and leave my room to head for his.

The door isn't locked, something that prickles my nerves.

Because it means I probably won't find anything interesting in here.

But he should have a laptop somewhere.

I pause just inside his space, my stomach igniting with flutters as his bookstore-like scent welcomes me home.

Closing my eyes, I simply inhale, enjoying the aroma. It's strange but I… I *miss* him.

Clearly, I'm insane.

That's fine.

I'll embrace it.

But I'm going to find a laptop in the process.

I learn the layout of his room first, taking in the modern decor and masculine touches. He has a large bed, one big enough for a party of five or more. But the sheets are crisp and tucked in. Something tells me Johan did that, not a maid.

It just goes with the rest of his space—organized and tidy.

I bet even his boxers are folded neatly in his drawers. I check and smirk. *Yep.*

I feel around inside, searching for any valuable tech.

Nothing. Just silky black shorts. I'm tempted to steal one, the inclination hitting me in my chest.

It would be soft in my nest. I shiver but decide to revisit that after I find a computer.

I don't have a nest here.

And I'm pretty sure I won't be building one.

Well, mildly sure.

Er, not sure at all.

"Focus," I chastise myself, shaking my head and forcing myself to move into the adjoining study in his quarters. Obviously, that's a better place to search for a laptop than his bedroom area, but I'm not sorry for snooping there first.

It only takes me a few seconds to find what I need in his cozy office space. However, I stay for a few minutes to admire his setup.

Four screens. All high-end. There's a controller that

suggests he often uses them for gaming, which explains the executive lounger chair.

He also has more than one laptop.

I take the one connected to the displays on his desk, deciding that must be the favorite.

"Don't mind if I do."

I tuck it under my arm, search for a mouse and a few other items, and then head back to my room.

Only to pause on my way past his bed.

"Hmm." It makes more sense to work in here in case I need something else from his den.

I shrug and climb up onto his bed, then create a makeshift work nest in the pillows.

And open his laptop.

It takes me over ninety minutes to crack through his login. *Ninety. Minutes.* I'm both impressed and irritated. It's never taken me more than thirty to break through login encryption before.

Yet this man has layers upon layers of security.

I'm barely even in his system now, and I've already passed through nine different screens. There are more security hurdles to access his files. But I don't need those right now. I just want to establish an internet connection.

Which isn't nearly as easy as it should be.

"Wow," I breathe, utterly enthralled by his programming. This isn't a normal laptop. No standard software. No apps. He's basically built this mainframe from scratch.

My thighs are slick with appreciation.

I love a man who knows how to program, and this is next-level amazing. Probably the most intricate work I've ever—

"Lark." Johan's deep voice travels through the room, startling a yelp from me.

I was so engrossed in his data web that I didn't even hear him enter.

Well, now that he's here… "Your laptop is a work of art," I inform him. "But I'm rewriting all your programming."

That's how I've decided to punish him for not responding to my messages.

And leaving me here for two damn days.

Which I almost comment on out loud, only he steps into view and I realize his black suit is soaking wet.

"Why are you…?" My eyes widen. "Oh my God, is that *blood*?" I set the laptop to the side and roll off his giant mattress. "Are you okay?" I ask, rushing toward him, trying to figure out where he's bleeding.

He looks down, frowning, then runs his fingers through his messy hair. It looks like he hasn't slept in days. And the haunted look in his eyes makes me wonder what the hell happened.

"It's not mine." His words are quiet. "It's…"

"Go shower," Lazarus says from the doorway. "I'll talk to Aurora."

Johan glances at him and nods. "All right." He starts toward the bathroom, his hands already unbuttoning the soiled dress shirt. "Don't be an ass, Laz." He sounds exhausted as he voices the comment, but his eyes resemble ice as he looks at the don. "Be *you*."

With that, he leaves the room, causing me to frown after him.

"If it's not his blood…" I swallow and focus on Lazarus, taking in his pristine suit. "And it's not yours…"

My heart starts to hammer in my ribs, my mind struggling to process what I fear might be true.

"Lazarus…" His name comes out like a warning. As though I'm trying to stop him from telling me something I don't want to hear. All while begging him to help me understand at the same time.

A soft vibration flows through the air, his purr seeming to swathe me in a blanket of false comfort.

False because I know something is wrong.

False because I don't trust him.

False because I'm *scared.*

"Everyone is okay," he tells me. "Aurora." He's suddenly in front of me, his finger beneath my chin as he forces me to meet his gaze. "*Everyone is alive.*"

My throat works.

Because something about that feels wrong.

"What happened?" I ask, my voice a whisper. "Tell me where you've been." On some deep level, I feel like it's my right to make that demand of him.

He's not mine.

I'm not theirs.

But if our futures are intertwined the way fate seems to intend them to be, then I want to understand everything.

"Don't treat me like a fragile doll," I add. "I'm not that omega."

"I know you're not," he murmurs, his touch leaving my jaw as his knuckles brush my cheek. "You're our intended queen."

"Then explain this to me," I say, my voice a little stronger. "Why is Johan covered in blood?"

His dark eyes hold mine, his expression hardening just the slightest bit. "Because something went wrong and Noah was injured in the process."

CHAPTER FIFTEEN

LAZ

I CATCH AURORA'S HIP, HOLDING HER UPRIGHT AS SHE SWAYS.

She seems to be unaware of the movement, her eyes a little dazed and unfocused before suddenly sharpening once more. "*What?*" It comes out in a startled shout. "Noah was *shot?*"

"Yes." No point in hiding the truth from her. That's not me being an *ass* like Johan warned me against; that's just me being straightforward. "But he's okay."

"Where is he?" she demands, sounding every bit like the mafia queen that I can't wait for her to become. "Why are you smiling at me? This isn't funny! Where's Noah?"

I didn't realize I was smiling. But now I feel my lips curling even more.

Because I like this feisty omega.

She's strong. Intelligent. An equal.

And about to hit me.

I grab her wrist before she can connect her fist with my face. Her hand wasn't in the air, but I could see the intention in her features. So I stopped her before she could even begin.

"Noah's in a workout room downstairs, burning off some steam. He's not allowed to be near you in his current state."

She gapes at me. "He was hurt enough to cause that much blood." She points in the direction of the bathroom door, clearly assuming the savagery decorating Johan's outfit was from Noah. Which isn't necessarily wrong, but not entirely accurate either. "And you sent him to the *basement*?"

That comment must mean that she explored the estate, like I suggested.

Although, I was surprised to learn she was in Johan's room. I only realized that because I caught her scent lingering in the air when he walked inside.

"What the hell is wrong with you?" she demands, taking a step to move around me.

But I still have a hold of her wrist, and I use it to pull her back into me. She snarls and lashes out, the jab of her elbow against my ribs unexpected.

And fucking hot.

I grab her by the waist and throw her on the bed, next to a laptop.

She bounces right up, ready to fight.

Only, I'm faster and already moving.

In the next breath, she's on her back and gasping for air as I pin her to the mattress.

"I need you to calm down, please," I murmur, my purr rumbling through my chest and into hers.

"*Calm down*?" She's like a damn wildcat beneath me. "Get off of—"

"Noah's fine," I interject, the authority underlining my tone slightly derailed by my continued purr. "He just needs to blow off some steam."

"He needs to see a doctor or go to a hospital," she returns, her winded voice rather erotic.

Except it's for all the wrong reasons.

Doesn't stop my lower half from reacting to the way she's rubbing up against me, though.

"He's seen the doctor, Aurora. That's partly why we were delayed. The bullet basically grazed his arm. He's physically fine." Mentally is another story entirely and the real reason we're just now getting home. "He's in a blood rage. That's why he's not allowed near you."

I can't trust him not to do something stupid like claim her with his teeth and his knot.

All without consent.

Because he assumes she's already his. And maybe she is, but I will not let their first time happen while he's in an unpredictable frame of mind.

"The bullet…? A… a blood rage?" Her brow furrows, her struggle ceasing. I'm almost saddened by that, as I was enjoying her fight. "I don't… What's a blood rage?"

I settle more on my elbows on either side of her head, my chest still vibrating in a soothing rhythm, one that will only ever be for her. "When Noah is triggered, he thirsts for revenge," I explain quietly.

This isn't something I would normally share.

But Aurora is important to us. She's our scent match and our intended omega. If she's going to become our queen, then she needs to understand all three of us in a way that no one else ever will.

"We went into the city the other night for a last-minute meeting with one of the Ricci brothers, but it was an ambush." A fact that still fucking pisses me off. "Johan doesn't typically attend with us, but his particular skill set was needed. Or so we thought."

Aurora probably has no idea how rare it is that I'm taking time to explain this all to her. I didn't even share these details with our crew.

However, I feel bad that we left her here alone for nearly three nights. That was never our intention. Nor is it something we intend to do often.

"It was a trick," I go on. "Johan was the target. Noah realized that a moment before it happened, jumped in the way… and then went on a killing rampage."

Her nostrils flare, but she doesn't otherwise react to the gruesome scene I'm trying to explain. Perhaps because I'm not providing enough description.

Or, more likely, because she grew up in this life. She understands the violence that comes with it.

Yet another reason she's our perfect queen.

"But Noah wasn't satisfied with the carnage. After the doctor fixed him up, he went on another rampage. That rampage is why Johan is covered in blood." He's not one to get physical, but when Noah caught up with Bastian Ricci—the one who betrayed us at the meeting—he helped Noah ask a few questions.

She swallows, her lashes fluttering a little. "Oh."

I smile. "Better?"

Her lips curl down. "I'm fine."

I take in the silky tank top she's wearing—it matches her tiny shorts—and meet her gaze again. "Indeed you are," I agree, my purr deepening into a low growl.

Violence always turns me on. Watching Noah work with Johan tonight just stoked my need even more.

Which makes being around this omega quite dangerous.

Fortunately, my control is resolute. But I'm not a saint, either.

That last part is why I don't move away from her, even though I probably should.

However, I rather like the way my cock feels nestled between her splayed thighs. She's warm, her pussy radiating a heat that calls to my knot.

I lean down to run my nose along her cheekbone, inhaling as her scent heightens. "You smell amazing," I admit in a whisper, loving her honeyed sweetness. "It makes me want to taste every inch of you."

I should stop.

I should pull back and let her breathe.

But the weight of the last few days holds me in place.

I just want to exist with her for one more moment. Lose myself in this sensual connection. Let her feel safe and wanted by me.

"I'll never force you to do anything you don't want to do," I promise her, my lips traveling to her ear. "And it kills a part of me to know that you fear me." Because I sense it in her tension. Smell the subtle sour note of it in her aroma. "I'm going to do whatever it takes to earn your trust, Aurora."

I press a kiss to her thundering pulse, my eyes closing as I inhale one more time.

Then I pull away from her and sit on the edge of the bed, aware that she needs space to process everything I've said.

Yet I can't seem to leave her for Johan to find alone. I just want to… be close to both of them.

Noah is probably beating the shit out of a punching bag right now or jumping rope so fast that the strands are threatening to break.

He might even be throwing knives at a target.

I would go find out, but he'll just invite me to spar. And in his current state, he'll best me. Something I don't really want to experience right now.

"Which Ricci brother did you meet with?" Aurora asks after sitting up and leaning back against the headboard.

I run my fingers through my hair, aware that it's a mess, and blow out a breath. "Bastian."

The way her mouth tightens tells me she knows him, or at least knows of him.

But it could also be the same way she's heard of me.

"Have you met him?" I ask, wanting to know for sure.

She nods, her lips flattening. "Unfortunately."

I arch a brow. "Am I going to be disappointed that he's already dead? Similar to how I feel about Gideon

Henderson?" Because I really want to go back and kill that bastard again. And if Aurora's history with Bastian is *unfortunate*, there's a good chance that I'm going to want him to die again, too.

She swallows, my attention catching the movement before lifting up to her full lips. I eventually return my gaze to hers, still waiting for a response.

"My father had a list of potential mate candidates, one he compiled when I turned sixteen." She grimaces. "Bastian and Stefano were on it."

"Was I?" I wonder out loud.

She doesn't hesitate. "Yes."

"He never informed me of it," I tell her.

"That's because he chose Stefano." Her eyes narrow a bit. "He wanted to strengthen alliances with the Riccis. I think that's why Gio never told him where to find me."

Well, that's interesting information. "Gio doesn't want to align more with the Riccis?"

She snorts. "No. He wants to go his own way. Or, well, he used to, anyway." Her lips twist. "I don't know his goals anymore. We haven't discussed family or business in a very long time. I just knew I would eventually have to come home."

Yes, that part I know as well because of Johan's snooping into her background. He found a very telling conversation between Aurora and Giovanni where he made a comment reminding her that her freedom was temporary.

That's one of the many details he used to coax her out of Widows Peak the other day.

"Perhaps alliances are something I need to discuss more with your brother," I murmur.

It's already my intention, especially with Aurora being my scent match. But I wanted this coupling before I even knew that part. She became our desired queen after she stole all that money from our organization.

"I don't want to be a mafia jewel," she informs me flatly.

"I've seen what that did to my mother, and I'm not interested in being used by a pack or paraded around like some sort of porcelain doll."

My eyebrow arches. "That's an interesting assessment." It also tells me a lot about potential misconceptions regarding our intentions with her. "For the record, I expect our omega to not only help us run the organization but also become the queen of it."

"I see." She picks up the laptop beside her and opens it, her eyes leaving mine.

I suddenly feel dismissed.

But I have no interest in leaving Johan's space. He's going to need me tonight. Hell, he probably needs me right now.

Only, I think Lark may need me, too.

"In case I haven't been clear, you're our desired omega, Aurora."

"Whom you expect to help you 'run the organization'?" she asks, putting emphasis on the repeated phrase.

"Yes."

She looks up from her computer. "Is that why you left me locked up here like a damsel in your palace? To help me learn more about your organization?" She cants her head. "Or is it because I wasn't needed as arm candy for your meeting?"

I scowl at that. "You will *never* be arm candy for a meeting. If someone so much as looks at you wrong, I'll fucking rip them apart. And Noah will help."

"Me, too," Johan says, returning to the room with a towel wrapped low around his waist.

That has to be the fastest shower he's ever taken, likely because he worried about leaving me alone with Aurora.

I try not to be offended by that realization. But it's impossible not to feel a slight pang in my chest. I'm not a soft alpha. Though, that doesn't mean I won't try for our omega, if that's what she requires of me.

"Isn't that the purpose of a mafia bride? To provide a visual distraction of sorts? Or entertainment, I guess." Her nose scrunches with that last remark, then she shakes her head. "Anyway, my point is that you left me here in your tower and didn't even bother to tell me that Noah was hurt. I think it's safe to say our definitions of helping to 'run the organization' vary."

Johan saunters toward her, his damp hair dripping down onto his sculpted chest.

Definitely rushed his shower. And didn't even bother to dry himself off properly.

Not that I mind the view.

But the reason still irks me.

As does Aurora's commentary.

"We—"

"No," I cut Johan off and meet his gaze. "This is for me to explain."

He stares me down for a beat, then dips his chin in acknowledgment.

Aurora has returned her focus to the laptop, making me feel dismissed for a second time. My eyes narrow.

Then I move to sit beside her on the bed, my legs stretching out right next to hers as I lean back against the headboard—just like her.

She tenses a little, the action one I feel since our arms are touching.

Aurora doesn't acknowledge me, just continues to type on the keyboard, bringing up back-end programming screens. It's all gibberish to me, but I've watched Johan do this enough times to have a high-level understanding of what I'm looking at.

I wait until she's finished typing, then gently place my hand over hers when she pulls up a new screen.

"You're not part of our pack yet," I tell her softly.

Johan makes a sound that tells me he disagrees with my approach.

But I'm not one to mince words. He knows this. Just as he knows that what I've said is true.

"Trust has to be earned on both sides, Aurora," I go on, watching her profile as I speak. She hasn't attempted to resume her work, her hand still trapped beneath mine. Though, she hasn't tried to move away from me either.

She's listening.

Which is good.

Because I have more to say.

"But we want you to join our pack. And us leaving you here without communicating our whereabouts or intentions wasn't a good way to convince you to join us."

I reach for her chin and slowly draw her attention to me.

When our eyes meet, I say, "I apologize for not contacting you, Aurora. That's on me. Johan's phone was broken. Noah was lost to the blood rage. I should have called you, and I didn't. That won't happen again."

She swallows but says nothing.

Not that I expect her to comment.

I'm not owed her forgiveness; I have to earn it.

"I meant what I said about wanting an omega to help us lead. You're not a pretty toy for us to show off, or *entertainment* for us to share. We're possessive men. Protective, too. If you attend a meeting or a function with us, it'll be because you want to be there. Understand?"

She jerks her chin a little, causing me to release my grip.

"We don't want a doll, Ms. Bianchi," I tell her. "We want a partner. Now I would appreciate a verbal response so I know you're not just listening but comprehending."

Consent and communication are important to me.

And it will only become more vital as we continue to get to know one another.

That's why I apologized for not calling her or messaging her. I knew better. To leave her here without a word wasn't okay. We were all caught up in the moment, and we're not used to having an omega to answer to.

She might not be ours yet, but she will be soon. Which makes it all the more important now to recognize and respect that times have changed.

"Are you asking me to forgive you for not calling me?" she inquires softly.

"No, I'm requesting confirmation that you understand what I'm telling you about our desires for a partner, not an omega puppet. If I wanted a female I could control, I would have accepted one of the dozen offers I've received from syndicate partners abroad."

"What if one of those offers was from my father?" Her question comes out sassy, nearly making me grin.

Whatever point she's trying to make or insinuate is punctured as I tell her, "I would have declined without ever bothering to meet you."

Her brow furrows, her brown eyes narrowing shrewdly as she formulates a response.

But I'm not done speaking.

"And that would have been a shame, given what I know about you now." I let my eyes roam over her silky pajamas. "You're a beautiful omega, Ms. Bianchi. But there's a lot more to you than looks, isn't there?" I look at the laptop. "I think I would enjoy watching you work."

Johan snorts. Because he knows what that means.

I watch him work all the time.

Then work him over afterward.

Intelligence is an aphrodisiac to me. Coupled with Aurora's scent, and my arousal is resolute. I will never not be hard around this female.

She owns me.

And she doesn't even realize it.

"My work would bore you," she informs me flatly.

"Oh?" I fold my arms. "Prove it."

She blinks. "What?"

I smile and issue a dare. "Finish whatever you were doing on your laptop."

"It's actually *my* laptop," Johan mutters.

"Not anymore." Aurora's singsong tone reminds me a bit of Noah when he's enjoying a taunt a little too much. "It's mine now."

Johan studies her, his ice-blue eyes narrowing a bit. "We'll see."

Amusement enters her expression. "You have others you can use in your office."

"Yes, but that one is my favorite."

She nods, a note of false understanding crossing her features. "Yes, I suspected it might be, which is why I chose it."

He hums and joins us on the bed, taking a position on the other side of her and sitting just as close to her as I am.

Aurora stiffens once more.

I wait for her to move.

She doesn't.

Instead, she nibbles her lip and starts typing on the keyboard again.

Johan's nostrils flare, his attention on whatever she's doing. After a moment, he breathes, "Fuck," and I realize he's aroused by whatever she's done to his laptop. He doesn't bother to hide it, his dick tenting the towel.

It takes physical restraint not to move to his side and free his pretty cock so I can play.

I know he needs to get off. Violence always puts us all in a mood. He also needs a reminder that he's safe. That we survived. That we're *here*.

But I don't want to interrupt his admiration of Aurora's work.

I also… kind of want to see what she'll do next.

"Who are these alphas?" he demands, causing my brow to furrow as I return my focus to the screen.

"A pack Aries asked me to run a check on," she says, her fingers flying across the keys. "They visit Widows Peak for business sometimes and are interested in joining her gym. But she needs to know they're harmless first."

I don't recognize any of the profiles she's running. "What kind of business?" I demand, confused as to why these men are unfamiliar.

I also really dislike that our omega is looking at images of other alphas.

Johan appears to be equally miffed.

We might be able to share her together, but not with pack outsiders.

The only way that would ever change is if Aurora demands it. But it'll be our life mission to be enough for her as a unit.

No matter what she needs, we'll provide it. Both in the bedroom and outside of it.

"Nothing that touches your world," she murmurs, making me frown.

Then I grasp that she's talking about the organization these alphas work for, and once I see the corporate name, I realize they're just standard business types. "Oh."

"Yeah, see? Boring, right?"

My lips twitch. "What they do for a living? Yes. Watching your beautiful fingers fly across that keyboard? No." I make a show of adjusting my pants. "In fact, seeing your hands move so fluidly makes me wonder what else you can do."

Her typing stalls, the only indication that she heard me. Then she shivers and resumes, but not before a faint pink glow highlights her cheeks.

I glance at Johan and find him admiring her, too. Then he meets my gaze over her head, his eyebrow inching upward like he's asking me what we should do now.

Or maybe he's inviting me to play.

Either way, I think it's time we show our omega what it

might be like to join us in bed. Our demonstration on the plane was just an appetizer.

What I plan to do to Johan tonight is the main course.

And if Aurora is good, perhaps we'll make her our dessert…

CHAPTER SIXTEEN
JOHAN

Fuck. I KNOW THAT LOOK.

Laz is about to devour me.

I should stop him. Tell him to give Lark more time to get to know us before dragging her into the devil's lair. But I'm too depleted to try.

The last few days have been exhausting.

Arousing.

Savage.

My emotions are shot. My body is tired. And all I want right now is a good fucking orgasm.

Which I know Laz can provide.

He's an outlet that sets my soul on fire. He knows exactly how to make me feel alive. How to make me submit. How to make me *plead*.

His dark eyes hold mine, burning me with his intentions.

Only for Noah to burst through the door with a bang that ripples through the space.

Fuck.

I should have anticipated he would come for me, too.

The darkness between the three of us is spiraling out of control, the carnage from the last few days tipping us over into dangerous waters. We were already balancing on the edge, knocked entirely off-kilter by finding our scent match.

Then Bastian fucking Ricci had to go and try to kill me.

For reasons we don't yet know or understand. Because the fucker wouldn't talk. When it became clear that nothing Noah was going to do would force him to reveal his secrets, Noah simply ended him.

Which means Stefano Ricci is due for a visit. He needs to answer for his brother's sins.

"You'd better fucking be ready for me," Noah says before rounding the corner and coming into view. I only knew he was the one who entered before because no one else would ever be bold enough to barge into my room without knocking.

Well, Laz does it, too.

But Laz was already here, meaning only one other alpha could be responsible for that brazen entry into my space.

An alpha who freezes on the threshold as he finds the three of us already in bed.

Me in a towel.

Laz in his slacks and dress shirt—with his fucking shoes on my bed.

Lark wearing a silky little outfit that I want to rip off with my teeth.

Meanwhile, Noah is naked.

Stark. Naked.

And very fucking hard.

"Oh, fuck yes. Our little bee has come out to play?"

"Aurora was just getting some work done and intending to leave," Laz cuts in, his body moving on the bed to block Lark from Noah's hungry eyes. Not because he wants to stop her from drinking her fill of Noah's exquisite form—which I definitely caught her doing—but to stop the enforcer from pouncing on our omega. "Isn't that right, princess?"

Lark looks at Laz, then down at the computer. She hits Send on the files she was compiling for her friend Aries, then closes the laptop. Going to her knees, I fully expect her to make a hasty exit.

But instead, she reaches across me—an action that brings her alluring body exceptionally close to my erection—and sets the laptop on the nightstand.

Then she plops right back down with a "Nope."

Laz glances back at her with a frown. "Excuse me?"

"*Nope,*" she enunciates clearly. "I was *not* intending to leave at all. In fact, I think I'm going to stay right here."

My lips twitch at her defiance.

However, the reality begins to play out as Noah walks purposely toward the bed and says, "Excellent. I'll come to you."

He places a knee on the bed, and Laz moves to intercept him. "She's not ready for this."

"Then talk me through it," Lark says before Noah can respond. "Tell me what to expect so I can prepare myself."

I blink, surprised. The little show of disobedience made sense—she wanted to piss Laz off by not playing along with his commentary.

But this… this is entirely different.

I expected her to hightail it out of here at the first show of aggression. Only, now I'm not sure she understands what's about to happen.

"Lark," I start, swallowing. "The mood the three of us are in… it's not safe for you here right now."

She glances at me. "I'll be the judge of that, thank you."

Laz again looks back at her, studies her face, and shrugs before returning to the space beside her. "Fine." His focus goes to Noah. "Demonstrate on Johan so Aurora can learn what to expect."

The enforcer narrows his gaze. But then his concentration shifts to me, and he begins to prowl.

Fuck.

I'm not wearing much, having grabbed a towel after the

quickest shower of my life and barely wrapped it around my hips.

"Actually," Laz interjects, causing Noah to snarl as he swings his attention to the taunting alpha. "Johan, our enforcer saved your life. Do you wish to thank him?"

I wish to do a lot of things.

Punch Laz.

Taste Lark.

Kiss Noah…

Maybe in that order.

No. Not in that order. Tasting Lark is definitely at the top. But I like Laz's suggestion that we show her what she's getting into with us.

The episode on the plane was just a way to take the edge off. Laz was violent, but he can do a lot more damage than simply fucking my throat.

And Noah… God, Noah is a damn sadist. He loves pain.

Which is why I know exactly how he would like to be thanked.

Not with my mouth. Not with my hands. But with my submission.

He'll want to use me.

Raw.

I'll let him because I owe him my life. And because I know this is what he needs. But it's going to fucking hurt.

"I don't need gratitude," Noah growls, coming toward me again. "Knowing you're okay is all that I need right now, boy genius." The variation of his nickname for me rolls off his tongue a second before he grabs me and yanks me into him.

It's rough.

It's hot.

It's overwhelming.

But I give in to his touch and open my mouth for his punishing kiss.

Except he's surprisingly gentle. Like he's trying to soothe

me. Or maybe he's soothing himself. Reassuring himself that I'm okay.

But as his tongue continues to stroke mine, I come up with a third possibility. One that has to do with the honeyed slick permeating the air.

Laz told Noah to demonstrate on me, to show Lark what he would do to her.

And Noah is doing just that—he's showing that even in his violent state, he'll be careful with her. Sensitive. *Gentle.*

He's *never* kissed me like this before, and I'm not sure I like it. This isn't how we fuck. This is… this is how he *loves.*

I yank back from him, my gaze narrowing. "That kiss isn't meant for me."

"I know."

"Then stop and kiss *me.*" I don't want to take away from Lark's experience. That embrace is meant for the two of them. And while Laz may have implied that's what he wanted Noah to do, it's not what Noah *needs* to do. "Fuck me, Noah. Fuck me or fuck off."

"You trying to tell me what to do, tech boy?"

Again with the damn nickname. Noah is always switching it up, using different versions to suit his mood.

But he's not going to distract me from my point. "I'm trying to remind you who you're touching, asshole."

"I know who I'm touching," he says, narrowing his gaze.

"Then why the fuck are you being so gentle?"

"Gentle?" he repeats, the word a low rumble of sound as he wraps his palm around my nape to give it a violent squeeze. "I'm not fucking gentle."

"Prove it," I growl.

And I'm on my back in the next second with his big body hovering over me. The towel is gone, his hand having ripped it out from between us so he could settle his dick right next to mine.

His palm moves from the back of my neck to my throat,

his grip punishing as he bends down to take my mouth with his.

This is how Noah usually takes me—with his fucking teeth.

Kissing me so hard that I bleed. He loves the taste of it, his tongue swiping at my lip before he dives in to destroy me.

Only a small gasp from right beside me causes him to pull back and evaluate Lark. His expression is positively feral, yet his hazel eyes soften a bit as he looks at her. "Am I scaring you, little bee?" he whispers, the question so unexpected that I freeze beneath him.

I can't breathe, his grasp cutting off my airway.

Yet he's speaking to her tenderly, asking if she's frightened.

But she shakes her head, then leans toward him.

Fucking. Leans. Toward. Him.

Like she wants to kiss him, too.

He notices. Because his nostrils flare. And his grip loosens just enough for me to breathe.

"You like the violence, pet?" he asks softly. "You want me to tongue-fuck your pussy like I'm kissing Johan?"

That brown-sugar-and-honey aroma grows, her slick likely saturating her silky shorts by now.

And fuck, that makes me so damn hard. I just want to roll into her and rub all over her.

But I'm trapped by Noah's muscular form.

"Ask nicely, and I'll give you whatever you want," he goes on. "Or maybe Laz will eat you out while I fuck Johan."

Her mouth parts, her tongue sneaking out to dampen her bottom lip.

Noah's chest vibrates in response, not with a purr but with a growl, and suddenly he's kissing me again. Brutally.

I give back just as fiercely, pressing my hips up into his. He reaches between us, his fist wrapping around my cock and giving it a savage pump.

Precum leaks from my tip on command, and I know exactly what he plans to do with it.

I pant against his mouth as he reaches beneath me to shove a finger into my ass without prep, the burn making me flinch.

"Aurora," Laz murmurs conversationally. "There's some lube in the drawer over there. I suspect Johan would appreciate you grabbing that for Noah to use."

I feel the bed moving, her heat disappearing, and I half expect her to leave the room. But then I hear her opening the drawer of the same nightstand she set the laptop on.

Rather than hand it to Noah and leave, she climbs back onto the bed, situates herself right next to me again, and says, "Noah." Her voice is soft but steady.

The big man pulls his lips from mine and looks at our omega. "Yes, my love?"

She shivers, the vibration one I feel against me. "I have some lube for you."

"I would much prefer the slick between your thighs," he replies. "Maybe you can slip your fingers into your wet cunt, then help me prepare Johan's ass for my knot."

My eyes widen.

And Lark releases a shuddering breath.

"Use the lube," Laz tells Noah. "She's watching tonight, not participating."

"I believe that's up to her," Noah returns, his grip returning to my cock to give it a cruel twist.

"*Fuck*, I'm not the one who made the rules," I remind him on a groan. "Don't take your irritation out on me."

"I'm not." He yanks again. "I'm trying to make more natural lube."

A groan leaves me as he moves his hand down to squeeze my knot. "*Noah.*"

"If our omega wants to help you, she will. Otherwise, this is how we're doing things," he replies, then goes to suck on my neck as he continues to abuse my knot.

I reach for the lube and take it from her, prepared to just

do it myself, but Noah grabs it with a growl and tosses it at Laz.

"That's how you two play. That's not how *we* play."

"I fucking hate you," I force out between my clenched teeth as my dick responds to his ministrations with more precum.

"No, you don't," he murmurs, kissing a path down my body. "But I'm happy to remind you *why* you don't hate me."

I thread my fingers through his hair, fully intent on yanking him back up my body. Only, he reaches my cock before I can try, and his mouth closes around the tip to steal the arousal with his tongue.

My back bows as he deep-throats me without hesitation, all while his hand continues to massage my knot.

A moan escapes me, tainted with a growl, my body on fucking fire. Noah knows how to bring me to climax quickly, and he's going to do exactly that.

Then let the cum dribble from his mouth onto my ass, which he'll use to prep me.

All while Lark watches.

God. Knowing she's here, knowing she's observing, knowing she's *wet*... It's killing me. All I want to do is kiss her. Bury my face between her thighs while Noah takes me from behind. Fucking live in her sweet pussy with my tongue.

"Fuck, tech boy, you're already about to come," Noah says, his amusement pissing me off. "Someone likes that honey-scented slick as much as I do."

"We all do," Laz says, his deep voice drawing my gaze to him. He watches Noah taking me into his mouth again, then looks at Lark to observe her reaction.

She's blushing.

But her lips are parted on a pant of need. One I recognize because my mouth is doing the same thing.

Laz leans down, his mouth near her ear as he softly asks, "Have you ever sucked an alpha's cock before, princess?"

She swallows and shakes her head.

"Mmm," he hums. "Then this is a good lesson for you. See how Noah's hand is wrapped around Johan's knot? How he's squeezing his base while taking him as deep as he can into his throat?"

Oh, fuck, hearing him describe it is going to send me over.

Except, no. Nope. Completely wrong.

It's Lark's *reaction* to his commentary that's going to send me over.

All she says is "Yes," but it's breathy and erotic and accompanied by a delicious wave of sweet perfume.

She's aroused. *Really* aroused. Like slick is pouring out of her to the point that I can not only smell it but *see* it bleeding through her tiny shorts.

Because her legs are on top of the blankets, and they're *clenching*.

"You like the idea of sucking Johan's cock, don't you, Aurora?" Laz says, his eyes meeting mine as he utters the words against her ear.

She whimpers in response, then nods. "Yes."

Fuck. I'm fucked. The burn in my balls reaches a crescendo, causing my body to tighten as I explode into Noah's mouth.

He doesn't swallow.

Because of course he doesn't fucking swallow.

He just lets my cum fill his mouth until he can't take any more, then he uses his hand to catch the rest.

I'm still quivering from the aftermath as he flips me, my face landing against the pillow with a grunt. I can't move. I'm putty. My body is shaking. My orgasm still rolling through me.

And fucking Noah is filling my ass with my own release, using his fingers to spear into me and prepare me for his massive dick.

"It's a dragon tattoo," I hear him say, the words presumably for Lark. Because I'm very fucking aware of his decorated shaft. "Feel free to trace it with your tongue sometime. Or your fingers. Whatever you like."

The head of his dick is already at my entrance, my ass nowhere near ready for him.

But he doesn't care.

He's all about brute force.

His hand is in my hair, pulling me off the pillow and forcing me to look at Lark.

Then he thrusts into me with a punch of his hips that has me shouting at him in response. "*Asshole*" is the word I utter the loudest. Followed by "*Hate you.*"

It's a lie.

I don't hate him at all.

And I fucking love the rough way he takes me. He always makes it good, even when he's in this savage mood.

Something he reminds me of now as he reaches around with his cum-drenched palm to grab my dick and massage my knot.

He's going to ensure I come again.

I'm on my hands and knees now, my face still angled toward Lark by Noah's grip. I'm just thankful he used his clean fingers to grab my scalp.

Not that it matters.

I'm going to need another shower after this anyway.

And I have no doubt that Laz will be joining me to use me in there.

I wish Lark would, too.

Something I try to convey as I stare at her.

She's watching me with wide eyes, her nostrils flaring, her pupils dilated. She's not even trying to hide her wetness anymore, her legs seeming to have spread like she wants to invite us to come home.

"I want to pull those soaked shorts off you, little hacker," I admit, my voice hoarse. "And *bury* my face between your thighs."

I want to die there. Suffocating on sweet, honeyed pussy. All while Noah keeps railing me.

It would be the purest fucking heaven.

"Do you want him to lick you, princess?" Laz asks, his mouth still near her ear. He's not touching her, just close enough to ensure she can feel his presence and his heat. Smell his interest. *Feel* his dominance.

That's who he is.

The one who is always in charge.

Even now as Noah exudes his own form of domination by forcing me to bottom for him. It goes against an alpha's instinct to submit. But Noah and Laz make it easy.

Fuck, Lark might even be able to top me.

Except the way she's watching me now suggests otherwise.

She's losing her mind with lust, just like me.

I can see her longing. Taste her need. *Feel* her heat.

"It would be the hottest reward," Laz is saying to her. "Johan's working hard for Noah, taking that big fat cock up his ass and letting our enforcer work out his furious need. It's painful, princess. But we do our best to ensure he experiences pleasure, too."

He presses a kiss to her neck, where I imagine her pulse is thundering.

"I would love to see you make Johan feel good," he adds, his voice low and coaxing. "Just a little taste, even if it's from your fingertips, would make his night so much sweeter."

She dampens her lower lip again, her gaze holding mine.

"You can kiss him, too," Laz murmurs. "Or just brush your knuckles against his cheek. He likes that."

"He also likes it when we choke on his cock," Noah grunts out, his hand leaving my hair so he can grab my hip. His thrusts turn harsher, his movements cruel as he pumps himself into me with a force that nearly sends me face-first into the mattress.

Only, Lark is suddenly there, her hands on my cheeks as she pulls my gaze back up to hers.

I didn't realize my head had fallen, the savage punch from behind having knocked me off-balance.

But she doesn't just hold me upright to look at me; she leans in and presses her lips to mine.

Fireworks ignite in my head, my mind losing all focus as Lark becomes the center of my universe. She's all I can see. All I can think about. All I desire.

I go onto my knees and reach for her, only for a weight from behind me to topple me to the bed with Lark beneath me.

I pull back as far as I can to check on her, but my head is pushed back down to hers, and her tongue enters my mouth.

Fuck. I can't process anything other than the feel of her silk-covered breasts pressing into my chest. Her thighs are against mine, too.

I don't know how we ended up here.

And I don't care.

All that matters is her mouth against mine. Her tongue. Her sweet heat against my throbbing knot.

Noah, I realize, my body forcefully grinding against Lark's as he drives into me from behind.

The sweet little omega pushes right back up into me, causing me to growl against her mouth. Not being able to feel her slick cunt against my knot is an exquisite torture. Yet my shaft is wet from her arousal, providing a delicious friction between us as she begins to writhe.

It's decadent.

It's addictive.

It's outright erotic.

I can't stop kissing her, my palm cradling her face. I wish I could do more, wish I could map out her exquisite curves, but I'm supporting my weight on my elbows, holding myself up so I don't accidentally crush her.

Except, *fuck*, I want to strip her naked.

Feel her tits with my bare hands.

Explore her.

But the force of nature at my back makes it impossible to touch her more than I already am.

I brace as Noah rides out his rut, taking out his agony and fury on my ass while I protect Lark with my body.

He would never hurt her. That much was evident in the way he kissed me at first. He was trying so hard to provide a clear demonstration of how he would treat her.

However, our intimacy is different.

He uses me and I use him.

It's a darkness. A craving. A twisted embrace.

Maybe one day she'll join us. *God, I hope so,* I think as our kiss intensifies. She moans against me, her thighs quivering as she clenches her muscles.

Fuck, she's going to come, I realize, feeling her vibrating beneath me.

It rivals the growl at my back, Noah close as well.

I'm trapped between them, lost to their mounting pleasure, doing my best to let them use me as they climb higher and higher.

And explode.

Noah shouts as Lark moans, the two of them detonating in unison. My knot throbs in response, Lark's silky pajamas leaving wet kisses along my shaft.

I bury my face in her neck as she continues to shake, her soft little pants music against my ear. I swear I hear my name. But she seems lost to her climax, the waves of pleasure overwhelming her gorgeous form.

Noah's hands are a brand against my hips, his lips in my hair. He's already massaging circles against my skin with his thumbs, his need to check in on me overriding the residuals of his orgasm.

He knows he was rough.

But he also knows I can take it.

I'm about to remind him of that when Lark freezes beneath me, her tension palpable. I glance at Laz, wondering if he's touching her.

However, he's studying her profile with a frown.

His dark eyes meet mine, and a sense of urgency radiates from the depths of his gaze as he jerks his chin, telling me without words to get off of her.

I push back against Noah, causing him to issue an irritated grunt, but he moves, taking me with him and to the side.

Lark lies there for a bit, her eyes closed.

Then she springs out of the bed and runs from the room.

I move to go after her, only to be held back by Noah and blocked by Laz.

"Let her process" is all Laz says.

I have no idea what that means or if it's a good idea to not chase her. It doesn't *feel* like a good idea. Actually, it feels very fucking wrong.

If she's hurt, I need to know.

Only, I know we didn't hurt her.

She kissed me. She pressed up into me. She *came*.

Noah was heavy against my back, but I braced most of the weight.

Still, what if it wasn't enough?

"I should go talk to her," I tell Laz and Noah. "Let me up."

"No." Laz presses his palm to my stomach, holding me in place on top of Noah, who is now running his hands up and down my sides while his cock remains in my ass. "I suspect that was her first time doing anything with an alpha. She'll come back to us when she's ready for more."

"She might be hurt," I argue, wrapping my fingers around his wrist. "Let me at least check on her."

Laz stares at me. "I'll go ensure she's okay. You stay here and accept aftercare from Noah." He looks at the man behind me. "Clean him up. I plan to spend the rest of the night with him after I'm back."

Noah sighs and kisses my shoulder. "Fine" is all he says. "But I might stay and watch."

"Fine," Laz echoes, then leaves.

I close my eyes. As much as I love putting on a show for Noah and Laz, it was Lark watching tonight that really set my soul on fire.

She… she completes something inside me that I never even realized existed. But it's there now, warming my heart and making me long for more.

I need her to be okay.

I need her to come back.

And I… I need her to do more than watch next time.

I need her to join us instead. Then stay. *For good.*

CHAPTER SEVENTEEN

LARK

I CAN'T STOP SHAKING.

It's like my limbs are electrified, my body vibrating with an intensity that feels unending. Like I'm still coming despite my orgasm igniting several minutes ago.

The sensation isn't exactly new. But it's something I typically only experience during my heat. *And with a very special toy,* I think, shuddering as I clamp my legs together.

I'm covered in slick.

Down my legs.

Again, just like during an estrous cycle.

But my heat isn't due for a couple more weeks.

This can't be happening. I can't be going into heat now. I… I can't handle it.

God, I could barely handle Johan kissing me.

I knew their scents might trigger me to go into heat early. I hoped I might be able to avoid it. However, now, I don't think I can.

I feel like I'm on the verge of *exploding.*

All I want to do is crawl back into that nest of masculine limbs, strip myself bare, and beg them to knot me. *Everywhere.*

Which is asinine.

I've never been with an alpha. Only ever a few beta males I've dated throughout the years.

And my toys… the ones I use during my heats… are nowhere near as large as the real deal.

Noah's cock is *huge*. I can't believe Johan took him up the ass.

Johan is well endowed, too. Not as long as Noah, but still thick and intimidating.

Then there's Laz and his monster dick, the one Johan somehow managed to swallow partly down his throat on the plane.

Maybe Johan is a magical alpha, I think dizzily. *He's just predisposed and capable of taking anything and everything.*

Part of me is jealous.

Part of me is in awe.

I… I don't know what to do with this information.

I need to take a shower, I think, pulling my silky top off. I try to yank the shorts off, too, but the fabric sticks to my skin. Growling, I bend to try to force it off and hear someone clear a throat behind me.

Oh God.

It's Lazarus.

I can tell by the scent alone. *Dark chocolate–covered cherries.*

I want to lick him all over. Memorize his muscles with my tongue. *Climb him like a damn tree.*

Because of the heat.

Or… or something.

I'm too coherent to be truly in estrus. Yet I've never been more turned on in my life. *I'm losing my mind.*

"Aurora?" he says, his low baritone causing goose bumps to dance along my arms. "Johan was worried you might be hurt. Are you?"

He's close.

I can sense him maybe a foot behind me now.

All I have to do is turn around and jump on him.

He'll help me figure this out.

Except.... except I ran out of the room because I didn't want to do something I might regret. I just can't remember what that was now.

My mind is clouded with Lazarus's presence. His dominance. His... his *purr.*

It's subtle, radiating from his chest like a damn beacon of power.

I turn, not caring about my strange state of dress, and basically collapse into the tower of protective muscle.

Lazarus catches me with ease, his palms on my bare waist as he pulls me into his vibrating chest. "Talk to me, princess," he whispers. "Did we push you too far?"

I snort. I don't think there is such a thing as *too far* when it comes to these men. Maybe *not far enough* is a thing, though?

I don't know.

I just feel... overwhelmed. Not like myself. A little lost to whatever this is that's brewing in my belly.

A heat, I think again, blinking in and out of cognizant thought. *God, it really is happening, isn't it?*

"Estrus," I whisper. "Maybe. Yes." It's an incoherent explanation. One I'm not even sure is right. This isn't how my heat usually starts. It's gradual, like a wave of warmth that spreads from between my legs to all my nerve endings.

This is all-encompassing instead.

Sudden.

Insane.

"Estrus?" he repeats, frowning down at me. "You're going into heat?"

I nod.

Then shake my head.

Tears pool in my eyes, confusion flooding my mind. "I don't... I don't know." And I hate it. I hate this. I hate feeling helpless. Hot. *Out of my mind.*

That's what reminds me of my estrus—the lack of control.

It's always like this, causing me to lose sight of who I am deep inside. Temporarily, yes. But I loathe the vulnerability associated with losing my self-restraint.

"Help me," I beg Lazarus, aware deep within how dangerous it is to ask this of him. But I don't know what else to do.

I ran.

He followed.

And now I just… I just want to feel normal again. *Like me.*

"I don't think you're going into heat," Lazarus murmurs, one of his hands lifting to cup my cheek. "But I'll help you." He leans down to brush his nose against mine. "We're going to take a shower, okay? Together. And I promise not to hurt you or take advantage of you."

I nod, accepting whatever he wants to do to me so long as it helps. "Anything."

"Not anything," he corrects me, a note of sternness underlying his tone. "I'm just going to take care of you, Aurora. Nothing more. Tell me you understand."

"I understand," I repeat immediately. Not because I really do, but because I want to obey him. To submit. To do whatever he desires.

For whatever reason, that makes him frown at me.

I don't like that.

I want to please him.

To make him want me.

Which, of course, inspires more stupid tears. *Ugh, I hate this!*

"Shh," he hushes, gathering me into his arms and carrying me. "I've got you, omega. You're safe with me."

I'm not.

I know I'm not.

But I don't have the energy to say so. Instead, I just bury my face in his neck, inhaling his decadent scent. "You smell so good," I tell him, my tongue sneaking out to lick his skin. It's not as sweet as his aroma suggests, the slightly salty flavor surprising me.

He tastes like a man.

An alpha.

My alpha.

I nuzzle him again, laving him once more and groaning as slick pools between my thighs.

Lazarus rumbles in response, his chest vibrating with a purr that's highlighted by his growl.

Yes, yes, I think, wanting more of that. "I want to feel you do that between my legs," I admit, feeling strangely bold. "Please."

He makes a noise, one I'm not sure means agreement.

Which has me pouting in response.

He shushes me again and sets me on a counter. The cool marble does little to dispel the warmth blasting through me—a warmth that actually burns hotter as he kneels to finish removing my shorts.

Lazarus is on his knees for me, I think, a fluttering sensation stirring in my lower belly.

He leans in to press a kiss to my thigh before standing once more, the light brush of lips not nearly enough. I reach for him, but he takes a step back.

A growl escapes me, one that turns into a moan as he begins to disrobe.

Because *yes.* Yes, this is what I want. A naked Lazarus. An alpha in his prime. A male who can help quell this ache simmering inside me.

I lick my lips, admiring the abs now on display, as well as the hard chest and impressive shoulders. He's like a work of art.

Something I think I must admit out loud because his lips twitch.

Or maybe it's just my open appreciation that amuses him.

Whatever.

He's fucking hot and he knows it.

All perfect arms. Strong. Lined with delicious veins along his forearms.

But his thighs… *Wow.* Solid muscle. He wasn't naked on the plane, just… mostly. Where it counted, anyway. However, his athletic legs are long and prove that he doesn't miss workout days. All parts of his body are honed to perfection.

Just like Johan and Noah.

I shudder, thinking about them. *Are they still playing in the other room?* I wonder, imagining Noah fucking Johan. *Oh, that was hot…* Feeling all that strength on top of me propelled me into a new territory of arousal, taking me higher than I've ever gone before.

I could almost feel Noah driving into me, his forceful thrusts pushing through Johan and directly into my center.

Insanity.

Amazing.

Bliss.

But it's Lazarus who picks me up now, his strength washing over me and lighting me on fire from within.

He's going to be even more powerful than Noah, I realize, shivering with the thought.

All three of them are alphas. However, Lazarus takes dominance to a new level of existence.

I wrap my arms around his neck and kiss his throat again, tasting him as my legs tighten around his waist.

It's then that I realize his boxers are still on.

My lips curl down, and a whimper escapes me. I want to be skin to skin.

"You're safe," Lazarus tells me.

Any other moment in time, that would appease me. But not right now. Because I don't want to be safe. I want to be *unsafe*. I want him to lose control. To fuck me into oblivion. No holding back. No control. Just an alpha claiming an omega.

Oh God, claiming… Yes. Yes, that. Teeth in flesh. *Biting.*

I nearly follow through with the desire, but water springs to life overhead, drowning me in a cold sea of reality.

I blink.

Then pull back to gape at Lazarus. "*A cold shower*?"

He smiles. "It's not just for you, princess." He walks until my back is pressed to the chilled wall, the temperature at odds with the heat blossoming between my thighs.

His dick is hard and throbbing against my center. The thin boxer shorts do nothing to keep his size contained, his shape perfect and pronounced as he rocks into me. "You were about to claim me," he murmurs, his lips ghosting along my cheek. "Do you know how difficult it was to stop you?"

My brow furrows. "You don't want me to claim you?"

He chuckles. "Ah, Aurora, I will boldly and happily wear your claim mark. But I want you to bite me in a willing state, not in a lust-drunk one." His lips meet my ear. "There will be no regrets between us. Ever. When we claim one another, it'll be for the right reasons."

His mouth travels down to my thundering pulse, his trimmed beard soft against my skin.

"Finding a place to mark you is going to be exceptionally enjoyable, Ms. Bianchi." He nibbles my throat, then begins a path down to my breasts.

His dark eyes seek out mine as he takes my beaded nipple between his teeth, then rolls it with his tongue.

My lips part, the image of him kneeling before me again so fucking erotic that renewed need shoots through me, causing my thighs to clamp together. "Lazarus," I whisper.

"Hmm?" he hums, still holding my gaze.

I want to ask him for something, but I don't know how to express it. I… I also kind of want to run. To hide. To… to… God, I don't even know.

Who am I kidding, anyway?

I'll probably end up running to Johan. Or Noah.

Why not just… see what Lazarus has in mind? See if he can help me soothe the torment growing inside me.

"If I'm in heat," I start, swallowing. "Can you… can you please… assist?" I feel so foolish voicing my request. It's ridiculous. But what else am I supposed to do? I don't have any of my toys. And suffering through an estrus without any relief will…

Well.

I don't want to find out.

I just don't.

"Please?" I press.

He smiles. "As beautiful as hearing you beg is, darling, you're not in heat yet. But after I've calmed your need, we can talk more about that, all right?"

I'm torn between growling and whimpering.

Growling because I'm annoyed.

Whimpering because he spoke those words against my breast, the vibration causing my nipples to harden even more.

I thread my fingers through his hair, hoping to hold him in place so he can give me more.

More kisses.

More nibbles.

More pleasure.

Pressing up against Johan drove me to orgasm, something that's never happened to me before. I can only imagine the euphoria Lazarus can inspire with his mouth. His touch. His hands. *His cock.*

"Tell me how to please you, princess," the alpha murmurs, still holding my gaze. "Do you want my tongue?"

I nod, the motion feeling frantic.

"Where?" he presses. "Here?"

I nod again, causing his eyes to narrow slightly.

"Verbal responses, please, Ms. Bianchi. Consent is important to me," he says. "Tell me you want me to lick your tits."

I swallow, my mouth seeming to go dry in an instant. "I… I want to feel your mouth on me. On my breasts, p-please."

His nostrils flare. "Only there?"

I shake my head. "No."

"Then where?" he repeats, the words a growl against my nipple.

I shudder in response, my eyes nearly falling closed. Only, his smoldering gaze demands that I focus on him, his dominance a pressure against my senses that captivates me entirely.

In this moment, I'm his. Utterly and completely.

"Ms. Bianchi," he says, pulling back just enough to make me miss the presence of his mouth near my stiff peaks. "Tell me what you want, and it's yours."

God, I wish it were that easy. I've been with a few betas, but nothing ever felt like this. Felt like *him*.

No, not even just him, but *them*.

My alphas.

My scent matches.

They're driving me mad.

They left me. Noah was hurt—though he looked just fine tonight. And now… now I'm in the shower with Lazarus Ferraro on his knees for me. Waiting for a command.

No, it's more than that. He wants permission.

Consent.

I would never have thought a man like him would value consent. He's nothing like I expected. Nothing like I could have imagined.

And I'm so tired of overthinking this.

I want to see what he can do. Learn more about who he is. Determine if he's the alpha he proclaims to be.

"Pleasure me, please," I whisper. "I want your mouth on my breasts," I reiterate. "And between my thighs." I can't say the word I know he needs to hear. I… It's too much. Too embarrassing. Too *real*.

But I can tell by his expression that he's about to demand clarification on *where* again.

"On my clit." The words rush out of me before he can ask. Then I nearly duck my head to hide. Only, his eyes still hold me captive, which is how I catch the smolder darkening his expression.

He's gratified by my words.

Moreover, he's *aroused* by them.

"You've been a very good girl tonight," he praises me. "And good omegas are rewarded. *Thoroughly*."

My breath catches in my throat, his words inspiring a fresh wave of slick to dampen my thighs. I squirm, feeling needier than seconds before as a plea leaves my lips. "Touch me, alpha."

He rumbles, deep in his chest, his irises seeming to morph into a black that rivals his pupils as he moves forward once more. "Happily, omega. *Very* happily." His lips close around my nipple, his tongue teasing the tip as his palms find my hips.

A cry of relief escapes me in an instant, my body so pent up with desire that I no longer know how to stand. But he presses me back against the wall, his hands holding me with ease as his mouth explores my breast. Licking. Nibbling. Sucking.

Not an inch is spared from his caress, his lips mapping every part of my chest. I'm a quivering mess by the time he's done, my center weeping with a need only he can satisfy. I'm about to use my grip in his hair to pull him downward, but I'm unexpectedly sliding up the wall as he lifts me off the floor.

My eyes widen, a yelp leaving me.

Only for him to command, "Legs on my shoulders, princess."

I'm so startled by the demand that I… I just comply.

And suddenly I'm pinned again, my back against the

marbled tile, his face between my thighs, and my legs… on his shoulders.

He doesn't give me a moment to evaluate the precarious position. He simply leans into my flesh and licks me deep from entrance to clit.

"Oh God," I moan, my head falling back against the wall.

"Laz," he corrects me. "'Alpha' and 'sir' work, too."

I'm about to reply to that when I all but swallow my tongue in response to him sucking on my clit.

Hard.

It hurts. It feels good. It… it's… *Oh, fuck…*

He rolls the tortured bud between his teeth, drawing a gasp from me, followed by a scream as he nibbles. "Mmm, claiming you right here is absolutely an option," he says, his words making me want to issue a protest.

But then he starts licking and sucking, and I forget how to speak. How to make any noises other than moans.

Because wow. *Wow.* This man… this man knows… what he's… *Ohh…*

His hands wander, his finger entering me without warning as he laves my clit with a skill that has my toes curling.

This is unlike anything I've ever experienced. Overwhelming. Consuming. *Brutal.*

He's destroying me in the best way.

Rewriting all my expectations.

Ensuring I remember him for the rest of eternity.

God, he doesn't even need to mark me. I'm pretty sure I'm his now. That I belong to him and his pack. To Noah. To Johan.

Why was I fighting this? I wonder, my head thrashing as Lazarus owns me with his tongue. His finger. *No, fingers… There are two. Twisting. Curling.*

"There," I breathe, my legs tensing as he touches me deep inside. In a place only my toys usually reach.

But something tells me his cock will do just fine.

And his knot… *Oh, fuck, his knot…*

It's going to feel so good when he's inside me, clinging to me, holding me to him, possessing every inch of me.

"Lazarus," I whisper, my hips writhing as he devours me.

"You going to come for me, princess?" he asks, then flattens his tongue and *hums.*

I'm so close. On the precipice. About to *explode.*

I feel it coiling, sense my insides tightening, anticipate the build, the impending explosion, the utter *madness.*

This won't be an ordinary climax.

It's going to be devastating. Just like the one I experienced while dry-humping Johan.

Only more somehow.

Incredible.

Soul-rearranging.

Life-threatening.

Lazarus is rewriting my version of reality. And I just… I just don't care.

"Mmm, that's it, omega. Come for me. Bathe me in your slick." His words are a rumble against my tormented flesh, and they coax me into a tremble.

A tremble that builds into a crescendo of sensation.

Until I can't stop quivering.

And the world detonates in an array of vivid colors and screams.

My screams.

I don't even know what I'm saying. It doesn't matter. Because I'm flying. Soaring. *Skyrocketing* to another plane of existence.

One where I exist in a series of violent tremors. Live in a puddle of pleasure. Breathe air warmed with chocolate and cherries.

I'm only vaguely aware of Lazarus moving, of my body being once again pinned between him and the wall.

Only, his mouth is on mine, forcing me to taste my slick as he grinds his hips against mine.

Part of him is still inside me. *His fingers. Three of them.* Strumming. Coaxing. Forcing me to stay in this euphoric state.

I struggle to inhale. Struggle to think. Struggle to do anything other than feel.

I'm so ready for more. For his cock. His knot. Except all he does is pleasure me with his hand, his palm applying pressure to my clit as his fingers continue to stroke me.

I groan into his mouth, irritated and elated at the same time.

I need more. I need him. *I need an alpha.*

But as I tumble off the cliff once more, a calming sensation steals over me, my ecstasy melting into a sea of soothing waves.

His purr, I realize. *He's purring for me.*

Pleasuring me. Taking care of me. Comforting me.

It's too much. Not enough. Too amazing. Terrifying. Beautiful. *Consuming.*

My head falls to his shoulder, his lips at my ear as he whispers praise.

"You're so fucking stunning when you come."

"Fuck, princess, I can't wait to feel you squeeze my cock like that."

"You're making it hard for my fingers to move. But I don't mind a little brute force, Ms. Bianchi. You'll take me. Eventually. And it's going to be fucking perfect."

"Yes, darling, just like that. Come one more time for me."

"Such a good girl for me, omega. So fucking good."

I'm lost in an oblivion that's owned and dictated by Lazarus Ferraro.

It's dangerous here.

Hypnotic.

Amazing.

I should want to run again, but my legs are too heavy to move.

Besides, he's already walking for me. Or… or something. I don't know. My eyes are closed. My head against his shoulder. His purr warming my heart. His fingers massaging my insides. His lips continue to voice words against my ear in that deep baritone that I'm starting to adore.

I yawn. Moan. Curl into him.

Exist.

And sleep…

CHAPTER EIGHTEEN
NOAH

JOHAN'S SOFT SNORES CAUSE MY LIPS TO CURL.

When Laz didn't come back, Johan tried to go hunt him down.

I provided an alternative activity.

Or rather, I forced him to stay.

Then fucked him until he passed out.

He's going to be pissed when he wakes up, covered in our cum. Johan always wants to shower after we play, then changes the sheets before going to bed.

Sometimes I fuck him again just to infuriate him.

Because the process starts all over and he eventually runs out of clean bedding.

But tonight, he was so exhausted by my antics that he didn't even try to shower.

Which means he's saturated in our joint fluids, something I play with now as I massage the substance into his skin. It's my way of marking him.

And defying Laz.

He told me to clean Johan up.

I made him dirtier instead.

Chuckling, I lean down to kiss his shoulder, then suck on his neck, curious whether I can rouse him into another round.

He swats at me instead, then goes back to his snore fest.

I heave a loud sigh. "Lightweight." It's not true. He gives as good as he gets. But I like to goad him anyway. "I guess a nap works. But I'm going to wake up hard and expect you to suck me off. You've been warned."

My lashes flutter, my eyes closing.

Only for a picture of Aurora on her knees to flood my vision.

Mmm. Or maybe she can suck me off instead…

Fuck, our little pet was absolute perfection beneath Johan, cradling him while I used him.

I *loved* that.

But then she ran.

Why? I wonder, my mind playing through the sequence of events. *Wait, I didn't scare her… did I?*

That thought has my eyes opening again, my lips curling down.

"No, that's not… that's not okay." I roll off the bed and go look for a pair of Johan's boxers. We're roughly the same size, so they fit.

It also adds to the list of things he can be annoyed about when he wakes up. Because he hates when I borrow his shit.

"Be back in a bit," I promise his sleeping form. "Got an omega to hunt down."

Johan knows I would never hurt her. Hell, he knows I would never hurt him, either. Even when lost to a blood rage.

It was Laz's idea that I go *work it off* before coming up to the residential quarters.

Yeah, that lasted all of fifteen minutes before I got bored and went searching for a better outlet.

When I found Aurora tucked in between Laz and Johan, I nearly growled with victory. But then it became clear that she wasn't there to play.

Which sucked.

But I liked Laz's idea to show her what she's missing. Or teach her. Or whatever the fuck he suggested. I just know I liked it.

At least until she left.

That… sucked again. Especially seeing Johan's concern.

I didn't understand his worry at the time, but now that I'm feeling more like myself, I get it. She practically ran from the room.

Was she hurt? I frown.

That would explain Laz not returning. But wouldn't he have come to get us?

Or maybe he thought I wasn't in the right frame of mind to help.

My eyes roll heavenward.

He seems to think I'm a psychotic killer when on a blood rage.

I mean, he's not wrong. But I can rein it in when I need to.

Like for our pet.

I can be gentle for her. I tried to show her that by demonstrating on Johan, but the fucker got all pissy with me about it.

So I railed him in response. Mostly raw. Because that's the way I like to fuck.

Aurora, though, I'll prepare better. If she wants me to.

That's why we still need a limits discussion. As my intended bride, I need to know more about her sexual expectations. Her wants. Her *needs*.

I adjust the boxers on my hips, trying to ease my now-throbbing knot.

Doesn't matter that I spent several loads on Johan. Just thinking about our luscious omega has me hard and ready all over again.

So let's see what you're up to, pretty bee.

I pause outside her door, my hand on the knob.

Her sugary scent is strong. *Really* strong. Like *I just came a thousand times* strong.

And it's mingled with chocolate and cherries.

My lips part. *No. He didn't…*

I push through the threshold, prepared to kill Laz. Only to find him curled protectively around our pet in her bed.

His eyes meet mine, his arrogant expression making my hands fist at my sides.

"You got first lick," I realize out loud, livid.

"Yeah. I did. And it's fucking divine." His voice is low, like he's trying not to disturb the sleeping omega in his arms.

My gaze narrows. "I get first knot."

"That's up to her," he says back to me.

"She's *my* fiancée."

"I don't recall her agreeing to that."

I snort and fold my arms over my chest. "Her pussy is gonna say yes. Just wait."

Laz shakes his head, his lips twisting upward into a smirk. "We'll see."

"We will," I promise.

Then I saunter toward the bed to pull the blankets back.

"What are you doing?" he demands, his voice still a whisper, but that baritone of his is hard to hide.

"Going to bed," I inform him, sliding in between the sheets. "If you're allowed to sleep with our omega, then so am I."

"She didn't ask you to be here, Noah." There's a note of authority in his tone that irks me. "She has to consent."

"I didn't say I was going to *fuck* her while she slept, Laz," I fire back at him. "I just want to cuddle."

And if she wakes up in the mood to do more, then I'll fuck her.

Because I'm going to be the first to knot her cunt.

Since Laz rudely stole my right to first lick.

Okay, maybe it wasn't my *right*.

But he's still a dick for getting there before me.

Johan got to kiss her first, too.

So it's obviously my turn.

Hopefully, our pet agrees when she wakes up.

"Noah," Laz starts.

"Fuck off, boss. I'm sleeping," I tell him, closing my eyes and snuggling as close as I can.

The asshole has his arm around Aurora, his presence like a damn barrier. But I don't care. I press my chest against his arm and ensure my warmth blankets our omega's back.

Laz sighs in response. "If she wakes up scared, I'm going to kill you."

"She has nothing to fear from me," I vow.

"What the fuck?" Johan demands, his sleep-laden voice sexy as sin and an invitation I *almost* answer to.

Almost.

But my knot isn't throbbing for him right now. It's throbbing for our pet.

"Come nap with us," I say, inviting him to join.

"I'm covered in your fluids," he hisses. "And why the fuck are you both in bed with Lark?" He sounds hurt. Like he's missed out on something.

"Because Laz ate her pussy until she passed out," I inform him. "Or I assume that's what happened. Now we're waiting for her to wake up so I can knot her."

"That's not at all accurate," Laz growls. "Well, the first part is, kind of. The latter half, no."

The bed dips as Johan joins us, only he doesn't cuddle like he should. Instead, he reaches over me to inspect Lark. "Is she okay?"

"She's fine," Laz returns, sounding irritated. "I took care of her."

"With her consent?" Johan presses.

"You're really starting to piss me off," Laz informs him.

"Then you know how I feel about you on a daily basis," I interject.

However, I'm ignored as Johan says, "I'm not trying to, Laz. I just want to make sure… she's okay."

"She thought she was in heat. She isn't. Not yet, anyway. She was just really turned on. So I helped her because *she asked me to*." Laz glares at Johan. "You, better than anyone, know how I feel about consent."

I can't see Johan, but given how Laz is boldly looking over my shoulder, I assume the two of them are staring each other down.

Yawning, I go back to snuggling.

Those two can work their shit out while I get my cuddle on.

"You're right," Johan finally says. "I'm sorry. I… I feel *protective* of her. And it's making me question things I wouldn't normally question."

I grunt at that. "There's nothing to question. She's ours. We should probably just start planning the wedding." My eyes open again. "*Oh.* I get to say 'I do' first. I proposed first. It's only fair."

Laz gives me a look like I've lost my mind.

Which really pisses me off. "Just because you licked her first, and Johan kissed her first, does not mean she's not also mine. If I want to marry her first, it's my right as the only one with enough balls to ask."

"She hasn't even said yes, Noah," Laz reminds me.

"Semantics." I resume my snuggles. "She's still mine, too. You'll see."

"Don't look at me," Johan says, clearly talking to Laz. "If Noah wants to marry her, he will. And I'll be the best man."

"No, you'll be too busy marrying her as well," I murmur. "Laz should be the priest, though. I'd enjoy that."

"I'm not going to be the fucking priest."

"Can you imagine him reading a sermon?" I go on,

ignoring Laz's comment. "It would be some shit about submitting. Then our pet would probably punch him." I smile at the fantasy unfolding in my head. "Nah, she'd *shoot* him, I mean. Because I'd give her a gun."

"She has one on her nightstand," Laz says conversationally. "Maybe she'll shoot you when she wakes up and realizes you've infiltrated her nest without permission."

"This bed isn't her nest yet," I murmur, yawning again, my eyes still closed. "Which we should fix. She needs supplies. I'll work on it after I get some sleep."

Meanwhile, I start a mental list of things we'll need.

The first item has me angling my head back so I can peek at Johan. "Don't change your sheets yet. She might want those."

He glares at me. "You're going to change them for me."

I nod. "Yeah, that's fine. Then I can give them to her as a present." Makes sense since I'm the one who did all the work to soil them. My lips curl as I return to my omega snuggle. "She'll love it."

"I really hope she shoots you," Laz mutters.

"Likewise, boss." Then I reach down to fix my boxers—or rather, *Johan's* boxers—because my knot is throbbing again. "I'm totally going to fuck her in a pool of your blood, Laz. It'll be so damn hot."

He growls something I don't hear, mostly because I'm no longer listening to him.

I'm too lost to the fantasy of a violent omega forcing him to his knees while pointing her gun at him. She wouldn't fatally wound him. Just… something superficial. Like that scratch on my arm.

Fucking Bastian.

Such a cheap fucking shot.

I'm glad he's dead.

His brother is probably next.

Depending on what I dig up on the hit on Johan, anyway.

That's tomorrow's task. Along with gathering nest items.

It's going to be a busy day.

One that I hope ends with my knot inside of Aurora's sweet, honeyed pussy.

Because yes, fucking please.

CHAPTER NINETEEN
LARK

Where am I? I wonder, lost in a sea of masculine intensity.

I heard them talking while I slept. None of it was coherent, just… deep murmurs and subtle growls.

They were arguing about something.

But I couldn't focus long enough to understand what or why. And I was too exhausted to care.

Now, though, I'm alert and very aware of the hot chest at my back. As well as the firm pec I appear to be sleeping on.

And the warm presence by my legs.

I'm surrounded by alphas.

That thought should startle me. However, the familiar scents… calm me.

These men intimidate me. Yet they're… they're mine.

I feel it in my soul. Know it in my heart. Like we're fated mates or some supernatural craziness.

Maybe I'm insane to accept our intertwined destinies. But those orgasms last night surely make it easier to embrace.

First with Johan.

Then with Lazarus.

Neither of them used me for pleasure. They only provided it.

And Lazarus helped calm me down.

I thought I was going into heat. Now I know it was all driven by hormones.

Which means my next estrus is going to be *explosive.*

It's also coming soon. I sense that I'm on the cusp of losing myself to that dreaded cycle. Early, as I feared.

Yet I'm not as scared now.

Because I don't think these alphas will hurt me. In fact, I'm rather certain they will ensure I experience the best heat of my life.

I shiver at the thought of having a real knot inside me.

No. Not a *knot*, but *knots*.

Can I take them all at once? I wonder, my thighs clenching.

Which is when I belatedly realize there's a leg lodged there, one that belongs to whoever is at my back.

"Morning, pet," a slightly accented voice greets me, telling me Noah is behind me. "Sleep well?" He presses his nose to my neck, his lips ghosting across my pulse. "Any good dreams you'd like to share? Perhaps one that led to that delicious scent blossoming between your thighs?"

Heat threatens to swallow me whole. Yet somehow I manage to ask, "Why are you in my bed?"

"Because Laz said we were having a cuddle party," he murmurs.

A rumble of disagreement sounds from the male in front of me, but it's the one near my legs that says, "Noah's jealous that he hasn't experienced a first with you yet. So now he's going to cling to you like a puppy dog until he gets what he wants."

I blink. "What?"

"I'm knotting you first," Noah tells me, causing my eyes to widen.

"*Excuse me*?"

"Hey, it's only fair." He moves and pulls me so I'm on my back and staring up at him. "I confessed my love, and I proposed. Yet somehow the first kiss went to Johan and the first lick went to Laz."

First lick? I repeat to myself, frowning.

Then I realize what he means, and I'm even hotter than before.

"So I'm claiming first knot," Noah goes on, clearly oblivious to my mortification. "Unless… unless you don't want me to knot you. In which case, I won't." His expression falls. "Do you not want my knot, little bee? Did I scare you last night? Because I promise I would never hurt you. I…"

Uncertainty taints his handsome features, causing my heart to ache.

This beautiful, psychotic male thinks I don't want his knot?

He thinks I'm *scared* of him?

Intimidated, maybe.

But scared? No. "No, I'm not scared of you," I say out loud. "Though, you are…" I trail off, considering how to phrase what I'm feeling. "You're very direct. Which is actually why I believe you when you say you won't hurt me."

Because he's been upfront about how he feels.

Even if he's a bit off-kilter.

Or a lot off-kilter.

"You can't love me, though. We barely know each other. And your proposal wasn't real."

His gaze narrows. "I do love you, and my proposal was very real. But I'll do it right next time. Get a ring and everything."

"You can't love—"

"Don't tell me what I can and can't do, little bee. Well, unless it pertains to your limits. *That* you're allowed to dictate. But my capacity for love is my own to manage. And we've been stalking you for years. So trust me, I know you more than well enough to be in love." He leans down and kisses me on the cheek. "Now, what would you like for breakfast?"

I blink at him, struggling to process everything he just said. *What does he mean by "limits"?* I wonder.

"Please say *cock*," he murmurs, making me blink again.

"What?" That's obviously my favorite word of the day.

"For breakfast—I'm asking if you would like my seed. I'll happily feed it to you." His hazel eyes glitter as they widen with excitement. "*Oh.* I can be your first blow job." He cants his head. "Unless you've sucked cock before?" His gaze goes to my mouth. "I'm guessing you have."

Murderous rage colors his expression in the next moment, making me wince.

"Give me names, little bee. I'll chop their dicks off and—"

"Noah," Johan interjects, cutting him off before he can tell me what he plans to do with these figment dicks.

Because no, I haven't done that with a man yet.

I've had sex.

But… but it's been pretty superficial stuff. Mostly to experiment and take the edge off. No oral.

Until last night, anyway.

"Let's give Lark a minute to finish waking up before we dive into personal questions, yeah?" Johan continues.

"So you're suggesting these previous experiences mean something to her? That they're *personal*?" Noah sounds furious. "I'm doing more than cutting off—"

"No," I force out. "*No.* There's no need for that. I… I haven't… I mean… *No.*" I shake my head. Because this is insanity. "You can't just chop off dicks for me, Noah."

He gives me an affronted look. "I assure you that I can and will, little bee. Feel free to give me a name so I can prove it."

"I would give you Gideon Henderson's name, but that's already done."

"*You gave Gideon Henderson a blow job?*" he demands. "*Willingly?*"

"No!" I shout. "I've never done that with anyone!" God, ugh, why am I yelling? "Noah, I'm saying…" Fuck, I don't even know *what* I was saying.

This alpha is certifiably insane.

And confusing.

And hot.

And… and… *Is he purring?* I gape at him, then swoon as I realize that, yes, he is indeed purring for me.

He also has a really goofy grin on his face. "See, little bee? I love you."

I just… I just stare. Because how am I supposed to even begin to respond to that? One second he's talking about chopping off dicks, then confessing his love in the next, and lastly emitting that hypnotic sound from his chest.

Yeah, I'm screwed.

How was I ever meant to say no to this pack? Why did I ever want to?

"Even though I really want to say the words, I won't ask you to marry me again yet. I'll get a nice ring first. Maybe some flowers or chocolate. Then I'll do it."

"I don't need a ring," I mumble. There's no point in commenting on anything else, so I don't.

"I'll also take you somewhere really nice," he adds, ignoring my comment. "Like on a proper date. Oh!" He looks at Lazarus, who is lounging alongside me with an arm tucked beneath his head.

Then he shifts his focus to the male lying longways across the bed near my feet. He currently has his head propped up on his hand, his naked form stretched out like he's waiting to be drawn on a canvas.

"Let's go out and show our pet a good time," he says, sounding boyish and hopeful. "Maybe a picnic at the park? Or one of those posh places Laz fancies?" He turns thoughtful. "I wouldn't mind going for a swim. We could fly down to the islands for a day or five?"

I gape at him. "How about a movie?"

His nose wrinkles. "You want us to buy a theater?" He glances at Lazarus. "Our girl wants a theater chain. You and tech boy genius should get to work."

"That's not what I meant," I sputter, a bit floored by his interpretation.

"Noah doesn't know how to do normal," Johan murmurs, his hand finding my ankle through the blankets and giving it a little squeeze. "He would give you the world if he could. As in, the entire planet."

"We're not acquiring a movie chain, and we can't fly to the Caribbean right now," Lazarus says, his tone underlined with finality. "Stefano's people reached out this morning, and he's demanding to know what happened to his brother. We need to address it and get to the bottom of why Johan was targeted."

I look down at the hacker lounging near my legs. I can't believe he slept there all night.

Or however long we slept, anyway.

He looks rumpled, his hair a mess on his head. Something tells me that's not his usual state of appearance. He seems too organized for it. But I like seeing him like this—vulnerable and unkempt.

I suspect I look the same since I'm naked under the sheets. But I don't feel exposed or nervous by it. Just… comfortable.

Which is a little crazy, given that I have three alphas in bed with me.

Three virile alphas.

Three scent-match alphas.

Three very dominant alphas.

My tummy does a somersault, my mind wandering as Noah responds to Lazarus. I don't catch the words, too focused on my thoughts to hear him.

Johan's ice-blue eyes capture mine, his lashes thick and abundant. I'm not sure which way I prefer him—with or without glasses. He looks good as both versions.

Handsome.

Sexy.

Mine.

Well, not mine yet. But… but soon, I think.

"Keep looking at me like that, Lark, and I'm going to make you my breakfast," he warns.

"Is no one listening to me?" Lazarus demands.

"Nope," Noah replies instantly, his face suddenly in front of mine. "May I kiss you, please?"

The request takes me off guard. Noah seems like the type to just do what he wants, not ask permission first.

So I blink at him.

Then give a little nod.

But Lazarus's hand on Noah's throat stops him before he can lean all the way down. "First of all, I was saying something important. Second of all, we don't do anything to our omega unless she *verbalizes* consent. A nod doesn't count." Dark eyes meet mine. "If you want Noah to kiss you, ask him."

This male and his need to force me to speak.

It's on the tip of my tongue to issue a sassy retort instead.

But one look at Noah and his hopeful expression has me considering otherwise.

This man really is like a puppy dog, just like Johan said.

A psychotic assassin, too, I think. *But a loyal, playful man as well.*

"Please kiss me, Noah," I say.

He throat-punches Lazarus, causing the other man to release his hold with a wheezed curse.

"Don't fucking stop me from taking our omega ever again," Noah growls at him. Then he grabs me and pulls me into him.

I expect him to be rough. Forceful. *Overeager.*

Yet his touch is unexpectedly gentle.

He barely grazes my lips with his. Then applies a hint of pressure while Lazarus coughs out another curse beside us.

I don't know how Noah can be so violent one second and so sweet the next. But I don't care. All I can focus on is his mouth, the way it slants over mine, and the tender way his palm cups my cheek.

It's like he's kissing someone for the first time. His touch is tentative. Explorative. *Appreciative.*

So different from Johan's kiss, which was also soft in the beginning. Yet his arousal was potent, too. He deepened our embrace with it, owning me with his tongue and providing a demonstration in sensuality.

But Noah is taking my mouth with care. Reverence. Like he's worshipping me with his lips.

And now his tongue, I think dizzily as he enters my mouth to tenderly explore.

It's erotic. Slow. *Thorough.*

I shiver beneath him, my nipples tightening as he settles on top of me. My legs automatically part around him, my body bending to his will. Not that he's being particularly demanding. He's just loving me.

Which is strange to think.

How can this male already be so obsessed with me? I marvel. *And why do I feel equally enamored with him? With* them*?*

I've never wanted to be a mafia bride. A toy. A pretty jewel left on a pedestal to be looked at and only touched when the alphas desire it.

Yet these males haven't made me feel that way at all.

It's still early, I remind myself. *And they did leave for three days…*

That's something I can't forget.

Yes, Lazarus apologized. Yes, they had a good reason. But that doesn't change what happened.

And it doesn't mean it won't happen again.

That's not how I want to live my life.

"What's bothering you?" Noah asks, his nose rubbing mine. "Talk to me, little bee. I can practically hear that mind of yours buzzing."

I startle, surprised that he noticed. Maybe… maybe he could sense the distraction in our kiss? I frown at that idea.

Mostly because I don't want him to think *he* is the issue. Because he's not. Not really, anyway.

Which makes me feel like I owe him an explanation. I don't want him to think he's done anything wrong, as he hasn't.

"Sorry," I whisper. "It's not anything you've done. I… I'm just confused."

He pulls back to stare down at me, his brow furrowing. "What are you confused about? Talk to me. Please."

"Us," Lazarus murmurs. "Talk to us. Unless you would like Johan and me to leave?"

I glance at him, see the concern in his features, and nearly groan aloud.

Actually, no, I *do* groan.

Because this is so complicated.

And stupid.

Well, not stupid. Just… just complex?

"Maybe we should try having coffee and some food first," Johan suggests, his words like a beacon of hope that I instantly cling to.

"*Yes*," I say, emphasizing my need. "Yes, coffee. Yes."

Noah's expression doesn't change.

But Lazarus's smooths out as he nods. "We'll arrange it for you." He grabs Noah by the shoulder and shoves him off me. "You and I are going to go dance in the gym for a bit."

Noah glowers at him. "If you fucking touch me one more time while I'm with my ome—"

"*Our*," Lazarus growls at him, the possession in his tone

making my thighs clench. "She's *our* omega, Noah. Not yours. Not mine. *Ours.*"

"Fuck you, *boss*. I know what she is to *us*." The words leave him on a rumble, his growl rivaling Lazarus's and causing slick to pour out of me.

Whyyyy is this so hot? I want to moan out loud.

All I want to do is submit to them both. Go up on all fours and beg them to fuck me.

Which is precisely the problem!

This isn't the life I desired.

I… I don't think so, anyway.

I can't be a kept omega. I have to do something more productive than be locked up in a tower and used for pleasure only.

"Hey," Johan murmurs, his hand traveling up my leg as he crawls over me. "Hey, Lark. It's okay. Let's go shower. We need to talk about what you did to my laptop. Might as well multitask, yeah?"

My lashes flutter as I stare up at him. "Your laptop?"

He smiles. "Yeah, little hacker. *My* laptop."

I frown at that. *Wait…* "It's *my* laptop now."

"Which is precisely what we're going to talk about. Because I don't remember agreeing to give it to you."

"Then you shouldn't have left me alone for three days," I fire back. "Or two. However long it was, I earned that laptop due to no communication."

He considers me for a moment. "How about I buy you a new one instead?"

I shake my head. Because now that he's trying to take it back, I want it even more. "Buy yourself a new one. That beautiful tech is mine now."

"I built that from parts, Lark."

"Then you shouldn't have left me alone with it for so long," I tell him.

He sighs, his forehead meeting mine. "Maybe we can share it."

Before I can reply to that, he kisses me. Not gently like Noah did, but passionately. Knowingly. *Intimately*.

I completely forget everything.

All I know is Johan.

His tongue.

His lips.

His hands roaming up my sides. The sheet suddenly feels too thick between us, his touch not hot enough because he's not stroking my bare skin.

But then it all stops, and he pulls back onto his knees, straddling me. "Let's shower, little black hat. I want to talk about that laptop." He rolls off of me and onto Noah.

"Good luck washing all that cum off," Noah murmurs against his ear, then nips at Johan's neck.

"I'm never letting you top me again," Johan informs him flatly, then continues his movements until he's standing.

It's then that I remember he's naked.

Very naked.

All of them are, actually. Except Lazarus, who has on a pair of boxers.

But Noah's comment has me looking mostly at Johan as I suddenly realize what he means about washing all the cum off of him.

He's… he's covered in… yep.

Wow.

Okay.

He definitely needs a shower. I… I don't need one as much. Except to wash off the slick pooling between my legs. But something tells me that isn't going to get any better with a shower.

"Say that again later tonight," Noah murmurs. "We'll see what happens, tech boy."

"Fuck you, Noah."

"Anytime," he returns with a grin.

Then he grabs me by the nape and pulls me into a kiss that's nothing like the one he gave me moments ago. This one is hot. Intentional. *Violent.*

Like he's trying to stake his claim, remove all essence of Johan from my history, and ensure only Noah remains.

I can't even respond. My tongue is simply mastered by his. Dominated. *Owned.*

By the time he pulls back, there's no doubt in my mind that I've been utterly branded by the assassin in my bed. "You can fuck me anytime as well, pet. And I'll happily bottom for you, too. But only you." He brushes his lips against mine, then nuzzles my nose.

But in the next moment, his fist flies through the air, only to be caught by Lazarus's as the alpha snarls at him. "The first time, you caught me off guard. Not this time, asshole."

Noah snorts, then rolls off the bed like Johan did and grins like a complete loon. "Let's play, *boss*."

"I'm going to fucking kill you," Lazarus returns sharply.

"Excellent." Noah practically preens. "I love it when you're all big, bad, pissed-off alpha. You actually put up somewhat of a challenge then."

With that, he skips—*literally* skips—out of the room.

I gape after him. He just taunted Lazarus Ferraro into a fight. And from the look on Lazarus's face, he meant it when he said he was going to kill Noah. "Please don't… actually hurt him…?" I request awkwardly, causing the mafia don to frown down at me.

"He's going to bleed for me, princess. But I won't permanently injure him." He cups my cheek, his expression softening only marginally. "This is how we play, Ms. Bianchi. And it's best you understand that now, because one day soon, you're going to be at the center of our ring."

Lazarus is suddenly in my space, just like Noah was seconds ago, and his mouth brushes mine.

Only, he doesn't kiss me like the other two did.

Instead, he takes my lower lip between his teeth and nibbles just enough to make me gasp.

"We're not easy alphas to love," he whispers. "We've also never been able to put someone between us in bed. It's too dangerous. But with you, there isn't going to be a choice. The battle has already started. So prepare yourself, Aurora. We love a good fight. And neither of us is afraid to bleed."

He nips me again, harder now.

I instinctively grab his nape, my nails digging into his skin. "You'd better not mark me there, alpha," I tell him, not ready for his claim, and certainly not wanting a bloody lip.

He grins. "I already told you where I'm thinking about biting you." He moves onto me, his cock easily lodging between my thighs as he skillfully presses into me. "Your clit is mine, darling."

My eyes widen, and my grip tightens on his neck.

He doesn't flinch even though I know I'm breaking the skin.

Instead, his smile merely grows wider. "You're fucking perfect for us, princess. Our wild queen. Don't ever feel like you have to bow to us. We want a partner, not a submissive toy."

He claims my mouth then, forcing me to take his tongue as he drives his hips against mine.

He's harsh. Hot. *Demanding.* Leaving no doubt behind about who the alpha of the pack is here.

And he's purposely pushing me.

Suffocating me with his presence. His scent. His intent to claim.

I slice my nails down his back, leaving my own mark on his skin, wanting him to understand that I might be the omega here, but I'm not his yet.

I'll be the first one to bite. Not him.

He growls.

I growl back.

Then I moan as he rubs his dick against my clit once more.

I'm soaked for him. For *them*. Writhing beneath him. Lost to the pleasure he's inflicting through pressure alone.

He doesn't stop, his tongue fucking my mouth as his body mimes the motion of taking me below.

He's driving me insane. Pushing me. Forcing me into a whirlwind of sensation.

Until suddenly I'm screaming and slick is pouring from my core.

I've never been more ready for a knot in all my life.

Every part of me is clenching, vibrating, *flying*.

I'm coming, yet I feel so empty. So bereft. So *needy*.

And the smirk he gives me as he pulls away from me tells me he's very aware of what he's done. "Enjoy your shower, Ms. Bianchi," he murmurs.

Then the bastard fucking leaves.

Forcing me to stare at his bloodied back as he walks away.

The scratches I left there glow violent and red.

Something tells me he did that on purpose just to piss off Noah.

I groan, my hands covering my face. *These alphas. These dominant fucking men.*

They're going to end up killing me.

Yet I can't even be mad about it.

In fact, I'm downright *thrilled*.

Lazarus said he and Noah have never shared a lover because it's dangerous. That should terrify me. But all I can think is, *Challenge accepted. I'm yours…*

CHAPTER TWENTY
JOHAN

LARK STARES UP AT THE CEILING FOR SEVERAL LONG MOMENTS before finally turning her attention to me.

While things are a little fuzzy without my glasses, I can definitely see her checking out my dick. I don't bother to hide myself from her view. I'm hard. And I'm covered in Noah's dried seed, a fact that makes my jaw tick.

Not because I'm embarrassed.

But because I fucking hate feeling unclean.

However, I don't rush Lark to move. If she wants to lie there and check out my knot, that's fine. "Want me to strike a pose for you, little black cat?"

Her brow furrows a little, her gaze lifting to mine. "Cat?"

"A play on *hat*," I murmur. "You are a black hat, right, *Lark*?" She's really not. But I know she understands the term because her lips twitch.

"From what I found on my new laptop, I believe the same could be said about you, *Mr. Aegean.*"

I grin. "That's more of an alias than a hacker name."

"As is Lark. In most situations, anyway," she points out.

"Touché, Ms. White." That's the last name she uses as

Lark. Not all that clever, given what her real last name means in Italian.

"Says *John*," she tosses back, teasing me about the first name I use with my alias.

"It's easy to remember."

"So is White," she returns as she slips out of the bed.

Any response I may have had to that disappears as she stands before me. Naked. Beautiful. *Covered in slick.*

I swallow, my throat dry.

All I want to do is lift her into the air and toss her right back onto the mattress.

Cover her with my body.

Slide into that wet pussy.

And rut her for fucking days.

"You're stunning," I whisper, feeling the need to say something. Compliment her somehow. Worship her.

My words feel… dull. Not powerful enough.

"The most gorgeous woman I've ever seen," I add, striving to make it better. Striving and *failing*. "You're like a goddess." Which sounds like a really stupid pickup line.

I wince.

"I'm fucking all this up," I mutter and run my fingers through my hair. "Let's just go shower."

I turn toward the door, then spin around in the direction of her bathroom because we should probably go there. Although, I have no idea what soap is in there.

Actually, no, I do know what's in there since I ordered it.

What the fuck is wrong with me?

I'm thirty-seven fucking years old. I know how to talk to women. Especially naked ones.

Granted, it's been a while.

But still.

I kissed her not even fifteen minutes ago.

And now I'm basically running to a distraction so I can

hide from the mortification inspired by my ridiculous commentary.

"Johan," she calls after me, causing me to pause on the threshold.

I take a deep breath—which fills my senses with the delicious scent of brown sugar and honey—and look at her over my shoulder. "Yeah?"

"You're stunning, too." Her eyes roam over me with interest. "And also one of the most gorgeous men I've ever met."

Fuck, I love her. A thought that sounds more like Noah than me. But fuck it.

I rotate to move toward her, no longer giving a shit about the shower, and pull her into my arms to kiss her.

She responds with her tongue, engaging me in a passionate embrace that has me lifting her into the air and carrying her into the bathroom.

It smells like honeyed chocolate in here, topped with a hint of cherries, telling me she and Laz must have played in the shower at some point.

That's fine.

I'm about to add my own scent to the mix.

Lark's mouth explores the stubble on my jaw before going to my neck as I pause at the bathtub to flip it on. Then I continue on to the shower so we can rinse off first.

Because I am not getting in a tub while covered in Noah's version of a claim.

Warm water rains down on our heads, causing Lark to bend back and catch some in her mouth. "Thirsty, sweetheart?" I ask her.

She smiles. "I'm starving, actually." Then she grabs my head and pulls me in for a hungry kiss, one that has my knot throbbing against her.

"Fuck," I breathe.

She hums in response, her fingers threading through my hair to keep me close. Her thighs tighten, too, like she's afraid I might set her down. I press her up against the wall instead, my dick gliding through her slick cunt and tempting me to slip inside.

I don't.

I won't.

I can't.

But if she asks me to… I might.

Noah will be pissed. However, he'll understand.

Saying no to our omega isn't an option. She owns us in a way no one else ever will. When she realizes that, she's going to comprehend what it means to be our mafia queen.

Her tongue skates along my bottom lip, her legs clamping down once more. "I feel so alive," she whispers. "Yet lost."

"Lost how?" I ask, holding her hips.

"This isn't what I wanted," she says, causing me to frown.

"Do you want me to stop?" I pull back so I can stare into her eyes. "Because I will, Lark. Just tell me."

"*No.*" The answer is emphatic. Immediate. "No, that's not what I mean. I… I want what Lazarus has said to be true. But you all left. I wasn't included. I didn't know where you went. You didn't respond to me. And I… I can't live like that."

I study her, my mind sifting through each of her statements. I've more than gathered that she's afraid of being a traditional mafia wife—only included when the don's pack needs her for something sensual.

But that's not us.

Except our actions the last few days suggest otherwise.

I know Laz explained this to her, told her that she's not part of our pack yet. However, I disagree. She's ours. We all know it. Even her.

We just have to embrace it.

Move forward.

Become a unit.

And communicate properly.

"I'm going to be very honest with you, Lark," I tell her, my eyes holding hers.

"Okay." The wariness in her tone matches the uncertainty in her gaze.

"There's a reason we've hunted you for years." I draw a circle against her hip with my thumb, the touch one that Noah often does to me. But it feels appropriate to do it now to her, to try to soothe her while I speak.

She swallows, the movement catching my gaze for a beat before I return my focus to her pretty brown irises.

"Laz was livid when he realized someone had stolen money from us. That's never happened before, primarily because he has *me*." My jaw ticks at the memory of the day I discovered that someone had hacked our system. "No one has ever been able to pull off something like that under my watch. *No one*. Until you."

Her cheeks pinken a little. But it's not from embarrassment. She's proud.

As she fucking should be.

"It took me years to track your work through the web. While I may not have been able to focus on it one hundred percent of the time, I definitely devoted a lot of hours to figuring out what the fuck happened. And when I finally did, I told Laz and Noah."

They were both ready to drop everything to track the culprit down and rain hell on the bastard's head.

Except I had to inform them that "Lark" was a woman, not a man.

And not just any woman, but Aurora Bianchi.

"It's one of the few times I've ever seen them speechless." I grin at the memory. "Noah demanded to see your profile, I think because he wanted a photo. Meanwhile, Laz said we'd found our queen. No hesitation. No debates. Just a declaration of intention."

"Because he wanted revenge?" she asks, clearly guessing at

his motives despite the fact that he already discussed some of them with her. He told her about the other offers he'd received and why he'd rejected them.

But I'll elaborate again for her now if it'll help her accept this. Accept *us*.

"He didn't want revenge. He wanted you because you bested him. And he loves that."

She blinks. "He does?"

"We all do," I inform her, my nose skimming hers. "We want an omega who will fight us and hold us accountable. Someone we can rely on to help our organization thrive. Who challenges us more than she submits. And who is strong enough to handle all three of us."

I pause, considering that for a moment.

"Well, primarily Laz and Noah," I amend. "As the only one who has been taking care of them these last few years, trust me when I tell you it's not an easy task. I'm very much looking forward to having some assistance in that area."

She frowns at me. "Why don't they just fuck each other? Or take another…?" She trails off. "I don't want to think about that, actually."

"They're too violent to fuck each other. As for the latter, you don't need to think about it, as they haven't taken anyone else to bed—other than me—since the night I revealed the truth about your hacker identity—the night they learned about *you*."

It just didn't make sense to any of us at that point. We were consumed with the desire to hunt her down.

But that didn't curb Noah's and Laz's urges. Same with mine.

So I saw to their cravings.

Lark stares at me. "They haven't been with anyone else since learning about me? Anyone other than… the pack?"

I nod. "There wasn't a purpose. We knew who we wanted, little hacker. *You*."

Her eyes search mine. "Because I challenged Lazarus."

"Yes."

"And because of my name?"

I consider that for a moment. "It's more about your experience in our world. The fact that you know what we're capable of yet you chose to steal from us anyway. That marked you as bold, intelligent, and daring. All traits we admire. You being a Bianchi just adds to the allure."

Laz already told her that he would have rejected an offer from her father, just like all the others he'd turned down.

"Can you just imagine for a moment how much you and I could accomplish together as a team?" I ask her. "Think about the jobs we could pull off. The protection we could weave around the various Ferraro organizations. We would be fucking unstoppable."

And just the thought of it has my dick throbbing all over again.

She's the root user to my server. Which is cheesy as fuck, but true. Because there will never be any firewalls between us.

"You know I'm not really a black hat, though, right?" she asks cautiously. "I consider myself more of a gray hat."

I smile. "Sweetheart, we both know you're a white hat, which just makes your last name all the more appropriate. From what I've seen, all of your jobs have been for the greater good. Just like mine." I pause. "Well, mostly. There are a few enemies we've absolutely targeted in nefarious ways."

But they deserved it.

And I don't elaborate on why.

Given Lark's experiences in life, she already understands that there's evil in the world that can only be taken down by dark deeds.

However, none of that matters.

All I care about is the future. About *us*.

"I want to partner with you, Lark. If you'll have me." It's

not a proposal like the one Noah offered, but it's my own form of offering commitment.

I want her in my life.

As my other half.

As my omega.

As my everything.

She studies me for a long moment. Then, in a very serious tone, she asks, "Does that mean I can keep the laptop?" The twinkle in her eyes is the only indication that she's teasing me.

Except, I think she's also serious.

So I sigh and shake my head. "That thing is worth a hell of a lot more than a diamond ring, Lark. I hope you know that." I lift my hand from her hip to her face, cupping her cheek. "But what's mine is yours, sweetheart. If you want the laptop, you can have it."

"If you're nice, I'll let you borrow it," she offers, smiling now.

"How generous of you," I deadpan.

Her resulting nod is solemn. "Yes. Sometimes I can be generous."

I snort. "Cocky, too."

"I did break through several encryptions," she points out. "My arrogance is well earned."

"As the one who programmed those, I agree," I admit, then press a kiss to her lips. "Now we should probably finish this shower before the tub overflows." Because I just remembered that I left it filling nearby.

It's a huge basin, so it shouldn't be too full yet. But it will be soon.

"So we're taking a shower and a bath?" she asks, her brow furrowing.

"Yep. Shower to get clean. Bath… to do other things." I waggle my brows at her. Then set her down on the ground so we can accomplish the first part.

She seems incredulous.

But that incredulity dies when I start lathering us up with soap.

I'm thorough.

Touching her everywhere. Along with myself—all while her eyes watch hungrily.

Then I rinse our bodies off, wash our hair for good measure, and ensure we're both suds-free by the time the shower ends.

Afterward, I pick her up and carry her to the bathtub.

"I'm capable of walking," she grumbles at me.

"I know. But I like the feeling of having you in my arms." I start up the two steps toward the tub, only for a bloodied Noah to run into the bathroom and jump into the bath before we have a chance to enter.

Water sloshes *everywhere*, drawing a curse from my mouth.

"Thanks, tech boy," Noah says as he surfaces. "This is *exactly* what I needed." He shakes out his wet hair like a damn dog, then holds out his arms. "I'll take that from you, too."

I glower and move backward a step. "Absolutely fucking not."

"Hey!" He pouts. "We're supposed to share. And it's very much my turn with the omega." He holds out his hands again. "Come on. Gimme."

I grunt at him and leave the bathroom instead.

He shouts something after me, but I ignore him, walking swiftly through Lark's quarters and out into the hallway to head toward my bedroom.

Only to be blocked by Laz.

"It's not like you to drip water all over the fucking hardwood floors, so I'm not going to bother pointing it out more than I just have. But I would like to remind you that there are staff who frequent this corridor, and I would personally be very displeased if they saw our omega in this state."

"Then perhaps you should move so I can safely hide her in

my room," I mutter at him as I try to step around the towering asshole.

He sidesteps with me. "I'm not finished."

Of course you're not, I think, irritated.

"Ms. Bianchi requires food. So whatever you have in mind is going to have to wait. Now take her back to her room so she can get dressed. Breakfast will be ready in ten minutes. Then we're having a pack meeting on how to handle the Ricci situation."

My back stiffens. "Has something else happened?"

He stares me down. "I thought that would have been obvious by Noah coming to get the two of you. Our sparring was cut short. And we need to talk."

"Noah failed to mention any and all of that," I inform him flatly.

"Hmm" is all the stubborn alphahole says. Then he adds, "Ten minutes," and walks away.

It's then that I realize he's still only wearing a pair of boxers.

Yet he gave us a hard time about being naked. "We should probably ask the staff not to frequent this hallway for a while," I call after him. "Seems safer than facing your wrath."

I don't wait for his response, just turn and head back to Lark's room.

When I go to open the door, I find her grinning up at me. "Something amusing you, little hacker?"

Her smile grows. "Life." That's all she says. She doesn't elaborate. And I don't press for details.

Instead, I give her a kiss and draw my lips to her ear. "I owe you a bath, Lark. And I promise when that happens, you'll have a whole new appreciation for *life*."

CHAPTER TWENTY-ONE
LARK

Stefano Ricci looks exactly as I remember, only with a few subtle age lines around his full mouth. His hair is still black, his eyes the same color. And he's tan, just like Lazarus, except Stefano has a yellowish tint to his skin.

Though, that might be from the lighting in this particular photo.

Johan flips to another, his laptop on the table in Lazarus's den.

Or, well, I guess this is considered the Ferraro family business space.

It's a large conference room that's clearly meant to host visitors from the outside, and it connects to Lazarus's main office.

Only, we're not meeting with anyone in person today. Just discussing the message Lazarus received in the middle of his sparring session with Noah.

All three men are showered now. Johan and Lazarus are in dress shirts and black pants. Noah and I went for a more casual look of jeans and a sweater.

I'm not sure if the plan is to be on a call soon or not. That's the debate.

"Stefano has set a meeting for three" was what Lazarus informed us of over breakfast. "It wasn't a request but a demand."

"In person or over the phone?" Johan asked.

"In person. But that's not going to happen," Lazarus replied.

That was his subtle way of dismissing the command of another don while asserting his own form of dominance by changing the location requirements.

It's always a dance between the families. A constant battle of measuring their knots against each other.

In this case, my money is on Lazarus's being the biggest, as I've not only seen it but also felt it against my clit.

A thought that naturally makes me feel warm all over.

Because the sensual activities with Johan were left unfinished.

Not that I think *finishing* would help.

These three men have awakened a hunger inside me that refuses to be sated. Just like a heat cycle.

Yet I'm very aware. And very… *willing.*

Which I never thought would be possible with this pack. But they've proved they're nothing like a typical mafia pack. Or at least the ones I grew up around.

And they're continuing to prove it now by including me in their strategic discussion on the Ricci family.

I listen as Lazarus discusses how he wants to handle the call, how he doesn't want to mince words and intends to be direct. "They started this war when they attempted to perform a hit on Johan," he says. "We were entitled to the kill."

"We're entitled to a lot more than that," Noah mutters, his thick arms folded across his chest. He has his dark red hair tied at the back of his nape in a fashion that would look ridiculous on most men. But Noah isn't most men. "I've only just begun our revenge."

"You took out over a dozen of his men," Johan murmurs. "That's not enough for you?"

Noah's head turns slowly to stare Johan down from across the table. "They tried to kill you. Fifteen bodies isn't enough payment. I require at least a hundred more. And I'll bleed them all into a vial for you to wear around your fucking neck."

"That sounds heavy," Johan deadpans.

Noah doesn't share in his amusement. "I'll also make a necklace for you with their teeth."

"And fashionable, too," Johan adds.

"Want a matching bracelet?" Noah offers. "A ring made of their intestines?"

Johan gapes at him. "How would that even work?"

"I'll take a knife and—"

"Enough," Lazarus interjects, sounding exhausted. "We're not killing anyone else until we talk to Stefano. His response to this will dictate our next move."

He doesn't wait for them to agree, just launches into the potential paths this meeting could take and how he intends to counter.

Johan voices a few additional items for consideration based on what he pulls up from his laptop—a different one from what I've commandeered for myself—and starts showing some financial numbers. "If they want to pay recompense, this is what we should ask for."

"Blood is far more fun to play with than money," Noah mutters.

Both of the other alphas ignore him, their focus on business only.

When they're done, Lazarus looks at me and asks, "You've been quiet, Ms. Bianchi. Do you have any thoughts you would like to share?"

Noah leans forward from his spot next to Lazarus, a hopeful expression on his face. "You're bored and want me to kill them all, right?" He's like a puppy dog begging me to let him off his leash so he can run out and play.

Unfortunately, I don't really want to watch him kill a bunch of Riccis.

Instead, I'm much more focused on everything Johan shared, which I was able to see since I'm seated right beside him on this side of the table.

"I think you need to talk to my brother."

Lazarus's eyebrow inches upward. "Is he involved in this somehow?"

"We all are, aren't we?" I counter. "The city is split three ways. If you're going to take from the Riccis, that's going to disturb the balance. Disturbing the balance leads to turf wars. Turf wars lead to bloodshed—"

"Fuck yeah, they do," Noah inserts eagerly.

Ignoring him, I say, "And bloodshed can be bad for business."

Noah makes a noise like I've shot him.

"I'm not saying it's always bad," I murmur, trying to placate him. "But in this situation, I agree that *fifteen* dead bodies is more than enough."

He narrows his eyes. "They tried to kill Johan."

"I know. But I think it's important to find out *why* they targeted him. Because from what I've gathered, you haven't learned the purpose behind the hit. So, what if Bastian was working alone? Or maybe there's something larger going on here? Regardless, we can't learn more about it if everyone is dead."

Noah's expression sours, and his glare turns to Lazarus. "You told her to say that to me."

"I didn't," Lazarus replies, his lips curling just a tiny bit. "But the fact that she did is why she's our perfect queen."

Johan leans into my side, his lips near my ear. "Laz told Noah those exact words the other day when trying to quell his blood rage."

"Oh." I just said what came naturally to me. Nevertheless… "I still think you should talk to my brother before you upset the balance. Or consider partnering with him against the Riccis."

"Giovanni isn't one to favor partnership," Lazarus says, his fingers lacing together on the mahogany surface as he shifts forward a little to hold my gaze. "But if you think we should reach out to him before we talk to Stefano, then we'll call him."

I perk up at that. "You will?"

He stares at me. "Yes. I don't make false promises, Ms. Bianchi. I also value your input and suggestions, so thank you for providing your insight."

Noah grunts again, causing Lazarus's attention to drift toward the clearly disgruntled alpha.

"Anything you want to add?" he prompts his enforcer.

The two men stare each other down for a moment before Noah says, "If Stefano ordered the hit, he's mine to kill."

"Shouldn't he technically be mine to take out?" Johan asks, arching a dark brow.

Noah considers him for a moment. "I'll hold him down while you carve your name into his chest and slice off his dick."

"Seems like a good way to leave evidence behind," Johan says conversationally. "Maybe you can hold him down while I simply stab him?"

Noah gives him an affronted look. "That's it? That's all you want to do?" His focus shifts to me. "This is why I'm in charge of the killing around here. These two assholes aren't creative at all."

Lazarus merely shakes his head, but I catch the smirk flirting with his lips.

"I can be *very* creative when I want to be," Johan argues. "I just choose to employ my creative genius in other ways."

Noah's hazel eyes glitter as they look over Johan from across the table. "Mmm, I suppose that's true."

"I'm not talking about sex."

"You should be, though," Noah argues. "Sex is fantastic." His gaze finds mine, his body leaning forward with interest. "Have you been knotted before, little bee?"

The abrupt change in topic leaves me a little bewildered.

Which is probably why I stammer out a truthful response of "N-no."

"Been fucked?" he presses, making me frown.

"Yes." *Kind of*, I want to amend. *Fucked* feels powerful. More intentional. Violent, maybe?

What I've experienced is just… well, plain sex. Not fantastic sex. Simply intercourse, I guess?

"Names," Noah demands, a notepad suddenly in front of him.

I gape at him. "*No*."

"Yes."

"Absolutely not."

"Absolutely affirmative and now, please," he counters, tapping the pen against his paper. "Johan will research locations. I'll handle the rest."

"You are *not* hurting my former… whatever you want to call them."

"Dead men," he tells me. "That's what I call them. Now give me the names, pet, or I'll knot them out of you."

My thighs clench at the prospect even while my mind screams in protest. "You can't just kill my former bed partners, Noah. They weren't cruel to me. Just… introduced me to some things. And I never claimed any of them."

"You also haven't claimed me," he points out with a pout.

"If I did, would that help soothe your murderous needs?" I demand.

He considers me for a moment before giving me a vague "Maybe."

I sigh. "There's no one else in my life. Just this pack, okay?"

Noah studies me for another long pause. "What about anal? You been taken there?"

"Are we seriously doing this right now?" Johan interjects.

"You want to know these answers, too," Noah fires back. "And since no one has had the limits discussion with her yet, I'm taking the initiative."

"We're supposed to be talking about the Riccis," Lazarus growls.

"We have," Noah stresses. "For the last ninety fucking minutes. Now we are moving on to a new topic. Unless you've already discussed limits and haven't shared with the class?" There's a note of accusation in his tone, one that Lazarus bristles at.

"I know how to *share*, Noah."

"Do you? Because you keep claiming firsts."

"I've literally claimed *one* first."

"More than I have," Noah mutters, a note of dejection entering his handsome features.

For someone so incredibly lethal, he certainly has a soft heart. Or maybe that tenderness is only reserved for me.

I kind of like that.

No. I *love* it. Which is equal parts terrifying and exciting.

I'm basically swooning over this powerful alpha who adores bloodshed.

Whatever.

If an insanity charge is in my future, I accept it.

"I've only had sex," I tell Noah, wanting to do something to help him feel more secure in our dynamic. "Nothing else."

"So no sucking cock and no anal," he reiterates. "Only in the pussy and it wasn't a knot."

Pretty sure my face is currently on fire. But I nod.

Which earns me a look from Lazarus.

So, out loud, I confirm with a "Yes. That's accurate."

And I really want to go hide forever now.

"How do you feel about anal?" he asks, his tone matter of fact and exceptionally businesslike. I suspect he talks about stocks in a similar manner.

Er, well, maybe not.

Noah doesn't seem like the investment kind of guy. Financial discussions are probably handled by Johan. Maybe Lazarus. But definitely Johan.

"Are you okay with the idea of taking a knot up the ass?" Noah presses, causing Johan to sigh beside me.

"You don't have to answer that," my fellow hacker murmurs.

"She does," Noah argues. "Because I need to understand what I can and can't do to her."

"We haven't even fucked her yet. Let's not force her to talk about what she may or may not want until she's ready."

"So you want to wait until she's in heat and just, what, guess?" Noah snorts. "I would much rather know what she likes and what she's open to me doing to her *before* she's an incoherent mess of need." He looks at me. "And I mean that description in the most loving way possible, pet, because I can't fucking wait until you're wet and begging."

Pretty sure I'm halfway there, I think, swallowing as my thighs squeeze together for the thousandth time since meeting these alphas.

"There are lots of things we would like to do to you," Lazarus murmurs, his body directly across from mine. He appears to be relaxed in his dress shirt, but I can see the subtle flex in his jaw. I don't know if the conversation is making him uncomfortable… or turning him on.

Perhaps both?

I certainly feel a mixture of discomfort and arousal. But the discomfort is being caused by the arousal. So…

I clear my throat. "I am open to experimenting," I start, trying to answer Noah's questions without repeating his phrases. "When my heat comes… I would just ask that I have what I need to stay hydrated and fed. And maybe… maybe some pillows for a nest."

Noah's expression brightens with excitement. "Yes, let's talk about your nest. What items do you need? Any fabric preferences? Scents? Do you want any of our clothes?" He starts taking off his shirt. "I can give you this. Want me to come in it for you?"

And I'm gaping at him again.

Not only because of everything he's just said, but because he's now shirtless.

"You're welcome to help me out, pet," he murmurs, waggling his brows. "You'll have to use your hands, though. If I put my cock in your mouth, I won't be able to pull out until you've swallowed my entire load. And if I'm in your pussy or ass, I'm keeping my cum inside you for a while. Oh, which brings me to knot-warming limits."

Johan shuts his laptop. "I'm going to get a drink."

"Getting hard over there, tech boy?" Noah drawls.

"Been hard for hours," Johan returns, standing.

And yep. There's a very obvious bulge in his pants.

This is… Well, this is a lot.

But I'm confused by something—*many things?*—Noah said. "What is *knot warming*?" I ask slowly.

"Like cock warming, only with the knot."

He says it so seriously, like I should just… understand him.

"I don't know what that is," I admit, frowning. "Like… holding your… umm… with my hand…?" That wasn't very eloquent. But I don't understand what it means.

However, the smile that crosses his face tells me he's very pleased. "Oh, I call first cock warming," he says, then looks at Lazarus and Johan. "Do *not* take that from me."

"You can't keep claiming firsts, Noah," the don informs him flatly.

"Says the man who has already taken the one I wanted."

"I called it first," Lazarus tells him. "And she consented." That last part seems to be for Johan more than Noah.

These three men are going to drive me insane. "Would someone please explain *cock warming* to me before I steal Johan's laptop and research it myself?"

Noah's eyebrows go up.

And Lazarus smothers a laugh.

"Go ahead," Johan urges me. "I'm curious about what kind of results you'll get."

I scowl at all three of them. "Stop treating me like I'm a naïve little toy and explain, or I'm leaving."

"I would much rather demonstrate," Noah says as Lazarus leans across the table.

"Aurora." The way my name leaves his tongue is hypnotic, mostly because he underscored it with a slow rolling of the *r*'s, almost like a purr. "Noah's asking how long he can leave his cock inside you after knotting you."

Noah nods. "Yes. I need limits for your pussy, ass, and mouth."

"I…" I have no idea how to respond to this. Or… or *that.* "I don't…. You want to knot my mouth?" I'm not sure that'll feel great. Actually, I'm pretty sure it could suffocate me and kill me.

"For your mouth, I would prefer that you use it like a pacifier and just suck on it for hours. In your pussy and ass, yes. I want my knot to live inside you. For however long you're comfortable."

Johan returns to the table then and sets a drink in front of me.

I don't even bother asking what it is, just pick it up and *drink.*

Noah groans. "Ah, yes, see, that kind of swallowing is *exactly* what I want to feel around my dick."

I choke on the liquid, nearly sputtering it everywhere.

"Well, maybe not like that," he says, sounding a little less pleased. "But we'll work on it."

Johan gently thumps my back, trying to help me breathe properly again. "I think that's enough for now, Noah," he says, a note of dominance in his tone. "Give her a break."

"Are you going to say that when you're mid-orgasm and she can't take any more?" Noah demands. "Our pet needs lessons, not coddling."

My eyes widen. "*Lessons*?"

He nods. "On how to take our knots." He sets his shirt on the table. "Come over here, and I'll give you one before the meeting."

Part of me wants to tell him to fuck off, irritated that he's implying I need to be *taught* how to take him.

But another part of me sees it as a dare I want to accept. If anything, just to prove him wrong.

I've not been with an alpha before. However, I understand the concept of it. I've read some books.

None of them talked about cock warming or knot warming, though.

Still, I'm an omega. I'm practically built to bring this man to his knees.

And he wants to teach me a lesson on his knot?

Maybe I can teach him a lesson instead.

In not underestimating me.

I may not be experienced. But I'm not one to back down from a challenge.

So I push back from the table and stand. "All right, Noah. You want to teach me a lesson? Then begin. I'm ready to learn."

CHAPTER TWENTY-TWO

NOAH

OHHHH, MY LITTLE BEE IS PRACTICALLY BUZZING WITH FURY.

I fucking love it.

"You can start by crawling across the table," I tell her, wanting to see how far I can push her before she lashes out at me.

Because the first night on the jet was fun. I loved that she attacked me even though I wasn't the one who'd pissed her off.

It felt good putting her beneath me.

And I'll very much enjoy doing it again now if she decides to launch herself at me like before.

She narrows her gaze, the subtle defiance in her features making my heart pound in my chest. *Oh, yeah. Here we fucking go.*

I'm ready.

Hands braced on the arms of my chair. Feet spread and planted on the floor, prepared to stand at any second. Cock hard. Knot pulsing. Balls full.

But rather than lash out at me or growl, she places her palms on the table, then her knee, and starts doing exactly what I asked.

Johan's eyes instantly go to her ass, his position behind her one I almost envy. Except I have a full view of her swaying breasts beneath her sweater.

I definitely should have told her to strip first.

Laz leans back beside me, an appreciative hum forming in his chest.

"If you fuck this up for me, I will put a blade in your groin," I warn him, my voice low.

He hears me just fine, though. As does Aurora. She pauses for a second, like she's waiting for Laz to reply.

"Focus on me, pet," I tell her. "I'm the instructor here."

Laz folds his arms but says nothing.

However, I know it's grating on his nerves to take a back seat.

Too. Fucking. Bad.

It's my turn to play. *Finally*.

And I have just enough time before our meeting to do so. Although, some of it might run over.

But that'll be intentional.

My lips nearly curl with the anticipation of what I want to do. The only reason I hold back is that I don't want to alert our pet to my plans.

Instead, I merely watch as she pauses in front of me on the table.

"Stand up and take off your pants."

Her brow furrows, and she moves like she's about to climb off the flat surface I now consider to be her stage.

"No, no," I tsk. "Stand up right where you are and give us a show, pretty bee. I want that pussy on display for all of us to see." I sing-song the rhyme on purpose, mostly because it's fun.

I also really like the way her cheeks redden in response, though that might be a result of what I've asked her to do.

"Tick tock, pet," I murmur. "Our meeting starts soon."

Her gaze narrows again, just like when I issued the challenge to crawl.

Then, ever so slowly, she stands.

She isn't wearing shoes. Just bare feet against the wood. But I would love to see her in a pair of heels at some point.

Preferably just a pair of heels.

We'll discuss it later.

Holding my gaze, she reaches down to begin lifting her sweater. It's on the tip of my tongue to tell her I only wanted her to lose her pants, but I'm not about to stop her from showing us her tits.

I catch her sweater as she drops it, then toss it to Laz for safekeeping.

From the corner of my eye, I see him bringing it to his nose to inhale her sweet aroma. I should have done that, too. But I'm about to have her pussy in my mouth, so I'll get my fill.

Leaving her bra on, she pops the button on her jeans, then draws down the zipper.

Johan hisses through his teeth as she bends to pull her pants off, his position providing an excellent view of her fine backside again.

"You thinking about knotting her ass over there, tech boy?" I ask him.

"Thinking about knotting her everywhere," he groans.

I smile. "I'll warm her up for you. Don't worry."

Her nipples harden as I speak, the stiff points evident beneath her lacy white bra and making her arousal obvious.

Just like the slick saturating the matching panties between her legs, I think, instantly starving for a taste of her sweetness.

"When you take that scrap of fabric off, I want it," I tell her, looking at her pussy.

She visibly shivers, then kicks her jeans aside. I grab them and throw them at Laz.

He growls.

Probably because her slick permeated the fabric.

Or maybe because he doesn't appreciate me treating him like a laundry hamper.

Whatever.

He'll live.

Aurora removes her lacy undergarments—starting with the lower half, then adding her bra—and throws them both at me.

It's sassy. Confident. And fucking magnificent.

Because she's naked.

And her panties smell like sugary heaven.

I inhale deeply, ensuring she sees it, then slide the sexy lace into my pocket. "For when I jack off later," I tell her.

Slick visibly pools from her sweet center, making my mouth water.

"Come here," I growl at her, standing and holding out my hand.

She steps forward, but I grab her by the hips instead and sit her on the table right in front of me.

"Place your palms on the wood," I instruct her. "And spread those pretty thighs."

She only barely opens her legs as I reclaim my chair.

That's fine.

She'll learn.

Using my grip on her hips, I yank her forward.

She yelps, her palms flailing and catching herself on the flat wooden surface.

I don't wait for her to stabilize, just dive down and place my mouth where it belongs—right on her fucking clit.

Another startled sound leaves her, followed by a moan as I suck the little nub into my mouth and *purr*.

"Ohhh," she whispers, her body tensing beneath my palms.

I run my hands down her thighs to her ankles, then set them on the arms of the chair on either side of me.

I want her all around me.

Owning me with her scent.

Saturating me with her slick.

Claiming me in a way only an omega can.

"Fuck, you taste even better than I imagined, little bee," I whisper against her slick flesh. "You're going to be my daily dessert. Breakfast, too. Shit, I may just eat you for eternity and subsist on honeyed pussy alone."

Her cheeks are a beautiful bright red.

And I decide to see how far I can make that blush spread.

I spear her with my tongue, then draw my touch back up her legs with one hand going to her hip to hold her and the other joining me between her thighs.

"I'm going to prepare you for me, pet," I tell her. "I'm big, so you need to be stretched." I slide two fingers into her, loving the way her tight sheath clenches around me.

Definitely a knotting virgin.

That's about to change.

Because I'm going to fucking live inside this perfect pussy for the rest of my existence.

Laz and Johan will just have to take her ass and mouth instead.

Mine, mine, mine.

"*Noah,*" she groans as I add a third finger.

"Oh, sweet bee, if you think that's a lot..." I trail off and suck on her clit again, helping to push her into a state where pain and pleasure combine.

She nearly falls back onto the table.

Which gives me an idea.

"Lie down," I tell her. "And get up there with her, tech boy. I want you to suck on her tits for me."

Laz can fucking watch.

Prick.

Always ruining my fun.

Let's see how he likes sitting back while someone else makes up the rules and runs the show.

Johan follows my command like the good fucking alpha he is and gets on the table, then helps to lean Aurora back.

Only, he doesn't suck on her breasts like I demanded.

Instead, he kisses her.

Which I only allow because it makes her even wetter between her thighs. I lap up her slick, growling as her decadent flavor hits the back of my throat. "You taste so fucking good, pet." I give her a long lick while my fingers work inside her.

"Just wait until she comes," Laz murmurs. "It gets even better then."

My hands itch to grab the knife tucked into my pocket so I can stab the asshole in the throat. I don't need the reminder that he did this first.

But he will absolutely bear witness to me knotting our omega on this fucking table.

And he will *not* be allowed to touch her.

It's my fucking turn with my fucking bride.

I drive that point home by nipping her clit, then laving away the sting as she cries out into Johan's mouth.

His hands are moving now, exploring her perky breasts and tweaking her rosebud nipples.

"Get your mouth on her tits," I tell him. "Before I kick you off this table."

He casts me a glare, then kisses a path down her neck before feasting on her beautiful peaks.

Her body bows off the wood, but I move my hand from her hip to her belly and push her back down, then add a fourth finger to her channel.

She squeals, but I don't relinquish her from my hold.

Instead, I force her to take it, all while ensuring she feels good with my mouth.

We really should have discussed safe words or some shit. But right now, I'll take "no" or "stop" as red flags.

Fortunately, she's not uttering anything like that at the moment. Probably because she's too busy moaning.

"Fuck, pet, you're drowning me in your slick," I tell her. "Something tells me you're going to very much like my knot lodged deep inside your cunt."

Her response is a wet kiss to my fingers, making it even easier to glide in and out of her.

"Beautiful," I murmur, loving her physical responses to my touch. I can't wait to take her. To own her. To master her. To *claim* her.

"*Noah*," she breathes, her fingers in Johan's hair as she holds him against her breast. "I… I…"

She doesn't finish her statement because I roll her clit between my teeth again, giving it a little bite.

Which sends her cascading into an orgasm so powerful that my fingers struggle to move.

That's going to feel so damn good around my cock, I think, my knot throbbing with expectation.

I continue licking her and stretching her but release her belly so I can use my hand to unfasten my pants.

I want to make this easy on her.

A choice. An ability to consent. A way for her to stake her claim without having to sink her pretty teeth into my skin.

My jeans loosen, the fabric opening enough to free my cock.

I could push them down farther, but I'm done waiting.

"I'm going to sit up now, but my knot's more than ready for you, little bee. All you have to do is slide off that table and come get it. Put it in your pussy. Your mouth. Or I'll take care of myself with my hand while you watch. The choice is yours, pet. So, what's it going to be?"

CHAPTER TWENTY-THREE
LARK

JOHAN KISSES A PATH UP MY BODY, HIS LIPS NEAR MY EAR. "WE all value consent, Lark. If you're not ready for Noah, tell him. He'll understand. That's why he's giving you a choice."

I love what he's saying and that these men are ensuring my comfort.

But I didn't start this dance with Noah just to back down in the end.

I want to blow his mind. Make him realize I'm the right omega to match his brand of crazy. And prove that I'm not afraid of his knot or anything he could do to me.

He's dangerous. Deadly. *Psychotic*.

Yet I don't fear him at all.

Threading my fingers through Johan's hair, I pull him into a kiss, one that I hope demonstrates my confidence and intentions.

I don't want him to think I feel coaxed into this.

I want Noah. I want all of them.

But it's Noah's knot I'm going to take first.

"I'm ready," I tell Johan. Just the admission out loud is enough to cause my insides to squeeze.

I'm still coming down from the climax Noah and Johan gave me. Yet I'm already preparing for another.

It's like I'm insatiable.

And maybe I am.

These alphas have been driving me crazy since we met. This moment feels inevitable. They're my scent matches. Of course I want them. It's only natural.

That I've managed to hold back this long is a miracle.

But I'm done fighting this pull.

Instead, I'm going to let them have me. Keep me. *Knot me.*

I kiss Johan again, his lips and tongue addictive. He's not gentle, but he isn't harsh either. He's just perfect. The way he treats me like an equal, not a toy. The way he makes me feel alive. The way he's tender while also ensuring that I know he's not afraid to push a little harder.

So very different from Noah and Lazarus, both of whom have their own flavors of sensuality.

Yet somehow all three of these alphas are meant to be mine.

I'm no longer terrified. I'm elated.

Maybe it's the captivity that's changed my mind. But I don't think it's that at all. It's simply them.

Johan palms my cheek, his forehead meeting mine. "I'm here if you need me," he says against my lips.

Then he rolls to the side and sits up.

I swallow, suddenly feeling exposed without his body covering mine.

But one glance at Noah causes heat to swathe my being.

He has his hand on his cock, lazily gliding it up and down while watching me.

"I haven't chosen yet," I tell him, glaring at his movements. "*That* isn't my choice."

He arches a brow. "You saying I can't touch myself, little bee?"

"I'm saying that knot is mine," I tell him, feeling possessive and pissed off that he's starting without me.

It's irrational. On some level, I recognize that.

But I can't focus on that right now.

Because this feels like a test I've failed.

He issued a challenge and doesn't think I can follow through.

And *that* pisses me off.

I slide off the table with purpose and move to straddle him. "Put your hands on my hips."

"Yes, omega," he murmurs, doing exactly as he's told.

"Don't help me." I want to prove I can handle him without assistance. It's important.

He needs to know I can do this. That I *want* this.

Although, my confidence wavers a bit as I reach between us and realize I can't wrap my whole hand around his thick shaft.

I allow myself a moment to stall, my fingers tracing the dragon tattooed into his skin. "Did this hurt?" I ask in a whisper, hoping he doesn't hear the quiver in my voice.

"No." His hand leaves my hip, almost causing me to protest, but he grasps my chin to pull my attention up to his face. "You're built to take me, little bee. To take *us*."

Ugh, I hate that he can see through me. He shouldn't know me this well yet.

Only, I feel like I know him, too.

That I can read him just as well as he reads me.

Because there's a hint of vulnerability in his expression, like he's worried I might decide not to do this. To not be with him. To run away.

And I don't think that concern is related to any sort of perceived cowardice on my part.

He seems to be more worried that I might reject him.

Because I didn't accept his proposal? I wonder, searching his expression. *Does he think I'm afraid of him?*

"Aurora?" he murmurs, studying me like I'm studying him. "Tell me what you need, little bee."

I lean in and kiss him, showing him rather than telling him that I want him. That all I need is this. *Him.*

My insane alpha.

So gentle with me, something I assume is an anomaly. Because there's nothing gentle about this male. He's a killer. An assassin. A being without scruples.

However, his tongue is hesitant in my mouth now. Coaxing, even. Like he's trying to evaluate my limits and tease me into taking more.

I release his cock so I can grasp either side of his face, then settle in his lap, my heated center right up against his groin.

He groans, the intimate kiss of our mutual arousal fueling the connection formed between our mouths.

Everything around us melts away as I simply exist with him.

And our embrace turns hotter.

Heavier.

More *intentional.*

His tongue is no longer tentative, but masterful. Teaching me. Owning me. *Possessing me.*

All of it just makes me wetter, causing my thighs to clench around his hips. At some point, he moved the chair arms up and out of the way, allowing me to fully straddle him. It's like this chair was made for sex.

I don't think that's the case.

But we're about to make use of it in that manner anyway.

Keeping my lips connected to him, I slide my hand down again to grab his knot. He growls a little against my mouth, the sound reverberating through me in an arousing caress. "Noah," I breathe.

"Aurora," he returns, the *r*'s a rumble as he growls once more.

"This is my first time touching a knot," I tell him, wanting him to be aware that he's getting one of the firsts now, since it seems to be a point of contention that he hasn't had one yet. "Now I'm going to put you inside me."

Or I'm going to attempt to…

He's just so big.

Hot.

Heavy.

And pulsing.

I can feel his knot preparing for me, the bulb seeming to vibrate against my palm as I lift to angle him toward my entrance.

There's a subtle growl from one of the other alphas in the room. Lazarus, I think. But I'm too consumed by Noah to look.

One challenge at a time, I decide, wincing as Noah's head slides into me. *God, this is never going to fit…* He's too big. Too wide. *And there's so much more of him to take.*

I start to come back off of him, but his hand leaves my face to grab my hip once more. "Take a deep breath for me, little bee," he says, his voice stern, his dominance resolute.

"Noah…"

"*Now*, Aurora," he demands.

I swallow. Then force my lungs to inflate.

"Good girl," he praises. "Now exhale."

I begin to obey, only for the air to leave me on a scream as he thrusts up into me. "*Noah*!" It comes out part shriek, part whine. Fury, surprise, and a hint of terror all underline his name.

Because I can't fucking believe he did that.

I want to kill him.

Except… except he's purring.

And I rather like that sound. It calms my raging emotions, causing me to melt into him.

It's then that I realize he's stroking my back, helping me to relax. His lips are at my ear, telling me how good I feel around his cock, how proud he is of me for taking him. "And soon, you'll take Laz, too." He kisses my temple. "We're going to double-knot you, pet."

I pull back, alarmed.

"Not today," he says with a smile. "I'm not ready to share you with that asshole yet."

Lazarus releases a low sound of warning, one that has Noah chuckling.

"Don't worry, boss. I'll help her learn how to multitask for you." The fullness inside me suddenly disappears, causing me to yelp as Noah spins me around in his lap.

"What are you—"

My words cut off on a yelp as he slams into me again, this time from behind.

I'm pretty sure I see stars.

Or fly to the heavens.

I… I don't even know.

He's inside me again, but I'm somehow *fuller* now.

And I'm looking at Johan.

He moved to take over my "seat," though his feet are planted on the floor and he's leaning back against the table for support.

His gaze is between my legs, his hands gripping the wood so hard that the muscles of his exposed forearms are bulging. I'm not sure when he rolled up the sleeves of his dress shirt, but I'm a fan.

I like the view almost as much as the bulge in his pants.

Noah moves below me, his hands guiding my hips up and almost off of him, only to yank me right back down. "*Fuuuuck,*" he groans as a gasp leaves my lips.

Fuck indeed, I marvel, dizzy from the way he's filling me at this angle. It's the fullest I've ever been.

And all I can think is *There is absolutely no way these alphas are double-knotting me.*

My body can't take that.

Noah's hands slide up my sides, reaching around to grasp my breasts. Then he pulls me until my back is against his chest. "Ready for your lesson, pet?" he asks against my ear.

"Hasn't it already started?" I breathe, feeling utterly exposed and very much on display for both Johan and Lazarus.

"Mmm, not quite," Noah murmurs. "You've taken a cock in your pussy before. Now you're going to take a knot—*my* knot. And you're going to let Johan fuck your mouth while I fuck your cunt."

My eyes widen. "*What*?"

"Laz wants you to learn how to multitask," he says, kissing my throat. "So that's your first lesson—taking two knots at once. Now be a good pet and lean forward to unzip Johan's pants."

All the hairs rise along my arms.

I thought the challenge was to take Noah's knot. But he just changed the game.

And rather than wanting to say no, I want to blow his mind by excelling at the task.

Which means pleasuring Johan with my mouth.

Something I've *never* done before.

I lick my lips and look up at the other man. His eyes are on my face now, not between my thighs, his gaze reassuring.

He won't make me do this if I don't want to. He also won't force me to take more than I physically can.

That actually makes him the right alpha for my first time doing this.

All of my scent matches have demonstrated patience, but Johan's understanding and compassion seem to exist on an entirely different level.

Even now, he's observing me with a note of calmness in his expression.

A calmness that's undermined by the heat in his gaze.

He wants this. He wants me. But he will absolutely restrain himself if he needs to.

It's with that knowledge that I lean toward him—just like Noah told me to—and reach for his belt.

Johan's hand covers mine, his touch warm and tense against my skin. "Be sure, Lark."

"I am," I answer without hesitation. "I can do this."

His eyes hold mine for a beat, his pupils dilating with exquisite need.

Then his touch slowly leaves me, letting me complete the task of freeing his erection.

Granted, Noah only told me to *unzip* Johan's pants. But I'm an overachiever. And I'm determined to prove to my pack that I can do this. That I can take them. *That I can multitask.*

I don't wait for Noah to issue another command. I simply grasp Johan by the knot—which is slightly smaller than Noah's—and bend down to put him in my mouth.

My lips stretch around his girth, but I'm going to do this right. So I think about how he took Lazarus that first night and force myself to take him as deep as I can.

And gag.

Holy fuck.

I yank myself back up, sputtering.

Which results in Noah chuckling behind me, a sound that really grates on my nerves as I cough in surprise.

"You have to relax your throat before you do that," he says, his chest meeting my back as he moves in the chair to wrap himself around me. "Here, I'll help you." His fingers thread through my hair. "Part those lips again for me, pet."

I nearly hiss at him instead.

But a drop of precum forms on Johan's head, causing me to stop breathing. I've never tasted a man in this way before. And I suddenly need to taste Johan. Like, more than I've ever needed anything in my life.

So I part my lips, just like Noah asked, and let him guide me forward to take Johan into my mouth.

Except Noah won't let me go as far as I want. He holds me so all I have between my lips is Johan's tip.

"Swirl your tongue around him, pet," Noah tells me. "Show him how much you appreciate his cock. Make him fucking beg for more."

I look up at Johan and he stares back, his eyes even more heated than before. It's like I'm the most important being in his universe, his own personal sun.

I just want to bathe in his adoration. *And make him moan…*

So I do what Noah demands, using my tongue to tease Johan. A curse leaves him, his muscles flexing along his arms as his grasp tightens on the table.

"Want more?" Noah asks.

I try to nod, but his grip in my hair holds me steady.

Which is when I realize the question was for Johan because he answers, "Yes. *Please.*"

"Yes, please, what?" Noah murmurs, his tone utterly casual despite his dick being buried inside me.

And something about that makes me want to push him to lose his mind the way Johan appears to be doing right now.

I clench my inner walls, curious.

Causing Noah to release a breath right by my ear. "Patience, pet."

Mmm, no, I decide, doing it again as I try to move my head forward to take more of Johan.

Noah curses. "So fucking eager. But I'm in charge here, little bee. Now swirl that tongue around his fucking cock like a good girl, and I'll let you take more of him."

I growl.

Which causes Johan to groan.

Yet Noah merely chuckles. "Do as I say, and you'll be rewarded with more precum."

His words are a taunt, one that has me obeying because I

really do want to taste more of Johan. I've only experienced a little bit, the salty flavor not nearly enough to satisfy my craving.

"Beautiful, pet," Noah murmurs. "Wrap your hand around his knot and give it a squeeze."

I do.

And moan when more of Johan's essence touches my tongue.

"Yes, little bee. Just like that." He pushes my head down more. "Okay, pet, relax your throat and hum a little."

I obey.

And Johan's cock jumps in my mouth as a growl echoes through his chest. "*Fuuuck.*"

Noah releases a noise of contentment. "Our omega's made for this, isn't she? Taking our cocks together, pleasuring us with her mouth and pussy." He kisses my neck, my pulse throbbing in response. "Want me to help her take more?"

"Yes," Johan whispers, his eyes meeting mine again. "*Yes.*"

I tighten my grip on his knot, loving the way more cum enters my mouth.

"Try rotating your wrist a little, too," Noah instructs me. "And take as deep a breath as you can."

When I move to pull back and breathe, he holds me in place.

"Through your nose, Aurora," he tells me. "You need to learn how to inhale while you have a cock in your mouth. It's going to be a very important skill in our pack."

My thighs clench, his dirty words doing something to me.

I shouldn't like what he's saying. I should probably be pissed that he assumes I'll be doing this often.

But I rather hope he's right.

Because this feels amazing.

And I really don't want to ever stop.

"Perfect," he whispers as I inhale. "Now hold your breath and try not to tense."

He pushes me down on Johan, causing the other man to hiss. His head falls back, his pleasure written in his features.

"See how much he likes this?" Noah says, his voice still low. "You're making him feel so fucking good right now, pet." His lips caress my neck, then move into my hair. "It's making me want to hold you just like this and drive into your slick cunt while you choke on his cock."

Knuckles brush my cheek, causing my gaze to flick to the side, where Lazarus has moved to stand right beside us. "You look beautiful, Ms. Bianchi," he murmurs, his praise making my clit pulse in response.

"She feels fucking amazing, too," Noah growls.

"I can imagine," Lazarus murmurs, leaning against the table beside Johan, close enough for their arms to touch. "Are you going to make her swallow?"

I'm not sure whom the question is for, but Noah answers, "Abso-fucking-lutely."

Johan merely groans, his head still tossed back in pleasure, but Lazarus threads his fingers through Johan's hair and forces him to focus on me. "Watch our omega," the don murmurs. "She's working hard for you. Let her see how much you like it."

Somehow I feel like Johan and I are both being dominated right now.

Maybe because we are.

I don't know.

But I love it. So much so that I clamp down on Noah's cock.

He growls against my ear, then thrusts up into me with so much force that I gasp. "If you're going to hug me like that, I'm going to fuck you," he says, doing it again. "Laz, take over our multitasking training."

Noah's hand leaves my hair, only to be replaced by Lazarus's.

Then Noah grabs my hips and starts driving into me with

abandon while Lazarus forces me to take more of Johan into my mouth.

I feel trapped.

Full.

Owned.

I don't know what to do. My hands are suddenly on Johan's thighs like I might try to push myself away from him. But instead I dig my nails into his silky pants and moan as Noah hits my G-spot.

Oh God… None of my prior experiences involved *that* sensation. I thought it was a myth. But no, it's… it's definitely… *Ohhhh…*

My eyes threaten to roll into the back of my head, but a tug from Lazarus's hand commands my focus. "Hollow your cheeks, princess. Yeah, just like that. Now breathe in and hold."

He shoves me down even more than Noah did, making me gag around Johan.

But there's nowhere to go.

I'm forced to embrace it, to swallow around Johan, to just *endure* the contractions in my throat.

Then he pulls me back and tells me to inhale.

I do so noisily, only to be driven back down again while Noah ruts into me. I don't even know how he's doing that from the chair, but his strong body is moving with mine while Lazarus controls my head.

"Good?" Lazarus asks.

I'm not sure how to respond, nor am I sure if I'm good or not.

But then Johan says, "So fucking good."

Ugh, why is that so hot? I wonder, panting as Lazarus lets me breathe again. There's something undeniably sexy about these men talking to each other as they fuck me.

"Touch your clit," Noah tells me. "Pinch it for me, pet."

My insides burn with his request, my body on fire for him. On fire for Johan. On fire for Lazarus.

This is insanity.

I love it.

I don't want it to ever end.

And as my finger finds my clit, my world ignites beneath another wave of fiery heat.

"So obedient." Noah kisses my neck, his mouth closer to my nape now as he angles my hips in a way that allows him to fuck me even harder.

I feel like I would fall right now if he and Lazarus weren't holding me. I'm so precariously perched. Speared by two cocks. *Trapped in a pack of alphas.*

I'm dizzy from the realization that this is somehow my reality.

Overwhelmed by the sensations that knowledge provokes deep inside me.

And lost to the male growls filling the air.

Johan's jaw is clenched tight, his eyes on me. I release my death grip on his thigh so I can grab his knot again, squeezing it and twisting the way Noah told me to.

It's clearly the right thing to do because Johan groans, then reaches for my nape to hold me to him. "I'm going to come."

"Swallow it," Noah demands, pumping into me. "Don't waste any of that precious seed, Aurora."

"I'll make sure she swallows," Lazarus says, his grip on my hair unrelenting. "Deep breath, princess. You're going to need it."

I do, but before I can finish, Johan is already releasing his essence into my mouth. I nearly inhale it, causing panic to quicken my pulse.

"Shh," Lazarus hushes, pulling me back a little to give me time as Johan's seed spills onto my tongue. "Swallow, Ms. Bianchi."

I obey him because his tone demands me to.

But I'm not sure how much I can take with so little air in my lungs.

He must see that because he pulls me back suddenly, making me sputter as I gulp in air. Then he's there on his knees, finishing the job for me and making Johan growl in response.

Lazarus still has a grip on my hair, though, forcing me to remain close as Johan completes his climax.

"We'll work on it," Noah says softly, his pace slowing.

I'm mad that I messed up.

Angry that I couldn't take all of Johan's seed.

But before I can fully embrace the emotion, Lazarus is suddenly kissing me and forcing the essence into my mouth with his tongue.

Startled, I swallow on instinct. Then moan when I realize he didn't take over for me but is helping me to finish it.

I kiss him with a fervor, trying to gain every drop of Johan's essence, needing to keep him inside me. To feel his intimate claim.

"That's it, pet," Noah murmurs, his hand reaching around to replace my own as he thrums my clit. "Take all the seed like a good fucking omega." He thrusts into me with the words, making me moan into Lazarus's mouth again.

I'm so overwhelmed.

So utterly captivated by these men.

So turned on I can hardly breathe…

"Going to knot this honeyed pussy now," Noah grunts out, pistoning his hips into mine. "Take it, Aurora. *Take. It.*"

I scream as he explodes, his knot locking him deep inside me, the sensation so different from all the toys I've played with throughout the years.

God, those toys were *nothing* compared to the real deal.

I'm instantly thrown into a spiraling climax, one that makes the world spin and my vision dim.

It's dark.

Then light.

And so impactful that I forget to breathe.

But Lazarus is there, kissing me still, grounding me, helping me *feel.*

His palm is on my breast.

His fingers tweaking my nipple.

While Noah plays between my legs, stroking my sensitive bud and forcing me to spiral some more.

I fall into another state of existence.

Oblivion possesses my mind, body, and spirit.

My heart ceases to beat. Then jump-starts with a new rhythm. One that sounds mysteriously like *pack, pack, pack.*

I haven't claimed these alphas yet, but they're very clearly mine. In the same vein that I'm theirs.

And we've only just begun to play…

CHAPTER TWENTY-FOUR

LAZ

My phone buzzes in my pocket, the vibration one I ignore as I continue to kiss our omega.

But when it starts up again, I pull back to take it out, fully expecting to toss it to the side.

Until I see *Stefano Ricci* on the caller ID.

I narrow my gaze. "Fucker is thirty minutes early."

Noah looks up from where his face is buried in Aurora's neck, his gaze meeting mine. "My knot isn't moving anytime soon."

Johan practically collapses back onto the table, his dick still hard and protruding through the opening in his pants. He releases something incoherent that sounds a lot like "G'luck." Which I take to mean that he's joining Noah in the "not moving anytime soon" category.

"Assholes," I mutter as the call goes to voicemail again.

A text message comes through a few seconds later that reads, *Call me back, Ferraro. Now.*

I roll my eyes at the demand. I should make him wait just to piss him off.

But I want answers.

Which means I need to keep him somewhat agreeable if I want him to talk.

Sighing, I focus on Aurora, noting her pink cheeks and blown pupils. She looks so pretty like this—freshly used and lost to the orgasmic bliss of Noah's knot. She did so well for her first time. Not being able to take all of Johan's load wasn't surprising. But as Noah already said, we'll work on it.

I lean in and brush my lips against hers.

"I'm so fucking proud of you, princess. You're amazing." I kiss her again. "I wish I could stay and play, but I need to return Stefano's call. Just lounge there with Noah and let him take care of you, yeah?" I trust him with her safety. He'll make sure she comes down from her euphoric high and see to her needs.

I've never actually watched him fuck or knot anyone before.

So that was an experience.

One I fully intend to witness again and perhaps join in on in the future.

Sharing Aurora with him will be… *explosive.*

Poor omega. She's going to feel like she's being ripped in half by our knots. But she'll take them. And she'll love every fucking minute of the experience, too.

Or perhaps every fucking hour is more accurate, I think, my gaze running down to where she and Noah are still connected. He's going to be inside her for a while.

"Jealous?" he asks, clearly noting the trajectory of my gaze.

"Extremely." I reach down to thumb her swollen clit, causing her to gasp and clench around Noah.

He growls in response, obviously enjoying the squeeze around his knot. "*Dick.*"

I smile. "You're welcome." I give Aurora another tender caress and catch her moan with my tongue as I kiss her soundly. "Make Noah and Johan come again while I talk to Stefano," I demand. "I'll join the three of you in a bit."

She releases a little squeak.

But Noah chuckles and shifts his hips, causing that squeak to turn into a shriek.

"Don't hurt her," I add, walking away. "And no claiming while I'm on the phone!" I yell back to him when I reach the door. Because I'll be fucking pissed if I miss that.

Noah's reply is muted by the slamming of the door.

He's a dick, but I know he won't disrespect me by disobeying a direct order. Not when it comes to the pack, anyway.

Aurora is our heart. He knows that as well as I do. We're a pack that's meant to protect her and cherish her. Which means marking her will be a joint activity, not a solo one.

Unless otherwise discussed, of course.

Settling behind my main desk in the den—which is adjacent to the conference area I just left—I pull up my computer and connect my cell phone to a nearby Bluetooth speaker.

Then I dial up Stefano using video conference technology so I can see the Ricci family don on my computer screen.

His frowning face appears in seconds, his dark eyes glowering at me. "I wanted an in-person meeting, Lazarus."

"And I wanted a calm meeting the other night with your men, Stefano. But they tried to kill my second-in-command. Clearly, we can't always have what we want."

His square jaw ticks, his gaze narrowing even more. "Bastian was a bastard, but he didn't deserve to die like that, Ferraro."

"If one of my men tried to kill your second, how would you respond?" I demand.

"He was my brother."

"And Johan isn't just my second. He's *pack*. I know you understand that. So cut the shit and tell me why Johan was really targeted. Are you trying to start a war? Because I'll gladly give you one." This isn't going at all like I planned. But my patience is suddenly incredibly thin.

All I want to do is rejoin my pack in the other room. Watch Noah knot Aurora again. Help her pleasure Johan with her beautiful mouth. Maybe convince her to indulge me in a round, too.

But instead I'm stuck on the phone with Stefano, talking about a dead man.

Brother or not, he earned his fate when he attacked Johan.

"If you're looking for an apology, you won't be getting one," I go on. "And if anyone should be apologizing here, it's you for targeting my pack first. Now tell me why I shouldn't set fire to your entire fucking world."

There are a few logistical reasons I can think of that prevent me from letting Noah go on another killing spree. But I'm sure we could find a way to properly navigate the shattered businesses and take over as the new owners.

Of course, Giovanni may have an issue with that. Which Aurora already commented on.

The balance between the three families only works because we respect one another.

But the Riccis just disrespected the Ferraros. And I can't let that go unanswered.

"My brother was an ambitious man," Stefano says slowly. "His desire to run the Ricci family empire wasn't a secret. He took great pride in telling me how he would one day replace me."

I say nothing, just fold my arms and wait for him to continue.

Because so far, I haven't heard a good reason not to kill him.

Rivalry among brothers is common in our world. But a good don knows how to command respect. If Stefano couldn't convince Bastian to support his leadership, then that's a Ricci family don problem. Not mine.

"We weren't close," Stefano mutters. "That's why I gave him an enforcer position out in the field, not in the family home. I also didn't know about the meeting he arranged with you until after it occurred."

I arch a brow. "The request came through your official channels."

"Yes, I'm aware." There's a note of irritation in his tone, one that doesn't appear to be directed at me. "I've handled that issue. It will not happen again."

Someone moves into the background, the all-black suit giving him away before his face appears near Stefano's on the screen. *Nazar Petrov.*

It was quite the scandal when Stefano named the infamous Russian assassin as his second-in-command.

I found it rather amusing at the time.

I assume, however, that Bastian did not share in that amusement.

The stoic male looks at me with his silver-blue eyes as he whispers something to Stefano. Then he straightens and leaves the frame.

"You're certain?" Stefano asks, sounding wary.

"Yes," the Russian replies, that single word seeming to be underlined in lethal intent. It reminds me of Noah. Except Nazar isn't quite as psychotic. He doesn't play or enjoy death. He simply annihilates. Efficiently. Swiftly. And effectively.

If he and Noah were to ever join forces, the world would weep with blood and tears.

Or they would end up killing each other in the end.

Unclear.

Nor does it matter.

"If you're going to waste my time with personal discussions, I'm hanging up," I inform Stefano, my voice flat.

"Nazar was just confirming that the information we

learned this morning is, in fact, true." Stefano leans forward like he's trying to ensure he has my full attention through the camera. "It seems my brother accepted the hit assignment from Giovanni Bianchi."

My fingers flex with the urge to create a fist against my desk. But I manage to maintain my composure—just barely—and give him a bored look. "That sounds like a convenient way to shift blame."

"Come now, Ferraro. Don't tell me you're surprised by this reveal. It should be rather obvious to you, given your current *situation*," the assassin says, his voice lacking the accent I know he was born with. But the man speaks at least a dozen languages. *Fluently*.

He reenters the frame, this time closer to Stefano, and leans down to meet my gaze.

"I hear you've kidnapped a mafia princess," Nazar murmurs. "Could that be why Giovanni has a bounty on Johan's head?"

"How much is it for?" Stefano asks, making my jaw clench.

"Are you trying to infuriate me?" I demand.

"I want to know how much was offered for my brother's betrayal," Stefano replies, then looks at Nazar. "Do we know?"

"From what I've gathered, Giovanni promised to help Bastian overthrow you."

Stefano snorts. "And how did the Bianchi don think he was going to accomplish that?"

"I don't know, but I intend to find out," Nazar replies silkily. "Lazarus, always a displeasure to see you. Until next time." He steps away, causing Stefano's gaze to drift as the assassin leaves.

"Stop checking out the Russian and tell me what else you know," I demand.

"The details of my brother's betrayal are still unfolding," Stefano says without looking at me. "I'll keep you informed."

The line goes dead before I can tell him that's not good enough.

A growl leaves me, one that echoes through my office and rivals one coming from the other room.

Does she know? I wonder, my mind shifting to a place I don't want to visit. One underscored by potential betrayal. *Does Aurora know that her brother has a hit out on Johan?*

We haven't been screening her calls or monitoring her. Johan felt strongly about protecting her privacy—which is ironic, given the developing situation.

But has she even tried to reach out to her brother?

I was very clear about rule number one—no sharing any details about our pack with anyone else, including our plans, location, and businesses.

Did she break that rule?

I run a hand over my face, not appreciating the way my chest feels in response to this line of thought. My heart feels strangely tight, like it can't properly beat.

She's our omega.

Our… our *center.*

Except, we never really gave her a choice. *Is she only pretending to want to be with us? Is she secretly working with her brother? Supplying him with information? Trying to take down our pack?*

My jaw clenches with the prospect, and I push to my feet, determined to make her answer some questions.

But I freeze in the doorway to the conference room when I see Johan bending her over the table to slide into her wet pussy.

Noah is standing beside him, fisting his own cock while he watches. "Doesn't she feel amazing?" my enforcer asks, his voice low. "Like the best pussy you've ever experienced?"

"The only one I ever want to experience," Johan grinds out, slamming home inside of her as she claws at the table.

Her eyes are closed, her lips parted on a pant. She doesn't look unhappy. In fact, she seems to be quite pleased by what Johan is doing to her.

But we're her scent matches.

Her destined alphas.

It wouldn't be difficult for an omega to feign interest in that situation.

So is she playing us? I wonder, my chest aching once more. *Have we fallen for the oldest trick in the book—a vixen spy?*

I swallow, my eyes narrowing.

If she's here to hurt us, she's in for one hell of a surprise.

Because she's ours now.

And we won't be letting her go.

Ever.

I quietly shut the door to return to my desk and pick up my phone.

Then I select Giovanni's number and hit *Call*.

CHAPTER TWENTY-FIVE
LARK

Johan isn't as long as Noah, but he's thick and impactful as he thrusts into me.

In and out.

Allowing me to become accustomed to his size. His pace. *His heat.*

He presses a kiss to my shoulder, then to my neck, before placing his lips near my ear. "You okay, sweetheart?"

I groan and shake my head. "*No.*"

He stills, then starts to pull out of me.

I reach back to grab his hip. "You're not moving enough," I whine at him. "*Fuck me,* Johan. Don't be gentle. I want—"

He slams into me, causing my back to arch as a scream of approval leaves me.

"That," I breathe. "*That.* Yes. More."

He chuckles against my ear, his hand covering mine on his hip, then he begins to truly fuck me right over the table.

I'm not even sure how I ended up in this position.

Oh, wait, no… Noah dared me to bend over…

More like challenged me, actually.

And I'm very okay with it.

"Mmm, I think we need to move this party to the couch," Noah says. "I want to lick her pussy while you fuck her."

A moan escapes in response to his words, my body going up in flames at the picture he's painting.

And then it's suddenly becoming a potential reality as Johan slips out of me, flips me around, and lifts me into the air to carry me over to a cushioned area of the conference room.

I wrap my legs around his hips and kiss him while he walks, my slick center right up against his groin.

Just like in the shower.

Only better because he's rubbing my clit with the head of his cock. Kissing me deeply. Holding me tightly. *Purring heavily.*

It's perfect.

It's hypnotic.

It's exceptionally arousing.

But just when I think it can't get any hotter, Noah takes me from Johan's arms and holds me against his pulsing knot.

I shudder, then sigh as his tongue slides into my mouth for a long, deep embrace. I thread my fingers through his silky hair, loving that his long strands are wild and loose. I've only ever seen him with his red hair tied back. But not now. He's untamed. Free. *Feral.*

"Sit on the couch, Johan," he says against my mouth. "I'll give you her pussy in a minute."

He shifts our hips and thrusts into me, making me groan with delight. But then he leaves me bare and wanting a moment later and starts to lower me to the floor.

Only it's not the floor I feel beneath me, but Johan's lap.

His hands clasp my hips as he guides me, his arousal waiting for mine. Noah goes to his knees to help, grabbing Johan's knot to properly angle his dick, and suddenly he's inside me, filling the space Noah just did.

This is unlike anything I've ever experienced. Unlike any sort of reality I could fathom.

My alphas are moving me in ways I didn't know I could be moved.

But I'm too lust-drunk to contemplate their methods.

My legs are straddling Johan, my back to his front, and he's thrusting up into me with a force that leaves me winded.

"Grab her throat," Noah tells Johan. "And hold her back. I want to feast."

"Happily," Johan murmurs, his palm moving up to my neck as his opposite hand goes to my breast. "You good, Lark?" he breathes against my ear.

I swallow. "Yeah."

"Okay, sweetheart. Just talk to me if that changes." He kisses my temple, then tweaks my nipple right as Noah takes my clit into his mouth.

My insides clamp down around Johan, causing him to groan deep in his chest.

"Fuck, make her do that again," he says, pushing up into me.

Noah does by using his tongue to swirl my bud, followed by a light nibble from his teeth.

Warmth and need spiral through me, making me squirm on Johan's lap.

I feel so full. So pent up. So *ready*.

Which is insane. I've already come more than once. I usually only achieve multiple orgasms while in heat. Yet these alphas are about to prove that my body can take so much more than I've ever imagined.

My estrus is going to be explosive in the best way, I marvel, moaning as Noah licks me again. His hand is near Johan's knot, doing something to it as he pleasures me with his mouth.

The sensations are intense.

The warmth is overwhelming.

Yet I feel safe. Cherished. *Properly taken care of.*

These alphas are driving me to a precipice I've never before experienced.

And I welcome it. Them. Their world. *Everything.*

"I can feel your orgasm building around my cock," Johan whispers. "The way you're squeezing me… *Fuck*, Lark. I'm going to explode with you."

Noah growls in agreement, his fingers massaging Johan's knot as he continues to abuse my clit with his tongue and teeth.

Everything inside me tenses, my veins suddenly on fire.

Johan releases my breast and grasps my chin, then tilts my head back and to the side. "Kiss me while you come, Lark." His lips brush mine. Then he claims me with his mouth, and my world explodes.

He swallows my screams, but in the next moment, he's growling out his own release. I moan as his knot locks us together, securing him to that place deep within that Noah recently occupied.

It feels similar. Yet different. Both alphas bringing their own intensity and size and touch.

I shudder, my body writhing in waves of pleasure that feel unending.

I'll never be the same after this.

These alphas have ruined me for the future, guaranteeing that the only ones who will ever be able to inflict this kind of ecstasy on me are them.

Only them.

My pack.

My men.

"I need your mouth, pet," Noah says, his fingers suddenly in my hair and taking my lips away from Johan.

Except it isn't Noah's mouth that meets mine. It's his cock.

Which I now realize he's been stroking.

His hand is on his knot while his other is in my hair, guiding me forward.

"Try to swallow," he murmurs, feeding me his engorged dick just as he begins to come.

I nearly inhale instead, my own orgasm still rocking through me. But I do my best to take his seed the way he wants.

Cinnamon fills my senses, followed by a sweet hint of hot honey.

It's Noah's essence, his scent and his taste, flooding me.

Just like Johan's coffee-like aroma.

If I could purr, I would. Instead, I hum happily as my throat works to accept everything Noah has to give.

"That's it, pretty omega," he murmurs, his fingers stroking through my hair as he twists his knot with his opposite hand.

He isn't deep-throating me, just sitting with his head on my tongue, allowing me time to take every drop from his shaft.

"Fuck, pet," he groans, another spurt landing inside my mouth. "You're doing so good, taking both of us like this. Just keep swallowing and try to remember to breathe."

Johan exhales against my neck, his lips ghosting along my pulse. "I want to mark you as mine so fucking bad right now," he admits, making me shudder and clamp down around him again. "*God*, Lark…"

"Mmm, she's a little busy at the moment," a deep voice says, traveling through the room. "I would show you, but I don't think you want to see your sister like this."

I sputter, my eyes widening.

Noah holds me to him, though, not allowing me to pull back. "Shh, finish your job, pet," he tells me.

But all I can hear is Lazarus saying "your sister."

Because that means he's talking to *my brother*.

"Swallow," Noah growls, causing Lazarus to chuckle.

Bastard, I growl in my head, not sure if I'm talking to the male still coming down my throat or the one fucking laughing.

Noah drives deep, forcing me to take him and to focus on his cock in my mouth.

"Unfortunately, no. Her mouth is currently… preoccupied. But I'll send proof of life when she's done servicing my enforcer and my second."

Oh God, I can *hear* my brother shouting from here.

I grab Noah's hips and dig my nails into them as I try to shove him backward.

"Let her go," Johan says.

Noah sighs but obeys, releasing my mouth so I can sputter and cough.

He keeps climaxing, though, and I belatedly realize the angle of my head has his cum landing in my *hair*.

I'm going to kill him.

No. Scratch that. I'm going to kill *Lazarus*.

Growling—or trying to, anyway, as it's hard when I'm still hacking from inhaling some of Noah's essence—I shoot my glare toward the smirking male in the doorway. He's just casually leaning there, holding a phone out in front of him.

I have no idea if the camera is facing me or him.

It had better be toward him.

I do *not* want Gio to see me like this.

"I'm going to fucking shred you, Ferraro," my brother seethes, clearly on speakerphone.

"Maybe you should have considered the consequences before hiring a hitman to take out my second," Lazarus answers coolly, his smile disappearing as he stares me down.

My brow furrows. *What?*

Johan also stills against me, clearly as shocked as I am, and slowly turns his attention to Lazarus. As does Noah.

"This is between you and me, Lazarus," my brother says after a long beat of silence. "Don't punish my sister for—"

"Oh, I will do whatever the fuck I please to your precious little sister," Lazarus returns, sounding lethal as he continues to hold my gaze.

I shiver.

Because that sounded like a threat, but also a promise.

And for some fucked-up reason, it excites me.

Except I don't think he intends to be kind about it.

In fact, he looks *livid.*

Because Gio hired Bastian to kill Johan? I question, dizzy with that information. *Why would he do that?*

Gio knows better than to start a war between the families.

Is it because of me? I wonder. *Oh God, does Lazarus think I had something to do with it?*

My heart kick-starts in my chest as I realize that, yes, he absolutely does think I have something to do with this.

That's why he's threatening to do whatever he wants to me. Why he's informing my brother of what's currently happening to me. He wants my brother to pay for nearly hurting Johan.

And he's going to make an example out of me as a result.

Every part of me freezes, my interest in his threat turning to ice.

Johan is no longer coming inside me, but his knot is still lodged deep within me, forbidding me from moving. Noah still has a hold of my hair.

Yet we're all frozen as Lazarus says, "Friday night, we'll have dinner at the Ferraro estate. If your sister survives what I'm about to do to her, I'll let you see her."

"*Ferraro,*" my brother growls. "You can't—"

"I assure you, I *can,*" Lazarus returns. "And more importantly, I *will.* Friday at eight, Bianchi. Don't be late." He hangs up, then slides the phone into his pocket while holding my gaze.

I feel raw.

Exposed.

Trapped.

"I didn't know," I breathe, hoping he believes me. Praying he doesn't hate me.

This is my pack.

My scent matches.

"I wouldn't do that..." I trail off, swallowing, my voice hoarse. I break his cruel stare and try my best to look at Johan over my shoulder. "I would *never*..."

The alpha slowly turns to look at me, his crystal-blue eyes searching mine. Then he leans in to brush his lips against mine. "Even if you did, I wouldn't blame you," he whispers. "We kidnapped you. Forced you to stay here with us. And we all know fighting back is in your nature, little hacker."

"But I didn't—"

Movement from the left has me abruptly quieting, my spine stiffening as Lazarus draws closer.

My throat tries to work, yet everything feels wrong. I can't swallow. I can barely even breathe.

And those sensations only worsen as Lazarus takes hold of my chin and forces me to look up at him.

Noah moves out of his way, taking a seat beside Johan and throwing his arm along the back of the couch. It's an action I only catch out of my peripheral vision. I can't tell if he's glaring at me the way Lazarus currently is or if he's just watching everything unfold.

"I didn't," I force out, my voice choked. "Why would Gio...?" I can't get out any more words, my chest too tight.

"Inhale," Lazarus tells me, his demand forcing my lungs to expand.

It's like he's taken control of my spirit and my will, commanding every aspect of my being.

"I'm angry," he murmurs, the admission unnecessary, as I can clearly see the anger written into his features. "But I'm not angry with you, princess." He leans down to place the softest of kisses against my lips. "Even if you had something to do with this, I would forgive you. Because you're *ours.*"

I tremble, his words undoing something inside me.

Something furious.

Something passionate.

Something *foreign*.

"Keep breathing," he tells me, his fingers gently stroking my cheek. "My threats were for your brother, not for you. We would never hurt you, Aurora. Not even if you betrayed us." He kisses me again, this time with a little more pressure.

I'm so confused.

I feel lost.

Yet his touch anchors me in the present, dominating me in a way I can't define.

He's like the primary source of my life. His words are grounding, redefining everything I thought I knew about this man. About this pack.

If this is his version of punishment, he's going to shatter me to pieces.

Because he's making me feel safe. And if he betrays that, I'll never be able to recover.

"Please don't hurt me," I whisper, aware that he just said he wouldn't, but I need him to hear my plea. "I promise I didn't have anything to do with this. I don't even know why Gio would try to hurt Johan. Starting a war between the families doesn't make any sense."

"He likely feels we started the war first by taking you," Lazarus murmurs, his lips a hairsbreadth from mine. "We'll find out more this weekend when we meet with him." His nose brushes mine, then he pulls back to look at Noah and Johan. "She needs another shower. Take care of her. The three of us will regroup after."

With that, he leaves without a backward glance.

I watch him go, my heart in my throat.

He never said he believed me. Just stated that he would never hurt me.

Except he just did—by walking away. By not *trusting* me.

Maybe I haven't earned his faith yet.

But I will.

Then he'll know that I never betrayed him or our pack.

Because that's not who I am, or who I'll ever be.

I'll show him he's wrong, I decide. *I'll prove my trustworthiness, force him to realize his mistake, and make him wish he never questioned my loyalty.*

And I think I know just where to start…

CHAPTER TWENTY-SIX
JOHAN

Giovanni Bianchi ordered the hit on my life.

That's what Laz learned on his phone call earlier with Stefano Ricci. And when he called Giovanni, he didn't deny it.

I rub a hand over my face, then pick up the glass of gin Noah made for me and take a healthy sip.

Noah's already fixing a second one, along with a glass of scotch for himself. He's usually a martini guy. But he clearly needs something stronger.

As did I.

Laz is the only one not drinking.

He's seated calmly behind his desk, his fingers on his keyboard as he sends out commands via secure channels.

There's already a small army surrounding the estate, but he's requesting more men, just in case.

And he's checking in on all of our business assets, ensuring that Giovanni hasn't attempted to attack us anywhere else.

I try to help from my laptop, but my nerves are fucking fried.

Leaving Lark alone in her room didn't sit right with me. She made a comment about understanding Laz's need to meet with just the pack, suggesting she didn't see herself as part of our unit yet.

We haven't claimed her, and she hasn't claimed us. So I suppose she's not officially ours, but my heart and soul already belong to her.

She's my omega.

My *center.*

If she wants to be, I think, taking another sip of my drink before slamming the empty glass on the desk.

Noah is there a second later to swap it with another helping, but I ignore it and fire up my backup laptop instead.

Lark has my preferred laptop.

Which has me wondering what she might be doing with it right now.

But I refrain from hacking in to find out. She deserves her privacy, even if she's contacting her brother right now for an update.

Fucking Giovanni.

Narrowing my gaze, I decide to go hunting. I want proof that he hired Bastian to take me out. And I want to see if there's any indication of why he chose me.

Because I'm the one who found his sister? I wonder. *Does he see me as a primary threat?*

That would normally be a compliment. But right now it just fuels my need to know more.

I start pulling up programs and screens, logging in with my usual protocols before diving into tracer logs.

I want his phone history, proof that he's even talked to Bastian. So that's where I start, drawing up all the records I can find for his various phone numbers. If he's smart, he used a burner. But there has to be a trace of something somewhere.

And I'm going to find it.

Data starts to populate, my eyes scanning, my sense of time slipping away as I pull everything into a database. Writing a few scripts, I begin sorting through the logs in a way that allows me to search for specific terms. Numbers. *Assassin codes*.

I'm familiar with the latter because of Noah. There's a whole dark web filled with bounties. He takes on special projects when he wants to hone one of his skills. Or if he despises whatever the mark did.

"I have standards," he once said when explaining what types of assignments he favors. "If they've hurt women or children, they meet those standards."

He has a particular hatred for men who prey on the innocent. It's why he was pissed when he couldn't join the Widows during their trip to the Henderson mansion last month. That place was full of marks that he longed to kill.

But Laz and I forced him to stay behind and observe.

"If something goes wrong, you can go in and help. Otherwise, stay put." That was Laz's command.

So I hacked into the feeds, and we listened from afar. Aside from a minor hiccup with Silva, everything went fine.

Noah was pissed, though, that he didn't get to go out and play.

Except, we weren't ready to take Lark yet.

And now I'm wondering if we were ever going to be ready at all.

I don't think she knew about the hit on me. But I meant what I said about not blaming her if she did.

She's a fighter. I respect that. Not too keen on being killed in the process. However, if she wants me to die for her, I will.

I pull up another screen, aware that Laz and Noah have been talking while I've been working. I've not paid attention, too busy searching the dark web for—

A message pops up, interrupting my flow and making me frown.

LarkFerraro: Check your email.

I blink at the username. It's pretty clear who sent it. Although, it's interesting that she's updated her handle from *LarkWhite* to *LarkFerraro*.

JohnAegean: Cute last name.

LarkFerraro: Careful or you might offend the boss.

I smirk.

JohnAegean: He doesn't scare me.

LarkFerraro: I wish I could say the same.

And my smirk dies.

JohnAegean: He meant what he said—he'll never hurt you.

She doesn't reply, which has me glancing up at the man in question.

"You have some work to do with our omega," I inform him, cutting off whatever he's just said to Noah about security parameters.

Ignoring them again, I open my email and gape at the information dump waiting for me.

After skimming a few threads, I flip back to the messenger screen.

JohnAegean: How did you find all of this?

LarkFerraro: He's my brother. I knew where to look.

Dots appear and disappear as she types and deletes.

"*Johan*," Laz says, the emphasis on my name yanking my gaze up to his from my computer. He's clearly been talking while I've been reading Lark's report. "Why do I have work to do?"

I frown at him. "What?"

His dark eyes narrow. "You said I have work to do with our omega. Why?"

"Oh, right, that. She's afraid of you. So you need to fix that."

Lark's messenger icon flashes, drawing my attention back to my laptop.

> LarkFerraro: I'm realizing now that this probably just makes me look more guilty. I was trying to do the opposite, to prove I'm not involved. Though, now you'll assume I deleted something, which defeats the entire purpose. Sorry.

LARKFERRARO HAS LEFT THE CHAT.

I frown, then connect directly to the laptop she's using to send her a response.

And I don't bother with my alternate identity handle, instead using my real name.

> Johan: You have nothing to prove to me, sweetheart. If you were involved, I forgive you. End of discussion.

I leave the computer before she can get angry with me for intruding on her privacy. Although, technically, that computer she's using is mine.

But she's slowly making it her own.

"What the hell are you doing?" Laz demands, his irate tone grabbing my attention.

I look at him. "Why are you yelling?"

He gapes at me. "Have you heard nothing I've said?"

"Pretty sure he's been ignoring you while flirting with a

certain hacker," Noah says. "Kind of jealous, if I'm honest. I would love a reason to tune you out."

"Fuck off, Noah."

"Happily," the enforcer returns, standing. "I'll just go knot our—"

"Is neither of you taking this seriously?" Laz demands. "We're at war."

"Yes and no," I murmur, pulling up the message exchange that Lark found. "It wasn't a true hit."

Which is why I didn't find any bounties with my name on them while searching the dark web.

Spinning my computer around to show Laz, I let him read the written exchange between Bastian and Uriah.

"It didn't even come from Giovanni, but from the elders who advise him. And it was meant to be a kidnapping, not an assassination. I assume their intention was to force a trade—me for Lark." I shrug. "Pretty standard."

"Where did you find all this?" Laz demands after he finishes reading.

Noah takes the laptop next, wanting to catch up.

While he skims the conversation, I reply, "Lark found it and sent it to me."

Laz's jaw ticks. "That's convenient."

"Yes. And if you read my conversation with her"—I take the laptop back from Noah to pull up that screen and flip it around to show Laz—"you'll see she already commented on that."

I let him read everything so he sees what she said about being afraid of him, too.

I know he's caught that part when his lips curl downward.

"She doesn't trust me," he says, mouth tightening.

"Do you trust her?" Noah counters before I can voice the same question. "Do you think she helped her brother?"

Laz considers it for a beat. "I don't know." He looks at Noah and then at me. "What are your instincts telling you?"

"That she had a good reason to want me dead in the beginning," I reply without missing a beat. "I'm the one who tracked her down. I enabled her capture, too."

He nods. Then looks to Noah for his answer.

"She was like a little angry hornet when she boarded our jet. Her fighting back is a turn-on." He shrugs. "I like that she's a strong mate. It'll help her survive our pack."

"But do you think she aided in the assassination attempt?" Laz presses.

"Does it matter?" Noah counters.

"If she were anyone else, it absolutely would," Laz points out. "So yes, I think it matters. Not because I want to punish her for it—at least not in a traditional sense—but because we have to decide if we can trust her."

Silence falls between the three of us.

"She can't have confidence in us if we don't have faith in her allegiance," Laz adds after a moment of contemplation. "And trust is vital for her approaching heat."

"Then let's talk to her," Noah suggests, being a voice of reason—which isn't his usual mode. "We'll tell her that if she tried to get Johan kidnapped or killed, we forgive her. If she didn't, then we've wasted time debating on how to proceed."

"I'm going to amend only slightly and suggest that Laz talk to her. Noah and I are not the issue here."

Laz arches a brow. "And I am?"

"Yes." I close my laptop and set it to the side. "You're the one questioning her loyalty."

I lift my hand to halt him when he starts to reply.

"I'm not saying you're wrong, Laz." I voice the words quietly, wanting him to hear me.

"Then what are you saying?" he demands.

"I'm pointing out that it's your responsibility as our don to protect the pack. And it's the pack's responsibility to be loyal to you. If you're questioning her motives, you're questioning her worth. So talk to her. That's the only way you'll be able to determine if she's truly meant to be ours or not."

Noah makes a noise of discontent, clearly disagreeing with the concept of her *not* being meant for us.

While I agree, I don't voice it aloud.

Because, as I said, this isn't my issue. This is Laz's query.

Noah and I have more than accepted our fate. Fuck, Noah's already professed his love and proposed. He might be psychotic, but he means every word he's said to her.

And I've been enamored with the woman since I discovered her on the dark web. There's no question in my mind that she's ours.

Laz is the only one holding himself back.

"Go tell her how you feel. Hear her out. And we'll determine how to proceed from there." I push out of my seat and grab my laptop. "Meanwhile, Noah and I will be in the gym."

I could use a workout after all this bullshit. And I know the only way to distract Noah right now is with a good sparring session.

"Or we could go knot our omega again," Noah says, glaring at me. "I would enjoy that more than kicking your ass."

My lips curl. "Kick my ass and I'll let you knot me there." It's an invitation and a promise, one that has his nostrils flaring.

It doesn't matter that we already went two rounds with Lark today. We're both pent up and on the edge of a serious rut. He knows that as well as I do.

The moment she goes into heat, we're fucked. Literally.

She's going to be ripped apart by our aggression. Assuming Laz comes to his damn senses and indulges in our omega's heat.

Though, even if he decides she's not pack—which had

better not fucking happen—Noah and I won't be able to stay away from her.

"She's ours, Laz," I tell him. "So go talk to her. Apologize. Earn her loyalty and respect. Kiss her. Knot her. Claim her. I don't fucking care. Just do whatever you need to do to resolve this doubt. Or it's going to destroy our pack."

I grab Noah by the arm to drag him out of his chair.

He flips a blade in his hand, the weapon one I didn't even see him pull. But he doesn't use it. Just menacingly twirls it between his fingers, likely because he's attempting to soothe his mounting rage.

"Ditto." Noah's statement comes out in a snarl of sound. Then he palms my nape, his knife dangerously sharp against my skin. "I'm in a violent mood, tech boy. You sure you're ready to handle that?"

"Give me a bō, and I'll handle anything you want," I return, the insinuation in my voice clear.

He smiles, but it's not a kind expression. Instead, it's underlined with lethal intent. "Then let's go play." He shoots Laz a glare. "And you go fix your mess."

"My mess?" Laz repeats, incredulity layering his tone. "*My* mess?"

"Glad to know you heard me, boss. Now *fix it.*" He drags me from the room without a backward glance, his blade breaking the skin with the force of his movements.

It's going to be a rough session.

But I welcome it.

Because I have no intention of holding back.

Bring on the rut…

CHAPTER TWENTY-SEVEN

LARK

What a mess.

I can't believe Gio tried to kidnap Johan.

Well, no. I *can* believe it, actually. It makes sense.

The error was in assuming Johan would attend a meeting without his pack. Though, that error was on Bastian's part, not my brother's.

"Ugh," I grumble, irritated. At least Gio wasn't trying to kill Johan. But still, he's made my life rather difficult.

I flip the phone in my hand, debating if I should call him.

Lazarus was clearly trying to punish my brother by implying that I'm being hurt by his pack. If I call my brother, I'll undermine that.

But I hate leaving Gio with doubts about my safety and well-being.

"This is ridiculous," I mutter, pacing the balcony just outside my room. I feel like I have to choose between Gio and my pack.

Or rather, my scent matches.

They're not my pack yet.

I'm not even sure Lazarus wants me as part of the pack. Actually, pretty certain he doesn't.

I cover my eyes with my hands—one of which still has my phone—and growl.

Only for a reverberation from the device in my palm to make me jump. I half expect to see Johan's name on the caller ID. But it's Luna's instead.

I frown. She usually checks in after dinner, which makes her call earlier than expected.

"Everything okay?" I ask after accepting the call.

"I was going to ask you the same thing," she replies, her nose scrunching on the display. "I just had a weird feeling that you may need a friend right now."

My lips twitch. "You and your cryptic intuition."

"So I'm right? You need me?"

I sigh. "Yes and no," I mumble. "I could use a distraction right now, if you have one."

"Hmm, let me see if I can think up something." She taps her chin, her russet-brown eyes thoughtful. "Lexi ate half a dozen maple donuts for breakfast today. Emmett was impressed for reasons I don't want to evaluate. Of course, Sloane made those reasons clear with his descriptive commentary..."

"I bet," I say with a snort. I don't know Lexi's alphas all that well, but from what I've observed, Sloane is quite the character.

Actually, I suspect Noah might like him. They're both... *blunt.* Only, in very different ways.

"Haven't seen Silva much recently. Pretty sure she's enjoying her new pack and the privileges that come with that. Briar has kept to herself, too. And Aries mentioned that you helped her vet some new alphas in town. Though, you obviously already know that. So, I'm not doing a good job, am I?"

My lips twitch. "Just hearing you talk helps," I admit. "I miss you."

"Just me?" she asks, brightening. "No one else?"

"You the most," I tell her honestly. "But I really miss everyone and Widows Peak."

"Then you should tell that sexy fiancé of yours to take you home," she suggests.

"Did you just call Noah sexy?" I demand, feeling stupidly annoyed. "He's *mine*, Luna."

Her dark eyes widen, her expression morphing from teasing to shock. "Are you seriously getting all proprietary on me right now?" She makes a show of looking her screen up and down. "Who are you and what have you done with my best friend?"

Part of me wants to growl at her. "I'm not getting *proprietary*." Okay. That's a lie. But I'm not going to back down now. "He's my alpha, though. They all are."

"Oh?" She arches a brow. "Does that mean you've claimed them?"

"Er, well, no," I hedge, my lips twisting. "Not yet."

"Why not?"

"Because it's been, like, a week?" I tell her.

"A little less," she informs me. "But who's counting?"

"Apparently you."

"I do like details," she says, nodding. "And speaking of details..." She gives me a knowing look. "Anything you want to share, best friend?"

"Seriously? You're pulling that card right now?"

"Well, you're clearly holding back on me. Is it because of rule number one?"

My eyes lift to the ceiling. "You're going to get me in trouble, and I'm not even the one who told you about that rule."

"No, my newest *bestie* did that," she murmurs. "Where is Noah, by the way?"

"In a pack meeting," I mutter.

"A pack meeting?" she echoes. "Shouldn't you be involved, then? Since they're *your* alphas?"

I bite my lip, not sure how to answer that.

But given the way she's looking at me when I meet her gaze again, I don't need to say anything.

She can read me like an open book. We might have our secrets—ones we'll never share with each other—but we've always naturally understood one another.

"Oh, Lark, if I could hug you right now, I would."

"And I'd probably push you away," I tell her.

"I know," she says, her smile sad. "So I'd just hug you tighter."

"Thank you," I whisper, acknowledging that, despite the fact that I would absolutely try to squirm out of her arms, I really could use a hug right about now. "They're mad at me for something I didn't do."

Okay, that's not exactly accurate. Noah and Johan definitely said they didn't "blame" me for betraying them. And Lazarus also mentioned that he was angry at my brother, not me.

So I rephrase by saying, "*Mad* isn't the right term. I can't really elaborate. But let's just say we're having a misunderstanding."

She considers that and nods. "Can you, uh, help them understand?"

"I tried that, and I think I made it worse." I hacked into my brother's communications to see if I could find proof of what he had done.

Instead, I found the kidnapping assignment, which was written in a bunch of cryptic commentary that I only understood because of growing up in this world.

So I sent that to Johan, hoping it would absolve me since I wasn't part of the chat or even mentioned in it.

Except, I immediately realized that he would just assume I massaged the communications to remove myself from the evidence.

"Hmm, well, I can't really help without much context.

But, in my experience, logic prevails. So if you can present facts to them, that should clear up the 'misunderstanding.'"

"Ironically, that's what I already tried to do," I tell her, sighing. "The problem is, I'm someone who can alter the facts, if you grasp my meaning."

She stares at me through the screen. "So they don't trust you."

I wince. It's a direct assessment, but that's Luna. She isn't one to mince words. Not with me, anyway. "Basically, yeah."

"Do you trust them?" It's a quiet question, one she utters with a bit more gentleness than her frank statement from a few seconds ago.

I don't immediately answer her, instead seriously considering her question. "This is going to sound kind of crazy," I warn her, swallowing. "But yes, I do. I… I know they're dangerous. I know they could easily hurt me. However, I don't think they actually will."

Lazarus scares me. Although, not in a traditional way.

"I'm terrified of what I'm feeling for them," I confide to Luna, the statement one I've barely admitted to myself. "I've never wanted to be a mafia bride. I've seen what that did to my mother. But I don't think they're anything like my father's pack."

Actually, I'm certain they're not.

"Maybe it's the scent match, but I… I really like them, Luna. Which is insane. How can I feel this way after only knowing them for a week?" I clear my throat. "Or slightly less than one," I quickly amend, aware that she's likely thinking that already in her head.

"Scent matches are rare and powerful," she says, her voice soft. "If you like them, then embrace it, Lark. Otherwise, you're just fighting fate."

"You believe in fate now?" I ask, incredulous.

"Pretty sure I never stopped," she replies, her expression holding a touch of sadness to it that she instantly masks behind a smile. "My point is that time is irrelevant. Follow your instincts. They've never failed you before."

She's right.

My instincts are what drew me to her that night thirteen years ago. I knew something was wrong. Then we were taken, and while I was certain we could escape within days, my instincts forced us to remain.

That led us to saving the other Widows.

Founding Widows Peak.

With the money I stole from the Ferraros.

Which has landed me here… in Lazarus's family estate.

Luna's comment on *fate* plays through my head again.

"I don't want to fight fate," I whisper, more to myself than to her. "Luna, I need to go." Because I need to talk to the pack, to tell them I'm innocent and make them *hear* me.

No more wallowing on this balcony.

I'm going to fix this by telling them they're wrong to distrust me. And I'm going to demand that they give me a proper chance.

"Thank you," I tell my best friend as I move away from the railing outside the balcony and step backward toward the house. "You helped me more than you know." She didn't really give me a pep talk so much as help me process the situation.

"Uh, Lark—"

"Seriously, I'm good," I cut her off as I spin toward the house. "I'll call you back later tonight. Normal time, okay?"

"Yeah, but—"

"Love you!" I hang up before she can say anything to change my mind and practically sprint toward my room. I'm going to convince—

I run right into the closed glass door.

"*Ow*!" I shout. I could have sworn I left that thing open!

I lift my hand to smack the offending object, only to find my wrist caught in a strong hand.

I blink, realizing I didn't run into a door at all.

I ran into Lazarus freaking Ferraro.

Shit!

My eyes widen. "I-I wasn't talking to my brother," I sputter. "I swear I didn't call him."

"I know you didn't," he answers calmly.

"I was talking to—" I frown, then look up into his dark eyes. "Wait, you know I didn't call him?"

"I've been standing here for the last five minutes, Aurora."

My eyelashes flutter again. "I… *what*?" *How the hell did I miss that?* "Did you knock?" Okay, that's a stupid question. So I shake my head and try again. "How much did you hear?"

He arches a dark brow, his thumb gently running across my still-captured wrist. "I stepped out onto the balcony around the time your friend mentioned maple donuts."

"So basically my entire conversation," I say, feeling oddly defeated. "What I talk about with my friends is meant to be private."

"I didn't hide my presence," he tells me. "And for the record, yes, I did knock. I'm guessing you didn't hear it out here."

My phone buzzes, causing me to glance down at it.

> Luna: There's a ridiculously hot, Italian-looking guy standing on the balcony. I'm guessing you figured that out by now.

My lips pinch.

> Luna: I was trying to warn you when you rudely hung up on me. So I'm not sorry if he startled you.

I sigh.

> Luna: Please tell me he's one of your scent matches.

I shake my head, but the dots on the screen tell me my friend isn't done sending me messages.

Luna: If he's not, I would like his name and number. Please and thank you.

My gaze narrows as I type back…

Lark: That's Lazarus Ferraro. And no, you may not have his number. He's mine.

The dots appear again, and I wait for her response.

Luna: Has he proposed, too?

I scoff at that.

No. He would have to like me to propose to me. And I'm pretty sure he hates me right now.

"I do not hate you." Lazarus's voice startles me, making me realize that I'm literally typing all this out in front of him. "Give me that."

"Give you—"

He takes the phone from my hand and starts typing.

"Hey!" I try to grab it back from him, but he's already walking away from me.

I chase after him as he disappears through the doors, his long legs carrying him to the bed before I've even entered the room.

He sits, and I leap onto the mattress next to him, then try to take the device from him. He lifts an arm, easily deflecting my movements.

I growl.

But the bastard ignores me and continues typing with one hand.

So I jump on his back and try to get to my phone

that way.

He spins while *still typing*, and suddenly I'm flat on the bed with him straddling me.

I'm not even sure *how* he accomplished that.

When I try to sit up, he pushes me back down and says, "There. That's better."

The sound of my phone locking follows, and he sets it on my nightstand next to the gun I haven't touched in days.

"Now let's chat." He settles on top of me, his elbows on either side of my head, caging me beneath him.

I gape up at him. "Have you lost your mind?"

He considers me for a moment. "My mind, no. My heart might be a different story, though." He leans down to brush his lips against mine, the motion so unexpected that I gasp.

Which he perceives as an invitation because he dips his tongue into my mouth and starts to kiss me.

I have half a mind to bite him and very nearly do.

But then realize I would be claiming him if I did.

Except… except that wouldn't be that bad of an idea. I *want* to claim him. To make him mine. To show him that I'm loyal to this pack. That I want him and the others.

Maybe that's a way to prove I wasn't involved in the attack on Johan?

It would be impulsive. Daring. And a way to take charge of this kiss.

The claim can't be undone, though. But I think I'm okay with that.

No, I *know* I'm okay with that.

In fact, I don't want it to be undone. I don't want *any* of this to be taken away at all.

I grab Lazarus's shoulders, feel the muscles bunch beneath the fabric of his dress shirt, and cling to him.

He deepens the kiss, likely assuming that I'm submitting to his touch.

I am to an extent.

But also not.

It's the latter part that has me clamping down hard on his tongue and drawing blood.

He stills.

I swallow.

And our eyes open at the same time.

He tries to pull back, but I bite down harder, ensuring my claim is resolute.

He'll forever wear this mark on his tongue, and some rebellious part of me is *very* pleased by that notion.

A rebellious and possessive part of me, I decide. Because I'm also ridiculously happy that he'll never be able to kiss anyone else without thinking about *me*.

His gaze narrows.

Mine narrows right back at him.

Then I release his tongue from between my teeth.

He pulls back, a growl rumbling through his chest.

"I'm not sorry," I tell him before he can speak. "Whether you like me or not, you're *my* alpha. Not even my death can change that."

He gapes at me. "You think I want to kill you?"

"I don't know. Do you?"

"Fuck, Aurora," he curses, jerking back and away from me. "I don't know where I went wrong with you, but I've clearly fucked this up if you think I could kill you." He leaves the bed, his fingers running through his hair as he paces.

Then he shakes his head.

And leaves the room.

I lie on the bed for a long moment, frowning while I wait for him to return from the sitting area.

But the sound of the bedroom door slamming shut is all I hear.

"Lazarus?" I call after him. It's a stupid desire. Except there's a naïve part of me that hopes he tried to leave and couldn't.

However, I slide off the bed to trail after him and find that he did, in fact, leave.

Crap.

I grab the back of my neck, irritated with myself. But also with him. With all of this. With *everything.*

"*Ugh.*" I stalk over to grab my phone, curious as to what he did to it.

And find that he sent three messages to Luna.

Lark: Hello, Luna. My name is Laz. I apologize for listening in on your conversation with Ms. Bianchi. It was rude of me. And I'm sorry for commandeering your friend's phone to send this message. However, "hate" is a strong word, and I feel the need to correct it.

Lark: I don't "hate" Aurora. I admire her. I'm obsessed with her. And I'm rather certain I'm in love with her. She's strong, independent, and intelligent. She's also beautiful and not afraid to stand up to the pack. The first time we met, actually, she pulled a gun on me.

Lark: Anyway, I just want you to know I don't "hate" her. I've clearly messed up, though. So I'm going to work on fixing that. If Aurora doesn't call you later, it's because I've occupied her time. Please forgive her. And thank you for understanding. Hopefully, we'll meet properly soon. —Laz

I blink as I reread the second message, where he says he's in love with me.

My lip trembles, the taste of his blood still on my tongue.

How can he send these messages after everything that's happened with my brother? He didn't let me join the pack meeting. He made it pretty clear he was furious with Giovanni and that he assumed I was working with my brother to hurt Johan.

Yet he wants to tell my friend he loves me?

"This doesn't make any sense," I mutter, throwing my phone down. "And you are *not* getting away from me that easily, Lazarus Ferraro."

I stomp off after him, determined to talk to him. To fix this. To… to do *something*.

Apologize, maybe.

Demand a reciprocated claim, also maybe.

Perhaps both.

Or neither.

I don't know.

But when I find him, I'll figure it out.

CHAPTER TWENTY-EIGHT

LARK

THE NEXT TIME I SEE LAZARUS, I'M GOING TO KILL HIM.

He left.

Left.

As in, vacated the estate.

And I have no idea where the fuck he went.

That was two days ago.

If he's punishing me for biting him, then consider me properly reprimanded.

Noah and Johan haven't told me anything useful. When I found them in the gym the other day, they said Lazarus stated that he needed to handle something.

That's it.

No elaboration.

The only thing I've been able to confirm is that "something" has nothing to do with Giovanni. Johan promised me that. But he wouldn't give me any additional details.

So I refused to let him and Noah stay in my room that night.

And again last night, too.

But their collective scents are driving me crazy. Plus, the

approaching deadline of my brother's arrival is looming over my head.

Gio will be here tomorrow.

Yet Lazarus is nowhere to be seen or found.

However, he's clearly coming back for the meeting. Which gives me maybe twenty-four hours to finish the statement I started working on this morning.

It's not a statement with words. But with actions.

I claimed Lazarus. He's *my* alpha. He wants to question my loyalty and run off like a coward? Fine. I'll "punish" him, too.

In my own way.

I evaluate the mess I've created of pillows, sheets, and clothing—both worn and washed. It's not enough. I need something recent.

Too bad I don't have that cum-covered shirt from the plane, I think, my lips twisting to the side.

I searched all three alphas' quarters to see if I could find something with their essence on it, but I came up empty-handed.

So I guess I'll have to craft something new later.

Tonight.

In the nest.

Once I'm done creating it.

That'll be the literal icing on top of my proverbial cake.

Especially since I'm making my nest in Lazarus Ferraro's bed.

Diving on top of the pile of blankets I've collected from the other bedrooms—the ones that belong to Noah and Johan—I start to put everything where it needs to go.

Against the headboard.

Along the sides.

The bottom of the bed—where I've set up the bench that I stole from Noah's room. That wasn't fun to drag down the hallway. But since the men have all left me alone again, I did it by myself.

Pretty sure Noah and Johan are working out. That's where they've spent most of the last two days.

Half naked.

Sparring.

Jumping rope, I think, shivering. *Shirtless. Doing rhythmic footwork… with a rope. While sweat drips down Noah's sculpted pecs onto those hard, muscular abs.*

My mouth is dry, my mind picturing him with ease. Apparently, he isn't into running or swimming or cycling or any sort of normal cardio exercise.

Nope.

He likes to jump rope to music. Like an intricate dance of hops and footwork.

And wow.

Just… just *wow*.

I watched him yesterday for an undetermined amount of time before forcing myself to leave.

It was that or yank the rope out of his hand and jump him.

Which I refuse to do until he or Johan tells me where Lazarus went. Since they're being silent, I'm being noncompliant.

Or nonsexual.

Or whatever they want to call it.

Regardless, this isn't how a pack is supposed to work. Communication is important. And they're not communicating properly. So I'm not packing properly.

Or… or *whatever* it should be called. Relationship-ing properly? Sexing properly?

I shake my head and focus on my task, ignoring my inane thoughts.

Well, not really ignoring them. I can't stop picturing Noah with that rope. *And Johan with that bō staff.*

It seems my hacker alpha isn't just good at computers. He's also a black belt martial artist.

Because of course he is. Why wouldn't he be skilled at basically everything he does?

My jaw ticks.

Do all my alphas have to be so damn perfect? So fucking attractive? So ridiculously alluring?

No wonder my heat is coming faster than expected.

I can feel it burning in my veins. I'm just hoping it'll happen *after* Gio's visit.

I should probably tell my alphas. Or maybe they already sense it.

That would explain why Noah showed up in my room first thing this morning wearing nothing but a towel. "Need anything, pet?" he asked me.

"Yes. Where's Lazarus?" I countered, causing him to sigh.

"The boss is off doing boss-related things."

I nodded. "And that's all you're going to tell me?"

"It's not my story to share, little bee. I'm sure he'll update you when he returns."

"Hmm." I slid out of bed and let him see that I'd slept naked. "Well, in that case, no, I don't need anything." I walked right past him, certain he could smell my slick. "Have a good day, *enforcer*."

His growl trailed after me to the bathroom, and I almost thought he might follow.

But he didn't.

And Johan didn't even attempt to come see me.

Which is when I crafted my idea to make a nest in Lazarus's space.

I fully intend to experience my heat right here in the middle of his bed.

If he's not here to participate, then he'll be surrounded by the scents of what happened. And *that* will be poetic justice.

I keep that thought in mind while I prepare my safe haven, my heart beating fast with excitement.

There are pieces of all my alphas in here.

It's Lazarus's bed.

I have Noah's bench.

And I put Johan's laptop on the nightstand.

Plus all their clothes and bedding throughout my pillowed heaven.

"It's perfect," I whisper.

"I disagree," a deep voice replies, causing the hairs on my nape to stand on end.

"Lazarus." The name escapes me on a breath, my body instantly on edge as I slowly turn to face him.

But then his comment registers, his *disagreement* with my statement.

I frown at him, then reevaluate the nest I'm kneeling in the middle of, searching for what's wrong with it.

Is he saying that because I made it in his bed?

The whole point was to fight back. To prove to him that I'm pack. To make him trust me.

But also to punish him for running away after I claimed him.

However, I never considered what would happen if he hated my effort.

"You don't like my nest?" I despise the hurt in my voice.

Maybe I deserve this for claiming him like I did.

Only, he's mine. He's been mine since he kidnapped me. *And he told Luna he was falling in love with me.*

I frown, utterly confused by the whiplash of emotions spiraling through me.

"Oh, I love your nest, princess," he murmurs, his fingers loosening the tie around his neck. "I merely disagreed with your assessment of it being perfect."

My frown deepens. "What's wrong with my nest?" I

demand, irritated by his evaluation. "I worked very hard to build this today."

I have no idea what time it is, but I know I've been in here for hours. And I don't appreciate him waltzing in here just to disrespect my nest.

"I can see that, Aurora. It's beautiful."

"But not perfect?" I demand, my eyebrow arching upward. "You're comparing my nest to others you've seen?"

That question makes me see red.

Because he's been with other omegas.

In their nests.

And they were better than mine?

The bastard must not see my mounting fury because he smiles and slowly takes off his jacket, the black fabric looking as expensive as the rest of him. He sets it on the bench without question, either not noticing the new furniture or not minding it.

"It's not perfect, because you're still clothed," he murmurs. "If you were kneeling like that naked with slick pouring down your thighs, *then* it would be perfect."

He finishes removing his tie and adds it to his pile on the bench, then begins to unfasten his cuff links.

"As for comparing it to other nests, that's not possible. Your nest is the first one I've ever seen, and the only one I'll ever experience." He walks around to place his cuff links on the nightstand. "Assuming I'm invited to join you, of course."

It's on the tip of my tongue to ask why he wouldn't be allowed in my safe haven when I remember why this all started.

Narrowing my gaze, I say, "I'll invite you in after you tell me why you ran away for two days."

His dark eyes meet and hold mine. "I didn't run away, Aurora. I went to make amends." He slips a hand into his pocket and pulls out his phone, then taps something on it before giving it to me. "Atonement number one."

My brow furrows as I accept his device and read the announcement on the screen. It appears to be a company memo informing everyone of a recent addition to the organization.

"Security Information Consultant," I read aloud, noting the formal title. "You're hiring me as an employee?"

"No, I'm taking you on as a *consultant.* But if you would like a different title or position, name it, and I'll make it happen."

"I don't understand," I say, setting his phone down. "Why are you hiring me?"

"Because you're amazing with technology," he replies, his nimble fingers working the buttons of his dark dress shirt.

I try not to watch. I do. But his tan skin peeks at me more and more with each unfastened layer, and all I want to do is lick him.

"I wanted to give you a permanent position in the organization," he goes on, "but Johan suggested the consultant role, as he thought you might be more comfortable helping in that capacity since it allows you freedom to pursue other avenues, if that's your wish."

Johan was right, I think, swallowing. Except… "What makes you think I want to help your organization?"

He shrugs. "If you don't want the role, you don't have to accept it. It's more of an invitation than a mandate. We want to include you in pack business, and this seemed like the best way to do that, as it'll give you unfettered access to everything Ferraro related." His eyes capture mine. "And I do mean *everything.*"

"Even the dark sides of the business?"

"Especially the dark sides of the business," he replies, and I don't miss the innuendo in his tone. It's clearly meant as a double entendre. "We don't want to hide anything from you, Aurora. You're pack."

"Am I?" I demand. "Because you left without telling me where you went. *Again.*"

He nods. "Yes, I did. And I'm sorry if that felt counterproductive to us building trust. But I was having something done that required secrecy."

"I see." I fold my arms. "I assume Noah and Johan were aware of this 'secret,' though, yes?"

Rather than answer me, he finishes unbuttoning his shirt and pulls it from his shoulders.

I'm about to tell him that sculpted abs won't distract me from my mission.

But I'm wrong.

Very wrong.

However, it's not just the abs that grab my attention, but the bandage across his chest.

I gape at him. "What the fuck happened?" I hurry toward him on the bed, awkwardly moving over the walls of my nest to the bench so I can kneel there and investigate his wound. "*Lazarus.*" My eyes widen even more. "Oh, please tell me you didn't attack Gio…"

He grunts. "If I had, I wouldn't be the one with gauze on my chest, Aurora." He grabs my wrists as I try to reach for him, his touch gentle yet firm. "I also don't intend on hurting Giovanni unless harm is warranted."

"What does that mean?"

"It means he would need to do something horrific to earn my brand of justice."

"Johan being attacked doesn't qualify?" I hedge, confused by his assessment. Noah went into a blood rage afterward. It's safe to assume my brother has more than earned the pack's wrath for his involvement in the situation.

It doesn't matter that it was meant to be a kidnapping.

The issue is that the Bianchis, who are under my brother's rule as don, put Johan in jeopardy. That has to be addressed.

"I didn't say I forgive your brother or that I'm not

displeased. I'm furious. And if Johan had been injured, I might feel differently. But I understand that Giovanni wanted to set up a trade. Bastian is the one who chose to alter the course of the assignment. He paid the ultimate price for that mistake."

I swallow. "But the Bianchi advisors set it all up..."

"And they will answer to our pack for that grievance," Lazarus assures me. "But you're a Bianchi, Aurora. That matters, and it changes things. So we'll attempt to work this out between the families and go from there."

I chew my lower lip. "Okay, if this isn't from Gio, then who were you fighting?" I again try to touch him, but he holds me back with his grip on my wrists. "Who hurt you?"

He smiles. "I hurt myself, darling."

My eyes widen. "*What*? Why the hell would you do that?"

"Atonement," he murmurs, using that word again. Then he releases me and takes a step back. "The gauze wasn't actually necessary, as there's a plastic film beneath, but I wanted to slowly reveal this to you."

And I'm frowning again. "Okay..."

He starts to unwind the fabric from his body, allowing me to see the plastic he mentioned.

Which shows hints of dark ink beneath.

My lips part. *A tattoo.*

But I can't quite make it out yet. "Is that... a spider?"

"A black widow, yeah," he says, the bottom half on display just above his right nipple.

However, he's nowhere near done.

He keeps unraveling until I realize the black widow is hanging from an *L*.

"Oh my God," I breathe. "You tattooed my name across your chest?"

And not my real name. But *Lark*. My hacker pseudonym. My chosen identity.

"Yes." He finishes revealing the beautiful script. It takes up all the space between his collarbone and the top of his pecs, making the letters huge. "Your bite marks are not visible unless I stick out my tongue. So I wanted something more prominent to show the world I'm yours."

I blink.

Then I reach up to gingerly trace the letters through the plastic.

"I wanted it to be a surprise," he says softly. "That's why Johan and Noah kept my confidence. We weren't trying to hide anything from you. I promise."

Tears fill my gaze.

Which is ridiculous.

This isn't something to cry about.

I'm just… I'm just so touched by his gesture. And also relieved.

"I thought you ran away from me," I admit in a whisper.

"I would never run from you," he promises, his palm settling over mine and flattening it to his chest. "You're my omega. My heart. There's nothing you could do to change that." His opposite hand grasps my chin, forcing my gaze to meet his. "I don't care if you helped Giovanni organize the kidnapping. In fact, I would respect you for it."

"But I didn't have anything to do with it, Lazarus."

He nods. "I believe you."

"Do you?" I ask, incredulous. "Because I don't think you do at all."

He cups my cheek, his opposite hand releasing mine so he can wrap his arm around my lower back. "Aurora, trust takes time. But you've said more than once that you didn't have anything to do with it. And I'm choosing to believe you."

I nibble my lower lip, considering his words. "Okay…"

He arches a brow. "It's my prerogative, darling. Just as it's your choice to believe me when I say I wouldn't care even if you were involved. That's the heart of trust—having faith in each other's words and actions."

He's right, of course.

Only, it's difficult to *choose* to accept someone else's word at face value.

Except, he hasn't given me a reason not to.

If anything, he's provided a myriad of examples of why I should think the best of him.

He's defied every expectation. The whole pack has, actually.

And he didn't run away. He went to have my name tattooed on his chest while also apparently giving me a job.

"One more thing," he says, his hand leaving my cheek as he reaches around me and into the nest.

I don't understand what he's doing until his phone appears in his hand.

"That farmland we flew off of last week has a lot of potential. So I have some designs I need you to review for our Colorado home." He looks up at me. "I assume you want a place where we can all stay to be close to your Widows, right? For when we visit?"

I swallow, my heart suddenly in my throat. "You're going to build a place outside of Widows Peak?"

"I thought you would prefer that more than us being inside Widows Peak, but we can do that, too." His lips twist a little. "It'll be a bit of a downgrade from what we were thinking. Although, we'll divide our time between there, New York City, and here. So it should be—"

I launch myself at him and kiss him. *Hard.*

His phone slips from his hand as he catches me, the dull thud barely registering above the rapid beating in my ears.

Never in a million years did I think he would allow me to return to Widows Peak, let alone agree to live there part of the time. Or near there.

I would be fine with a few days a year, if that's what he'll give me.

Only, he seems to be offering a lot more than that.

This man.

These men.

My alphas.

I don't know when I fell for them. But I have.

And it's so much more than a scent match.

These men are rewriting everything I expected from a mafia pack.

It could all be a lie. However, it's like what Lazarus just said—it's my choice to believe them.

I do, I decide. *I do*.

It feels like I'm agreeing to a lot more than simply putting faith in Lazarus. Maybe I am. Maybe I'm not.

It doesn't matter.

I just want to exist in this moment.

And invite him into my new nest…

CHAPTER TWENTY-NINE
LAZ

AURORA'S LEGS SQUEEZE MY HIPS, HER PUSSY HOT THROUGH her tiny shorts.

Her heat is imminent, something I realized the moment I walked upstairs. Her scent was so fucking strong that I nearly came in my pants.

I shot a text to Noah asking him why the fuck he didn't warn me.

His response was a kissy face.

Jackass.

I decide to return the favor by not inviting him to come play in our omega's new nest. He'll figure it out when he's done exercising with Johan.

Until then, I'll take care of our omega.

"You're going to have to talk to me about limits," I say against her mouth. "I want to make sure we properly care for you during your estrus."

She shivers. "I don't know what limits to set." Her arms are around my neck as she leans back to look at me. "I just want to be claimed. That's all I ask."

My chest rumbles in response, my grip on her hips tensing. "Claimed while in heat or before you lose your senses?"

"Before," she answers immediately.

I nod. "By all three of us?"

"Yes." There isn't a hint of hesitation in her features. Which is exactly what I want to see. "How do you feel about Noah and me sharing you? Knotting you at the same time?"

I don't bother to ask how she feels about me and Johan having her together. She handled Noah and Johan together without even blinking. Thus, she'll be fine with me and Johan.

Noah and I, however, will provide a very different kind of experience.

"He's going to want to stretch your cunt and see if you can take our knots together." It's a blunt statement, but a true one. "Likely your ass, too. I need to know you're okay with us… trying. Or if you want us to take you solo rather than as a unit."

"He…" She swallows. "When he said double-knotting, I assumed he meant one of you in the front and the other… in my mouth or… or elsewhere."

"Oh, he means that, too, darling," I promise her. "But I know Noah. He's going to want to see how much you can take. And I fully expect him to demand sharing your cunt with me or Johan. Likely me."

Mostly to push my boundaries as well as Aurora's.

Which is fine.

I welcome the experience. But only if she desires it.

The way her thighs are clenching around me right now—as well as the fresh wave of slick dampening her shorts—suggests she's interested. Though, I want to hear her say it.

"I could barely take just him and Johan," she whispers.

I nod. "They're big." I press against her. "And I'm the biggest." Not a statement designed to stroke my ego. Just a fact. "But when you're in heat, your body will be capable of taking a lot more than you can imagine."

I've never actually pleasured an omega through her heat.

Neither have the others. It's something we've all waited to do with our mate.

Which means we're going to rut her until she can't walk.

Because we have *years* of pent-up cravings to take out on her.

I say that as well, needing her to understand just how intense the next week of her life is going to be. "It will be hard for us to hold back," I inform her. "However, if you set limits, we will respect them."

One of us might have to remain sane and fight the urge to rut—and that someone will likely be me, as I'm the pack leader—but we'll do whatever she needs us to do to keep her safe.

"Everything you want to do to me will be for mutual pleasure, right?" she asks, her voice soft.

"Absolutely," I tell her. "Noah and I have some sadistic preferences, as we both get off on power plays that involve pain. Though, our true desire is to provoke a euphoric response to that pain."

The way her brow furrows suggests she doesn't understand.

Which stirs an idea in my head.

"Would you like a demonstration, Aurora?" I ask softly, my thumbs drawing slow circles against her hips. "Perhaps an introduction into what I mean when I refer to my sadistic cravings?"

Her pretty brown eyes study me for a moment. "I can handle anything you want to do to me, Lazarus."

My lips curl. "Of that I have no doubt, Ms. Bianchi. But it doesn't hurt to have a better understanding of what I want to do to you, what *we* might do to you together. Yes?"

A fresh wave of honeyed slick flavors the air, making my mouth water for a taste.

"How about we play?" I suggest, my voice deepening as my knot begins to throb. "And if you want me to stop, say *wasp*." I pull that word out of my memory because Johan mentioned that he used it to describe Noah when sending him off to retrieve her from Widows Peak.

It's also a play on her beelike scent.

"Wasp," she echoes, her nose crinkling. "Seems like a strange term to use."

"That's exactly what makes it a safe word, Aurora." I press my lips to hers, giving her a sweet kiss. "The point of it is to make everything cease between us and to tell me I've gone too far. You can use it with Noah and Johan, too." I kiss her again. "We don't want to hurt you, darling. Not really, anyway."

She gives me a dubious look. "That sounds ominous."

"It should," I murmur, my hands slipping down to her thighs to pry them away from my body.

She starts to slide down, but I grab her hips and toss her into the nest.

"Strip," I tell her. "I want you naked and wet for me in the center of that beautiful nest."

The way she glares at me from her back makes my dick even harder.

"Now, Aurora." I place my hand on my belt. "I expect you to go up on your knees again and bend over so I can see that slick pussy. *That* is how I want to be invited into your bed."

Technically, it's *my* bed. But she's marked it as her own.

And I fucking love that.

She can have whatever she wants from me.

Bed. Room. *Knot.*

Fuck, I'll even hand over the entire Ferraro fortune. She can buy hundreds of cities and turn them into omega safe havens.

All she has to do is name her wish, and I'll grant it.

Aurora slowly sits up, her gaze challenging mine.

I wait.

Then I make a show of unfastening my belt. She watches

every move, her tongue sneaking out to dampen her lower lip as I pop the button on my pants.

I gradually draw down the zipper, careful because I'm not wearing anything underneath.

And smile when she takes in an audible breath.

Her tits move with the inhale, her aroma deepening as she claims my space with her sweet slick.

"Aurora," I murmur, toeing off my shoes, then bending to remove my socks. "If you're not naked before I am, I'm going to be very disappointed."

She's staring at my cock when I straighten again, her hands still unmoving.

"If you want my knot, then you need to obey, princess."

"And if I don't?"

"Then I'll pin you to the bed and make you watch while I pump my seed all over your face," I tell her honestly.

"That sounds like a reward."

I smile. "You'll feel otherwise when I don't let you finish, too."

Her gaze smolders in response. "You wouldn't do that."

"I absolutely would, princess. Test me and find out."

What I don't clarify is that I would eventually coax an orgasm from her. And then I would keep her in a state of orgasmic bliss for hours until I felt she'd learned her lesson on obedience.

That's part of the pleasure-pain process.

At some point, the climaxes feel so good that they're almost agonizing. I can't wait to introduce her to that sensation. It's going to blow her fucking mind.

"What's it going to be, Aurora?" I ask, my hand on the top of my pants as I begin to push down. "Are you going to be a good girl? Or are you going to be defiant and force me to teach you a different kind of lesson?"

She swallows, her gaze running over my body with interest.

I honestly have no idea which way this is going to go.

She could easily choose to misbehave, which is part of what makes this dynamic with her so exciting. Most omegas simply submit.

But not her.

She likes to challenge her pack. To make us work for the reward of her submission.

I'm happy to do whatever it takes to bring her to her knees.

Including following through on my threat.

"All right," I murmur, pushing my pants down. "We'll do this the hard way."

I can see her nipples protruding from beneath her tank top.

She likes defying me.

Likes that she doesn't know what's about to happen.

"Remind me of your safe word, Ms. Bianchi."

She frowns, and the expression is almost adorable. "You're the one who gave it to me."

"I know. I want to make sure you remember it."

Her eyes return to that burning smolder as lightning flashes in her gaze. "*Wasp*."

"Well, at least I know you were listening," I say. "Now invite me into your nest."

She considers me, then goes up onto her knees and pulls her tank top over her head.

For a moment, I'm dumbfounded.

Because she just fought me on the undressing part, basically inviting me to come all over her pretty face instead of in her cunt like I originally intended to do.

My lips part when she removes her tiny shorts, too.

She throws them at me, and I catch them, my need to smell her arousal overriding every instinct. I inhale deeply, then growl as she goes up on her hands and knees and presents her wet pussy.

Just like I told her to do before.

"*Fuck*, Aurora." I don't even know what to do with this sassy female.

She disobeyed me, just to obey me on her own terms.

"You said this was how to perfect my nest." She glances back at me over her shoulder, her expression exuding an innocence I almost believe. Except her brown irises are radiating triumph.

Vixen, I think, hissing a breath between my teeth.

"Am I doing it correctly, *sir*?"

Jesus. Fucking. Christ.

She's going to make me come like a newly presenting alpha.

"Are you going to accept my invitation, alpha?" she asks, her sultry voice making my cock leak with precum.

"*Aurora*," I growl, which makes her pretty pussy glisten in response.

This female is threatening my control, something no one in my history has *ever* done.

All I want to do is mount her.

Ride her.

Rut her.

But I promised this female a lesson.

Only, I have no idea which one to deliver. She disobeyed me, then executed my requests fucking flawlessly.

She's infuriating.

She's stunning.

She's perfect.

I crawl onto the bed from the bench—something I recognize as belonging to Noah—and prowl toward her, my dick bobbing ominously.

She's still watching me with that sensual expression, her ass high, her cunt weeping.

I grab her hips from behind, line myself up with her

entrance, and thrust into her without preparing her for my size.

Her gorgeous eyes widen, a scream escaping her as she falls forward onto the mattress. "*Lazarus.*"

"Sorry, darling, did that hurt?" I ask, my voice a growl. I pull out and do it again.

She claws at the bedding in response, her own growls escaping her.

She's *pissed*.

As she should be.

I'm sure that hurt.

Her body is made for me, though. Made for this. And she's on the edge of her heat, which means she's extra wet and already loosening for her alpha's knot.

Which is why her furious sounds turn to moans within seconds. All it takes is a few well-positioned thrusts that hit her G-spot, and her anger melts into passion.

Just as it should.

Bending over her, I press my lips to her ear and whisper, "*That* is an example of sadism, princess. And you took your introduction to it *very* well." I kiss her thundering pulse.

"That *hurt*," she snarls at me.

"Mmm, yes," I hum. "But how does it feel now, darling?" I drag my dick almost completely out of her, then shove right back in, hitting her so deep that she shudders.

"*Good*," she moans. "*Again*."

"No." I pull out of her and flip her. "I'm not done playing with you yet."

She issues some sort of retort that I don't catch because I kiss her. Hard. My tongue spearing her lips and forcing her to revisit the claim marks she left on me.

Her protests die again, her resulting pleasure warming the air between us as she sucks on the tip of my tongue.

She likes that she claimed me there. I do, too. I'll forever feel her presence now. Just talking reminds me of her vicious little bite. And I fucking love it.

When she threatens to do it again with her teeth, I pull back and draw my lips down her neck to her luscious tits.

Her fingers thread through my hair, tugging at the strands like she's trying to dictate what I do to her.

"Topping from the bottom can be hot," I say against her nipple. "But, princess, *I* am the alpha here." I sink my teeth into her breast to the point of pain, but I don't break the skin. Because this isn't where I want to mark her.

Though, I do leave a nice red welt behind, one I lave with my tongue before repeating the action against her opposite tit.

"Lazarus," she pants, squirming beneath me.

"Oh, darling, we're only beginning. I'm going to make you *beg* before I let you come." I expect tears. Pleas. *A promise to do whatever I want if I let her fall apart.*

She's going to be a writhing, soaking mess before I put my cock back inside and knot her to oblivion.

I want her to scream so fucking loud that Noah will hear her in the basement and run up here to join.

Then I'll get to share her limits with him.

Of which there appear to be none.

But we won't be exploiting that.

We'll slowly introduce her to our preferences, just as I'm doing now, and let her tell us if it's too much.

However, I really fucking hope she'll let us double-knot her cunt. It'll be a first for all of us.

Maybe Johan can take her mouth at the same time.

Or, hell, I might even let him take my ass.

That's how much I want to be inside her with Noah.

One step at a time, I think, my hand wandering up her leg to the sweetness between her thighs. My other palm goes to her breast, squeezing the fleshy mound while I abuse her opposite nipple with my teeth and tongue.

She's panting. Shaking. Whispering my name.

Not enough, I think, deciding to drive her mad.

I slide three fingers into her tight sheath, needing her to feel full but not quite full enough.

I curl the digits in a way that strokes her G-spot while my thumb plays with her clit.

It's just enough to coax her into a blissful state without letting her fall off the cliff.

Pairing that with my assault on her pretty rosebud nipples, she starts to issue demands.

Demands followed by pleas.

Pleas followed by vows of killing me if I don't give her more.

Vows followed by whimpers.

Which lead to begging phrases.

And only then do I kiss a path down to her gorgeous pussy.

"You're so fucking wet, darling," I tell her, showing her my soaked hand. "But all this slick is just the beginning, sweet girl. I want this bed *saturated* with your need before I let you come. So give me *more.*" I verbalize the word with a deep growl, one meant to entice an omega.

Specifically, *my* omega.

She growls back in response, but her body does exactly what I command it to do—*it fucking weeps*.

So I rumble again, this time with my mouth against her sensitive nub.

Then I push four fingers into her, working her up for a fist.

Because if I have it my way, we'll introduce her to the double-knotting before she goes into heat.

Or maybe that'll be what coaxes her into it.

I don't fucking care so long as we get there.

"*Lazarus*," she hisses, jerking beneath me as I push her further with my hand and mouth, sucking and plunging into her soaked cunt.

She's losing herself to the lust, just like she will to her heat.

But I know she's still with me because of the way she curses.

I smile against her core, my tongue teasing her throbbing clit as I bring her close to the edge for what has to be the tenth or eleventh time. Not that I'm counting. I wait until she clamps down on me, then pause and only apply the barest of pressure to her pulsing nub.

"*Ah!*" she screams at me, making me smile. "*If you don't knot me…*"

I wait, but all that follows is a bunch of unintelligible words.

"Finish that threat, darling," I say, edging her some more. "I want to hear what you'll do to me if I don't let you come."

Her response is a groan, one that turns into a furious grumble when I repeat the exercise again.

And again.

And *again.*

"Lazarus, please," she cries, her body shaking with the effort of trying to come and not being allowed to.

"Please what?" I ask softly, the words a purr against her damp flesh.

"Please let me come!" she screams, her fingers yanking at the strands of my hair. "Or… or I'll do it!"

"You won't," I murmur, catching her hand when she tries and pushing it against her belly. "Keep it there, Aurora, or I'll make this worse."

She lifts her head to glare down at me, her eyes positively beautiful with tears in their depths.

I purr again, approving of the sight and the murderous way she's looking at me. "This is what we call 'edging,'" I inform her softly. "You earned this punishment when you didn't obey me earlier. But don't worry. You'll thank me for it soon enough."

Because her orgasm is going to be the most intense one she's ever experienced.

"This is what you like? Torturing me?"

I smile against her pussy. "Yes and no," I say, purposely brushing her tender bud with the words. "I want to drive you to a point of agony so great that your pleasure brings you back to life and redefines your meaning of breathing."

I give her a kiss, adding some tongue, causing her head to fall back as a moan escapes her.

That moan turns into a real sob when I stop, my fingers stilling inside her.

"Lazarus," she breathes. "*Please*, Lazarus. Please let me come!"

"That wasn't the point of the experience, though, was it?" I whisper. "I wanted to introduce you to agonized ecstasy, hmm?"

Every part of her stiffens. "Lazarus…"

"Now would be a good time to use your safe word, Aurora," I tell her honestly. "Because I'm about to deliver your lesson now."

She seems to freeze, then ever so slowly, she looks down at me, her face a beautiful mess of tears and pink skin from blushing.

I wait.

But all she does is lie back down before saying, "Teach me, sir."

Fuck. This woman's mouth and the words that she speaks…

"You're perfect," I inform her, loving that she knew exactly what to say to make my knot pulse with need. "So. Fucking. Perfect."

I close my lips around her clit and circle it with my tongue, preparing her once more.

Her insides squeeze my fingers, her orgasm already mounting.

However, just before she reaches the peak, I *bite* down.

She comes alive beneath me, her resulting scream louder

than anything else she's given me, and I hold her down while I finish leaving my mark right on her fucking pussy.

"*Lazarus*!" She sounds ready to kill me.

But then the rapture hits, the claiming bite accompanied by a slew of hot emotions and euphoric sensations.

My name leaves her again, only this time it's on a moan of extreme pleasure, her torment erased by the oblivion crashing through her.

I smile, wanting to keep her in this state for as long as physically possible.

So I crawl up her vibrating form, remove my hand, and replace my fingers with my cock.

Then I *rut.*

Fucking her hard.

Hitting her G-spot.

Rubbing her abused nub.

Holding her in a rapturous release while I take her to new heights.

She claws at my back, tears streaming down her face as she tells me to stop. But on the heels of that statement, she says she'll kill me if I listen to her. "*Keep going*," she demands, making me chuckle. "*Fuck, Lazarus. Fuck*!"

I don't bother to point out that I'm already doing that.

I just growl her name and tell her to keep coming for me like the good fucking girl that she is.

"You feel so tight, princess. I can't wait to own you with my knot. Then I'm going to flip you and let Noah try to force himself inside you, too. Whether it be in your ass or your cunt, I'm not sure. But we're going to take you together."

"Fuck yeah, we are," he says, clearly having heard our omega's mating call, just like I wanted.

I felt him enter a few minutes ago, which is why I chose to utter those words.

I want him to know that he's absolutely invited to join, just as soon as I finish.

"You're going to take my knot and keep coming, Aurora," I say against her parted lips. "You understand me, darling? I want you in this state for *hours*. And I want to feel Noah inside you with me."

She shudders and moans, her head shaking a little like she's in denial. But I swivel my hips in a way that has her staying lost to her euphoria.

"Fuck, it's like she's in heat already," Noah breathes.

"She's not," I murmur. "She's just fucking made for this."

The vixen clenches her walls around me like she wants to voice her own opinion and prove me right with her pussy.

"Keep massaging me like that," I demand. "Beg me for my knot, princess. *Beg. Me.*"

She starts to cry again, the pleasure too much.

Poor darling. We've only just begun.

She won't be able to walk when we're done.

That's fine.

I'll carry her wherever she wants to go.

"Lazarus," she whimpers, her hips bucking into mine. "It's too much. It's… I can't… I don't… Oh… *Oh God…*"

Her insides clamp down again as she spirals deeper into the throes of another orgasm.

"Impossible," she breathes, arching into me.

"You have no idea what we're going to do to you," I whisper back to her, very aware that what she's experiencing is absolutely fucking possible.

And I'm about to make it that much more intense.

I lick up the tears on her cheek, then take her mouth with my tongue and force her to join me in a cataclysmic state of bliss.

With my hands on her hips, I drive myself deep until my knot starts to pulsate and shift. She's begging me to stop now, but not saying her safe word. She's just lost to the darkness. To the intensity. To the *craze*.

Because she's also telling me to keep going, like she can't quite make up her mind.

Then her nails scratch down my back as she fights, her legs tightening around mine.

And she *growls*.

"*Fuck*, that's hot," Noah says, his presence right beside us as he falls into the nest. "Knot her, boss. *Knot her*."

He doesn't need to tell me twice.

Nor does he need to say it at all.

Because I already fucking am.

Our bodies lock together as my orgasm hits with a tidal wave of fervor. Heat. *A lavalike claim.*

I growl, my lips suddenly on her neck.

And I bite *again*.

Because once wasn't enough.

I need this omega to be mine. To know she's pack. To believe I want her. Respect her. *Love her.*

She screams in response, her body trembling violently. Only to go quiet as she passes out from the pleasure.

But I know she'll be right back with us.

And when that happens, we'll begin again.

With a double-knotting.

Right in her fucking cunt…

CHAPTER THIRTY
NOAH

OUR OMEGA LOOKS AMAZING ON LAZ'S COCK.

He's rotated to his back, holding her to his chest as he continues to come inside her. Yet somehow he's able to talk and give us an update on her chosen safe word, as well as the lack of limits.

"We'll ease her into it," he says, his eyes closed while he strokes her spine.

Johan is to his left, having run up the stairs with me when we heard our female screaming with need. We stripped in the fucking hallway, ready to barge into her room. Only, her scent was stronger near Laz's quarters.

I knew she was playing in here today, but I wasn't sure what chaos she was crafting for Laz.

Now I see that it was a nest.

In his fucking bed.

With my fucking bench.

And all of our fucking clothes.

"What did she say about breeding?" Johan asks, the question taking me by surprise. "Does she want a baby?"

My dick is fucking hard with the notion of our pet growing with our seed. "Oh, hell yes. *Dibs*."

Laz's eyes open. "I'm literally filling her right now."

"She's not in heat yet," I point out.

"Still, you're *not* calling dibs."

"Do we even know if she wants a baby?" Johan interjects, being the voice of reason as always.

"We didn't discuss that aspect," Laz says, sighing. "Only limits, double-knotting, and a brief lesson on sadism."

"Brief," our pet repeats, sounding half drunk with lust. "That's considered brief?" It comes out in a mumble. "Mmm. What's long?"

Laz chuckles, his lips parting on a reply.

But I beat him to it by saying, "My cock. That's long." I lean in to kiss her shoulder, which causes her eyes to flutter open as she stares at me. "Hey there, gorgeous pet. Can I put a baby in you?"

Her pupils blow wide. "I... *What?*"

"A baby," I repeat as Johan makes a strangled noise of discontent.

"Noah is trying to call dibs on whose seed you're going to take during your heat," Laz informs her, his tone flat. "I already said that's not how this is going to work."

"And your bossy vote doesn't count," I tell him. "This is up to our little bee." I waggle my brows at her. "So, you, me, and a baby bee?" My lips part as I picture it. "Oh, fuck *yes*. I will one thousand percent be dressing you up as a mama bee for Halloween."

I sit up to look at Johan.

"Can you picture it?" I demand. "Her cute baby bump with a bee on it?"

That has to be the most adorable fucking image I've ever envisioned.

"We could even give her a little stinger, like a blade," I go on, loving this concept. "I'll make it sharp and—"

"*Noah*," Laz growls at me. "Can we find out first if Aurora even wants a child?"

My lips curl down, my brow furrowing as I return to my lounging position beside them on the bed. Meeting our pet's gaze, I say, "Sorry, pet. I got excited."

Here she is, still coming on Laz's cock, and all I can think about is getting in there with my own seed to make a baby.

"If we have a little omega, I hope it's a girl with your hair and eyes," I whisper, dreaming again about the potential future. "Although, Johan's eyes are pretty, too. I guess Laz's are all right."

"Jackass," he mutters.

"Hey, you can give the kid your tan, though. That's fine."

Laz rolls his eyes and shakes his head. "Aurora, if you want us to make arrangements—"

"That's not necessary," she cuts him off, glancing up at him with a lazy smile before focusing on me again. "If the pack wants a baby, I want a baby."

"The pack wants what you want," Johan says before I can start celebrating.

Aurora lifts her head and looks at tech boy. "I've never really considered it before because I didn't have a pack. But now that I do, I… I wouldn't mind a baby, too." She looks at Laz. "It's all about having faith, right?"

He smiles at her, the comment clearly related to something they've discussed. "Yes, princess. That's exactly right." He threads his fingers through her hair and pulls her into a kiss. "I've brought them up to speed on your limits. But still need to discuss the double-knotting."

"You only want to do that so our sperm have to fight for dominance in her womb," I say, narrowing my gaze.

"I don't care who impregnates her, jackass. We're a pack. The baby will be *ours* regardless of who the father is," he bites back at me. "And I want to double-knot her because I want to see if she can take us."

I consider his words, then admire our omega's sweet body. "Oh, she can handle us." She doesn't really have a choice since we're pack. And I'm *dying* to share her with Laz. "Tell him, little bee. Tell the bossy don that you're more than ready for both of us."

She glances between us, her expression holding a touch of uncertainty until she locks eyes with Laz.

He's staring at her with a hint of concern, which royally pisses me off. Because she was literally born for this. She's our scent match. Fate wouldn't put us all together if she couldn't indulge in joint knotting with the pack.

Laz knows that. Yet the dick is looking at her like he expects her to say no.

She sees it, too, because her jaw tightens as her gaze narrows. "I'm not afraid of taking you both."

"You sure?" Laz presses, making me want to punch him in the fucking face.

"Yes, *sir*, I am," she sasses him. Then she focuses on me. "Stretch me. I want to take both of you."

My lips curl, satisfaction slamming into my gut. "Fuck yes, little bee. I can't wait to feel you swarm between us."

She rolls her eyes at my pun.

But I'm too excited to care and already moving to kneel behind her. Meeting Laz's gaze, I try to figure out where he wants my legs.

Which is when I realize the bastard just played our pet.

Because he's fucking smirking.

He was never concerned. He just pretended to be because he knew it would provoke our pet into accepting his challenge.

Well played, I tell him with a glance.

The fucker winks at me. Any other time, I would growl in annoyance. But right now, I'm too fucking pleased to react to his cocky bullshit.

"My knot is about to subside," he tells me.

"Sounds like a you problem, boss," I reply. "Better keep yourself hard because I need you to stay inside her while I stretch her."

"That won't be a problem." His voice is all confidence. "Come here and kiss me, Aurora." He yanks her up to him and takes her mouth, causing her to moan in response.

Seeing her like this, all spread out over him, has me briefly considering taking her ass instead of her pussy.

It would be a somewhat gentler way to introduce her to being shared by me and Laz.

But neither of us is particularly gentle.

Besides, Johan has more than earned first anal, given that he's sitting this one out.

Or, well, he's not necessarily *sitting* so much as *lounging*. Though, he seems perfectly content to watch, his hand stroking his stiff dick while he observes Laz and Aurora's embrace.

"Want to help me prepare our pet?" I ask him.

He leans in to press a kiss to her shoulder, then sits up and starts kissing a path down her back. I move to let him work. I thought he would offer a literal hand, but it seems he has something else in mind.

Laz growls when Johan reaches Aurora's bottom half, his mouth and hands doing something I can't quite see from this angle.

He's getting very friendly with her adorable rump, though his mouth seems to be focused closer to the place where she's joined to Laz.

I move to get a better view, realizing that he's licking Laz's balls and continuing up to where they're connected, lapping up her slick and the alpha's spilled seed.

But he's also using the fluid to push his fingers inside her, right along Laz's shaft.

"Fuck, that's hot," I groan, grabbing my knot and giving it a squeeze. "You should put your dick in her first, help ease her into taking me."

He's thicker than me, but I'm longer. It'll be a good way to ensure she's ready to take me.

"Spread your legs," I tell him, moving down to his groin. "I'm going to suck on you while you prepare her for us."

He growls, his agreement palpable as he shifts his body to give me access to his dick.

I don't go easy, just take him into my mouth and deep-throat him in the first go.

"*Fuck*," he breathes against Aurora's slick core.

"Focus on your task, tech boy, and let me work," I demand.

Then I take him even deeper and swallow around his head.

He hisses, so I drag my teeth along his engorged shaft and chuckle when he rumbles in response.

Aurora releases a little sound, one that suggests Johan may have been a little rough.

"Sorry," he whispers, the apology confirming my suspicion.

"She can take it," Laz assures him. "Right, princess?"

"Yes, sir," she replies, the title making my dick leak.

I like hearing "sir" on her tongue even if it's not directed at me.

Rather than comment on it aloud, I celebrate my pleasure by sucking hard on Johan.

He curses, a bit of precum slipping from his head.

I debate catching it on my tongue and bringing it up for Aurora to swallow, but instead keep it for myself. Maybe Johan can come down her throat while Laz and I knot her.

I daydream about it as I continue to work Johan with my mouth, my mind losing track of reality and time until he's forcefully pulling me off his dick.

I'm about to issue a protest when he moves upward to align himself with our omega's cunt and starts to work himself inside of her.

Laz curses and Aurora moans, the combination making my knot pulse against my palm.

It's just so fucking hot.

I give myself a good pump, my eyes fixated on the mess of limbs before me.

"Shh," Laz hushes. "Relax your inner muscles, princess. Let us both in."

She starts to whine, resulting in Johan purring as he leans down to kiss her shoulder. "You can do this, Lark," he encourages her.

Our girl starts to shake her head.

I frown and crawl toward her on the bed. "Need a distraction, little bee?" I ask, taking hold of her hair and guiding her face to my cock. "Here. Help me get good and ready to knot your pussy."

Her eyes widen, her nostrils flaring.

"Trust me," I tell her, my knuckles brushing her cheek.

She's a defiant little thing who loves a challenge. If I try to choke her with my cock, she'll forget what's happening below. I'm sure of it.

"Feel free to leave some claim marks on me, too," I encourage her. "I would love a ring of teeth around my shaft."

She gapes at me.

I press my head to her lips instead.

"Open up," I demand.

She rebels with a growl, then moans as Laz reaches between them to pet her where she needs it.

Her mouth parts, granting me unintentional access that I fully take advantage of. She chokes, her pupils dilating as she glares up at me.

"You can bite, pet," I remind her. "Of course, I'll enjoy that."

Her glower positively simmers, causing my balls to throb as Johan continues to work himself into her slick heat.

"Fuck, this feels so good," Laz says, arching up into her.

She squirms in response, a hint of panic crossing her

features. I study her reactions, ensuring we're not taking this too far.

And sure enough, pleasure chases away her worries, her cheeks reddening as she starts to lose herself to the rocking motions surrounding her.

Johan is fully inside her now, sharing her pussy with Laz. The two of them are making her feel good while I use her mouth.

It's an erotic dance and just the beginning of what's to come. Her heat is almost here, her sense of awareness slowly slipping.

I just hope she claims us first. "I want to feel your teeth in my skin so fucking bad, pet," I admit. "Do you want me to beg?"

Her eyes are on me, her arousal palpable. She can't reply with my dick in her mouth, but she doesn't have to. I can see the response in her eyes.

"Please, pet," I whisper. "Please mark me with that pretty mouth."

She draws her teeth along my shaft, teasing me without biting.

I want to curse.

I want to growl.

I want to *purr*. Because I fucking love that she's trying to top me while being taken by three alphas.

"Careful, little bee, or you're going to make me come down that pretty throat of yours. And then we'll have to start over." I mean every word. I'm so fucking close to drowning her with my seed.

"Stop fucking her mouth and lie on the bed," Laz tells me, his order nearly eliciting a growl in response.

Of course he chooses *now* to assert his dominance.

"Always making the rules," I mutter, sliding free from Aurora's lips. "I'm only obeying because I want that sweet pussy around my cock."

Johan is the next to move, not waiting for Laz to command him. His dick is glistening from Aurora's arousal, making me sit up and grab his hips to yank him toward me.

He groans as I lick the slick clean from his shaft, her flavor on his skin my new favorite dessert.

But Laz shoves the man away from me and uses a hand to knock me back to the bed.

I growl, ready to return the favor with my fist, only to have Aurora suddenly in my lap.

"Put him inside you," Laz demands. "Right fucking now, princess." He's already shifting to take a position behind her as she struggles to obey, her limbs shaking with exquisite need.

Our omega grabs my knot to position me, her brown eyes meeting mine.

I swallow, utterly lost for this woman, and I let her see that on my face. Let her see her effect on me. Let her *know* how I feel with my gaze alone.

Love.

Adoration.

Obsession.

Possession.

I want her to know it all. To feel it all. To embrace it all.

She shudders once more, then begins to slide down on my shaft, her wet heat a kiss I'll forever crave. Her body falls over mine, her mouth on my neck and trailing a path to my pec.

I wonder if she's about to lick my nipple, something I never thought to ask for, when suddenly her teeth are in my skin and the little rebel is *biting* me.

Pleasure shoots through every inch of my being, spreading through my veins like rapid fire and making me growl with euphoric need.

A claim.

My omega has claimed *me.*

Right over my damn heart.

How fucking appropriate.

"I'm going to tattoo that to my chest," I hiss out, thrusting up into her at the same time Laz lines up his cock with her opening. "*Fuck*, Aurora." I can't fucking breathe. I'm so elated. So proud. *So damn hard…*

I grab her hair and yank her up to me, then sit up as far as I can so I can sink my teeth into her tit.

It forces Laz to push out of her, the angle not conducive to what he needs. But this isn't about him. It's about me and my omega. He can wait a fucking second.

She screams, her pussy walls closing around my shaft as she contracts and writhes.

Then Laz, being the dick he is, pushes her back down, his hand over mine in her hair as he forces her mouth up to mine. I kiss her, not caring at all that Laz is controlling this. Because this is my omega and she deserves to be worshipped. To be held. To be cherished. To be given whatever she wants and desires.

I try to convey all of that with my tongue. With my hand sliding down to her nape. With my cock pulsing inside her. With my heart beating for her and her alone.

I feel her melt.

Then tense as Laz starts to push himself inside again.

He purrs, as do I, both of us trying to ease her into this intensity.

Johan adds his own rumble, his hand tracing her sides as he kneels beside us. I feel him more than see him, my focus on our pet. But he's there, his presence warm and comforting as Laz threatens to split her in two with his massive knot.

Fuck, this is going to be amazing.

Laz is already starting to slide in and out, taking over the rhythm and setting a steady pace. It's gentle, something I suspect is only temporary as our little bee gets used to feeling so full.

I do my part by kissing her and distracting her with my tongue, loving the way her breasts feel against my chest.

And fucking reveling in the fact that I can feel my claim mark and hers with each movement.

Mine, I think. *My omega. My mate. My fucking pet.*

"Marry me," I whisper against her mouth. "Please fucking marry me."

She giggles. "You're incorrigible."

"I'm *obsessed,*" I counter. "Marry. Me."

"Only you would propose while another man is inside her," Johan says, obviously amused.

"I'm inside her, too," I point out.

"Oh, I know," he murmurs. "I'm watching and I'm *very* envious."

"Then get up here and fuck my ass," Laz tells him. "Or take our omega's mouth. Your choice."

I arch a brow, then stop kissing Aurora to glance at a stunned Johan. I'm willing to bet Laz never offers to let him top. But from Johan's expression, he's torn on what he wants more.

"Can I have you in my mouth first?" Aurora asks softly, also looking at him. "I just… I just want to feel *full.*"

"*Fuck,*" Johan breathes. "Yeah, sweetheart. You can have anything you want."

There's a hint of deviousness in her gaze. There and gone in a flash as Laz thrusts a little harder into her. But it's enough to make me wonder what she's thinking.

Johan can fuck Laz later, when our omega is in heat. For now, we need to indulge her needs as she's aware and voicing them.

Laz helps to pull her up a little, the angle driving us both deeper into her and causing her to moan in response.

She's no longer in pain. She's fully stretched and ready to *fuck.*

But she's missing Johan's dick.

"Open your mouth wide," Laz growls.

She obeys, and he grabs Johan by the knot to feed him to our pet.

It's fucking intoxicating to watch her work. To be here with Laz. With Johan. *As a pack.*

I feel suddenly whole. Like we're finally a finished unit. A beating heart. *A circle.*

Ridiculous tears threaten to form in my eyes, the emotion unexpected and very fucking unwelcome.

I'm not that man. I don't do the feelings shit. But I *love* this unit. My two best friends. Our omega.

This is our life.

Our home.

Our family.

And there's nowhere else I want to be. No one else I desire. Just these three. *Forever and fucking eternity.*

CHAPTER THIRTY-ONE

JOHAN

I'M HYPNOTIZED BY LARK'S EYES, HER GAZE HOLDING MINE with some unspoken question. I can see her mind working, which is a feat considering what Laz and Noah are doing to her.

But she's focused.

Intent.

And moaning around my cock.

When Laz offered his ass, I was temporarily dumbfounded. He *never* gives that up willingly. And the notion of joining their motions while taking Lark was all I could picture.

Until he mentioned her mouth.

Those pretty fucking lips.

I've been mesmerized by them for years, her pictures inspiring countless fantasies. Yet they all failed to live up to the real deal.

Then hearing her ask to suck me off? Begging to be *full*?

Yeah, I was fucking gone for her.

She's licking and nibbling and still watching me, her pupils dark with need, her nostrils flaring as she tries to breathe around my girth.

But there's something else happening.

Something I'm trying to decipher as I feel her teeth skim my head.

Oh, fuck, I think, a curse leaving my mouth just a second before she clamps down and *claims* my damn cock.

That's what Noah asked her to do to him.

Yet she's doing it to me instead.

And I can't help but feel that's purposeful on her part, like she wanted to leave her mark on me in a place that shows I'm hers so that whenever Laz and Noah play with me, they think of her, too.

It's unnecessary on her part. We'll always fucking think of her. We'll always invite her in, too. Because she's our center. We might enjoy playing with each other in our own ways, but she's the star we rotate around. The focus of our universe.

In time, she'll understand that.

"Fuck, that's hot," Noah breathes as I fall out of Lark's mouth. There's blood on my tip, which she proceeds to wipe away with her tongue.

"*Now* you can fuck Laz," she tells me, her voice sultry and so fucking seductive that I grab her hair and slam back into her mouth.

"No, I fucking can't," I tell her. "Because I'm taking your mouth instead."

Delight stares up at me from her alluring gaze.

Noah snorts.

And Laz fucking chuckles. "A possessive omega is so fucking hot." He kisses her neck, then brushes his lips across my hand in her hair. He's still holding her, too, his touch hot beneath my palm as he applies pressure and makes her take more of me into her mouth. "Swallow him, darling."

She does, her throat working around me in a delirious movement that has me groaning deep.

I want to mark her. To claim her. But I can't from this angle. So it'll have to wait until we're done.

That realization drives me faster, making me want to come so I can flatten her on her back and choose a place to make her mine.

I want it obvious, too.

Somewhere the others see every time they play with her. Just like she's done to me.

Noah already claimed one of her tits.

And I'm pretty sure I caught sight of bite marks on her pussy from Laz—because of course the bastard chose her clit.

That leaves me with a few other interesting options.

Her inner thighs.

Her other tit.

Her nipples.

Her ass. I gaze down at where her rump is pressed up against Laz's groin as he ruts into her with abandon.

She's still a virgin there.

"I want first anal," I announce, the words leaving me on a possessive rumble.

"It's yours," both men say in unison.

I love that they probably already knew I would want that. Or perhaps felt it was my due, given everything we've shared.

Regardless, I'll be taking our omega there and marking her in the process.

It's perfect.

Just like her.

Just like *this.*

She grabs my knot, giving it a squeeze that has my muscles straining in response. Her slick has permeated the air for several days while I've held back from touching her, from seeking her out. I wanted Laz to be able to surprise her, just like he desired. And I knew I would ruin that if I spent too much time with our omega.

I don't like keeping secrets from her, even the good kind.

So I tortured myself with her scent instead and refused to jack off.

Which means I'm pent up and on the edge of a serious rut.

I want to fuck her so hard. See her through her heat. Fucking live inside her for a week. Fill her with our seed. Make her round with our child.

The future is so fucking bright right now. So tangible. *So ours.*

"Johan's about to come, princess," Laz says against her ear. "I know you've been practicing, so let's see if you can take his load down your pretty throat."

He shoves her face into me, causing me to go deeper than before, and forces me to erupt.

I fucking hate that he knows how to do that. Knows how to read my body's cues better than I can. But I can't deny the absolute rapturous nature of the sensations ripping through me.

"*Aurora*," I growl, aware that I usually call her Lark. However, her real name is what leaves me now as I unleash my passion into her mouth.

She swallows. Sputters a little. But keeps trying to take everything I'm giving her while massaging my knot.

It's again too much, a realization that makes her grumble in annoyance when she has to pull back. So I just release the rest of my seed on her tits.

Then Noah goes up onto his elbows to clean her up while Laz loses control behind her.

He's fucking her hard, his movements furious and fast and borderline violent.

It's driving Noah's orgasm onward, too, the friction between the three of them a dangerous dance of eroticism and mutual appreciation.

Lark starts to cry out, her orgasm already spiraling.

Then both men rumble in unison as they join her, their knots connecting inside her pussy to force her into a state of absolute oblivion.

A moment of panic overtakes her expression.

Then disappears behind a wave of intense pleasure as her climax shoots her into another plane of existence.

She's writhing.

Moaning.

Screaming.

There are tears. Scratch marks. And a cyclone of scents. All of which originate and swirl around our omega. Our mate.

She pants from the exertion, then collapses onto Noah, and her eyes fall closed. I reach forward to check her pulse and find it raging, her body still shuddering despite having lost consciousness to the power of her ecstasy.

Noah purrs, holding her with ease, his lips ghosting across her hair as Laz collapses against her back and kisses her nape. "So fucking good," he marvels, sweat dripping off him from the effort of fucking her to oblivion.

"We're doing that to her ass, too," Noah says on a sigh. "*While* she's in heat. And after Johan takes her virginity."

I sprawl out beside them and lean in to kiss his shoulder and then Lark's. "Her heat is probably going to start the moment she wakes up," I say, sensing the shift in scents in the air.

"It'll start when you mark her ass," Laz murmurs, obviously aware of my intent despite me not actually vocalizing it. "But yes, it'll be tonight."

"Then we should probably cancel that meeting with Giovanni tomorrow," I suggest.

He grunts. "Yeah, we'll need to."

"Are we going to tell him why?" Noah asks.

"We'll tell him that his sister has gone into heat. But we're not giving him any more details than that. We'll let him think she's locked up in a room and being tortured for a week." He looks at me. "Seems like a fitting punishment?"

I nod. "Not sure Lark will like it, though."

"Oh, she's going to love her heat," Noah inserts. "We'll make sure of it."

"I meant about her brother," I growl at him. "She's not going to like that we're emotionally punishing him."

"She had an opportunity to call him over the last two days and didn't." Laz looks at me, and I realize he's asking me to confirm that statement even though he didn't actually voice it as a question.

"I've been monitoring Giovanni's communications, and I haven't seen anything come through to him from her, so I think that's accurate, yes."

Although, I wasn't spying on him to see if his sister would reach out to him. I was monitoring his chatter to ensure he wasn't planning anything nefarious for tomorrow.

Laz nods, clearly pleased. "That suggests she agrees with the punishment."

I stare at him, not sure I feel the same way. "Or she thought she wasn't allowed to call him."

He considers that for a moment, then shakes his head. "I never said she couldn't. And she's too clever not to try. There's a reason she held back, and I think it's because she knew it would undermine my punishment. Which means she respected the pack's desires and our intentions."

"Mm-hmm," she hums sleepily. "Good intentions."

Noah chuckles. "Someone's drunk on our knots."

"Very. Yep. Good. 'Kay." Her incoherent babble causes my lips to twitch.

She's fucking adorable.

"Aurora," Laz murmurs. "We're going to cancel the meeting with your brother for tomorrow, as you're clearly about to go into heat. Okay?"

Seems a little unfair to ask her that when she's lost to her lustful state of mind. "Don't want to see Gio like this," she mutters. "Definitely not. *Ugh.*"

"So you want me to cancel the meeting?" Laz presses.

She releases a soft sound of agreement.

"I'm not going to insinuate that she's in harm's way," I tell Laz. "I'll just message to say she's in estrus and we'll reach out when she's better."

Laz looks at me.

"It was my life on the line," I remind him before he can try to push his decisions on me. "This should be my choice, and I don't want her brother punished this way. He's already spent two days thinking we're raping her. I'm not letting that continue."

Lark winces, clearly not liking that word. "I've consented."

"We know you have, pet," Noah murmurs. "And you *consented* very well, too."

Of course he would turn that word into something dirty.

I ignore him and focus on Laz, waiting for him to acknowledge my request and agree to it.

He dips his chin, giving me the go-ahead.

Yet I take great pleasure in saying, "Words, Laz. I expect words."

He glares at me. "I *consent* to your choice," he tells me through his teeth.

"Good boy." I pat him on the ass and roll out of the nest before he can grab me.

His growl makes my cock throb with anticipation.

He *hates* to bottom.

Which is why I add, "And I'm taking your ass later. Since you offered it so sweetly."

"I'm going to fucking destroy you, Johan."

"Not anytime soon, since you and Noah are currently stuck inside our omega. Try to play nice while I go make some calls, hmm?"

I start to leave when I notice my laptop on the nightstand.

The laptop Lark commandeered.

Hmm. It would be much easier to just use that to send a note to Giovanni.

So I flip it open and start working my way through her login screens—all of which she's cleverly redone.

For fun, I add a few layers of my own, knowing that she's going to be pissed when she's aware enough to play on this laptop again.

My dick hardens as I think about her growling in response to my antics.

We're going to have a lifetime of playing in this manner, and I can't fucking wait.

She moans on the bed, the two men starting to play with her once more while I work.

It's hot and fuels me to type faster.

Your sister is going into heat, so we need to postpone our meeting. We'll be in touch in eight days or so. Just know that she's in good hands, Giovanni. You're going to have to learn how to trust us… now that we're family and all. I'd show you the claim marks, but they're in places you don't want to see. Speak soon. —Johan

I send the message with a tap of my finger, aware that it's coming through from Lark's phone number.

Dots appear within seconds.

But I don't bother to wait for his reply.

Instead, I fire off instructions to some of our crew, ensuring the compound is well armed and protected in case Giovanni decides to go on a suicide mission.

Then I rejoin my pack in the nest.

Where Lark is already being prepared to take me.

Noah says he wants to be in her pussy while I take her ass.

I tell him he can be wherever he wants, then settle behind her and lean down to finish preparing her with my own hands.

She's a writhing mess, barely coherent, and begging for our knots.

But I ensure she's cognizant enough when I kiss a path down her spine.

Her brown eyes meet mine as she glances over her shoulder, her cheeks pink from exertion.

"Ready, Ms. White?" I ask her, not just about my claim, but about the heat this bite is going to push her into.

"Yes, Mr. Aegean," she breathes, the returned use of the nickname confirming she's still with me.

So I sink my teeth into her pretty flesh as Noah drives into her from the front.

She moans my name, then his, and falls into a squirming mess of slick need.

It makes entering her from behind exceptionally easy.

And it forces my knot out of me so much faster than I anticipated.

But as I'm filling her with my seed, joining Noah in the throes of passion, I realize that this moment couldn't be more perfect.

Because we finally found our hacker. The one who stole from us for a good cause. Hid from us for years. And finally allowed us to ensnare her in our web.

Our very own black widow.

A white hat.

Our omega.

Ours.

CHAPTER THIRTY-TWO
LARK

THREE CLAIM MARKS.

My breast.

My clit.

My ass.

I feel them all combining together in some sort of magical pattern that lights fire within my veins. Maybe that sensation is a fabrication in my mind, or maybe it's caused by my mounting heat. Regardless, I feel complete. Whole. *Cherished*.

Noah is kissing me, his knot still locked within me.

Johan fills me from behind, too, his lips a caress against my shoulder.

And Lazarus is lounging alongside us—watching and *waiting*.

Every part of me burns for him. For *them*. For everything that's coming. For everything that we're going to create together.

"Mmm, little bee, you're practically *buzzing*," Noah murmurs against my mouth. "I can feel that pretty pussy clenching around me, begging us to stay locked forever. I want to give in and live here for the rest of my damn life."

Johan makes a soft noise of agreement, his lips traveling to my nape. "Her ass feels fucking amazing, though. You might change your mind once you knot her here."

Noah hums, his hands roaming up and down my sides. "Should I take your ass next, Aurora? See if Johan is right?" He kisses me before I can reply, his purr igniting in his chest and lulling me into a state of comfort as I hold both his knot and Johan's within me.

I can't believe how full I feel.

How *safe* I am.

This is why I made my nest. I didn't need my mates to help me because I wanted this to be a tribute to them.

And an invitation.

For my heat.

As well as a way to punish Lazarus. Though, now that I know why he left, I'm not upset. That tattoo on his chest is *hot.*

I want to lick it. *Once it's healed*, I decide.

Until then… I can lick the dragon on Noah's shaft.

A notion that has me squeezing around him now, my heart kicking into overdrive. "I want you in my mouth, Noah," I tell him, suddenly needing that more than anything else in this world. "*Please* let me suck your cock."

He rumbles, his purr morphing into a growl that has my insides clenching around him and Johan.

"You'll have to release my knot first, omega," Noah tells me.

I'm not sure that's how it works.

But I try.

And whine when I can't figure it out.

Because all I want to do is *squeeze.*

"*Fuck*," Johan groans, his lips skimming my throat as he draws his mouth up to my ear. "That feels so good, sweetheart. Do it again."

Noah follows up that demand with a pinch to my clit that has me spiraling into an unexpected state of oblivion.

I never thought I would enjoy pain like this. But there's

something intensely euphoric about the afterburn, the way his thumb makes me feel better as he draws circles against my abused flesh.

"Keep our omega in this state," Lazarus murmurs. "I'm going to go grab some supplies."

"There's a cooler in my room," Johan tells him. "Full of frozen fruit for our girl."

"Fresh blankets and sheets in mine," Noah adds. "And check the fridge—I added water last night."

"To yours or mine?" Lazarus asks, his question barely registering as my world spirals with pleasure and *need*.

"All of ours. Aurora's, too," he growls. "I wasn't sure where she'd choose to nest."

"I'll gather them all," Lazarus replies. "Any other requests, princess?"

I blink, then look at my very naked and aroused alpha don. He's leaking precum. "That," I whisper, licking my lips. "I want *that*."

He arches a brow, his arrogant expression making me want to growl. "That being what, Ms. Bianchi?"

I narrow my gaze. He knows what I want. "Don't tease me, alpha."

"I'm always going to tease you, Aurora," he says, his voice silky and deep as he utters words I don't like.

Only, he's on his knees now and coming toward me.

That I like. *Very, very much…*

"The best orgasms are brought on by *teasing*," he adds, his cock near my mouth. "Now part those pretty lips for me so I can give you a taste of what's yours."

Oh God. My muscles tense, my insides on fire even though I'm pretty sure I'm still coming.

I'm just a ball of sensation, lost to my alphas, yet needing more. *So much more…*

I don't just part my lips—I widen them and lead with my tongue.

Because I have to indulge in his flavor. His seed. *His knot.*

I grab him by the base, feel that part of him pulsing with life, and try to suck him in as far as I can.

He curses, his fingers threading through my hair. "Fuck, princess," he whispers, the awe in his gravelly tone stroking something deep within me.

I make him curse again by twirling my tongue around him, taking every drop he'll give me, and swallowing it down right along with his cock.

I feel starved. *Parched.* Like I need his seed more than I need air.

Some part of me registers that it was Noah's cock I intended to lick, but it's Lazarus's taste that I need now.

Please, I think, looking up at him, my soul on fire with a craving I can't define.

It's my heat.

A logical part of me is aware of that, which means I haven't fully fallen into my estrus yet.

But it's here.

I'm absolutely ready for my pack to take me to new heights. Increase my limits. *Claim me* on a primal level with more than their knots and their teeth.

I... I don't know exactly what that means, just that I *need more.*

I want to bathe in their essence. Be truly marked inside and out. Simply exist as their omega in my new nest.

Scent it properly.

Make it truly mine. *Ours.*

But first, I need Lazarus to come. To let me swallow him. To *taste* him.

I twist his knot while begging him with my gaze.

"Darling, the way you're looking at me right now is the sexiest view of my life," he marvels, his dark eyes smoldering. "Tell me what you want, Aurora. Say it around my cock, and I'll give it to you."

"*Cum.*" It leaves me in a gargled mumble. I'm not demanding the action but requesting the substance. And the way his nostrils flare confirms that he understands.

"Squeeze my knot, princess," he murmurs.

I do. Massage it. Twist it. *Milk it.*

He releases a low growl of approval. "That's it, Aurora. Now take a deep breath. I want you to swallow everything I give you, okay?"

My throat automatically responds, closing around him as I try to preemptively accept his essence. But then his words register, and I force myself to inhale deeply.

The blend of our collective fragrances makes me dizzy, my males providing me with inexplicable pleasure through scent alone.

And then Lazarus is feeding me his seed, his growl one that vibrates between my legs as Johan and Noah keep me locked between them.

I'm fairly certain they could have released me by now but have somehow chosen not to.

I don't mind.

I'm happy to remain full like this for *days.*

I don't need any of those items they were talking about. *Frozen fruit? Ugh.* I just want sex. Euphoria. *Alpha seed.*

Lazarus's grip in my hair is unyielding as he continues to come down my throat. His eyes are on my face, his gaze intense as he watches me swallow.

I realize that he's ensuring I'm safe. And knowing that has me leaning into his touch and simply giving in to the moment. Taking everything I can. Loving him with my mouth. Massaging his knot with my palm while intimately squeezing my other two mates.

All of my males groan.

Then growl.

Then begin to *move.*

It's like they were waiting for an opportunity to take me together, to *rut* me as one.

I don't know.

But I'm suddenly so full of them that I can hardly breathe.

Because Lazarus is still *coming.*

Yet he's fucking my mouth, too. Causing his seed to spill over my lips, dribbling down onto my breasts.

Where Noah bends to lick me clean.

Oh, alphas…

I'm lost to them.

Gyrating.

Moving.

Indulging in their various lengths. Their strokes. *Their virility.*

Their colognes increase, causing my own perfume to honey the air. Or maybe that's my slick. I… I don't know. Don't even care. I just feel so good. So full. *So owned.*

These alphas are my safe haven.

My pack.

My future.

"Fuck, this is so hot, watching you take all three of us like this," Noah groans. "You were absolutely meant to be ours."

"No fucking question," Johan agrees, his lips a brand against my neck. "You're perfect, Lark."

"And stunning, too," Lazarus murmurs, his touch loosening in my hair as he combs his fingers through my strands. He's no longer coming down my throat, just lazily drawing himself in and out of my mouth while I suck on his tip.

A little more cum slips out, likely because of my hand on his knot, and he remains hard, but he's not actively fucking me anymore.

None of them are, actually.

They've all slowed their pace, just letting me feel them. Learn them. *Know them.*

It makes me feel cherished and possessed at the same time.

I love it.

I just want to exist in this moment for eternity. Feeling their hands on me. Their mouths. *Their cocks inside me…*

They seem to understand my desire, their pace barely existent as I just revel in the sensation of their ownership.

I don't know how long it lasts before Noah growls. "I need to lock us again, little bee. I need to fill you completely. Do my part in helping to create our future baby."

Lazarus hums and Johan growls, all three of my men renewing their thrusts with vigor, like they all want to participate in the act.

Their aggression is almost rut-worthy.

I love it.

Want more of it.

Demand that they keep going by rocking my hips back into Johan and forward into Noah, all while devouring Lazarus with my mouth.

I feel hot all over. Boiling with need. *Borderline feral.*

I barely recognize myself. I've never experienced a heat like this. An estrus so utterly mind-blowing that all I want is to claw up my alphas and demand their knots *everywhere.*

Please, I say with my eyes, staring at Lazarus.

Please, I try to convey with my hands as I dig my nails into Noah's shoulders.

Please, I echo as I clench around Johan.

All three of them growl in unison, then they give me what I need, each of them locking me to them in their own way.

Except Lazarus.

Instead, he pulls out of my mouth and leans down to kiss me as Johan and Noah explode inside me again, their bodies shuddering around mine as I orgasm with them.

Lazarus kisses me through the euphoric explosion, his lips seeming to ground me in the moment and remind me to breathe as pleasure threatens to swallow me whole.

I didn't even realize I needed him to do that, my mind so utterly consumed by my oblivion that I forgot about the importance of inhaling.

But a subtle exhale into my mouth prompts my lungs to expand, my need to take in Lazarus's scent and essence overriding everything else.

I resume normal breathing, all while he kisses me. My lower half clings to my other mates, our bodies coming on rapturous waves of endless sensation.

Their seed is hot inside me, making me feel even warmer than I already do.

Tears fill my eyes.

Sweat dots my brow.

And dizziness overwhelms my vision.

"She needs a cool bath or shower," Lazarus says against my lips. "And food. Try the chocolate."

"Hmm?" I reply, confused.

"I would go start it, but she's clinging to me," Lazarus goes on, deepening my bewilderment.

She who?

Oh, me, I realize in the next moment, my nails no longer in Noah's shoulders, but in Lazarus's now. *Why is he talking about bathing and feeding me?*

I need more knotting.

More fucking.

More seed.

I try to inform my alphas of that by writhing my lower half, but I can't seem to move. I'm stuck on their knots. Trapped between their muscular forms.

Mmm, yes. I like this very much. I lean into Lazarus to kiss him again, but his mouth curls against mine.

"You're on fire, princess," he murmurs. "Even your lips are hot." He dips his tongue inside before I can reply, his embrace causing me to blink out of existence once more.

Because all I am now is a bundle of feelings.

Of warmth.

Of pleasure.

Of intensity.

Someone hums.

Another male purrs.

Then, suddenly, I'm being carried. I have no idea how I ended up in Noah's arms, but I snuggle into his rumbling chest. He feels so good. Like comfort and safety.

Johan is with him, too. I feel his hand stroking my spine, checking on me as the pair of them converse about something I can't quite hear.

I'm too lost to my blissful state.

No, hold on. That's not right. I'm *hot.* Too hot.

I whine, needing something to fix—

Cool water falls over me, startling me into opening my eyes—eyes I didn't even realize I'd closed.

Oh.

Oh, that's… that's nice.

Though, it's not exactly what I wanted.

Actually, it's not what I desire at all.

I want more knotting. More seed.

More alpha, I think, growling.

Noah chuckles, the sound at odds with the annoyance mounting inside me. "Calm down, little bee. We'll give you *more alpha* soon."

I frown. *Did I say that out loud?*

Maybe.

Who cares? I think in the next blink. "Knot me," I demand.

"Oh, I will," Noah murmurs. "Right against the damn wall if you want. But I need to cool you down a little more first."

I growl at that. I don't want to be *cooled down*. I want to be fucked. "*Knot. Now.*"

Noah just chuckles again, his purr loud and almost enough to pacify me. *Almost.*

Leaning in, I sink my teeth into his chest.

His purr morphs into a groan, and I'm suddenly pressed up against the shower wall, just like he said, his dick brushing my clit. I rub against him, trying to get him where I need him, then deciding that this is fine, too. I like the friction. It's… it's good. Nearly perfect. *Mmm…*

"You claimed me twice," he breathes, his mouth drifting across my cheek to my mouth. "Fuck, pet." He kisses me, his tongue slipping inside for a quick taste. "*Fuck*, my blood is on your…" He trails off, embracing me again, deeper now, his body rocking into mine.

The water moves, the chilling spray touching my arm and giving me a dose of coolness. It feels good, the juxtaposition against Noah's warmth making me feel grounded for just long enough to understand that I claimed him again.

"I'm not sorry," I tell him clearly, my arms wrapping around his shoulders. "I'm going to bite you a lot."

"Fuck yes, little bee," he whispers. "Bite me as much as you want." He drags his teeth along my lip. "Just be prepared for me to return the favor."

My nipples tighten against his chest, the cool water slipping between us and somehow making me burn hotter.

I love the mixture of temperatures. The heat inspired by Noah's touch. The fire stoked by Johan's nearness. *The slick pooling between my legs.*

Only it's not just slick.

There's alpha seed, too.

From Johan and Noah.

I nearly reach down to stroke myself but instead use Noah's shaft, grinding my clit against him and groaning as pleasurable sparks ignite along my nerve endings.

"More," I whisper. "*More.*" It turns into a demand, my nails clawing at his shoulders just like before. Only with increased intensity.

Because he's not inside me.

Where he belongs.

I'm empty.

"*Knot.*"

He doesn't chuckle this time, instead repositioning his hips and thrusting into me so hard that I scream.

But then the wall disappears, only to be replaced by Johan's chest as he holds me for Noah to fuck, his own cock a brand against my backside.

I'm about to demand that he join me when Noah says the words for me. "Get in her pussy, tech boy," he growls. "Help me double-knot our needy little pet."

Moans escape me, followed by shrieks of pleasure as I'm expanded to accommodate them both.

It feels divine.

Insane.

Perfect.

Only, at some point, I pass out from the euphoria and wake up… in bed. Or maybe I blacked out from the heat-driven high. I don't know.

But I stir with Lazarus nestled between my legs, his skillful tongue licking me to completion.

I grab his hair to pull him up to me, needing more, and sigh as he slides into me.

Then he turns me until I'm on top and says, "Reach back to part those cheeks for Johan, princess. He wants to knot you, too."

I obey, presenting myself intimately to Johan.

He slides into me, my body slick and ready.

His strokes are long and thorough, creating a delirious pattern with Lazarus as they both knot me into oblivion.

I feel like all I do is come. Scream. *Beg.*

There's so much cum.

It's perfect, my nest scented with my mates.

Where they're focused on me. My body. My orgasms. *My needs.*

It's amazing.

I never want it to end.

Which I say out loud.

For hours, I think. *Or days.*

Time is irrelevant.

My only desire is to exist in the moment. Indulge in my mates. *And fulfill my version of a happily-ever-after…*

CHAPTER THIRTY-THREE

LAZ

Aurora's blissed-out expression warms me all over, her pleasure a gift I will forever cherish.

But it's more than her ecstasy that makes my soul feel complete.

It's seeing her sandwiched between Noah and Johan, the three of them resting in a pile of sweaty limbs in the nest.

This is my pack.

My reason for breathing. The heart of my whole world.

For the first time in my life, I feel like I'm finally breathing. That my veins are actually pumping. That my universe is officially perfect.

I thought I was happy before.

I was wrong.

This is joy.

Being with my completed pack.

Protecting them.

Loving them.

Respecting them.

We've always possessed a unique dynamic, our friendship forged from decades of established trust and mutual appreciation.

But Aurora takes our bonds to a whole new level.

She's going to teach us the meaning of being a proper pack. I can already see that just from the last few weeks. I've never felt closer to Johan and Noah, the roots of our friendships having strengthened even more through this experience.

We're ready for whatever the future may bring.

Ready to protect our omega and our unborn child—which I have no doubt we created this week.

Ready to embrace whatever twists and turns lurk in our intertwined paths.

Aurora has inspired a renewed purpose, a gift I don't think she'll ever realize she's provided. But I'm going to spend my entire life thanking her for it.

Appreciating her.

Worshipping her.

Loving her.

It's what all of us are going to do. Because she's our heartbeat. The soul ours needed to create a permanent pack.

Together, we'll ensure she's forever cared for and always adored.

I crawl forward between her legs and lean down to kiss her belly. "We'll love you, too, sweet little one," I whisper.

"That's a weird nickname for her pussy, but I can agree to the sweet part at least," Noah murmurs, his eyes closed in what's clearly a fake sleep.

"I was talking to our child," I mutter back at him

He peeks one eye open at me, then two. "Our child," he repeats.

I half expect him to issue some sort of asinine claim about it being *his* daughter or son.

But instead, he smiles and says, "Yeah, I like the sound of that. *Our* omega. And *our* child." He closes his eyes again. "Our little beehive filled with humming babies. In a nest. Covered in sweet slick."

I blink at him. "Now you're the one saying strange things."

"I'm tired," he replies, yawning. "Someone moved on the bed and stirred me from my beauty sleep."

I snort at that. "We both know you're always on edge, *enforcer*."

"Not when I'm with my pack," he replies honestly. "This is where I know I'm safe, Laz. I only woke up because I thought you might be able to lick our omega's cunt, and I wanted to watch."

"I can still do that if you want," I offer, more than willing to oblige that notion.

"Yes, please." That comes from Johan, his hand stroking his dick. "She's going to be out of her heat soon. Best to ensure she's fully satisfied by the time it's done."

"Our little bee deserves the best," Noah adds, agreeing. "So get to work, boss. I want to hear our pet scream again."

I don't typically appreciate being told what to do.

But in this case, I happily obey.

Because this is for Aurora.

Pleasing her is my purpose in life.

The only thing I want to do is see her smile.

And make all of her dreams… come true.

EPILOGUE

LARK

Six Months Later

Gio glances up and down the street, instantly on guard as strangers roam all around. He's not pleased about having to leave his enforcers behind at the house. But I told him there was no way Silva and the others would be okay with him sauntering into Widows Peak with a fucking mafia entourage.

It's hard enough to visit with my pack, and they've all been vetted.

Or rather, forcibly accepted.

Since they're mine.

Though, I'm pretty sure Syrus still watches Noah like a hawk every time he enters the town limits. Lazarus, too, for that matter.

Johan seems to be the only one my friends don't fear. Maybe because he's the most like me. Some of the other widows have even started sending him data requests instead of me. However, I think that's because they're preparing for my maternity leave.

Gio jumps as Noah claps him on the back. "What's wrong, bro?" Noah drawls. "Feeling out of your element in that ridiculously expensive suit?" He looks over my brother's Italian import and whistles. "Seriously, I did suggest some jeans, didn't I?"

"I hate it when you call me *bro*," Gio mutters at him. "I'm not your brother."

"That ring on your sister's hand says otherwise," Noah sing-songs, drawing attention to the diamond glittering on my finger. It's a triangle shape with three adorning jewels—one blue, one black, and one multicolored.

Noah says they represent each of my men.

Blue for Johan.

Black for Lazarus.

Multicolored—"the best, obviously," according to Noah—for Noah.

"I can't believe you married this psycho," Gio says to me.

"I can," I reply, smiling at Noah. "He's pretty awesome."

"I *am* pretty awesome," Noah agrees. "And the father of that baby in her belly. So feel free to start calling me *Daddy* if *Bro* doesn't work for you, G-man."

"No. *No*. We are not doing *G-man*," my brother says, rounding on Noah. "What is with you and nicknames?"

"I don't know. Maybe *Lark* can answer that." Noah gives me a look.

I lift my hands. "Leave me out of this." I've only recently admitted to my fellow Widows that *Lark* is a hacker name, not my legal name.

None of them cared.

Which is good because it meant I didn't have to elaborate on the past, including the source of funds used for this town.

Johan has been quietly funneling more into the infrastructure over the last few months, helping out businesses in sly ways, just ensuring Widows Peak remains happy and comfortable for everyone.

And, most importantly, *safe*.

We visit when we can, which isn't as often as I want, but

Lazarus recently suggested we plan for my maternity leave to take place in Widows Peak.

That's why we're currently here. We're finalizing our home, including the baby's room, and meeting with the local doctor.

Lazarus is still with her, peppering her with questions.

Or, more likely, *demands*.

I left Johan behind to try to smooth the waters, as I know Lazarus can be pretty demanding. But the clinic here specializes in omegas, just like the town. I'm sure everything will be fine.

Pressing my palm to my belly, I feel the little one inside kick.

I don't know if it's a girl or a boy. Nor do I know who the father is. And I prefer it that way. I want it all to be a surprise.

Besides, each one of my men already refers to himself as *Dad* anyway.

Or, in Noah's case, *Daddy*.

He and my brother bicker a little more as we walk. I listen without really hearing them. I'm just glad Gio has given my pack a chance.

Things were a little bleak there in the beginning, his lack of acceptance evident in the way he growled at Lazarus throughout our initial meeting.

Of course, Gio was pissed because he assumed Lazarus and his pack had forced me into this mating. But he's since realized that we were all destined for one another.

Scent matches.

Happy mates.

A perfect pack.

I sigh and glance up at the blue sky above. It feels like a good omen. A rebirth. *A step into the future.*

Everything has changed, not just for me, but for some of my fellow Widows as well.

Even Luna has experienced a new chapter. Aries, too.

Our safe haven continues to grow.

Marking Widows Peak as more than just a home.

It's a sanctuary. A place for new beginnings. A safe town to start over and explore different paths.

I never thought my destiny would lead me back to my origin, to the mafia families I once feared.

But fate has a unique way of coaxing us in the right direction.

My steps led me to Lazarus, Noah, and Johan.

And now I can't picture life without them.

My alphas. My men. *My pack.*

"Come dance with me, little bee," Noah murmurs, dragging me toward Club 21. "Laz will play with Gio."

I frown, realizing that Lazarus and Johan are coming toward us.

"I have no desire to *play* with Giovanni," Lazarus states flatly.

"Likewise," my brother agrees.

"Which is why you two should bond," Noah says, pulling me away. "Come on, Johan. You can dance with us, too. It's not like Gio or Laz has any weapons. They'll be fine. Pretty sure they owe Stefano a call, anyway. Something about a new business venture they've all decided to share."

"What's he talking about?" my brother demands.

"I fucking hate you," Lazarus growls at Noah.

The enforcer feigns a confused look, then snaps the fingers of his free hand—the one not holding on to me. "Ah, right, *my bad.* That's what you wanted to talk about later at dinner. Oh well. Might as well kick off the bromance now, yeah?" He waggles his brows at Gio. "Enjoy!"

I'm aware of the merger Lazarus wanted to discuss. It has to do with an acquisition from France. A clothing line that focuses on maternity wear.

But of course Noah made it sound like a big deal by dragging Stefano's name into it.

The truth is that Lazarus outbid Stefano's second, Nazar, at a recent fashion show.

That's it.

Though, I do wonder why an assassin like Nazar had an interest in maternity clothing. But at least the families seem to be getting along.

For the most part, anyway.

There will always be tensions.

And Noah is likely going to enjoy exploiting those tensions for the rest of our lives.

At least I'll never be bored, I think.

"Play nice," I tell my brother. Then I look at Lazarus. "You, too, sir."

His lips twitch.

And my brother sighs. *Loudly*.

I'm not ashamed at all, something I show by giving Lazarus a big smile before letting Noah carry me the rest of the way to Club 21.

Some of the other Widows are there. Some are not.

It's a new way of life, one we're all embracing in stride.

Because this is our present.

Where we're safe and loved.

And I've never been happier…

BONUS EPILOGUE
NOAH

One Month Later

"Are you sure we shouldn't add a little blood?" I ask, feeling very uncertain about Johan's vision of our pet's new nest. "I really don't mind killing those fuckers on the list and adding their skulls as ornaments."

My best friend gives me a look that says I'm not going to like his response. "Lark already said you can't kill her former bed partners, Noah."

Yep. I read that look right. Because I *hate* his reply.

"Call them bed partners one more time," I dare him.

He rolls his eyes. "Dead men. Fine. Whatever. You can't kill them with—"

"I can—"

"*Without* upsetting Lark," he interjects, overriding my own interruption. "She's been very clear about that. And given her fragile state, I suggest you obey her wishes."

"Don't let Aurora hear you call her fragile," Laz mutters as he enters the room. "She'll lose her shit and show you just how unbreakable she is."

Johan glances at him. "You tried to make her breakfast again today, didn't you?"

Laz scowls. "I just wanted to help cut up the fruit. She grabbed the knife and attempted to stab me with it, just to prove a point."

I smirk, amused. "I would have enjoyed watching that."

Laz ignores me. "It's going to be difficult to get anyone to staff this home with Aurora insisting on doing everything herself."

"She's pregnant and nesting," I murmur. "And everything is brand new. Once she's settled, we'll be able to move over some of her favorites from the Ferraro estate. Like Chef Harmony."

Our pet seems to like the chef. But since moving into our newly built ranch—only ten minutes from Widows Peak—Aurora has insisted on doing everything herself.

Which is why she's either going to love this nest…

Or shred it apart.

"I still think blood would help," I mutter, shifting the conversation back to our current task. "At the very least, a blade decorated with the blood from those fuckers who dared to touch her first."

I have the names.

Well, it's a list Johan supplied, anyway.

A very short list.

With two names.

Both of whom are known acquaintances of our pet. Only, we're not actually sure they're the ones she's been with.

But I plan to ask first.

Then I'll kill them.

And present Aurora with their heads.

In a basket.

Right on this pillow, I decide. "Yeah, definitely needs blood." I turn toward the door, only to be blocked by Laz.

"Have you heard anything we've said?" he demands.

I blink at him. "Was it something important?"

He releases a long sigh and pinches the bridge of his nose.

"There isn't time to add blood, Noah," Johan says as he comes up behind me. "Lark's going to find us all in here and wonder…"

"What are you all up to?" a suspicious voice asks from the doorway.

I curse. "You led her here." The words are for Laz.

"Your combined scents led me here," Aurora corrects me as she pushes past Laz's suit-clad form.

She pauses just inside the room, her pretty brown eyes wary. It's cute.

But not nearly as cute as her baby bump.

"You're wearing my favorite dress," I whisper, loving the pattern around her midsection. It looks like a flurry of bees chasing hearts.

And it instantly brings me to my knees before her.

I plant a kiss right in the center of the bump, then hug her and our baby. "I love you, little bee and super-tiny bee."

Aurora runs her fingers through my hair, glancing down at me. "We love you, too. Now tell me what you all are doing."

"Making you a nest," I answer without hesitation. "If you hate it, you can destroy it. Or we can change it. Or we can help you make a new one. Whatever you want, pet. We're yours to command."

Johan and Laz voice their agreement with dueling purrs.

"We had to bring in all new material, as we didn't want to risk moving anything incorrectly from our Hamptons estate," Laz tells her softly. "But we ordered similar fabrics, then scented them ourselves."

"However, the frame is pretty different from the four-poster one you built your original nest in," Johan adds.

Aurora's attention goes to the canopy bed we built this week. It's not a normal size, but one meant for a pack of five or more to sleep in. And it's surrounded by little fairy lights that remind me a bit of bees.

Hence the reason I insisted on installing them. I threaded them into the lacy curtains to almost give the room a starry-night experience, one I really hope our pet likes.

It was a risk.

And would look better if I could splatter some violence onto it.

Maybe.

Though, it would ruin the delicate appeal.

Hmm.

Depends on our pet's mood, I suppose. If she wants violence or sweetness.

"Perhaps sweetness in appearance, but violent sex in the nest?" I think out loud, looking at Johan. "Is that why you nixed the blood? You want it pretty to look at so we can have fun ruining it with a hard, fast rut?"

He stares at me. "Our omega is pregnant, Noah. There will be no violence in the nest."

"Why?" she demands. "Because I'm too 'fragile' for it?" She shoots Laz a glare with that word.

"I never called you fragile, darling."

She puts her palms on her shapely hips. "You didn't have to, Mr. Ferraro."

He holds up his hands in surrender. "I only wanted to help, *Mrs. Ferraro*."

It's technically Mrs. Dragon-Ferraro, but I'm not given a chance to interject.

"Because I'm too pregnant to handle a knife?" she counters. "And I'm too pregnant for violent sex?" That last part she throws at Johan. "Have you all lost your minds?"

"Not me," I promise her. "I will happily rut you, Aurora. You can even bring a knife to use on me if you'd like."

I consider her pushing a blade against my throat and instantly harden at the prospect.

Well.

I get *harder*, anyway.

Pretty sure I'm constantly erect in her presence.

"Then you can show me the nest," she says, clearly pleased with me.

Smiling, I hop up from the ground and hold out my hand. "My sweet bee." I give a little bow. "I'm happy to be of any service you desire."

Her cheeks pinken, her honey scent strengthening.

Being pregnant has made our omega insatiable. And I'm fucking here for it.

She's just over seven months, which means we still have plenty of time to play before the tiny bee arrives.

I'm pretty sure it's biologically mine. Not that it matters. All of us are the fathers. Regardless of the genetics, I'll be teaching him or her how to fight.

And later, how to kill.

Those are important life lessons for survival.

Aurora takes my hand and lets me lead her to the nest.

The lacy netting falls all around, reminding me a bit of a translucent waterfall flickering with the afternoon sun. "I threaded in those lights," I tell her quietly. "I thought they added a majestic appeal. But I can remove them if you want me to."

She says nothing, simply admiring our work.

"And like Laz said, the material is the same. The brands, too. We also scented everything."

I show her the pillows.

The comforters and layers of sheets.

Then point out the clothes we've hidden throughout the massive space.

"And, um, that little bee is from me." I gesture to the stuffed animal sitting in the middle of the bed. "Your gun is under that pillow beside the bee, too." It's an upgraded weapon that Laz bought for her, one engraved with her hacker name on the handle. "There's also a gift from Johan in the corner there."

The metallic top peeks out from where I indicate, causing Aurora's forehead to pucker.

She releases my hand to slip into the bed.

I know better than to follow.

This is her safe haven now. If she chooses to accept it, of course.

We'll only ever enter with her permission.

Aurora crawls across the bed, her belly swaying a little with the movement. It makes me want to pursue her and play with her from behind.

But I don't want to intrude on her exploration.

We've spent weeks preparing for this surprise, and days building it ourselves.

Laz even put a fridge in the corner of the room, stocked full of all her favorite cravings. There's an entire shelf devoted to just chocolate-covered strawberries.

She loves those.

And I love feeding them to her, too.

Especially while keeping my knot warm inside that beautiful cunt of hers.

We've been working on her knot-warming limits, building up to hours of fun. Though, lately, that's changed because of baby stuff.

Which is fine.

We'll just work on it again after the little one is here.

I will forever be okay with teaching Aurora how to take my cock.

"What did you do?" she demands as she pulls the shiny object free, her hands quickly flipping it open. "*Johan*."

He says nothing, just folds his arms and smiles as her fingers start flying across the keyboard of the brand-new laptop.

Her eyes widen.

Her pretty lips part—which has my cock leaking in anticipation.

And that flush on her cheeks travels down to the neckline of her alluring dress. I want to remove that fabric with my teeth and admire her tits.

I bet that gorgeous blush is highlighting my claim mark right now.

I reach down to adjust myself, eager to play.

But this particular moment is for her and Johan.

While Laz and I slaved away at building the bed, tech boy genius has been busy doing… whatever the fuck he did to that laptop.

Aurora settles on the bed, folds her legs, and pulls the item into her lap. Her eyes are glued to the screen as her fingers continue to move impressively along the keyboard.

Laz clears his throat, not to grab her attention but because he seems to be getting a little uncomfortable. The alpha has a fucking hard-on for intelligence. I've seen him jump on Johan enough times to know that our don enjoys watching his lovers work.

Johan, however, just seems to be amused, his icy blue eyes smiling behind his dark-rimmed glasses.

"This is amazing," Aurora breathes, her focus shifting to Johan. "You built this from scratch."

"I did."

She stares him down. "It's better than the one I claimed seven months ago."

"Yes." He nods. "Yes, it is."

"How long have you been working on this?"

"For a while," he says vaguely. "I started shortly after your heat, when you went back to Widows Peak to see everyone. While you were getting approval for us to visit the town."

She gapes at him. "When you said you kept yourself busy, I thought you meant with the building plans."

"Well, that's true, too. But Laz handled most of that while

Noah worked out the security." He glances at us. "We've all been… preparing for our new life here."

Originally, we planned to try to split our time between New York City, the Hamptons, and our new estate outside of Widows Peak.

But after a lot of discussion—and witnessing Aurora's friendships firsthand—we decided that we needed to prioritize living here, with the other homes being used for business purposes as needed.

Which we haven't exactly told her yet.

We mentioned that we would prefer her pregnancy and maternity leave to take place in this home, saying that it made the most sense due to her comfort with the Widows Peak omegas and their hospital clinic.

However, our intention was to make this more permanent.

For her. And for our pack.

It's not inside the town limits, but it's close enough for her to visit as often as she wants. Yet far enough away for us to ensure no one feels uncomfortable with our… business practices.

The perfect compromise.

"You mean for the baby's arrival?" she asks, her nose scrunching adorably. "That's the new life here, right?"

"No, he means *our* new life here," Laz murmurs. "As in *our pack's* new life in Widows Peak. Or, well, just outside of it, anyway. It'll allow us to better protect your friends in our own way. Quietly. Just as you've done over the last ten years—with money flow."

"And it gives you an opportunity to stay close to your friends," Johan adds. "Our work will require us to travel back to the East Coast frequently, but this will be our new primary estate."

"Security is already in place," I tell her, just in case she's concerned. "They're being quiet about it, but we're safe here, little bee. All of us." I look at her belly. "Especially the tiny bumble baby."

"We're making plans to stay, princess. Even after your maternity leave," Laz concludes. "Just making sure that part is clear. Assuming, anyway, that this is what you want."

Tears start to form in her eyes, the glistening one I've gotten a little too familiar with these last few months as her pregnancy hormones have raged.

My own eyes widen, my body already moving toward her.

Because I *hate* when she cries.

"Oh, little bee, we're sorry," I rush to tell her, aware that I'm probably making it worse by invading the nest without permission—something I just noted I would never do. But when our omega cries, I break all the rules. "Tell us how to fix this. Tell us what we did wrong."

"Noah," Johan starts.

I don't pay him any mind, my focus entirely on our omega and the tears now falling down her cheeks. I try to catch them, to put them back or hide them or *something*. Except my hands flounder, and I end up cupping her face and nearly falling on top of her instead.

But I manage to hold myself up on my knees, my body awkward as I palm her cheek. "I'm sorry," I repeat, though this time I'm talking about my clumsiness. "I want to make it better, pet. Tell me what to do."

She stares up at me through her wet gaze, then slowly closes the laptop and sets it safely to the side. "The only thing I want any of you to do right now is kiss me." She moves into me before I have a chance to respond, her lips already finding mine. "Kiss me and knot me, alphas."

I growl, more than approving of those requests.

Except I'm confused. "But you're sad," I whisper.

"I'm happy," she tells me. "So unbelievably happy." Her nose brushes mine. "I just can't control these damn hormones.

Or my eyes. But trust me, Noah, I'm *very* pleased. And now I want your knots inside me."

Her hands are on my belt, then my zipper, her nimble fingers easily freeing my cock.

"Fill me, alphas," she whispers. "Help me scent this nest properly and make it *ours*."

Laz releases a growl.

Johan purrs.

And I simply stare down at our omega in awe.

She's utterly perfect.

"You like our nest?" I ask, needing to hear the words.

"I *love* our nest," she promises me. "Thank you for preparing it for me."

I close my eyes and press my forehead to hers. "I love you, little bee. We all love you."

"I love you all, too," she replies. "My alphas."

"Our omega," I murmur back to her.

"Our little hacker," Johan says, joining us in the bed—already naked.

"Our heart," Laz adds, moving to our other side in only a pair of boxer shorts.

"Our queen," I whisper, bowing to Aurora and giving her everything she needs.

We all do.

Because she's the center of our universe now. We'll forever orbit around her. Protect her. Worship her. Pleasure her. And love her.

For the rest of our lives.

And beyond…

THE END

USA Today Bestselling Author Lexi C. Foss loves to play in dark worlds, especially the ones that bite. She lives in North Carolina with her family. When not writing, she's busy crossing items off her travel bucket list, or chasing eclipses around the globe. She's quirky, consumes way too much coffee, and loves to swim.

Want access to the most up-to-date information for all of Lexi's books? Sign-up for her newsletter here.

Lexi also likes to hang out with readers on Facebook in her exclusive readers group - Join Here.

Where To Find Lexi:
www.LexiCFoss.com

www.ingramcontent.com/pod-product-compliance
Lightning Source LLC
LaVergne TN
LVHW050923080826
845145LV00001B/189

* 9 7 8 1 6 8 5 3 0 4 0 6 5 *